BOOKS BY JEREMY HODGSON

HISTORICAL ROMANCE

Dance on the Terrace

ADVENTURES IN RESEARCH

Curing Emily

Secret in the Seas

ROMANTIC AFRICAN ADVENTURES

Leap of a Lifetime

We Are One

EGYPTIAN SAGA

Take Me Instead

AERIAL ADVENTURES

Breathe On Me

SCIENCE FICTION

Tarik

The Madonna and the Medallion

A Historical Mystery

Jeremy Hodgson

© Jeremy William Hodgson, 2025

All rights reserved. No part of this book may be reproduced or transmitted in any form or by any means, electronic or mechanical, including photocopying, recording or any information-storage or -retrieval system, without permission from the copyright holder.

ISBN: 978-1-0370-7860-6
e-ISBN: 978-1-0370-7861-3

Jeremy William Hodgson
Villa 99, Tamarina Golf Estate
Black River, Mauritius
90922
jwhodgson42@gmail.com

This is a work of fiction. Names, characters, and some places and incidents are either products of the author's imagination or are used fictitiously, and any resemblance to persons living or dead, business establishments, events, or locales is entirely coincidental.

Structural evaluation by Wesley Thompson
Proofreading by the author
Cover by Nikki Meier
Maps by Louise van Wyk
Typesetting and ebook by Liquid Type Publishing Services

For my Granddaughter Manon

The improbable will never happen; the impossible always does. What is Destiny other than the inevitable consequences of a supernatural coalition of natural circumstances?

– Asad bin Rachid Al Said, mathematician

Prologue

From *Legends of Madagascar*. Chevalier Ferdinand de la Motte. 1683

> A man named Boraha went fishing, and a whale dragged him out to sea. He drifted for hours, but a fish called a *Sorokay* saved him. The fish carried him to dry land, an island. He gave his name to the island he discovered; *Nosy Boraha* means the Isle of *Boraha*.
>
> It is *fady*, forbidden, for the *zafin-boraha*, the descendants of *Boraha*, to eat a *Sorokay* fish.

1710

A ship left Jakarta for the Netherlands in October. Two years later, the port clerk stamped his copy of the ship's document file:

> *Lost* – Presumed sunk.

The file remained in sealed archives for centuries until it was collected by the owner's successors and shipped to the Netherlands. Technicians scanned the file and added the data to digital records. Marked '*Lost*', it attracted no attention from historians.

Another ship sailed the same sea in November, departing from another port. Three years later, the port clerk incinerated the departure documents. Hence, the ship's visit remained unknown, except for an order and a delivery note for supplies to the vessel, placed the day after collection in a company's archives, where they would remain untouched and unseen.

1716

The Administrator had years to think about his death. He prepared for it. It took two years to build his tomb – a stone cube on a gran-ite slab with a stone armchair inside, facing west and the view from the hilltop. On the top slab, chiselled into the granite, was a name, a chiselled skull, and crossed bones below it. The date came after his death.

PEGLEG JON
PYRAT O CARIB
1716

Three hundred years later, in Djibouti, the crossroads of Africa and Arabia where traders have bought and sold for thousands of years, a sixteen-year-old schoolboy visiting one of Djibouti's many souks received a coral block as a gift when his father bought a roll of Muga Silk, once reserved exclusively for the Moghul Emperors. He took the coral block home and placed it on his trophy shelf with awards, prizes and items he had collected from an early age in dif-ferent towns and countries.

1

2021

Leo entered the dining room in a company-owned house on the Isle of Wight. He was frequently a non-paying guest as his father was a director of the company.

'Hi Dad, why are you dressed up? Another meeting for the IFC?'

Leo knew his dad worked for the International Finance Corporation, a UN agency.

Louis *blended*, his suit styled to resemble a thousand others by an exclusive tailor, a plain dark blue tie, and a shirt that hid behind a smidgeon of off-white thread instead of glaring. He had a suit in each country he visited that blended with those countries' businesspeople. His dark hair, cut short and neat with a parting, matched a million others, his height of a metre eighty-one and a face that appeared ordinary made him unremarkable. If he looked directly at an observer, his brown eyes revealed a powerful intellect and gave the impression they could see into depths better hidden. When Louis smiled, it transformed his face, for his eyes smiled, too – he rarely smiled at meetings and kept his eyes averted.

'Yes, Leo, a chopper will be at the hotel in an hour to take me to Battersea. The UN Food and Agriculture wants a preliminary assessment of an irrigation dam project in Liberia; the IFC agreed to assign me.'

'Will the chopper bring you back and then return to Battersea?'

'Yes, about four o'clock. Do you want a lift to school?'

'Please, Dad, it's much faster.'

'Okay, be ready. I'll send an ETA, and you can meet the chopper at the Priory Hotel. I've been meaning to ask, what will you do when school ends this month?'

'I'll take a gap year, Dad. I'm a year ahead of the other students, and some are taking a gap year; I'll still be eighteen when I begin university.

'I have some work to do at the palace. My computer centre's construction is due to start, and then I'll hike.'

'Where? Around Europe?'

'No, too many people, especially in summer. I'll do the same as my last hike from Arusha to Victoria Falls: take a backpack, walk and hitch. This time, though, I'll visit Madagascar; it'll take me months to travel around it, even if I take buses. And there's a stack of things to see.'

'Check with Private Wings; maybe they have a jet going south with a spare seat.'

Leo didn't find this odd. His dad's clients always paid for a private jet flight. Private Wings, based in Dubai, knew Leo well as he had often travelled with his parents. They knew him as Leo Poussin, for his father had told him once he was old enough to understand.

'Leo, Omanis may call you Highness, but outside Oman, tell the kids you're Leo, and your dad works for the United Nations; many kids want to be friends with someone called Highness, but not with you.'

Leo landed in November on *Nosy Be*, a holiday island beside the northwest coast of Madagascar. He shouldered his backpack and took a taxi to Ambatalok, the nearest beach area, to gather information. The taxi driver advised Leo to walk south along a rickety-looking walkway on stilts above the beach, and after a short distance, he left the walkway to an open-air bar for a beer. The bartender was helpful. 'If you're looking for a place to stay, there's a wide choice as you walk south. Some are cheap but noisy at night; others are much better. At the end of the beach, Gerard and Francine own and run a clean hotel.'

Leo realised why the bartender had used the word '*clean*' as he walked. In one area, a maze of wooden structures, he walked along raised rickety walkways between bars with music already booming and doorways occupied by skimpily dressed young women leaning against the doorposts.

'Mister, cheap room. Full service.'

Leo saw several rats below as the tide was out and kept walking. Gerard and Francine had a room and a terrace for meals. There, he met another traveller who waved at him.

'*Bonjour*, you look like a newcomer. Come and join me. I'm Georges Vassail.'

'Leo Poussin just arrived for a casual stroll around Madagascar.'

'That's impossible. Order a beer; Don't trust the water unless you know it's clean. The most common beer is Three Horses, then I'll tell you why.'

Although raised as a Muslim, Leo's mother was the Minister of Health. As he grew up, she had told him several times. 'If you don't trust the water, don't drink it. Mohammed banned the consumption of anything detrimental to health. A light beer may contain a small amount of alcohol, but that sterilises it. Every hospital uses alcohol to clean the skin. Do not drink spirits or too much beer.'

When the beer arrived, Georges continued, 'Madagascar has highways only along the island's central spine, and the coast is accessible by spur roads. Then, once at the ocean, the only possible route is to return to the major highways, although that is a flattering term. Coastal travel and trade are maritime.'

'Are there buses?'

'Works the same way; the buses route between the major towns, like from the north to Tana, but they stop wherever there's a branch road to the coast, and you can ride a local bus from there to the ocean and back.

'The ferry from Hellville will take you to the first bus on the mainland. Please don't stay in Hellville; its name now describes the town. Admiral Hell would have a fit if he saw it.'

The following day, Leo took a taxi to Hellville and then the ferry to the mainland. Six weeks later and five kilograms lighter after five hundred kilometres, much of it on foot, some rides in bullock carts, ferries in small pirogues, and the occasional dilapidated and groaning truck, he reached the port town of Mahajanga that feeds the capital, Antananarivo, in the central highlands. It was Christmas. He spent six days relaxing on the beach, eating massive prawns at La Terrasse restaurant, an open-air *bistro*, and then joined the New Year's Eve beach party that ended in 2022.

He left for Morondava when he learnt he could visit the Tsingys, an eroded limestone plateau with only rows of jagged teeth up to a hundred metres high.

He saw the Tsingys and visited the most photographed site in Madagascar, an alley of Baobab trees on either side of the road to Morondava. Leo was on the beach a week later for his eighteenth birthday party that continued until dawn. He slept through the next day before returning halfway across the island and then south again to Toliara; travel was easier thereafter. The road was never far from the coast as Leo passed along the south coast and through the old French port of Fort Dauphin, renamed Tolagnaro. Leo visited his third forest of lemurs and reached Farafagano, where the canal he had read about began. His plans included a cruise up the channel, for six hundred kilometres, to Foulpointe, where he hoped to find a ferry to St. Marie Island. Although officially *Nosy Boraha*, everyone called it St. Marie.

In their Rixensart, Brussels house, on an unusually cool June evening, Gaston Calmette, an epidemiologist who worked for the World Health Organisation, called, like all the UN agencies by their initials, said at dinner, 'Rose, the WHO wants me to organise a vaccination campaign in Guinea.'

'Oh no, Gaston, not another year in Africa; Lisa can't leave now; these are the most important years of her education.'

Lisa had lived with her parents in many countries; her mother, a doctor, went with her father to help him by organising vaccination centres. The International schools in major cities and the French schools in capitals enhanced Lisa's education through daily contact with children from many countries. A polyglot and mild extrovert, she adapted quickly to local languages. As maturity is a function of experience, Lisa was more mature than most girls her age. For the last three years of schooling, the boys at the school gave her the name 'The Ice Maiden'. At first flattered, Lisa had thought it was because she had Nordic blood and was tall with blonde hair and grey eyes, like her father. She imagined herself as a reincarnation of the goddess Freya, but much later, she began to suspect her dislike of the boys was the cause. When, as she usually did, she asked for her mother's opinion, Rosemary replied, 'Lisa, those boys have far less world experience than you do. They sense their inferiority, and teenage boys need to feel superior; they blame their feelings on you. You will meet a different kind of man in a few years.'

Gaston replied, 'I know, Rose; I was going to talk to you and Lisa about her next year anyway, but I think we should discuss it now that the WHO has made the request. Lisa, are you still sure you want to study medicine?'

'Yes, Papa, nothing else interests me, although the recommendations of the school careers officer are attractive. She said I'm too bossy to be a GP.'

'You mean about hospital management and administration?'

'Yes.'

'She might be right; GPs must be empathic; most diagnoses develop from a patient's description. That's why I specialised; you may be the same. But every manager must first learn what he must manage, and if you want to manage medical people, become a doctor first.'

What he said about himself didn't surprise Lisa; although she knew him to be cuddly, others sensed authority, not sympathy.

'Has the Free University of Brussels accepted your application?'

'Not yet, Papa; I had to wait for the entrance exam results before applying, so it will be at least another week.'

'I'm sure the university will accept you; being fifth in the exam will count. Did you apply to Leuven as well?'

'No, I don't want to specialise; at the Free University, the bachelor's degree is three years, then the masters three more. If I quit the medical courses after three years, I'll at least have a bachelor's degree. I could then study hospital management.'

'Rose, whether I accept or refuse the UN commission, Lisa must live in a student's residence. So, her education is unaffected.'

Rosemary surrendered. 'Alright, Gaston, as soon as Lisa's eighteenth birthday party is over, take us for a holiday where you'll have no work.'

'For how long?'

'I expect it's the only holiday we'll have together for a long time, so how about a month? Somewhere warm, with palm trees, a beach, and few people. Lisa can choose.'

Lisa chose St. Marie Island in Madagascar and announced, 'This is the place, Mama.'

'Why?'

'I don't know, but after reading about it, I'm fascinated and feel I must visit. Although we don't speak Malagasy, it is an ex-French territory, and the people also speak French.

For Leo, the canal was part adventure and part pleasure; a pleasure when he could travel in style in a tourist boat, view the activities along the canal banks or cross a short strip of sandy forest to swim in the Indian Ocean off an endless beach. When there was no tourist transport, he shared the space in a boat with goats and chickens, firewood, sacks of rice or bundles of clothes. – But every day brought surprises – like a man asleep beside the canal with a fishing line tied to a toe.

Leo had to bypass Toamasina as the canal had ceased to be usable, so he walked, then paid a few Ariary for a ride in a three-wheeled ricksha pedalled by a sweating rider. On the north side, he found the canal again.

Nine months after leaving *Nosy Be*, Leo arrived in Foulpointe, where the canal ended, discovered the ferry to St. Marie departed from Soanierana farther north and had to decide whether the side trip to St. Marie was worth the trouble. It took only seconds to decide. *It's a shame to miss it after coming this far. A quick trip there and back won't take long.* He hitched a lift on a truck carrying supplies for St. Marie.

After an unforgettable night in a palm-leafed room with woven reed walls, a tired bamboo bed, no door, a stereo booming out rock rhythms in a nearby bar, and three offers of love from bare-breasted maidens that he turned down, Leo reached the island on an overcrowded ferry the following evening. Asking the ferry captain, who thought he had little money to spend, brought the response, 'Walk or take a *tuc-tuc* south to *Chez Nath*, a backpacker's lodge. *Chez Nath* will, hopefully, meet your budget.' Although Leo camped and slept wherever he wished, a daily shower in the hot climate, often with another at midday, was one of the pleasures he refused to abandon.

2

A week after Lisa's birthday party, she and her parents landed on the island of *Nosy Boraha*, the long, thin barrier protecting a large bay on the northeast coast of Madagascar. Lisa had read a brochure on the Island's history; it was named Santa Maria in 1503 by Portuguese explorers, became St. Marie under French rule and reverted to *Nosy Boraha* years after independence.

It was warm, palm trees were everywhere, and the beach was ten metres from the bungalow verandas.

Lisa wryly smiled as she thought, *and a few people.* Two days later, she thought, *they've done it again!*

Instead of sunbathing on the beach, her parents had become involved with a group of biology graduates studying the whales that came to breed annually in the St. Marie waters. The students were all five or six years older than Lisa, and though they welcomed her, like any eighteen-year-old trying to find her way in the world, she didn't want to be with them and her parents all day.

Leo's first evening with a backpacker travelling south supplied information; one item was the pirates' cemetery less than two kilometres away. So, the following day, after a lazy morning on the beach, he ate a mixed salad with *Poulet Gasy*, a variety of chicken with such long legs that Leo had first thought they were baby ostriches. He then showered, shouldered his backpack, and headed for the cemetery. He left the road where a dilapidated sign, hanging at a drunken angle, revealed the path to the *Cimetière des Pirates.*

The deserted cemetery, overgrown with banana palms and Ravenalas, the tree commonly called the traveller's palm, although not a true palm, had a small soft grassy patch in the rays of the afternoon sun beside a pirate's tomb that delighted him.

Leo parked his pack on the tombstone, read the inscription, and then unrolled his groundsheet and sleeping bag. He stripped as he did whenever he could sunbathe in a secluded spot, then, naked, lay down on his back, watching the warm sun as it descended towards the mountains on the mainland, sharply outlined against the deep blue sky in the clear, pure air.

On the same day, after a morning swim and a late breakfast, Lisa turned down the offer of a boat ride to count whales and, carrying a small bag and a bottle of water, flagged a *tuc-tuc* on the only island road. She knew that the name referred to the noisy eastern three-wheeler, and it took her to the only town, Ambodifototra.

The town stirred memories. The dirt, potholed roads, and dilapidated buildings of Ambodifototra were familiar; what interested her were the people and what they did. She found an open-air café for food, bought a large carry bag, colourfully decorated in woven straw, and added sundry trinkets. She found a tiny *boutique*, although it was just an alcove in a wall, where two women made shell necklaces and other items for the tourists.

While eating an enjoyable lunch with unripe papaya and lemon as a dessert, she read a tourist brochure from a rack on the bar. The article she found the most interesting was a paragraph about the pirates who used St. Marie as a base in the late seventeenth century. The article recommended visiting the pirates' cemetery.

After lunch, Lisa visited a dress shop without a display window or door, with the roller shutter fully rolled up. She ordered a loose dress in colourful cotton, which was ideal for the climate. By three o'clock, after finding a man selling flower essences from a doorway with a cupboard but no shop, where Lisa bought two tiny flasks after smearing a little on each wrist, Lisa decided to walk towards the hotel. She had learnt the pirates' cemetery was on the other side of the bridge the *tuc-tuc* had crossed when coming into town. On the way, Lisa met two small boys on the roadside selling model cars and trucks made from aluminium beer cans and bought two. She missed the path to the cemetery, but only thirty metres farther, a woman making table mats from used crown corks told her to return thirty steps. Lisa bought a table mat. *Nothing,* she thought, *goes to waste.*

She found the sign, displaying terminal rot, pointing downwards. *Cimetière des Pirates* was readable once she tilted her head to match the slope, but the skull and crossed bones burnt into the wood at one end had almost vanished. Only if you knew it was there could a mind have imagined it. A path from the road to the cemetery wound through palms and tropical creepers in lush undergrowth, across a dozen stepping stones at the edge of the lagoon inlet, and finally climbed a small hill. Lisa found the graveyard on the hilltop; she missed the first tombs, lost in the overgrowth; the gravestones had suffered centuries of weathering and the predations of tropical vegetation. She worked her way along the path, looking at each one, and stopped at the fifth. The tourist brochures mentioned Madagascar's enormous variety of chameleons, from two centimetres in length to half a metre. Beside the tomb, a young banana variety plant struggled for its share of sunshine, and a chameleon about eight centimetres long on the stem of a leaf was examining Lisa. She could see its eyes, tiny black circles in the peak of a conical hat, twisting and turning, up and down, side to side, as they scanned her.

She placed her Malagasy cloth bag with her day's purchases on the tomb, leant on one hand, and reached over to put a finger in front of the chameleon. After its eyes swivelled for a careful look, it hesitantly placed a foot with its distinctive claws on her finger and then walked aboard. Lisa stood and looked at the minute creature; she knew its eyes, moving independently, gave it the ability to judge the direction accurately and the distance to shoot its tongue, the length of its body, from its mouth. With a sticky ball on the tip, its tongue would snap back like a released rubber band, carrying the luckless prey into its gaping maw.

Lisa picked up her bag, walked on with the chameleon on her finger and noticed a large tomb ahead at the highest point, with something on top. As she approached, it became easier to identify a well-used backpack with a military water bottle on the side. No one was there, the silence undisturbed except by the occasional tweet or caw, the discreet rustle as a lizard ran through the fallen leaves; even her feet were silent on the moist carpet of leaves. When she saw the far side of the tomb, she stopped with a sudden intake of breath.

Leo had decided to sleep in the cemetery; he liked the missing roof and had almost fallen asleep when he heard a gasp. He casually turned his head to see who was there.

The young girl looking at him seemed surprised; *I suppose that's not strange, but I was here first.* He saw the chameleon on her finger and watched as she turned away, stepped to a small palm tree and waited patiently while the chameleon walked slowly and tentatively onto a leaf.

Lisa's initial reaction, to run away, was cut short when the chameleon dug its claws into her finger to avoid falling off as she began to turn. So she stepped over to a palm to let the chameleon leave.

When she turned to face him, he was smiling. As she said nothing, he moved to one side of his bed, patted the vacant spot in invitation, and turned to watch the sunset.

Her mind was whirling as she studied the boy. *Oh my. No, not a boy, definitely a young man.* She placed a hand on the tomb to steady herself. Then, she thought oddly: *It's daylight; he's naked and barefoot; I can run away, so he's not dangerous.*

She didn't run. Instead, she had another thought: *Why should I consider an invitation to sunbathe?*

As she stood with her hand on the tomb, looking at the naked figure, the instinct to flee died and running away seemed childish. The choice between leaving and staying didn't solve itself, but it raised a tricky question. *If I stay, should I take off my clothes? That would be a new experience.*

She didn't ask herself why she contemplated doing so with a stranger, as she felt a thrill of anticipation and thought, *it's like the beach where I sunbathe topless.* She put her bag on the tomb, kicked off her shoes, and slipped off her dress, but she kept her bra and panties.

It sounds like she undressed! I didn't expect that.

She saw he was wearing a silver medallion, so she kept her gold chain. As she lay down, being careful not to touch him, the young man, still silent, reached out an arm so she could rest her head on it to watch the sunset.

Nice perfume.

Tense at first, but as the sun warmed her and he said nothing, she relaxed and felt a growing languor and peace until any thought of moving vanished. *I could lie beside him forever, but he hasn't looked at me once.* After a few minutes, she thought, *I should have removed my bra; I'm sweaty under my arms.* She unclipped and removed it.

She relaxed again and thought, *the boys always peeked when I sunbathed topless, and he hasn't. Maybe he's gay.*

When the last gleaming sun bead flared and then winked out over the jagged mountain peaks, she sensed his movement as he turned his head, so she turned too until they were looking at each other, their faces almost touching.

She's young and beautiful. I must be careful.

He smiled. 'Hello, girl, you have grey eyes and are good company.'

'Hello, man, but I haven't said anything; yours are azure.'

'Most people talk their heads off and never see, feel, or hear what's happening around them. You have the gift of silence unless it's necessary. I like you.'

'Thanks. Do you come here often?'

'It's the first time, but I'll return daily because the pirates make me feel welcome. Is it your first visit to St. Marie?'

'Yes, and I don't know why I feel welcome or why I dared to lie down beside a naked stranger.'

'Perhaps we're alike.'

Lisa purposely looked downwards, then, looking into his eyes, she smiled and said, 'No one would agree with you. I don't have one of those, and you don't have these.' She touched a breast.

'Don't tease; you know what I mean. We're in a cemetery where eternal calm banishes our fears to the outside world. We both feel it. Without chaperoning fears, we sense the tranquil depths of each other.

'It's time to dress, and I'll take you to your hotel; the night falls quickly in the tropics and the temperature drops. What's the perfume you're wearing?'

'Ylang-ylang on your side, vanilla on the other.'

'That's unusual. Do you do that often?'

'Only when I try perfumes before buying. I bought little bottles in town.'

'The ylang-ylang is exotic and lovely. Now let's go.'

When he reached over the tomb for his bag, Lisa asked, 'Whose grave is this?'

'I read the inscription on the top; it's PegLeg Jon, a pirate of the Caribbean.'

'I hope he doesn't mind us sunbathing naked by his tomb.'

'I'm sure he doesn't; I feel he approves.'

Odd, me too. Am I sharing the feeling?

He let her lead the way to the road, then walked beside her.

'What's your name?'

'Elisabeth, but call me Lisa. I've lain beside you half-naked for over an hour, and only now do you ask.'

'Names are unimportant; you know that; you haven't asked me for mine; it's Leo. Have you seen much of the island?'

'No, I arrived two days ago; I've only seen the town.'

'I arrived yesterday, and all I've seen is the cemetery. I want to visit the Ile aux Nattes tomorrow. I'd enjoy your company.'

'But not if I talk?'

'Whatever you say will be worth hearing, so talk all you want.'

'I'll meet you in front of my hotel at nine,' she said, looking up; they were at the gate. 'That means right here.' She faced him. 'Good night, Leo.'

He raised her free hand to his lips. 'Good night, Lisa,' then turned and walked away. She watched him for several paces, raising the hand he kissed to her lips. Then Lisa walked through the hotel gate. Five steps in – she met her mother.

'Ah, there you are. We were beginning to wonder where you were. Did you have a good day?'

'Yes, Mama, I'll show you the things I bought, and I have a dress to collect in two days; you'll love it. I also went to the pirates' cemetery; there's a collection of old tombstones, all assorted sizes and higgledy-piggledy, only a few of which are readable, but the view of the sunset is lovely.'

Lisa wondered. *Did Mother see Leo?*

That night, Gaston asked Rosemary, 'Where was Lisa today?'

'Shopping, and she met a boy at the pirates' cemetery.'

'How do you know about the boy?'

'She was happy when she returned, and I saw him say goodbye. He kissed her hand. When she told me about the cemetery, I remembered what I was like at eighteen. She told me about the tombstones but didn't mention he was there, although her voice told me.'

'He must be of good family to have learnt the hand kiss; do you think she'll be alright?'

'Yes, she said she's going to the Ile aux Nattes tomorrow, and I'm sure she'll be with him. She's eighteen now; we can't watch over her forever, Gaston; we must let her find the path to follow.'

'What's he like, Rose?'

'Fair or blond hair, half a head taller than Lisa, slim but well built. It was dark – I couldn't see anything else. I did see him walk away; you know the impression that can give.'

'Yes. Fit, healthy, muscular, controlled, graceful.'

'Exactly. All of those: coordinated, silent and smooth.'

Leo and Lisa visited everything they could on the island and the adjoining islets: swam in the sea, Scuba dived with a dive school, walked the beaches hand in hand, snorkelled in the coral gardens, and sunbathed naked on the grass of the pirates' cemetery. On the third visit, she thought, *It's stupid to keep my panties on.*

Leo asked her, 'Tell me about your parents, Lisa; what are they doing?'

'Normally, they work for the WHO. Dad's an epidemiologist, and my mother is a doctor who helps by organising vaccinations. They should be relaxing on the beach, but are counting whales and recording the sounds they make. That's the kind of people they are.

Now that you ask, I realise I may be more like my mother than I thought.'

'Can you explain that?'

'I wasn't there, so I can only remember what they told me.

'My Dad's Gaston Calmette. He qualified as a doctor, but he's tall with steely grey eyes and an air of authority. That's not the ideal image of a sympathetic family GP, so he decided to study epidemiology. Although Belgian, he studied infectious diseases at the Pasteur Institute in Paris, where he met my mother; she was Rosemary Challant, also a doctor and had applied to research vaccination at the Institute.

'Dad told me that he saw my mother leaving a shop on the Boulevard Pasteur with two large dress boxes, and her "derriere" mesmerised him, so he followed her. My mother said he was clumsy, bumping into people, and had to run to keep up, so she stopped at a shop window to see what he would do, and he walked up to her.

'Mother said she had difficulty holding back laughter when he asked if he could talk to her, and when she asked why, he replied truthfully, "Because you have the most beautiful *derriere* I have ever seen."

'He invited her for coffee and told her he worked at the institute. She accepted, and their discussion about vaccination and epidemics lasted through lunch and dinner. He took her home, and she said, "Gaston, I must learn if what I feel is true. Take me in your arms and kiss me."

'A minute later, Dad proposed, and Mother replied, "Yes, Gaston, but we have much to do to be sure our marriage will work.""

'That's rare but not unusual. So tell me, why do you think you're like your mother?'

'Because she didn't hesitate, most women wouldn't have agreed to the coffee and might have hit him with their handbag. I accepted your invitation to sunbathe the first time we met.'

'Why do you wear that pirate medallion? Are you a Biker?'

'No, Lisa. I'm sure it's a real pirate's medallion. I'll tell you the story, though you might not believe it.

'Two years ago, I was shopping for souvenirs in a Djibouti souk, and after buying a roll of Muga silk for my mother, the shop owner gave me a flat-top lump of coral. You could see a skull on the surface when lit at an angle.

'I had it x-rayed and found a box inside with three medallions like this, in silver, bronze and copper. I have the metal analyses, but I don't know if those can tell me much. They're dated 1710. On a trip two years ago, I wore the bronze one, and on the way to Lubumbashi and Victoria Falls, I traded it with a giant and his wife for a gemstone necklace. After returning home, I tried the copper one, but it stained my skin, so I replaced it with the silver one with the initials RJC on the back.'

'I can believe all of it except the giant. How big was he?'

'Over two metres, maybe two-twenty'.

'That's not excessive; some basketball players are that tall.'

'Yes, but not over a hundred and eighty kilos!'

'I'll accept that might qualify as a giant.

'I told you about my folks, how about yours?'

Dad told me not to talk about him or the family.

'Just ordinary folks, Lisa; Dad's like your dad, a consultant to the International Finance Corporation, a UN agency, and my mother goes with him because he has to attend receptions.'

Then Leo chuckled. 'And to make sure he's presentable!'

Lisa collected cowrie shells. Each time they visited the cemetery, she added two of the best shells as decorations to PegLeg's tomb.

'He doesn't have any flowers, Leo, and we're invading his space; it's the least we can do. I'm sure he likes them.'

They talked about themselves, their past, desires, ambitions, and the future they hoped would come, and one day, after she placed two more cowrie shells on the tomb, she asked, 'Do you know who PegLeg Jon was? He must have had a real name.'

'I've no idea; he was likely English or French, Jean or John, but he could have been any nationality.'

'Leo, would you have been a pirate if you had lived when these pirates did?'

'Possibly, Lisa, I've read much about them. Most describe how heartless and cruel some were, but some descriptions of individuals show they refused the rules and classifications of a rigid society and loved to be free. That's how I feel, too. There were also women pirates.'

'I don't think I could be a pirate.'

'Neither did they when they were young, but they fought against the restrictions imposed on women in a male-dominated world. They captained ships and even fleets. One day, you might do the same.'

'Leo, to learn about PegLeg now is impossible, but I wonder who he was. He was a woman's son. Was he another woman's husband?'

Leo replied, 'Nameless, unidentified people pack history, but one day, we might learn from something we read or hear.'

While walking along the beach two weeks later, they met and talked to a man with a boatload of fish; at least Leo talked while Lisa stroked a beautifully coloured fish. The angler gave Leo the names of the species he had caught. As they left, Lisa asked, 'Leo, were you speaking *Malagasy* with him?'

'Sort of, Lisa; I've been travelling here for over nine months and learnt many words and phrases. It's not difficult because, like all evolving languages, they've borrowed words from Arabic, Dutch, French and English. Just like Swahili.'

'How many languages do you speak?'

'Four main ones: Arabic, French, English, and Swahili. Some Spanish, Italian, Russian, Kazakh, Dutch, and German, plus another twenty or thirty dialects from developing countries.'

'Why so many, and why Arabic? I thought you were French?'

'My mother speaks Arabic; she's Omani. My father is French, so they raised me with both. English is natural from schooling. Dad is a financial consultant to companies and governments; I spent several months each year in different countries for years. A dam or power station takes years to build. How about you?'

'I can't count that many European languages, French, Dutch, Flemish and English, and like you, Swahili and a dozen or more dialects.'

While lying by the tomb, Lisa asked the following Friday. 'Leo, can we visit the church on Sunday?'

'Because it's Sunday?'

'Yes and no. There are people at the church on Sunday, and Nomena in the hotel spa says the churchgoers sing on Sundays. I'd like to hear them singing in *Malagasy*. The church will be closed on other days; the priest won't be there. Like most Belgians, I began life as a Catholic; however, after schooling in a dozen countries with different religions where the only common denominator, though not always, is one God, I'm non-practising. So don't worry, I don't want to pray.'

'I wouldn't worry if you did. I'm nominally a Muslim, and when the occasion arises, I visit a mosque and pray to Allah. Sometimes, I attended a Christian church service and prayed to Allah. The atmosphere feels the same.'

'What does nominally mean?'

Leo had to pause and think… 'Lisa, do you believe in God?'

… 'Yes, but I know nothing about Him. He's not what any religion I know tries to define.'

'Then we're on the same wavelength. Nominally means I believe in Allah or God. But the conflicting writings of thousands of Imams since Mahommed preached in Mecca and Medina leave me cold. Reading them, I learnt that Allah's intentions in 622 are not what he intends today, yet no prophet has appeared to tell us that.'

'I feel the same. Do you eat Halal?'

'I try, Lisa. The prophet essentially banned the consumption of anything detrimental to health. At the time, Haram defined detrimental foods and healthy ones as Halal. So I eat healthily. It's not difficult to do.'

'But you drink beer.'

'Only a little, Lisa, because I never drink water from a suspicious source, including a bottle without a sealed top. That's more likely to poison me than a beer.

'My parents are both Muslim, although my father is French. My mother told me to drink beer if I was unsure of anything else. They travel extensively and have no choice but to compromise.'

Lisa asked, 'I know you could marry a Jew or a Christian, are those the only two?'

She must have read that on the web.

'Christians and Jews have the same God. Mohammed was specific about that.' Leo grinned. 'I believe the later interpretations that insist they must be blonde.'

She chuckled. 'That lets me off the hook; my hair is dark, and I use a blonde dye.'

Leo smiled. 'You forget Lisa, you're naked!'

'*…Damn!*'

'So we'll visit the church?'

'Of course, I'll check on the times.'

'I asked Nomena, and she said ten-thirty, but if we arrive before ten, we can meet the priest and visit the church.'

'I'll meet you at nine, and we'll walk or take a *tuc-tuc*. Now, we must dress before the chill sets in.'

When they arrived at nine-forty-five, the smiling man wearing a black cassock on the church steps was the only priest. Lisa had his name from Nomena, so she greeted him, 'Good morning, Father Benjamin, we've come for the service and to visit the church. I'm Lisa.'

'And I'm Leo, Father.'

'You're welcome; unfamiliar faces bring pleasure to my small world. I'll guess you're both on holiday before beginning further studies.'

Leo grinned. 'Dead right, Father, although we've been studying this island for two weeks.'

'And had to come here because of the altar?'

'Is there something special about the altar?'

'Please, come in; most visitors have read everything in the guidebooks and leave me with little to say. It'll be a joy to tell you the church's history.'

Leo and Lisa followed Father Benjamin into the church, where he said, 'Although this was the first stone-built church in Madagascar, it came after wooden buildings on this site or closer to the town centre served as a place to pray. I doubt any priest was there to consecrate them, but the people would have called them churches.

'The first consecrated church in Madagascar was in Tolagnaro.

'In 1644, France landed a group of colonists nearby. The colonists would have built a shack for assemblies and prayer, but an island of heathens to convert was so attractive to St Vincent de Paul, who had founded the religious order in France called the Lazarists, that he dispatched a group of Catholic missionaries in 1648. They found the colony had moved to a peninsula for safety against the warring inhabitants and had constructed a fort, which they named Fort Dauphin.

'The Lazarists worked hard, and they built a church and school, and in 1650, the Paris headquarters dispatched a painted wooden statue of our Virgin Mother and child, with more missionaries, and consecrated the church.'

'I've visited Tolagnaro,' interjected Leo, 'and the Catholic church; it's now an impressive set of buildings, but there's no painted Madonna in the church, only a stone statue.'

'That church was built long after the colonists left in 1674.'

Lisa asked, 'Why did they leave?'

Father Benjamin smiled at her. 'You could say adultery – most of the French were men living with Malagasy women. The cultures may be different, but some things are not. In October 1672, the *Dunkuerquoise* visited Fort Dauphin on its way to Reunion Island. The ship had a dozen female transportees for Reunion, but the women had other ideas and escaped. The colonists who switched to French wives sent their Malagasy companions home and married the French women, although I doubt they were church marriages.

'The Malagasy women banded together, complained to their king and demanded he punish the French, which he did, killing half of them indiscriminately in one night. The French lived in the closed fort for two years until the *Blanc Pignon* arrived and took them to Reunion.

'The Antanosy, the local ethnic kingdom, set fire to the fort but not the church.'

Leo remarked, 'I've heard of similar things. It's far safer to leave a place of worship alone than to annoy the Gods. But what happened to the Madonna?'

'That we don't know. We can only guess. Come, we'll walk to the altar while I talk.'

4

Lisa asked, 'What is your guess, Father?'

'Have you heard of Abraham Samuel?'

Leo answered, 'I have; he's part of Tolagnaro's history. They tell tourists he was a dark-skinned pirate.'

Father Benjamin knew more. 'A Caribbean mulatto. He came here from Aden in 1697, then sailed on to Fort Dauphin, where the elderly queen declared he was her son, crowned him as king, and then Samuel spent eight years fighting the neighbouring local groups and pirating any ship that came close. Samuel wasn't a Christian, and in 1698, a rumour made the rounds amongst the Christians in Madagascar that Samuel wanted to give the Madonna away because statues as religious symbols horrified him. The rumour expanded into believing that the Madonna would come to St. Marie.

'In 1699, the captain of a ship that visited Fort Dauphin and then here told a senior port official that the Church there no longer had the Madonna.'

'Then it's lost forever,' Lisa remarked.

'Yes, we think so, too, although hope never dies. But now something unusual, this is our altar.'

The massive black altar impressed Leo. 'Is it a basalt slab?'

'No, it's a unique gift from the French Empress Eugénie de Montijo; it's a naval scrap iron casting from a foundry in France.'

'Then you have a unique altar. Is the cross and Jesus also from France?'

'No, that was carved by a man in Toamasina when a previous church burnt down.'

After looking at the iron altar, Lisa's eyes drifted to a smoothly curving palm tree trunk about two metres tall standing on a plinth to one side, with an arched alcove in the stone wall behind it. 'I think that carved palm tree is also unique.'

'It is because it's the only one the artist carved. Take a careful look and tell me what you see.'

'Leo, what do you see?'

'The first two metres of an ancient palm tree and months of work. Your turn, Lisa.'

'It's a Madonna and child carving. The posture, leaning forward over her child, comes from the curve of the tree; the carving is minimalist, just enough for the figures to take on life. When I first saw it, I wanted to touch and caress her. Now, I can't; that would be indecent.'

Leo had more to say, 'I feel she's beautiful and must be respected, but why is she too tall for the alcove behind her? Also, who's the artist, and when was she carved?'

'I'm glad you feel as you do, but I must disappoint you. As each wooden church deteriorated, caught fire or fell, the residents built a new church and moved the palm Madonna to the new building. It took her a hundred and thirty years to find a home here. So she's about three hundred years old, and we will never learn the artist's name.'

'And the alcove?'

'After the St. Marie congregation learnt that the Madonna from Fort Dauphin might come to them, they insisted on including the right size alcove to await her arrival every time they rebuilt their church. I told you the hope never dies, so this church has an alcove waiting to welcome her since 1857.'

'If another statue, only a little different, came, would anyone know the difference?'

'Of course, records must exist in Lazarist archives in Paris, for they ordered her fabrication. But I believe people would know when they saw it.'

Lisa asked, 'And where would the palm Madonna go?'

'This building needs renovating; we have limited our services to Sundays as we worry about a stone falling from the roof and injuring someone, and we no longer play the organ to avoid unwanted bass vibrations. If a collector or museum buys her, she'll save this church.

'I must welcome my flock; they should arrive now. Leave something on the pew where you want to sit and follow me.'

Leo and Lisa stood to one side while Father Benjamin welcomed each congregation member, including the children. Leo counted the men, and Lisa counted the women and children. Before the last worshippers entered the church, Lisa said, 'I counted fifty-three women and forty-eight kids.'

'Forty-eight men, so a hundred and one adults and half that number of kids.'

'That's a fair congregation for a little island like this. I think no more than two hundred can squeeze into the church. Is there nothing they can do to repair it, or will the people find themselves without a church?'

'I don't know, and as the chance of the missing Madonna miraculously popping up from nowhere is nil, they must soon choose between a church without a Palm Madonna or no church at all.'

'Leo, am I being silly to say that if I could help, I would do so?'

'No, Lisa, my parents explained to me that such feelings should be respected and admired but warned that it would be many years before I could reliably judge the merit of giving such gifts or help. They were adamant that I should never feel pride or importance in what I did and to evaluate the possible consequences of such an action. Would you know how to help this church and ensure the people think they saved it? Without a powerful attachment to the church, it will die anyway.'

'Then it needs a miracle.'

'It does. Miracles are a reward for years of devout prayer, so the people themselves are responsible.'

Leo and Lisa had left their straw hats on the last row and were the last to enter and sit. For Lisa, the ceremony was a relaxed version of those she had attended in Brussels, more like others she had attended as a child in different countries. Apart from a few Latin phrases, the service was in Malagasy.

With no organ or other musical instruments, the choir, a group of twenty individuals ranging in age from eight-year-old girls and boys to one white-haired grandfather who led the singing, impressed Leo. Several of the choir didn't sing but harmonised a rhythmic background chant. Leo glanced at Lisa and saw she had closed her eyes.

The service was familiar to Leo, who had attended Catholic services, particularly ones in the Orthodox countries, and he bowed his head obediently when Father Benjamin said, 'Let us pray.' He could understand more of the Malagasy sermon than Lisa and understood three phrases clearly.

'In the rear pew are two *Vahini*; they're no longer children and begin their journey through the world where God will teach them what adults must know. I have asked them to look for our Madonna as they travel from place to place, for we need our Madonna's help to save our church. Let us pray for Leo and Lisa, ask God to grant them health and happiness, and guide them to our Madonna.'

As the prayer finished, many of the congregation turned and

smiled at Leo and Lisa, and she whispered to him, 'What was all that about?'

'Tell you later,' was his whispered reply, 'You can go up for communion.'

The last hymn impressed Lisa: the congregation sang in Malagasy, but the last three rows of people joined in with the choir's harmonised background chant. The volume began to grow, and their feelings overtook many people who started to sway and tap their feet. She saw Father Benjamin raise his arms and gesture like a conductor for less volume. *The building must be more fragile than I thought.*

Leo and Lisa had expected a collection bag and came prepared. The twenty thousand Ariary banknote, the highest value in issue, was worth four Euros, so each had a tight roll of notes.

Leo observed that everyone remained until the collection was over; Father Benjamin offered the collection bag with a short prayer of thanks and then walked down the aisle to the door. When he passed Leo and Lisa, he said, 'Please, join me outside. I'm sure many people would like to meet you.'

Lisa whispered urgently, 'Leo, tell me what he said in the sermon.'

'He asked the people to pray for God to look after us and teach us to be good people as we experience life as adults, and he asked God to guide us to the missing Madonna.'

'*Whew!*'

'That's about right.'

Father Benjamin blessed each member who came from the church, and then, broadly smiling, most came and shook hands fervently with Lisa and Leo. When everyone had gone, they thanked Father Benjamin and said goodbye.

Leo sensed the end of their time together approaching as Lisa stayed closer, a reaction against pending separation. He, too, was reluctant to see her leave and thought about how they could separate without hurt.

When the final day came, she said, 'Leo, I want to visit the cemetery earlier today.'

They stripped, as they had done every time they sunbathed, and lay down on Leo's bedding. Then Lisa asked, 'Leo, can Muslims have four wives and five hundred concubines?'

'Have you been reading stuff on the web again?'

'Yes, you're Omani, and an article mentioned an Omani Sultan had five hundred concubines.'

Leo laughed. 'Lisa, those are ancient descriptions; five hundred may mean "more than I have ever seen". Perhaps ten, but concubines were a way of life in many communities until the early twentieth century. I believe it's possible to say the rules were necessary to protect women and children before contraception became reliable. Increasing numbers of men don't obey the injunction against multiple partners or pre-marital sex. Trying to impose rules without justification will drive believers away.'

'Thanks for being honest, Leo.'

Lisa lay tight against him, watching the sunset, and then the August full moon rose.

'Lisa, I know you're leaving tomorrow.'

'How do you know?'

'I can feel you're upset; you don't want it to end.'

'You're right, Leo. I can't help it. Please, you haven't kissed me since we met; hold and kiss me now.'

'Lisa, I don't want it to end, but the world is bigger than us. Come.'

She turned towards him, and he took her in his arms; their kiss was tentative at first, and then passion took control. Caressing each other, waves of ecstasy came from nowhere, and each tried to weld to the other until twenty minutes later, he hesitated, and with eyes locked together, gazing into the depths of each other, she raised her hips and pulled. Then they lay motionless, each savouring the feel of the other in the intimate embrace until she started to move, experimenting with her sensations...

She was on a pirate ship closing on the shore, tossed by waves and breakers; on the beach stood a pirate with azure eyes.

She knew the ship would run aground. Suddenly, an enormous wave lifted the vessel and hurled it towards the beach; she screamed as it hit the land, and she felt the shuddering and shaking.

Eyes closed, Lisa whispered, 'Did I faint?'

'Yeah, us both. Lie still.'

A half-hour passed, and Leo said, 'Lisa, I want to say something.'

'Not now. Kiss me again; I want to know what it's like with me on top.'

'Me too.'...

Caught up by the ecstasy, their movements grew and became abandoned until, suddenly, they froze, straining breathless in a strangling embrace as the surrounding palms shivered and rattled their fronds in susurrating applause.

As the setting moon touched the high mountains to the west, with the first pink and yellow blush of the new day oozing from the ocean into the eastern sky, Leo, with Lisa in his arms, asked, 'Please tell me your thoughts. Do we walk away from each other and wrap our memories in a packet that we unwrap and remember each time we feel low?'

Lisa said nothing for over a minute.

'If you ask me to marry you, I'll say yes, and we can see Father Benjamin in three hours. So don't because it would destroy our lives.'

His cry was almost anguished, 'Why, Lisa?'

'Written on my bedroom wall is a quotation: "*You deserve to live the life you want to live, not the life others expect you to live.*"

'I want to study for a medical degree; you want to study maths, then a doctorate. Six years of study ahead of us and then years of experience before we know what life we want to live and with whom we want to share it. We must be free to learn, so you mustn't call me and ask for commitments I can't make, even if they're only temporary. I don't expect a social life for the first five or six years of medical school, and when I'm ready to commit to marriage, I don't know if we will feel the same as we do now.'

'So, is it goodbye, Lisa?'

'It should be, but I remember the first time we spoke. Do you re-member what you replied when I asked, "Do you come here often?"'

'Like yesterday, I'll never forget. I replied, "It's the first time, but I'll return daily because the pirates make me feel welcome."'

'Do you still feel the same?'

'Even more so, I feel we belong with each other and here with the pirates.'

'Leo, do you remember my saying, "I wonder who PegLeg was?"'

'Yes, Lisa, you said, "He was a woman's son. Was he another woman's husband?"'

'So you *do* remember! It's ridiculous to say this, but he welcomed us. He wants us to learn who he was. Why, I don't know. He may have a hidden secret, a task he never completed, which has kept him locked in the tomb instead of pirate heaven.

'We must separate; we have no choice, but can we say *au revoir* – until we meet again, not goodbye? And can we promise we will try to discover who PegLeg was and what he did? We won't call or message each other for any reason except to tell the other about a discovery. Then, if we feel it's right to do so, we can meet to discuss what we've learnt about PegLeg.'

She's a romantic, and I love her. 'Lisa, I'll promise whatever you wish if it might bring us together. But can we make another promise to each other?'

'I asked, so you can.'

'When I feel ready to marry, I'll tell you, then I'll come here on the day of the August full moon, hoping to meet you.'

'Why, Leo? That's like a promise not to marry before we meet here again.'

'For me, it's a promise not to marry until we have PegLeg's approval. If we meet here, we'll know and won't live our lives wondering what might have been.'

'Do you love me, Leo?'

'If the pain I feel at the thought of you leaving tomorrow is any indication, I love you more than I ever imagined possible.'

'Hold me tight; I feel the same.'

....

'Leo, stand up; we must ask PegLeg to witness our promise. I'm sure he approves.'

They stood, and he placed his medallion on the tomb. 'Put your hand on my medallion, Lisa.' Leo covered her hand with his and said, 'PegLeg, witness my pledge to Lisa; I shall try to learn your history, and I'll not marry until I have told Lisa and have visited your tomb on the night of the August full moon to meet her. I promise to come if she tells me she's coming.'

'Now you, Lisa.'

She repeated it but added, 'PegLeg, we'll be studying for at least four years, so you must wait until then.'

Leo kissed her again. 'Lisa, how do I tell you if I learn something?'

'I'll give you my email address; you can mail me the information. Don't expect a reply.'

Two can play that game. 'Lisa, I'll mail you a phone number; you can SMS me if you want me to call. It only accepts SMS messages.'

'Why only SMS?'

'Because there's no signal on the oceans, in an aeroplane, or the deserts of Oman. I collect messages once a day with a satphone.'

'That's unusual.'

Leo took her to the hotel before daylight and then returned to *Chez Nath*; he knew her flight was at 15:15, so she had enough time to sleep.

Leo didn't sleep but went for breakfast in the *Chez Nath* bar area after a shower. As he had not eaten dinner the night before, he ordered a copious breakfast, including eggs and *Zebu* sausages. Leo could see the beach and the enormous lagoon between the palm trees from his table.

Against the wall beside his table stood a wooden parrot carved by a local artist and painted in garish colours, perched on a long stick stuck in a flower pot. It gave him an idea. He asked if he could borrow it and if there was a cardboard box he could cut up. Armed with a stapler and some scissors from the office, he went to his room and made a three-cornered pirate hat using a cap as the base. Some more cardboard and a piece of string made an excellent eye patch. He cut up a black T-shirt to cover both, using paper glue and was quite proud of the result. *Now I look like Long John Silver from Treasure Island.*

Leo was at St. Marie Airport that afternoon before the flight to Antananarivo left. He went for one reason; Lisa said calling her might ruin her memory of their time together. Leo hoped seeing him at the low fence overlooking the aeroplane parking apron would reinforce her words, "until we meet again." He saw her walk from the airport terminal with her parents, and then halfway to the plane steps, she stopped and turned to search the faces of the spectators at the barrier fence. The figure with the pirate hat, eyepatch and parrot stood out. Leo stood straighter and waved, smiling broadly. She smiled a glorious smile; he blew her a kiss and raised the banner he had written in bold letters.

Until we meet again

He saw her mouth her reply, and then she waved and climbed the steps into the plane, her mother in front, her father behind. Her father turned at the top of the steps to look at him, so Leo saluted.

Rosemary let Lisa sit beside the window and sat beside her. 'Your young man came to see you off; why didn't you go and say goodbye?'

'We said goodbye last night, Mama; Leo came to remind me of our promise to the spirit of PegLeg Jon; he was a pirate, and his tomb is in the cemetery.'

When the seat belt sign went off, Rosemary asked, 'What promise did you make, Lisa?'

Lisa told her, and Rosemary asked, 'Whose idea was it?'

'I thought it was Leo, but now I'm unsure; maybe PegLeg wanted us to make the promise.'

There was a ten-hour delay in Antananarivo before the flight to Paris at one am. Gaston had booked rooms at the Relais des Plateaux rest house near Ivato airport, where he had stayed during an earlier visit.

Lisa, who had gone to her room for some extra sleep after the sleepless romantic night, fell asleep thinking, *I shall learn Arabic. Leo speaks it.*

After Lisa left the room, Gaston asked, 'What was that pirate stuff about?'

Rosemary explained what she knew, then added, 'He didn't make any false promises to Lisa. I hope we'll meet him; he took the trouble to make the pirate hat and find the parrot to make Lisa happy about leaving. I can't guess what the future might bring, but who knows? She thinks the spirit of PegLeg Jon might be behind the promise.'

Rosemary didn't say she was sure her daughter was no longer a virgin and hoped Leo and Lisa knew what they were doing.

Leo watched the plane take off and then thought about what he would do next for the first time in a month. The backpacker he met the first day had said, 'I travelled as far south as possible on the coast road from Diego Suarez and discovered that I had an eighty-kilometre walk, a hundred with deviations, along terrible tracks through the hills and valleys. They said it would take two weeks. Instead, I returned to Antalaha and paid for a ride on a fishing boat to Mananara, six days of hell.'

Returning to Toamasina or Antananarivo, then taking the road north to *Nosy Be* to complete his circle of Madagascar, was accepting defeat. Leo went into the terminal building to find an Air Madagascar official.

'Excuse me, what destinations do your flights serve?'

'Only one, Antananarivo, and sometimes we fly to Toamasina first. Where do you want to go?'

'Antsirabato.'

'I'm sorry, I can't help you; you can fly to Tana and see if a flight is going from there.'

Leo began to turn away when the rep added, 'You could ask Fifou if he's going that way.'

'Who's Fifou?'

'He owns the Princess Bora Lodge and the Cessna in the parking.'

'Thanks, I'll do that.'

Leo walked the short distance to the lodge and the reception, a building near the road, where he asked for Fifou.

'Down the path there, you'll find the restaurant, bar and pool. Fifou comes there every afternoon; he'll be with the whale watchers now. Ask the bartender.'

Leo bought a beer and relaxed on a lounger beside the pool until a voice from behind said, 'Hi, Andry said you were asking for me; I'm Fifou, and I'm surprised you're here. I thought you would have left with Elisabeth Calmette.'

Leo turned and looked up into a tanned, smiling face with blue eyes and short-cropped blond hair. *About a metre seventy-seven, his eyes smiling.* 'Why did you think that?'

Princess Bora shirt and shorts, owns a hotel on a tropical island and an aeroplane. Women must adore him.

Fifou grinned. 'After spending every day with her for a month, it seemed obvious. Why did you ask for me?'

'I didn't know it was so obvious.'

'Oh, this is a small island; everyone knows everything, and her parents seemed pleased she had someone her age to talk to.'

So, her parents knew about me and said nothing.

'Then I guess I must reveal all. I came here on the ferry and met

Lisa. I'm Leo Poussin, taking a gap year in my studies and backpacking around Mada; I'll study at Cambridge when I return to Europe. Lisa wants to be a doctor, so she and I have many years of study ahead of us. We will meet again in ten or twelve years, but now she's gone, and I want to continue my trip. I've learnt there's no road north and no flights. You have a plane, and the Air Mad guy said I should talk to you.'

'Well, her parents helped with the whale research, and I have a couple of officials to take to Maroantsetra on Monday, so promise you'll come to Princess Bora on your next visit, and I'll take you there and then on to Antsirabato. The roads are passable from there going north. Don't forget to see the Tsingys before Diego.'

It surprised Fifou when Leo said, 'I'll promise that with pleasure, but I didn't ask for a free ride; I can pay for it.'

'I'm not a licensed charter company; it's my pleasure. Advertising to the right people is a problem; just telling the students at Cambridge what a wonderful place we have here will be enough.'

'Thanks, I'll start now; if you have a spare room, I'll stay until we leave. And if someone can visit *Chez Nath*, pay the bill, and collect my backpack, I'll stay and ask you to drink with me.'

Fifou stayed and talked about the hotel, whale research, his travels, and his family in Switzerland. His stories about skiing in Kazakhstan were interesting, especially when he mentioned, 'I can also fly helicopters and fly one for a Heli-ski operation, taking rich Russians to the top of a mountain to ski down.'

'Why Kazakhstan? I thought you had a Swiss background.'

'I do, but I don't like skiing in Switzerland. There are too many people on the *pistes* and far too many in the resorts. In Switzerland, it's mostly a social scene; the skiers are there to show off their outfits and wealth and enjoy alcohol, food and sex. They ride the ski lift and spend the day watching others doing the same thing at the upper restaurants. You can't ski after an alcoholic and sleepless night in a disco.

'Kazakhstan will one day be the same, but for now, it's local families and keen skiers. If you leave the marked trails, you don't have a supervisor yell at you. The ski resorts are not luxurious, with no Chanel and Givenchy boutiques, but the girls like foreign pilots, some restaurants serve decent food, and you can ski on virgin slopes with few others, especially the high black slopes. If you ski well, you should try it.'

Several days after returning home, Gaston phoned Fifou.

'Fifou, Gaston Calmette here; how are you?'

'Fine, Gaston, we miss you at the research station. How can I help?'

'Fifou, I expect you know my daughter spent her holiday with a young man?'

'Of course, he has a reputation here; Leo is a very unusual young man. He flew me to Antsirabato two days ago, though I can't tell you where he is if you're looking for him.'

'You flew him or the reverse?'

'He flew; he's a superb pilot.'

'I'm not looking for him, Fifou; I would just like to know his name.'

'Poussin, like the baby chicken.'

'Thanks, Fifou. I hope to meet you and stay at Princess Bora again.'

Gaston found the time later to research the name Poussin. He found the web full of articles about Charles de La Vallee Poussin, a mathematician, nothing about Leo, and two entries about Louis. It seemed there were two different men with the same name. The first, years old, said Louis was French and had a son, Leo. However, the second, slightly more recent, said that L de La Vallee Poussin was an Omani citizen married to a daughter of the royal family, with a son called Asad and a daughter named Amina.

Then Gaston remembered that Asad meant 'Lion' in Arabic.

Satisfied, he left it at that; he had met Louis and might meet him again.

He told Rosemary. 'That boy Lisa met is Louis Poussin's son. Fifou told me he was using his gap year to walk around Madagascar and was coincidentally on St. Marie with us.'

'Coincidences happen for a reason, Gaston. Remember, I was shopping at a boutique on the Boulevard Pasteur and decided to leave the shop at the exact moment when you were about to walk by.'

'How do you know I hadn't been stalking you for weeks?'

'I told you; you were so inept at following me that I spotted you in seconds!'

6

When Leo arrived in *Nosy Be* a month later, he sent an SMS to his father.

> Trek finished Cambridge next, with Gerard and Francine in *Nosy Be* for my return.

Two days later, he stepped down from a jet at Farnborough airport, dressed as a pilot in the captain's spare uniform; Leo's hiking garb was disreputable. A waiting helicopter took him to his father's house on the Isle of Wight, a thirty-minute flight instead of three or more hours.

'Hello, Leo. How was your trip?'

'Hi, Dad, I made it all the way around; I have a thousand photos to sort to make a slide show for Mom and you. It was hard in places, but it's a fascinating country. Like most of Africa, it struggles for traction and momentum to develop.'

'Yes, I know, and unfortunately, riddled with clan factions.'

Louis looked carefully at Leo; he seemed to have grown up during the year. 'Did you meet any girls?'

'Yes, Dad, one at the Princess Bora lodge on St. Marie. She's blonde, with grey eyes, and beautiful. She'll be special when she's older.'

'It could be like you and Mom if I meet her again in ten years.'

Leo saw the faraway look in his father's eyes and knew he was remembering the story of his parents' meeting that he had heard years ago from his mother.

His father had attended a meeting in London in February 2002 at the Omani Embassy. From the outside, the building resembled many others in London, a stone Georgian mansion in the centre of a small garden with high wrought iron railings all around, but stepping inside led to an Arabian palace. Graceful pointed Islamic arches replaced interior walls, creating an impression of space; the decorations would have delighted the Hollywood producer of *Ali Baba*.

The boardroom where the meeting occurred was traditional, with British oak wainscoting and a polished oak table and chairs, men only, wearing business suits and ties.

Louis was there on behalf of the IFC to investigate a new port project proposed by Oman. The designated contractor sat at one end of the table with his engineers to support him. The Minister of Finance for Oman and his advisors sat at the other end, with Louis in the middle. Louis knew the minister was the Sultan's son – his English was perfect, his pronunciation precise, and he spoke without hesitation in a baritone voice. Still, Louis heard the overtones of Emirati Arabic.

Louis was unhappy – there were flaws in the project, and the pricing was wrong.

He was sure the minister sensed his mood. After Louis received another packet of documents from the contractor and promised to study them, the minister invited them to enjoy a cocktail in the reception area.

Louis didn't drink alcohol; he asked a waiter for a glass of fruit juice and then turned to look at the group. The Minister arrived a minute later. He had changed and wore a white *Thobe* and a *Keffiyeh* with a gold *agal*. Louis recognised his tailor, a specialist in Sharjah who made clothes for the royals of the Emirates. The fabric, a mixture of silk and the finest cotton, made the cloth a blinding white that hung creaseless from his broad shoulders. It highlighted his dark eyes, above sharply defined cheekbones and a strong jaw. A young woman dressed in traditional Omani clothing with a head-scarf but no veil entered the room and joined the Minister. Louis thought he was telling her who the visitors were, then she turned slightly to look at him, and what should have been a glance became a stare as their eyes met. Louis smiled.

After what seemed an eternity, she said something to the minister, and then they walked a few steps to Louis. She said, speaking perfect English, 'My father has agreed to introduce us; I'm Soraya.'

Louis dragged his eyes from Soraya and turned to the minister to reply in Arabic, 'The desert of Oman must be fertile to grow such a beautiful flower. You do me a great honour, your Highness. May the blessings of Allah continue to fall upon you.'

His speech startled the minister, whose sharp eyes had noted that Louis drank fruit juice. 'You follow the prophet?'

'Badly, I fear. I have Allah in my heart. I need someone,' Louis glanced at Soraya, 'to guide me.'

Reassured that Louis knew how to behave and hoping Soraya might have an influence, unexpectedly, the minister excused himself and left them alone.

Soraya switched to English and asked, 'Mr Poussin, can you tell me what you think of the project?'

Louis was always honest. 'I can, but it is not a good opinion. The numbers are too vague. Although I understand the importance of the project to Oman, the proposal is unsuitable and, consequently, overpriced; it needs study and revision.'

'Have you visited Oman?'

'No, I have business in the Emirates and visit regularly, but not Oman. I would have visited long ago if I had known it had beautiful flowers.'

'Then you must come and visit our country; you can study the port project – and the flowers.'

Louis replied, in Arabic, 'If I come, it will be to pick one flower.'

Soraya's eyes were laughing as she replied, 'There are so many that it might take years to choose. I'll ask my father; he's returning.'

Soraya asked in Arabic. Her happy eyes gave her away. Her father said he would send a request to the IFC.

After the guests left, her father asked Soraya. 'You have rejected every suitor I presented, yet you liked that man. Would you marry him?'

'If he asks, I shall say yes.'

'Then, if he's suitable, we shall make him ask.'

'I feel that won't be difficult.'

The minister investigated Louis and discovered extraordinarily little.

The IFC cooperated and asked Louis to visit the proposed port site, so two weeks later, the minister learnt that seven men from the IFC had booked into the Sheraton Hotel three days ahead.

The minister sent a car to the Sheraton and an invitation for Louis to dine at the palace. When the jet with the UN logo landed at Muscat's Seeb airport, three pilots and four men wearing business suits went to the hotel. The minister received a report from the airport that no passenger named Poussin was aboard.

The car was already at the hotel, and the minister received another report when it left. His guest was on his way. Louis had accepted the invitation and changed.

The minister and Soraya met Louis, and as soon as the formal greetings were over, Soraya exclaimed, 'Mr Poussin, you weren't on the plane; how did you arrive in Oman?'

'I'm the third pilot. No one notices pilots.'

It told the minister more about Louis than he had uncovered.

'Excellency, I'll not hide my intentions; I wish to marry your daughter.'

'I like your frankness. We will discuss your proposal. If Soraya agrees, I'll sanction it, but you must become an Omani citizen and build a palace here. Your children may one day be heirs to the sultanate, and you and Soraya must raise them to take on such responsibility. But how can you be so sure? It is only the second time you have seen her.'

Louis turned to Soraya and smiled. She smiled, too. 'It is the will of Allah; we know this is true. Whatever conditions you impose, we shall obey.'

Asad bin Rachid Al Said, Prince of Oman, was born eleven months later; the palace was nearing completion, and work on a new port had begun.

Leo sensed his father return to the present.

'Leo, are you still determined to do math at Cambridge? Have you registered, and when do you start?'

'Yes, and months ago, they accepted me, and the term starts October 8.'

'Are the Cambridge residence requirements for Maths still minimal?'

'Yes, Dad, I chose Cambridge because it's married to the tutorial system. The minimum is a continuous term each year for a degree. I can visit my team here if necessary.'

'Then you have a spare five weeks. Anything planned?'

'Not yet, Dad; although I might visit Cannes, Raoul Delgado is there and invited me to visit.'

'That's the man who taught you to sail. Is he still sailing?'

'Yes, a pro sailor; he's crewing on a classic yacht in the Cannes races. But that will take less than a week.'

'Then go to Florida or somewhere in the southern USA and train for a commercial pilot's licence. Your UK private licence will convert.'

'Why, Dad?'

'Leo, I was a paid employee when I started doing project evaluations and flying on scheduled flights. Over time, I built up my fortune with your mother's help, and I learnt several things from meeting rich men and their families. Would you have enjoyed a childhood where a bodyguard or two stood outside your classroom? Would you enjoy taking a girl home to your flat, knowing a guard stands in or outside the front door? And another at the rear? Or that a third is in the room adjoining your bedroom?'

'Shit, no! Is it like that for rich people?'

'Yes, Leo, the only way to avoid it is *never* to allow anyone to *suspect* you're wealthy or important. The first step I took was to qualify as a commercial pilot, and whenever I flew in a jet, anywhere, I was always a third pilot, wearing a uniform. Pilots are common at an airport, paid employees, so no one notices them. Don't fool yourself, Leo; at every airport, reporters are watching to find out if anyone, even a little famous, is going somewhere. Seeing the same person boarding a private jet several times leads them to investigate.'

'Do they investigate you now? You don't wear a uniform.'

'Not always, Leo, but the aircraft does.'

'The UN logo?'

'Yes, so I'm a paid employee. It's not my jet.'

'But if you aren't flying on a UN mission?'

'I tell the proper UN person I'm going, and I use my UN passport – that's allowed. The plane still has a UN logo; Private Wings has stock from all the different agencies; no one checks who owns it if I have a UN passport, but I still wear my uniform. I also have another reason.'

'What, Dad?'

'UN aircraft have internationally agreed-upon overflight rights for all countries; most don't require landing permission. I can fly somewhere without waiting for flight clearance. UN personnel have diplomatic immunity, don't need visas, and can use small airports without customs and immigration. Reporters don't hang around them. I also file my flight plan by radio when airborne or taxiing to takeoff, so reporters have no advance information.'

'I'll pass that com licence; I don't want a bodyguard sharing my bed.'

'Do a chopper licence while you're about it; they're good for short hops, and no reporter will investigate if you wear a uniform.

'When you have the licences, tell the boss of Wings; he'll let you fly left-hand seat, book jet time, and earn certification on different jets.'

Leo guessed his dad, as a hidden investor, owned half of Private Wings. He remembered the poster on his father's study wall in the Oman palace.

It was a set of rules. He had read them many times over the years, and only now were they beginning to make sense. He had another to add. He would put it in as number three in the copy Louis had given him when he was fourteen after opening investment accounts for him in five distant countries.

Leo had managed his funds since then, tripling their value with the help of his programs.

1. Having money is a problem – hide it. But always pay your bills on time.
2. Don't appear wealthy – do you want to go everywhere with a bodyguard?
3. Spread your assets worldwide in different countries and banks, but not in your name.
4. Don't own a private jet. Take free rides from a jet rental company you own and put a UN sticker on the tail.
5. Tell everyone you are a scientist or teacher; never reveal the truth about why you are doing something. Doing so makes it easier for others to shoot you down.
6. Cheap hotels have fleas; luxury ones don't match a teacher – three stars in city centres, four stars on the outskirts.

7. Don't own a palace. You can't occupy more than four rooms. Own a four or five-room apartment in every country, never in your name but a company name.
8. Carry a UN passport.
9. Don't cheat, don't steal. Keep your promises. A deal is a deal.
10. A handshake is a deal, a contract to honour. Make sure the other knows what you'll do, and you know what the other expects, for the other might want marble floors when you have allowed for bare concrete.
11. Don't allow any nation to tax you or your companies on what you earn in any other country, but pay your taxes where you earn the money.
12. Use a Satphone.

Leo inserted a new number three. He read the result and moved Lisa's rule to number zero. *It's more important than the others.*

0. Lisa's rule: Live the life you want to live, not the life others expect you to live.

Leo visited Cannes on his way to the USA.

Although Raoul Delgado was eight years older, he and Leo had established a firm friendship when Raoul coached eleven-year-old Leo to sail, culminating in winning the Cannes Sailing Club junior championship at thirteen. Their reunion was emotional, and Leo agreed to sail the last race of the week on the *Anemone*.

The navigator cried off sick at the last minute, and Raoul pressed Leo into taking the job. They won the race, and Leo had to participate in the photo session afterwards wearing a Jolly Roger tee shirt and pirate hat before an emotional departure and a promise to meet Raoul in the Caribbean.

Lisa had to attend the Free University on September 15. She didn't have the luxury of the Cambridge tutorial system. The winter and spring breaks were two weeks, and the summer was six weeks, but if she didn't need to resit any exams, she would have four more holiday weeks before the second year. The daytime lectures with evening and weekend revision allowed no time for other activities. The eight bank holidays in the year eased the revision but allowed no opportunity to relax focus.

Leo earned his two pilot licences and reported to Cambridge on time, wearing casual clothes and carrying his battered backpack, now decorated with twenty-three country flag patches. His hair was long enough for a casual observer to decide – *Hippy*.

He had done something unusual in his evenings while waiting for a training flight at the flight school. After searching the web, he found Lisa had a Facebook page. It wasn't difficult; although his search produced thousands of Lisas and Elisabeths, only one mentioned Madagascar. He read her posts and learnt he was a 'Great guy.'

I won't check her page daily, but will set up an alert.

Leo created a Facebook profile for Brunhilde Ericsson. Brunhilde's interests were like Lisa's. He felt Brunhilde should live somewhere that Lisa would never visit, so he chose a small town in Sweden called Gavie and an address. During the month of his training, Lisa posted several times, and Brunhilde, using Leo's finger, tapped the *like* symbol. Lisa felt she had another friend. After Leo had passed both licenses, Brunhilde asked to be Lisa's friend, and Lisa accepted immediately. Notified after that of every post, Leo knew where she was going and, usually, when and with whom.

A year earlier, he had told his father that he was a year ahead of his class. Although a year had passed, he was still a year ahead of the new student intake. It gave him sufficient time to work on his private research project and cover some second-year work.

7

Lisa's first term was agony; she had an on-campus one-bedroom student apartment with a sofa, a small table, a large desk, and filing cabinets. The mini kitchenette, designed for one person, allowed her to make breakfast and a light supper.

She walked to the Erasmus Campus each day, about a kilometre.

The heavy workload left no time for anything else, and she had yet to build supportive relationships. Ten days after lectures began, she lost focus on the lymphatic systems book she was reading; her mind blanked, and five minutes later, she returned to the present. *Did I fall asleep?*

She went for a walk in the cool evening air. *I must think about what happened. Is this programme too much for me?*

Lost in her thoughts, Lisa nevertheless managed to follow the paths she had run for ten days. *Maybe I should try something else. I know what Mother would say. What would Leo say? I said he mustn't propose; would he propose if I gave up?*

Minutes later, as she reached the halfway point of her daily run, she thought, *Do I return or go somewhere else?* Lisa stepped off the path onto the grass and stood silently, gazing into nothing, her mind idling like a car waiting for an instruction to move. Then the sound of waves breaking on a shore grew from a whisper, and a window onto a world of serried waves expanded and focused. A sliver of moon rose, and before her, she saw the slow glint of wave-tops in the moonlight. A shadow grew to one side, followed by the pirate ship she recognised; the pirate with a wooden leg and three-cornered hat stood on deck, and as it passed, he saluted and then pointed ahead.

PegLeg says I must continue. Leo would, too. I must pace myself, avoid doing anything unnecessary, and not stress. At school, the teachers regulated what we learnt. It was easy to stay ahead, but now I must decide how much to learn each day.

A habit developed early; the loneliness of an impersonal apartment at the weekend and the annoying disturbance of her studies when other students knocked made her return home on a Friday evening, where her mother inevitably asked how she was doing. The Friday after her blackout, Lisa told her mother, and Rosemary exclaimed, 'I had much the same experience. Let's look at your programme, and I'll tell you what I did.'

Lisa's apartment never became more than *my flat*. Her home was where her parents lived in Rixensart; she was usually there on the weekends for the atmosphere suited her, although once she had firm friends, she would sometimes spend the weekend at her flat with another girl, studying.

Although several male students suggested a coffee, she turned them away with a short refusal. 'I'm sorry, I'm here to study and not interested.' Before the year ended, she would use the blockbuster her friend Olivia recommended, 'I'm here to study. I have a child to support.'

Her first significant interaction was with another girl. Lisa was sitting on the grass in the late autumn sunshine, reading a document on her tablet, when a sheet of paper, blown by the wind, plastered itself against her face. She retrieved it and then looked around to see a girl several metres away, hastily grabbing loose sheets that had blown away. She waited until the girl had collected them all, then halloed, '*Yoo Hoo!*' – and waved the paper.

Close up, the girl reminded Lisa of someone she met in Katanga, a province of DR Congo, and her accent rang a bell when she said,

'Oh, thank you, if I had lost that sheet, I would have had a problem. I didn't realise there were unglued sheets in the borrowed book.' *Shorter than me, with wide-spaced brown eyes and a lovely smile. Muscular and graceful. A hockey player who might have walked many kilometres as a child.*

Lisa replied with a smile, '*Hujambo, unatoka Lubumbashi?* – Hi, are you from Lubumbashi?'

'You speak Swahili?'

'A little, but not well.'

'Well enough; how did you guess I would understand?'

'You remind me of a girl I met in Lubumbashi.'

'You lived in Lubum?'

'Only for a short while; my parents were doing something there. I was much younger then. Sit and tell me what it's like now; I'm Lisa Calmette, doing first-year medicine.'

'I might have seen you in lectures; I'm Ashina Kisula, doing the same. You're the first person to talk to me since I arrived in Brussels.'

'What do you mean?'

'Oh, you know, from the immigration at the airport onwards, everyone is polite, but they don't see me, just a body. I'm sure the supermarket cashier only looks for a skirt to say *Monsieur* or *Madame*.'

Lisa laughed. 'Ashina, I know what you mean, but all big cities are like this. The people must stay distant to avoid stress and violent reactions.'

'But even in a small group, no one has talked to me. It seems racist.'

'It's not racism; they can only allow closeness to people amongst their family or established friends; that's why there are ghettos in all big cities.'

'Is it the same for you?'

'Yes, although sometimes someone tries to start a conversation because they think I might be part of their social group. They break it off when they find I'm not.'

'So that's why it's lonely in the cities?'

'Yes.' Lisa was about to say 'you' when she thought: *I'm the same; we don't belong here. I may have Belgian nationality, but I'm not a Belgian person. I must remember this.*

'We don't belong here, Ashina; we're not part of this world. We've not had years of schooling here, so we haven't developed the habits or absorbed the rules of those who have.' *And we must marry a similar man, like Leo, and live in a place that suits us.*

After a pause to reflect on her thoughts, Lisa continued, 'We should help each other. My mother warned me how intense the study programme is in the first year, but it seems worse than she said.'

'I'm glad I'm not alone thinking that. Is your mother a doctor?'

'Yes, but not in Belgium; she partners with my father on medical missions for the WHO.'

'World Health Organisation?'

'That's them.'

'Is that what you want to do?'

'Not exactly; I hope for a scholarship from the WHO to study hospital and clinic management in developing countries. Dad is an epidemiologist, and my mother organises vaccination campaigns. I don't want to do either. Will you return to Katanga?'

'I must; my scholarship is for three years to a bachelor's degree. With that, I can apply for a junior doctor's appointment in a Lubum hospital and register as a GP after three or four years.'

'You could apply for another scholarship. The WHO awards several every year.'

'I know, but most scholarships are for research, and I know that's not for me. Besides, students from prestigious institutions usually receive them.'

'When we've earned our bachelor's degrees, you can ask my father when I do.'

Leo hadn't come to Cambridge to play; he had come to study and intended to continue for a fourth year to a master's degree, Part III of the Cambridge Tripos; he would also pursue research in his project. It left him little time to exercise, which he did by playing squash and five-kilometre runs beside the river Cam.

However, he remembered his promise to research PegLeg Jon and began by studying the list of professors in the history department. After reviewing for three weeks the professors and assistant professors listed as staff members, he settled on *Professor A G Restolomew – Post Renaissance History, 1500-1800*, after reading four papers he published.

Leo went to see Restolomew's secretary.

'Good morning, Ma'am; I'm Leo Poussin from the math faculty. I want to make an appointment to see Professor Restolomew.'

Leo thought she was intrigued. 'Why, Mr Poussin?'

'A tomb in a Madagascar cemetery.'

The secretary was apologetic. 'That *is* a historical subject. I'm sorry, Mr Poussin. The Professor is on a sabbatical and will return for the Easter term. I suggest you return then. Is there anyone else who can help? I've heard Mr Farquhar is interested in Madagascar; he's keen on pirate history because there are islands named after an ancestor, and he tells horrifying stories about them.'

'Well, I could try him. Is he here?'

She turned to look at a list of the day's activities on the cupboard beside her. 'I expect he's in the staff room; I saw him arrive. He has a supervision in fifteen minutes. You can go to the tearoom at the end of the passage and try.'

'Thank you, Ma'am, I will.'

The door had '*STAFF ONLY*' on a plaque. Leo knocked twice and opened the door.

The only occupant, with long hair over his ears and a pair of rimless spectacles, a cup of tea in his hand, looked up. 'Who are you?'

'Leo Poussin, sir, the secretary told me to come here. Are you Mr Farquhar?'

'I am. Are you a student?'

'First-year math, sir, but I have a history question.'

'Then spit it out.'

'There's a tomb in the St. Marie pirates cemetery, inscribed PegLeg Jon; I want to know about him.'

'I can't help you. I've seen the tomb; it's the big one, but it's before the period that interests me. I went once to see if there were pirates whom I might research.'

'Like William Kidd?'

'Not him; England hanged Kidd in 1701. We don't know who the St. Marie William Kidd was or if that tombstone is a memorial. That's what I believe it to be, but I have never read anything that suggests who erected it.'

'The date is correct, sir.'

'That's why I believe it's a memorial. St. Marie would have learnt of his hanging years later, and the tomb before his is dated 1704 and the one after 1711.'

'Sir, if it's a memorial, the person who commissioned it must have been a friend. Is there nothing in Kidd's papers that indicates who it might have been?'

'As it's not my period, I haven't tried to clarify the question. If Kidd had a friend, he might have been someone who sailed to Madagascar with him on the *Adventure Galley*. If you're interested, all the documents from Kidd's trial will be in the Old Bailey

Archives or, more likely, the British Museum.'

Leo asked, 'The secretary said you're interested in pirates; anyone special?'

'Olivier Levasseur, the notorious *La Buse*. I remain convinced he sank his treasure in a Farquhar lagoon, but searching a hundred and sixty square kilometres is a mammoth task. I'm trying to narrow it down.'

'Then I wish you luck, sir.'

'And you too, Mr Poussin. Unwrapping the past takes years and, without luck, lifetimes.'

I hope it won't. I don't have that long. I'll ask for an appointment with Restolomew after Easter.

8

As November ended, Leo phoned Lisa and learnt a lesson when she answered.

'Hello, man, what must you tell me?'

'Hello, girl. I requested an appointment with the History Professor, but he won't return until after Easter. I'm going to Almaty to Heli-ski at the end of December and want to ask if you would like to ski.'

'Leo, I told you, don't call unless it's about PegLeg. I'm working a twelve-hour day and can't do anything except study. Ask me again in a year or two. So goodbye.' *I wonder if he will invite another girl.*

'Bye, Lisa.'

I'm an idiot; I shouldn't have called.

On December the first, Leo received a satphone message, 'Sat+4.'

He knew it meant his father's time was four hours ahead of Greenwich Mean Time and that he wanted a call at eleven pm or seven am, their pre-arranged times, so he used his satphone that evening at seven.

'Hello, Leo; thanks for calling. Your mother wants to know if we will see you during winter break?'

'I'll be coming straight home, Dad; I have stacks of data to analyse, then after the new year, I'll ski.'

'I'm surprised; you've never been a person to enjoy the social scene at the ski resorts. Is there a girl involved?'

'No, Dad, Fifou in Mada recommended Almaty for serious heli-skiing; we'll be a small group.'

'Fine, Leo, I'll tell your mother.'

When he went home to Oman for the Christmas break, the flight didn't follow a straight line. Leo was in the Captain's seat.

'Captain, I have a no-fly weather warning from the Indian Ocean Satellite watch.'

'Warning about what?'

'A major sand and dust storm is inland from Muscat. It's unusual, extensive and will affect our descent.'

'Is there an alternative route?'

'Yes, cross the coast south of Aden, out to sea about thirty miles offshore, descend and then enter Seeb airspace from the East.'

'Set it up and notify Jeddah UIR.'

As the aircraft drifted out to sea after it crossed Djibouti and then the Somali shoreline south of the Gulf of Aden, Leo looked out the cockpit side window and remembered his visit to Djibouti. He reached up and fingered his medallion. *It must have come from a ship that a storm wrecked on a reef. How can I learn what ships sailed this ocean and never arrived? The Dutch East India Company must have records, as will the Portuguese, French and British.*

Then he had another thought. *Is it possible to discover where the coral came from?*

Leo, alias Asad, an hour after landing, was in his laboratory, a cool, vast, artificial cave.

Leo rapidly found a solution to his coral question. The Living Oceans Foundation, started in 2000 by Saudi Prince Khalid bin Sultan Al Saud, conducted studies of the coral reefs in the Seychelles, Maldives and the Chagos Islands. The Cambridge Coastal Research Unit was a partner in the Seychelles investigation.

Leo decided to take his coral box to Cambridge when he returned. *But I should check if the box would sink. It might have floated a thousand miles before sticking on a coral reef.*

The workshop made a new box and a glass tank filled with seawater.

Leo watched through the glass when Shuchang dropped the box containing the two remaining medallions and an identical bronze disc into the water. They expected it to float. It didn't, but turning to the angle of least resistance, it reached the bottom in fifteen seconds, where, strangely, it remained upright, with tiny air bubbles issuing from the upper join.

'Shuchang, that's conclusive; coral covered it where it first sank.'

'It's a guess, boss, but if it remained upright long enough to wedge in a crack while water surged around, it would have remained upright.'

'I agree; I don't think it eventually broke away; a coral collector saw it and kicked it. That doesn't explain the skull image.'

'Maybe the box held poisons before the medallions and had a skull engraved on the front, so the coral grew unevenly.'

'That's possible.'

Leo spent long hours in front of computer screens with two programming experts for the first four holiday weeks. He hoped the program they were designing would make sense of the data he had and hoped to collect. However, he managed fresh air and exercise with three Omani childhood friends on hikes and camel rides in the Oman mountains.

His father asked him one day, 'Leo, what are you trying to do?'

'I have an idea. It might seem nuts, but you'll understand. I think a country's problem with development projects comes from being unable to budget properly. I did a rough check using data from seven countries where you have assessed project investment. The budget provision for many items is just the previous year plus an added percentage each year, and they rarely achieve the budgeted expenditure. There must be formulas to give better forecasts, so I'm analysing past budget data to discover the best ones and invent new ones. Each country is working in isolation. If I can include the best of every item in one theoretical budget, I'll have a service I can sell and a title for my doctorate.'

'Are you doing it for the money?'

'No, Dad, although information in advance is a massive investment advantage, I'm fascinated by how people guess instead of calculating. If I can understand how they do it, my investment program will be a winner. As a secondary consequence, if developing countries budget correctly, their economies should improve; poor people will be better off.'

'That's a massive task.'

'I know; I've ordered two supercomputers, I have workers expanding the cave for them, and a contractor will double the solar farm.'

'Why two?'

Because I'll need to search for PegLeg clues, but I can't tell him that.

'I'm looking ahead, Dad, to when I have more than one country to analyse.'

'Can you find the data?'

'Not the details I need, but once I know what I require, I'm counting on you to help.'

'How?'

'For approval by the World Bank as a researcher and for the bank to recommend me to any countries that ask for loans.'

'I'll do my best, Leo; let me know when you need help.'

After four weeks in Oman, Leo left for Almaty as the third pilot in a private jet with one of many UN logos on the jet's tail. *I can't waste*

my life flying airlines. The three pilots entered the terminal, and an hour later, two returned to the aircraft that left thirty minutes later. Leo changed in the toilet, and a casually dressed tourist took a taxi to the Hostel Shymbulak in the ski resort of the same name. The room was clean, the bed wide enough for two, and the bathroom adequate. It was one of twelve rooms on the second floor, six on either side of a central corridor.

For Leo, the first day brought pleasure and exercise; he spent the day refreshing his skiing skills. He did four down runs, feeling unused muscles waking up. After a snack lunch at the high-altitude restaurant, the return along a combination of red and black runs left enough time for another black run, which, thoroughly warmed up, he did at top speed.

The gym beckoned, not for exercise but for the physiotherapist who spent an hour easing the muscles that would otherwise stiffen after the renewed stress of skiing.

After a hot shower and an hour talking on his satphone to his Oman crew, Leo went for a pleasant dinner at the Grelka restaurant. He planned to be on the ski slopes early, so instead of visiting a nightclub, he returned to his room and prepared for bed.

Leo had just removed his last shoe and sock when he heard a noisy argument in the room on the side where two bathrooms separated the rooms. He entered his bathroom to brush his teeth, and the voices, loud but muffled through the thin panelling, sounded Dutch or Flemish. Then he heard the room's entry door open, some angry words, and a slam.

Leo went to his door to the corridor and cautiously peeked out. A young woman wearing a bathrobe, looking lost with damp eyes, stood barefoot in the corridor.

Leo opened the door wider and asked quietly in English, 'What's wrong?'

She whispered a trembling reply, '*M-my*-my boyfriend threw me out.'

Leo continued to whisper, 'Why?'

'That's *p-p*-personal.'

'Well, you can't stand barefoot in the cold corridor; come into my room.'

'Are you *n-n*-normal?'

Peculiar question: the boyfriend must be weird. 'As far as I know. You'll be safe with me.'

She stopped trembling when she moved. 'What's your name?'

'Leo, what's yours?'

She approached his door, and he stood back to let her enter as she said, 'Lieke, I'm from Amsterdam. Thank you for opening your door; most people would have ignored the row.'

As she walked past him, Leo thought, *I recognise that perfume.*

Leo closed the door after he followed her in and stopped whispering, 'Well, I'm not like that; I stick my neck out when others don't. Lieke, I must know, will you return to him?'

'No, I need to fetch my case and things, but I won't try until tomorrow after he goes skiing.'

'Then it's serious. Shall I ask if there's a room available for you at the hostel?'

'Can I sleep here? I paid for my air ticket and skiing; he paid for the hostel and food, and I don't have enough spare money.'

'Aren't you taking a risk?'

She looked at him for half a minute. 'I don't feel I am, and beggars can't be choosers.'

'Then you can. Tomorrow, you can rebook your air ticket to Amsterdam.'

'I must retrieve my case and bag first; the ticket is in it.'

Leo heard a door open and raised a finger to his lips. '*Shushhh.*'

They listened to footsteps in the corridor moving away from them. 'Lieke, climb into the bed and hide under the duvet.' They heard knocking. A door opened, followed by a few spoken words before it closed. Leo stepped into the bathroom, retrieved a toothbrush, slipped off his shirt and dropped his trousers; then, as the footsteps halted before his door and the person knocked, he flushed the toilet and returned in his boxers with the toothbrush protruding from his mouth.

'*Momento*.'

Leo could see Lieke in the bed, the duvet up to her chin, grinning. He gestured to her to hide under the duvet as he approached the door and left the security chain in place as he opened it.

'*Qué es?*'

The man in the corridor tried English. 'Has a young woman knocked on your door?'

Leo frowned, looking puzzled. '*Aquí no hay prostitutas.* – You want?'

'No, no, okay.'

The man turned away, so Leo closed the door and turned to look at the bed as he heard stifled amusement. He stepped forward and lifted the duvet to look below it and saw Lieke had stuffed a corner into her mouth to muffle her laughter. Leo could see the tears in her eyes. She removed the now soggy corner of the duvet and asked, 'How much do I charge?'

Leo grinned. 'So you understand Spanish? I don't know, do you?'

'No, come to bed, you're fabulous, we'll try to work out a price...'

'Lieke, what perfume are you wearing?'

'It's LilyLang; I had a French boyfriend who bought it in Mayotte.'

....

'Leo, you're not just fabulous, you're marvellous. I won't charge.'

'Thanks, Lieke.' *Her perfume kept me thinking she was Lisa.*

9

When the noises of skiers clumping down the corridor to breakfast and the day's skiing echoed in their room, Lieke said, 'Leo, he'll ski at eight,' then asked, 'How do I fetch my clothes?'

'When does the maid service come to do the room?'

'I don't know. I haven't seen any room staff. We only arrived yesterday.'

'Then I'll dress and find someone.'

Leo showered, dressed, left, and returned fifteen minutes later. Lieke had showered while he was away. 'Lieke, come.'

A middle-aged cleaner was in front of the next room door. 'Leo, what did you tell her?'

'That he tried to torture you, and you escaped.'

'Good guess.' The cleaner opened the door, and Lieke followed her in. Leo returned to his doorway. Lieke took only four minutes before reappearing with a handbag and suitcase. After the cleaner locked the door, Leo gave her a generous tip before taking the case to his room.

'Thanks, now that's done. Leo, what's next?'

'Dress and breakfast, then you can book a flight home.'

I like her, and she came to ski; leaving will be a big disappointment.

With a grin, Leo added, 'However, after last night, I'll offer to extend your employment until you leave. I promise no torture.'

'Or kinky stuff? I leave on Sunday.'

'That's fine. You said *good guess*, what did the nutcase want?'

'Bondage, and I didn't ask what else would happen if I were helpless; I've never tried or will try the kinky stuff. The creep must have thought he could insist on whatever he wanted outside the Netherlands. How do we avoid him?'

'Are you at the beginner's ski school?'

'Yes, he's a poor skier, but not at the school.'

'Then tell the school instructor to look after you. Ski poles in the hands of an expert can do serious harm.

'Come, I'm hungry.'

The second day polished Leo's skills; after the first day's stretching and physio, his muscles allowed the exhilaration of painless exertion. He repeated his first day's programme, but feeling improved coordination, his speed on the slopes grew.

Happy after his day's exercise, he collected Lieke. She was bubbling. 'Leo, I had a marvellous day. We had a lesson, then skied down a short slope to learn how to slow down with the snow plough, and then more lessons to learn how to turn. I fell several times, so I'll have bruises all over, but it was great fun, and on the last run, I didn't fall once.'

Leo grinned at her. 'I've had a day of serious exercise. There are always physiotherapists at ski resorts who are experts at relaxing tired muscles and easing bruises. Would you like a massage?'

'That's a great idea.'

When they returned, the door of the room Lieke had left stood open. Leo looked in while Lieke carefully skirted him. The cleaner was there and had stripped the bed of bedding. '*Gospozha*, has the man left?'

Her reply, attached to a disapproving sniff, was '*Da*.'

Leo followed Lieke. 'He's gone, Lieke. I'm not surprised.'

'Why?'

'I suspect he didn't come to ski but to indulge in sexual fantasy once he had you isolated.'

'It was a tense moment, but I needn't fear meeting him now. I'm hungry; where do we eat?'

'The Grelka restaurant is the only good place to eat in the resort; we'll eat there every night. The others are suitable for breakfast and lunch. I'll call and check if we can book a table.'

'Then I'll bathe first.'

After they had ordered, Leo asked, 'Lieke, what do you do in Amsterdam?'

'I'm studying Dutch history at the University.'

'Any special period?'

'The first year is general; then I want to specialise in the polder's history.'

'I know nothing about them; you'll have to tell me. Have you visited the Hague?'

'Of course, Leo, that's part of Dutch education. Why do you ask?'

'You, being Dutch and a historian, reminded me about the *Vereenigde Oostindische Compagnie* archives; what do you know about them?'

'You pronounced that well, Leo. – Very little. Farmers first built polders in the twelfth century, but during school, we learnt about the later VOC period when the Netherlands was a world power. The records are all digitised. Every newspaper carried the news of the project's completion. The VOC historians collected records from all the places Dutch ships visited. I found it fascinating that apart from personal mail, a ship's official documents weren't lost if it sank en route; they kept copies at its departure point. I imagined a vast room with hundreds of scribes making handwritten copies.

'I thought you were studying math?'

'I am, but I must investigate something as a favour for a friend.' *I reckon I'm a good friend.*

'During the school visit last year, a professor told us that anyone can apply for access to the digital records, but only accredited researchers with references from academic institutions have access to everything.'

'Then I'll ask the Cambridge history professor to back my application.'

After dinner, back in their room, Lieke said, 'It's been a marvellous day, but I'm exhausted. Do you mind, Leo?'

'No, Lieke, I'm tired too.'

I wish she didn't smell like Lisa.

The rest of the week gave Leo the thrill of several slopes the helicopter could reach.

On Saturday, Lieke's last day, Leo took Lieke on the slopes; he was careful but impressed with her progress. After four runs down blue slopes, he asked her.

'Lieke, if we take it slowly, and you follow me and do what I do, I think we can do a red run. Would you like to?'

A flushed and happy Lieke didn't hesitate. 'Yes, let's try.'

It had snowed during the night, so Leo let it rip on the smooth powder slopes, confident she could manage the speed, but wherever the angle steepened, he slowed and zig-zagged to keep the pace down.

'Leo, it was a fantastic, marvellous week, and I wish we could stay longer. I didn't expect to meet someone who would look after me like you have.'

'Lieke, you've also learnt to speak some Russian. You can now ski anywhere on your next holiday.'

After Lieke waved to him as she climbed into the airport bus, Leo returned to his room to call Oman. The satellite signal was poor, so he went to the bar veranda with a sky view and sat between two massive gas heaters. He began by collecting his SMS messages and saw one from Lisa. She had sent it an hour ago, after one pm her time.

He called her. When she replied, he thought she was tense.

'Hello, man. Are you okay?'

She's upset and panicky. 'Hello, girl, of course, why not?'

'Haven't you heard the news?'

'Lisa, calm down, everything's fine. Please tell me what you're so upset about.'

He heard a deep sigh. 'I was worried, Leo. On the news, they couldn't stop talking about a woman lost in the Alps; she was skiing. When they eventually found her, even though thousands of skiers were searching, she had died of exposure. I know you're skiing, and it's remote, so it worried me.'

'Didn't they have search helicopters?'

'They said they had several but couldn't see what was under the trees.'

'Did they say it was her fault for leaving the piste?'

'They did, and you said you were going Heli-Skiing, which means far from the pistes.'

'But never alone, Lisa, we ski in pairs.'

....

'Oh...'

'So don't worry, Lisa. I'll have my satphone with me, and if anyone has a problem, I can call the rescue team. Tomorrow's my last day. I'm going to Oman and will return to Cambridge in four days.'

'I feel much better now. Bye, Leo.'

'Bye, Lisa.'

That's a new development. Lisa cares about me.

Leo entered the bathroom at the airport.

The young pilot exited the bathroom, walked to the VIP terminal, and left for Oman in a waiting jet. He had two days to check on the progress of his data analysis before returning to Cambridge.

Pilots have time between radioed progress reports for private thoughts during a three-hour flight. Leo could reflect on what he had learnt, and finally, before beginning the descent into Muscat, he concluded.

I must remember to ask Prof Restolomew for authorisation, and if PegLeg installed that memorial, he might have been a shipmate or a friend of Kidd. I must attend a London Mathematical Society meeting to sign the members' register. I'll visit the British Museum then.

He didn't forget to pack his coral-clad box.

10

Two days after he arrived, Leo went to the Cambridge Coastal Research Unit laboratory, where he explained why he had come. The secretary was abrupt. 'Mr Poussin, the CCRU is a research unit with several projects; we aren't a commercial laboratory. I cannot help you.'

Leo called his mother. 'Mother, can you ask Grandad if he knows Prince Khalid bin Sultan Al Saud?'

'Why Leo?'

'Khalid founded The Living Oceans Foundation, and it has worked in the Seychelles with the Cambridge Coastal Research Unit. I went to ask the CCRU here to analyse my coral block and tell me where the coral grew. The secretary almost threw me out the door.'

'Call me in two days, Leo.'

'Hello, Mother.'

'Hello, darling. Prince Khalid is a distant cousin. If you return to the CCRU, they'll be far more accommodating. You're a researcher; the coral block belongs to my father.'

'Thanks, mother. I'll tell you what I discover next time I'm home.'

The secretary was effusive. 'Mr Poussin, I apologise; you didn't say why you wanted the analysis. I'll call the Director...

'The Director will receive you. Go straight down the corridor to the end office.'

The Director, Emeritus Professor of Coastal Dynamics, a smiling man of sixty-three, opened the door when Leo, carrying a leather Gladstone bag, knocked.

'Mr Poussin, welcome; I've had a request to offer you whatever assistance you require. My secretary says you're an undergraduate in mathematics, so what I can do for you is a mystery.'

'I'm only the courier and the intermediary, Professor. I've brought a lump of coral, usually kept in a lounge, because it has a unique feature. This request is frivolous, spurred by the need to reply to the inevitable visitor's question about its origins. I must discover who can examine the coral and propose an area where it might have grown.'

'Why did you choose us?'

'Because the Indian Ocean is the most likely, and the CCRU has researched the Indian Ocean islands.'

'On what do you base that? Why not the Red Sea or the Persian Gulf?'

'The person in Djibouti who sold it to a family member claimed it was carried to him by a man from Zanzibar.'

'We cannot ignore such clues; however, we have a database of coral types. We can do a microscopic analysis and hopefully obtain some DNA. How long has it been out of the sea?'

'I don't know, sir. It began growing on the original wooden box it surrounded in 1710 or shortly after; that's the radiometric date of the inner surface. The sale was three years ago. I would guess between three and four years.'

'Can we drill cores?'

'Of course, on the underside as much as you wish. The top, which has an image visible in angled light, is the unique feature that makes it an object of interest to visitors.'

'What is the image?'

'A skull, sir.'

'That's certainly unique. Do you have it with you?'

Leo took it from his Gladstone bag and laid the tissue-wrapped coral on the desk.

'The email address for the report is under the tissue, sir.'

'Then leave it with me. I have the right person to do the work. I estimate about two months. You do realise it will be an area, not a location? Although if there is embedded plant or mineral matter, that might provide more precise evidence.'

'The best you can do is all I hope for, sir.'

Leo grinned. 'A romantic story about its origins might grow from your report.'

The professor laughed. 'That is always the risk geographers must take, although mathematicians may not fall in the same category.'

He stood, Leo shook hands and left.

He called Lisa that evening.

'Hello, man, I hope this is about PegLeg.'

'Hello, girl, yes and no. I told you about my medallions and the coral they were in. I brought the coral box to the Cambridge Coastal Research Unit.'

'Why?'

'The medallions have a link to pirates, and remember, we promised with our hands on my medallion, so finding where they came from might give us a lead to PegLeg and keep him happy.'

Now I'm talking about him like she does.

'The CCRU will analyse the coral and its DNA and tell me where it grew. It'll take two or three months.'

'That's fantastic, Leo, please tell me what you learn. I have two more hours of study and then bed. I now have a rigid routine that my mother imposed. It works for doctors.

'Bye, Leo.'

'Bye, Lisa.'

Asking for the coral analysis brought the PegLeg problem forward, and he remembered William Kidd's memorial. *I'm visiting London next week. I'll visit the British Museum after signing the Mathematical Society register.*

The Museum door guard indicated the direction to the reception, and then, after asking for the archives, an usher took him to another office, where he had to select the archive type from a list. He chose '*Legal*', printed his name on a form, and another usher took him to the '*Assistant Chief Archivist (Legal)*'.

Sixty, he has been here all his life but has a nice smile.

After Leo explained why he was there, the archivist said, 'Mr Poussin, you're in the right place, but the task you describe is monumental to impossible. Do you know what we do?'

'No, sir, please tell me?'

'I will. We did have all the documents from William Kidd's trial. I know little about him except that the prosecution took years – the document pack would have been massive.

'However, after the First World War, the museum directors decided to place the archives in an underground storage area, safe from fire and potential bombing. At first, funds to build the necessary storage were impossible to raise. Microfilm and microfiche technology made a smaller depository possible, and we began photographing all the archives. Every item has an ID number and is listed in an inventory, classified by legal case number, category, and place. If the technician understood what he was photographing, he added comments. There is also a case list and a short report for each case, which lists the categories and places used. The index and the reports are now in digital format. We incinerated the originals.

'In your case, the difficulty arises from language. None of the documents are available as adaptations, and the legal language of 1700 differs markedly from today. Other documents will be in the colloquial language of the period and, in Kidd's case, from places where the colloquial languages differed. OCR scanning will be erratic, so the documents are not machine-readable.

'We can allow access to the index and reports if you provide a recommendation from Cambridge; however, paging through them will take weeks; then, if you find an item, you may request a copy of the microfiche, but I doubt you will comprehend the language used.'

'Thank you, sir, I'll apply; at least I can take an initial look.'

It took a week to obtain approval for access, and then Leo spoke to Shuchang using their conference program.

'Shuchang, I'll mail you the login and password for the British Museum. Have one of our team members access the case list to find the William Kidd prosecution. Then, the individual items in the microfiche index. The AI must look for any item that might refer to a list of people who sailed with Kidd: crew, employment, health, immigration or anything else it finds. Once completed, send me anything highlighted.'

The most likely ship they sailed on is the Adventure Galley. 'Include anything that mentions the *Adventure Galley* in a second run.'

Leo remained in Cambridge for the Easter break.

Before it ended, he downloaded the emailed CCRU report from his Seychelles server.

Investigation to identify the location
where a coral block grew

Preparation:
Lab technicians drilled eight diamond cores to full depth, three millimetres in diameter.

Initial observations:
At low magnification, no striation bands were visible. Coral blocks in coastal waters show such striation because flooding rivers cover coral with silt and plant debris.

Conclusion: The coral grew far from any flooding rivers.

Plant particles, visible at high magnification, are scattered in the coral at random depths, and DNA analysis of the plant material corresponds to a known seaweed from tropical waters.

Conclusion: It confirms the coral grew in pristine marine waters, and the most likely environment is an island atoll.

Microscopic examination:
Only two species of coral polyps exist. A predominant species built the structure; a secondary grew in available interstices.

DNA analysis:
The DNA of each species indicates growth areas that overlap, defining a growth area in the Indian Ocean between latitudes three and ten degrees south. Possible islands in this area are the Seychelles, Chagos and outlying islands. The Maldives have only one species, and Madagascar only the other.

No other indications exist that will narrow the area.

Leo called, and she answered.

'Hello, man, what's new?'

'Hello girl, I have the report about my coral box. I'll send it to you. It confirms it grew in the Indian Ocean, not near a coast, but on an island. So that doesn't help much.'

'Why not?'

'Seychelles has a hundred and fifteen islands; searching for a shipwreck would take our entire lives, although if you're with me, it would be a life in heaven.'

Lisa sounded as if she was laughing as she replied, 'Have you been reading chick-lit romances?'

'No, my darling, that's my romantic subconscious taking charge.'

'Bye, Leo. *Darling* is banned.'

'Bye, Lisa.'

The day after Leo arrived for the Easter term, he again requested an appointment with Professor Restolomew. He expected a reply in a month, but nothing came.

Leo continued his project research with daily conference sessions with Shuchang and his assistants in Oman, but he studied the second-year textbooks to stay ahead.

A pop-up message appeared on Leo's screen:

> [Shuchang requests a conference call. *Click here to begin.*]

Leo clicked.

'Hello, boss; we may have struck gold on the first try.'

'What?'

'The AI has highlighted forty items, but two are marked *Adventure Galley*. Both mention a crew list, but they're from separate ports. One is London, and another is Tortola.'

'Does the site provide instructions on how to buy a microfiche copy?'

'Yes, boss, I can order for delivery to your address.'

'Then please do so. Thanks, Shuchang.'

Before the term ended, Leo's father called, 'Leo, I hope you haven't planned anything for the summer break, at least not in the first month.'

'Why, Dad?'

'Your grandfather has asked that you join a group of guards; a French archaeological expedition is planning to travel the Frankincense trail from Ubar to Tarim.'

'Why me, Dad?'

'He thinks it will be good for you, Leo. They are your people, and you haven't had much contact with them. The expedition is a Ministry of Culture and Tourism initiative, so your grandfather supports it.'

'How long for, Dad?'

'I don't know the details; I think it will be short. You will travel by camel caravan to the Yemeni border post, no farther than Shihin. The Yemenis take over from there. The starting date needs confirmation, but it's supposed to be June 27 and finish before Hajj begins on July 15.'

'Well, that would work. I'd have a week to prepare, two weeks on guard duty, and several weeks with the computers, and then I would like to climb Kilimanjaro before term starts.'

'Why do you want to do that?'

'I want to climb a mountain while I'm still single, and Kili because I could see it when I started my hike to Victoria Falls, and a man in Arusha said the moonrise over Africa from Kili is an item every man should have on his bucket list.'

'Is that girl in Madagascar turning you into a Romantic?'

'No more than are you and mother.'

'What is she doing?'

'Studying to be a doctor, but if I'm right, she will do far more than that. She's like me and grew up in developing countries. Like you and mother, we can't banish the desire to help those people develop.'

'Thanks, Leo; I'll tell your grandfather.'

A few days later, an SMS arrived announcing an appointment with Professor Restolomew on the last day of term.

Leo had seen Professor Restolomew from a distance in the street. The Cambridge history faculty data gave his age, sixty-three, and a lengthy list of achievements. Up close, Leo noted his greying hair cut short and his steely blue eyes under bushy eyebrows. *Overweight, but not a person to mess with.*

'Good morning, Professor.'

'Good morning, Mr Poussin. Your request for a meeting puzzled me; what does a math student need from history?'

'Sir, it's not the reason I came, but math history was a childhood interest, and I've read many treatises by Arab mathematicians; the logic displayed in those histories interests me.'

'You surprise me, Mr Poussin. Respect for history is unusual in your field of study, so why did you come?'

'Sir, there is a tomb in Madagascar, in St. Marie, or *Nosy Boraha* cemetery, with the inscription "*PegLeg Jon*"; he was a pirate, and the tomb is dated 1716. Do any historical records mention him, or where can I find out? I have found nothing on the web.'

'Why are you curious?'

Leo decided to be honest; he liked the look in the professor's eyes. 'My girlfriend told me to discover what I could about PegLeg and posed the condition that I can't call her for six years unless I have something to tell her about PegLeg.'

The professor chuckled, and his eyes crinkled in amusement. 'I hope you will learn to treat women carefully; they can be dangerous. As you've repeatedly tried to see me, I must offer to help.

'I've heard that name, but I don't have an answer. There are several PegLeg somethings in history. I can post your question to my colleagues in our history forum; one of them must have mentioned him in our discussions. I'll let you know if I learn anything. It may take years. One of my colleagues may call or email me, but I'll certainly ask when we have our annual forum meeting. Unfortunately, the next meeting is a year ahead.'

'Thank you, sir, I have another question.'

'Go ahead.'

'Who can identify the foundry that made ancient coins? I have the metal analyses of a copper and bronze coin I found in Djibouti.'

'What is special about the coins?'

'They have a skull and crossed bones embossed on one side.'

'*Good God!* There were unproven rumours about a pirate republic. You may have uncovered a blockbuster. You need to visit Istanbul or Constantinople as it once was. At the university, a professor of archaeology has studied coins for decades. For historians, tracing the travels of something provides a window into the past. Coins travelled; a Roman coin in San Francisco is interesting.'

'Or proves someone from San Francisco picked it up on holiday and dropped it in the USA.'

Professor Restolomew laughed. 'We ignore the outliers; we need several cases, but you've illustrated my point: a person travelled from Italy to San Francisco, not the coin.

'Look for Professor Demirci online; you can use my name for an interview.'

'Thank you, Professor; I'll leave my contact number with your secretary.'

I should tell Lisa, but I'll wait until I have something more concrete. Last time, she said not to call for two years.

Leo opened the postal package with the British Museum logo and name on the back. Reading the microfiche text without a magnifying glass was impossible, so he took them to a photographic lab and asked for enlarged A2-size prints. Later that day, he collected them after buying a powerful magnifier on a stand.

He had no difficulty reading the names and the crew titles: Seaman, Bosun, Navigator, etc...

He read the names carefully; none stood out. He noted the column 'Mark', with many scrawled Xs, and a few others with a carefully written name in childish handwriting, often only a first name.

He switched to the second list, noted that it was the Tortola one, and read it from the top. He was almost at the end and feeling desperate when he saw the last entry.

Jon – Lieut. Qtrmast.

Is that PegLeg Jon?

Then he looked at his mark. Puzzlement followed disappointment as he read:

Y Jon.

PegLeg's surname is Jon, or this is not the same guy. Why do I feel he must be?

He took the original microfiche from the envelope, placed it under the magnifier, and adjusted the knobs to focus on the mark. It became one letter that filled an A5-sized screen.

That's an odd way to write a Y. It's a small U with a leg in the middle.

Then comprehension dawned, and excitement exploded. *It's an artificial leg that fits on a stump. The Quartermaster of Kidd's ship signed as PegLeg Jon!*

I have something worthwhile to tell Lisa.

Shuchang saw the pop-up:

[Leo requests a conference call. *Click here to begin.*]

When Shuchang's face appeared on the screen, Leo spoke, 'Shuchang, congratulations. I received the microfilms, and there are two crew lists. The second one at Tortola contains the name I wanted to find. I'll send you the films and the enlarged prints. Please have someone read them and file two digital lists. We might need them again.'

A month before the first-year finals, Rosemary asked, 'Lisa, have you made plans for your summer holidays?'

'No, Mama, why?'

'The WHO has asked your father to speak at a conference in Nairobi during your summer break at the end of August. Would you like to come if I can persuade him to take us to see the wildebeest migration in the Masai Mara reserve? You won't lose focus over a few days.'

'Of course, Mama. The exams will be over, and I should take a break. We missed the migration in Tanzania, and I've always wanted to see it. Where will the animals be?'

'Probably south of the Kenya border, but they should be moving into the Masai Mara in August.'

'What's the conference about, and can I come? At least to Dad's presentation.'

'We won't understand it; it's about modelling the dynamics of an epidemic to aid decision-making. I might meet some of the people I've worked with, and you might meet a nice young doctor.'

'I haven't the time for a man, Mama, nice or not.'

'Well, that's up to you. Would you like to invite Ashina?'

'She has family visiting her during the summer break; maybe we can invite them for a Sunday lunch if we're here.'

'Of course, Lisa. I'll twist your father's arm to take us on safari after the conference.'

Leo learnt of the plans made by his grandfather once he was home in the Oman palace. The expedition would leave in four days with five archaeologists, many porters, camel herders, and the guard.

His mother told him his grandfather was coming for lunch the following day and showed him the clothes she had ready for him.

'Mother, they're super but too good for camel riding and camping trips.'

'You're Prince Asad bin Rachid of the house of Al Said. You can't let the Omani people see you barefoot in dirty khaki shorts; you're no longer a child and must wear the proper clothing. A white *Dish-Dasha*, a white *Mussar* wrapped on your head, a pair of polished sandals, and a *Khanjar*, our ceremonial dagger. After all, it was Oman that created it five hundred years ago.

'Your grandfather will present you with a new rifle and a pale or white camel. It is your heritage; be proud of it, as I am. I know you want to pass unnoticed outside Oman, like your father, but here in Oman, you're safe from spying reporters, so enjoy it. Wear dark sunglasses if you wish; you'll be unrecognisable with a *Mussar* on your head.'

'Mother, I must become used to being Asad bin Rashid one day; I'll start now.'

He remembered his first camel:

His grandfather had led the camel to Asad. He said as he handed Leo the rope to its nose ring, 'Asad, a boy's first camel marks when his parents judge him to be responsible and capable of caring for a beast that has allowed us to survive for thousands of years, providing wool, milk, and meat and carrying us safely across the sand seas. An Imam will lead a prayer imploring Allah to bless you.'

Asad remembered his pride as his grandfather continued, 'You must learn to care for your camel. We have camel herders with a history they can trace as far back as the Al Said's, in the dim past before Islam and Christianity, but the responsibility for your camel's health is always yours.'

He remembered saying that many people don't have camels, and then his grandfather's words made him determined to excel. 'Regretfully, traditions die if they aren't kept alive. Sometime in the future, your elders of the Gulf royal families will show their respect by addressing you as Sheikh; without this ceremony, that may never happen.'

He also remembered asking if girls had camels and his surprise when he learnt that girls with camels married, and those without became concubines who rode in a *Utfa* with the children.

'So I must marry a woman with a camel?'

Asad had not considered the woman he would marry, so the reply became the first item on his 'Marriage Qualifications list'. One he would never forget.

'Traditionally, that is true, but as a Prince of Al Said, there will be ceremonial occasions when your wife should ride a camel beside you. You may give her one, but she must ride it without assistance.'

Leo's mother continued, 'Your grandfather has not told me, but I suspect at least two guards have orders to teach you how to use your rifle, and there will be a falconer with the group to teach you how to fly a falcon. Please learn, for the men of Oman respect these skills.'

It isn't easy being two people; I think of myself as Leo Poussin; will I become Asad one day? I never thought of it; which one will marry? And where will I find a woman with a camel?

Accompanied by two guards and mounted on his near-white camel, Leo rode away to join the group and spent fourteen days with the guard. They were an elite group of soldiers, and he thoroughly enjoyed his evenings around a campfire under a sky full of stars, discussing various subjects. They taught him to shoot, and he marvelled at their ability to distinguish a tiny target at great distances. Raised as a Muslim, Leo prayed with them and felt peace doing so.

Leo won several camel races staged by the guards; he didn't fool himself; either his camel was the fleetest of them all, or they held back. The falcons flew, and he learnt to train them and avoid their sharp beaks. He became a welcome member of the elite Oman guards.

At the first ruin site after Ubar, after explaining to the guards that his grandfather wished him to learn the history of Oman, Leo visited the archaeologists during their investigations and then did so at every site.

They told him the history of the Frankincense trail, which he found fascinating, and he watched with interest when they used ground radar to map the underground vestiges of ruins. The clearly defined images were far better than he expected. His mind, which linked observations in odd ways, brought the thought. *Could that radar see objects buried under coral?*

That night, he called Shuchang using his satphone.

'Shuchang, I have no web access out here. Can you investigate ground radars or other devices that can identify objects inside the seabed coral? The archaeologists have one that works on dry land.'

'You mean like your coral box?'

'Yes, that and bigger coral outcrops.'

'Okay, boss, I'll check.'

At the second site, Leo decided that the only woman archaeologist was interested in more than ruins; she had a solitary tent set apart from the others, and he was sure she wanted company. He could tell by the way she looked at him. Leo remembered what his father had said about bodyguards in the next room. He knew she was out of bounds, for the guards would know and report it to his grandfather.

He made another satphone call and received a reply two days later; she was married to a chemistry researcher, so he avoided lengthy conversations with her. *There are things a prince can't do.*

When a Yemeni team arrived to take over, Leo went to say goodbye to the scientists, thanking them for the information he had received.

The woman stayed until they were alone; it gave Leo a moment to say, 'I'm sorry; in different circumstances, I might be interested in you, but your detailed files, both professional and personal, are with the authorities. I don't play the fool with married women.'

'I'm sorry too; you're an interesting man.'

Leo didn't ride his camel back to Ubar; He gave detailed instructions to the camel herder, for he loved his camel and believed she loved him. Once across the border into Oman, he and two guards climbed into a Land Rover. He didn't argue with his grandfather's instruction; he planned another adventure.

On returning to his cave, Shuchang came to him with a slip of paper. 'Boss, I struck lucky; after trying radar, I searched for "Sonar for archaeological purposes," and I found this.'

The paper had a title and a paragraph.

Sub-bottom profiling

Powerful low-frequency echo-sounders can provide profiles of the upper layers of the ocean bottom. One of the most recent devices is Innomar's SES-2000 quattro multi-transducer parametric SBP, used in Puck Bay for underwater archaeological purposes.

'I've asked the company for full tech specs. When the specs come, if they're what you want, I can confirm with a description of your requirements.'

12

Leo arrived at Kilimanjaro International as the third pilot in a new Gulfstream G650; Private Wings had collected it a week earlier.

After an early breakfast, the tour guide and driver took him to Machame Gate, where the day's hike began after a cup of coffee. Leo had studied the programme; they had two days of walking where the altitude would be less than he had experienced in a small plane for hundreds of hours, then on the third day, they would climb higher than an unpressurised aircraft should fly. Oxygen deficiency would only begin then. They would stay a day at that altitude. The first signs of altitude sickness would show after that. He expected to reach the summit on the day of the August full moon.

Lisa and her parents arrived in Nairobi for the conference. The Kenyan Standard would, naturally, report the conference as a roaring success. Gaston thought it would be, but only for those like him who were at the forefront of fighting epidemics and with powerful computers to back up their decisions.

For the others, it was a typical 'See what contacts you can make and information you can gather' conference, where success or failure had little to do with the conference itself.

Lisa attended the sessions. Gaston wasn't sure how much she understood, but he thought the questions she asked him each evening showed a reasonable notion of the speakers' proposals and the benefits that could flow from them. Medicine was evolving; epidemics were growing, and better tools to fight them were a blessing. Gaston noted the scheduled session in which Professor Lubyankov would present a paper on his Antimicrobial Resistance (AMR) research.

'Lisa, I think you should attend Professor Lubyankov's session. He'll speak about his research into the DNA changes occurring in microbes to resist the medicines we prescribe. AMR will soon be a major enemy in hospitals.'

'Are you going?'

'No, I've heard him before and read his paper, and there is another session on epidemic dynamics.'

'If you think so, Dad.'

Leo was climbing. Passing the four thousand metre altitude, other climbers began to drop out as altitude sickness took its toll. There were many quick stops to rest and admire the view, so Leo stopped with the others and became friends with a man only a year or two older, a South African called Jacob de Vries. Once at the Barafu camp, Leo invited Jacob to share his tent. 'It's much warmer with two in it.'

They talked, and Leo learnt Jacob had spent four years in the army and now considered the French Foreign Legion might offer more opportunity.

Lisa and her parents drove out of Nairobi in a safari vehicle with a driver and an Askari; Lisa learnt it was Swahili for a guard, although he did a bit of everything. They stopped for lunch in Narok at the Seasons Hotel, just off the road, and after relaxing for two hours, continued to the Keekorok lodge in the Masai Mara.

They changed lodges twice. On the first day, they looked for lions and elephants. However, Lisa had spotted a more exciting but tamer species. The young lodge ranger allotted to them introduced himself as Kurt, took one look at Lisa, and then couldn't take his eyes off her. He never stopped explaining what they saw, except when they had to be quiet. His behaviour amused Rosemary and Gaston, and it flattered Lisa. Kurt was attractive, a Kenyan from an English colonial family, enthusiastic about the wild game, and delighted to tell her about his childhood and Kenya. Still, Leo had entered her life only a year ago, and like many young girls after their first love affair, Lisa had convinced herself she would marry Leo and that the time was not far ahead.

Kurt took them to a square-topped hill with a fantastic view, and on the top was a commemorative bronze plaque attached to a tombstone.

Myles Turner

1921 – 1984

In remembrance of a life
dedicated to the wildlife of Africa

Kurt explained the history of the Serengeti and how much it owed to Myles Turner, the first Game Ranger.

Lisa listened but felt uncomfortable.

That night, she dreamed the pirate dream again. The pirate ship passed her, its sails billowing in a gale-force wind, with the one-legged pirate staring steadily at her from the bow rail. When she woke, she wondered if the Myles Turner tombstone had reminded her of PegLeg Jon or if there was another reason.

Then, they drove to another lodge.

On the way there, they saw the migration herds, vast numbers of wildebeest and zebras, and the lions, hyenas, and jackals stocking up from the moving larder.

Leo and Jacob summited. Jacob had struggled, fighting nausea, but with Leo's help and insistence, had managed the last four hundred metres. They found they were the only two tourists there.

After a photo session with the famous sign on Uhuru Point behind them, Jacob, Leo, and then both, with and without their guides, the guides urged them to begin the descent, 'You'll feel better after eating something warm and a night at three thousand metres.'

On the lodge veranda with a sundowner drink in her parents' hands, Lisa said, 'Mama, I'm going to watch the sunset.'

As she moved away, Gaston asked Rosemary, 'Shall we watch too?'

Rosemary shook her head. 'Not tonight; she needs to be alone.'

Lisa was unaware that Leo was less than three hundred kilometres away.

But he knew she was in Kenya. He and Jacob reached the camp at sunset.

'Jacob, I'll wait to watch the moon rise and make a phone call.'

'To Lisa?'

Surprised, Leo asked, 'How do you know her name?'

'You said her name two or three times last night. I guess you were dreaming; low oxygen must play havoc with sleep. I'll turn in; you won't wake me.'

Lisa had moved to the far end of the veranda, away from any people, and stood leaning against a pillar, her eyes fixed on the setting sun. When it finally dipped, she switched her gaze to the opposite horizon, where the full moon rose.

She remembered.

Please, Leo. Don't forget me.

Her phone rang.

Startled, Lisa's hand darted into her bag at the first ring; she lifted her phone into view and saw the twelve-digit satphone number. She felt her stomach clench, and her breathing stopped. *It must be Leo.*

She was breathless as she said, 'Hello, man.'

When he heard her voice, Leo shut his eyes and let the ripple of remembrance flow to his toes and up again. 'Hello, girl. When can I use darling or dearest?'

'When I do, and not before. Why did you call?'

'I didn't. My phone heard your request and dialled without my help.'

'That's ridiculous.' *However, I did ask him to remember me.* 'Do you have anything new to report about PegLeg?'

'No, it was PegLeg that called. I've asked the history professor if historians know anything about PegLeg. It may take the rest of my life to find something relevant, as there are millions of reports in the maritime archives of four countries.'

I must ask.

'Where are you, Lisa?'

'I'm on the veranda of a game lodge in the Masai Mara. I watched the sunset, and now the full moon has just risen, so I was remembering. Where are you, Leo?'

'If I had the eyes of an eagle, I might spot you. I'm three thousand metres up Kilimanjaro; I watched the moonrise too.'

Lisa felt warm, thinking he was so close. 'Why Leo?'

'I told you about trading my medallion with a giant. I started that hike in Arusha, within sight of Kili, and promised to climb it. I keep my promises, even to myself, and if I can't be with you on our anniversary, I can at least share the moon with you. What are you doing there?'

'I'm with my parents; we joined a medical conference in Nairobi. Dad said I should attend and learn what medical research is like. I learnt something interesting from Professor Lubyankov. After his lecture, he asked if I had learnt anything useful. When I said that before his lecture, I had thought that genealogical websites used DNA; he told me they collected data on people by name and tried to link them together using historical documents. When I finish my degree, I may have the time to investigate PegLeg.'

'That's a great idea. How will you start without a name?'

Lisa remembered her dream and Myles Turner again. 'We didn't check on the other tombstones in the pirates' cemetery. Do you think there might be someone buried there who knew PegLeg?'

'That's very possible. Do you remember William Kidd's tomb?'

'Yes, he's famous.'

'Well, that's a memorial placed there years after his death, so I checked if he knew PegLeg and found that PegLeg came to Madagascar with Kidd as the Quartermaster on the *Adventure Galley*. I found nothing else but one of the others might have known PegLeg.'

'That's wonderful, Leo. I'll see if there's a list of the residents.'

'I don't know where to find one.'

'Lubyankov mentioned church records of births, deaths, and tombstones; I'll call Father Benjamin tomorrow; he might know.'

'Good luck, Lisa; I'll ask the history professor if he knows someone doing genealogical research. I know you passed the first year. Are you still determined to follow the medical degree?'

'How do you know I passed?'

Lisa felt pleased when he replied, 'I scanned the results at the Free University.' *He cares.*

'I'll continue, Leo, but after the bachelor's, I'll consider hospital management.'

'I'll stay with math, stats and macroeconomics. Would you like to meet?'

'Of course, Leo, but we mustn't until it feels right.'

'Then, Lisa, enjoy the migration. Bye.'

'Bye, Leo.'

When Lisa returned to her parents, she couldn't hide her happiness, so her mother asked, 'Did he call?'

'Yes, Mama, although he said PegLeg placed the call.'

'Stranger things have happened.'

At Mweka gate the next day, Leo gave Jacob the name and number of Tariq bin Hasher. 'Call this guy; I was at school with him. If he likes what you tell him, he'll offer you a job that will pay better than the Foreign Legion. You can save, buy a farm, and marry a *Meisie*.' They said *Totsiens* or goodbye with a firm handshake and a backslap. *Jacob's a nice guy, but I'll never see him again.*

Leo returned to the SG resort for the night and, after dinner, selected the best photo of himself and Jacob standing before the beacon at Uhuru Point. He would send it to Lisa after he returned home.

After breakfast, he changed into his pilot's uniform, handed his baggage to a courier, and took a taxi to the airport. His holidays were over, and the jet was waiting on the apron.

When Lisa arrived in Brussels, she phoned Princess Bora for Father Benjamin's number; they had it in a brochure about the island.

'Father Benjamin, good morning.'

'Good morning, Father, it's Lisa.'

'Lisa, what a pleasure, it's been a year now, how are you? And how's Leo?

'I'm well. Leo was on the top of Kilimanjaro a week ago. He's probably in Oman by now.'

'That must have been exciting. Why did you call?'

'I want to know where I can find a list of the graves in the pirates' cemetery. Do you know if anyone in town would have such a list?'

'You've called the right person, Lisa; I do, or at least there is a list in the church archives. When the priests consecrated the church, it had no cemetery; the people buried the notables in the pirates' cemetery, so they also consecrated that. Before doing so, they asked for a census of all the burials. I must search for it. It will be hand-written, so it may be difficult to read.'

'If it's fragile, I can arrange for an expert to collect and preserve it for you, but if not, photographs will do. I'll SMS my email address; tell me its condition when you find it.'

'I will do, Lisa, I'll say again, it's a pleasure to have you call.'

Five days later, the email from Father Benjamin arrived.

Lisa, it may be better to send your expert.

She SMSed Leo, and he called to learn why.

'Hello, man, I've found the list, but it must be collected and preserved.'

'Hello, girl. That's brilliant; how did you manage it?'

'It's in the church archives; Father Benjamin found it and says it's fragile.'

'Then leave it with me, my darling. I'll take care of it and send it to you when it's safe.'

'Didn't we agree, no darlings?'

Lisa grinned at his reply, 'Slip of the tongue, my darling.'

'You're incorrigible. Bye, Leo, and thanks.'

'Bye, Lisa.'

Lightly loaded and with only reserve fuel as the runway is short, the G650 landed the following day at St. Marie, and Leo phoned Father Benjamin.

'Leo, what a surprise! I sent a message to Lisa yesterday.'

'I know, Father, and she phoned me. As I was in the area, I came to collect the list.'

'Then come to my house; I have it here. I'll put on the kettle.'

Father Benjamin's office resembled many others Leo had visited in developing countries. However, his office had a distinctly clerical air. In good repair but ancient, his desk must once have graced a government office. He sat on a stool. Four other chairs, all roughly carved, had shiny leather straps, a witness to the number of backsides that had sat in them. One wall had reprints of religious pictures; another had two cassocks hanging on pegs. An elephant ear plant, Colocasia, stood in a corner in a handmade earthenware pot.

Father Benjamin handed Leo a cup of tea, then took a box file from a shelf behind him.

'This isn't the original cover; I had to remove the file labelled *Consecration* from the bottom of a pile. It's so old that I haven't opened it, but I found this box file and placed it inside with crumpled tissue paper to stop it rattling around.'

'That's perfect, Father. I'll preserve the entire file and return it to you. You may then frame the papers and hang them in the church for visitors to read, with a collection box beside them for church repairs. Some history might improve holidaymakers' visits. Inform all the hotels; they will encourage visits.'

'Then I'll look for other exhibits. Thank you, Leo, you've given me hope. God bless you.'

'I must leave, Father; my pilot will have refuelled by now. I'm going home and then to university.'

'Then Godspeed, and thank Lisa. I hope she finds what she's seeking.'

Five weeks later, after a visit to an antiquarian outside Paris, a courier delivered the preserved original consecration documents to Father Benjamin. DHL delivered photocopies to Leo and Lisa.

Leo phoned.

'Hello, man, I've received the docs. Have you looked at them?'

'Hello, girl, I have. I've also loaded the cemetery census into a spreadsheet and sorted it by the death date. Then, I compared the list of names with the crew lists of the *Adventure Galley*. PegLeg Jon is common to the crew and cemetery lists, but so is Dylan Jones, a cook; he died in 1704. I'll send it to you. He must have known PegLeg. I see only two more possibilities. Others died much later, and as dying young was typical, I doubt they knew PegLeg. One earlier is dated 1714, so he's likely, and the one who died in 1721, Butterfly Bill, looks the most probable. However, that might be because of the unusual name.'

'His name won't be Bill, more likely William or Guillaume. How do we find out?'

'When you have time, try the Genealogical websites for the others; they're English names. Dylan Jones is unlikely to have written anything; his mark on the crew list is an X. I'll set up a computer search for the name Butterfly Bill or Naturalist-William appearing in scientific papers; he must have been a naturalist to have a nickname like that. Google has zero hits, so I'll ask the history professor for advice.'

'Thanks, Leo. Bye.'
'Bye, Lisa.'

The secretary knew Leo; she replied, 'I'm sorry, Mr Poussin, he's overseas attending a conference and visiting a university. He'll return in January. I'll ask for an appointment and let you know.'

Leo returned to his studies and research.

Leo spent the winter break working on his project and working further ahead in the second-year subjects.

While waiting for the professor to return, I'll search for the other two names in the British Admiralty records.

13

Days after Leo returned to Cambridge, Professor Restolomew's secretary called, 'Mr Poussin, can you attend a meeting with the professor at four pm on March the third?'

'I will do, Ma'am.'

'Mr Poussin, I'm surprised to see you. Regretfully, I have no news from my colleagues; I hope you have a different matter to discuss.'

'I do, sir; my girlfriend, Elisabeth Calmette, has found a list of the tombs in the St. Marie pirates' cemetery.'

Restolomew exclaimed, 'Fantastic, but why? And how did she manage that?'

'She has a theory that one of the persons buried there would have known PegLeg and might have left letters or reports that mention him. She asked Father Benjamin at the Catholic Church in St. Marie. She learnt that when the priests consecrated the church in 1857, they included the cemetery and, before doing so, completed a census of those buried there. Father Benjamin found it in the church archives.'

'Marvellous. Where is the list?'

'I had the file's contents restored by an expert in Paris and then returned the file to the church.' Leo handed the professor a copy of the list and said as he gave him another, 'This is the list sorted by date. Three entries interest us, one before PegLeg's death and two after; the most likely person to have known PegLeg is Butterfly Bill, who died in 1721. Lisa will try to find the others on genealogical sites. I have tried the Admiralty records without success, but Butterfly Bill implies a naturalist, so I thought I should ask you for advice as Google has no response.'

'I admire your deductive ability. The proliferation of worldwide naturalist expeditions only began in the early 1700s; however, we know of a few prominent naturalists before that. One of them, James Petiver, who died around 1718, had many amateurs, mostly botanists, send him items for his collection. There may be an indication of a collector in East Africa in one of his papers or documents written by others mentioned by him. The Natural History Museum has at least a part of Petiver's collection of insects and plants, although I have heard he was careless about preservation.'

'Thank you for providing a starting point, Professor; I shall read his publications.'

When Leo arrived home for his Easter break, Louis asked, 'Are you going to ride your camel?'

'I'm sure I will, Dad; I'll need exercise. Why do you ask?'

'Your grandfather mentioned the 240-kilometre race a few days ago; it's due this year. If he asks you to compete, you must. So, ensure your camel is ready and trained. When you return to Cambridge, leave instructions with the camel herders.'

Leo continued his project work and studies but had another interest – James Petiver's papers and those of others Petiver mentioned. Ten days before returning to Cambridge, he had exhausted everything he could find. Leo decided that visiting the Natural History Museum to find unpublished Petiver papers was the only remaining research path. He switched to working on the camel training programme.

For the Gulf Royals, status is everything. For centuries, this race brought the respect of the people for their rulers and the respect of the other royal families. I must win it for Grandfather and the Omani people if I can.

When Leo left, everything he had planned was underway, and he had agreed upon the camel training programme with the chief herder, who had explained the simple rules.

Each rider had only the camel he started on; the rider would not stop to help anyone in trouble because race marshals who could help would follow the riders. Such help meant disqualification. Disqualification automatically followed a non-finish within the allotted twelve hours. The race organisers would hang a twenty-five-litre bag of water, weighed by the scrutineer, on each side of his saddle. It was the only water allowed for the camel and its rider.

The course was across the desert in an oval loop, following markers with red flags, finishing where it started. The race was 125 *al-mīl*; using the ancient measure, Leo knew it was just short of 240 kilometres.

During the Easter break, Lisa stayed in her apartment revising. Her parents were out of the country on a vaccination drive, and the flat had two advantages: Ashina was nearby to assist, and the canteen was available for meals and tea. A jog to the canteen and back several times a day broke the growing stress before it ruined her concentration. She was not alone, so she met some students she had never seen during the term.

One day, when Lisa felt saturated, she accepted a theatre invitation.

Armand had seemed pleasant and cultured until they took their seats in the theatre.

As he lowered the seat, folded up to allow patrons to shuffle past to their allotted places, a spider, taking its evening sleep in a comfortable, warm spot between the seat and the chair back, suddenly found itself in the limelight. It scuttled across the seat cushion to find a hiding place.

Armand had a fit; he reared back and screamed, 'A spider, I can't *stand* spiders, *kill it, kill it!'*

Embarrassed by the sea of faces looking at them, Lisa said, 'Armand, it's only a little spider.' Then reached over and flicked the petrified spider off the seat.

'It'll crawl up my leg, *kill it, kill it.'*

Lisa looked down, stamped a foot and said, 'There, Armand, it's dead.'

The grateful spider found a hidey-hole until the end of the show.

Armand calmed down, and Lisa enjoyed the show. As they crossed the theatre foyer to the street, Armand asked, 'Lisa, will you come for a drink?'

'No,' Lisa replied, 'I'm going home. I'll take a taxi,' then walked away.

When he asked her again a week later, Lisa replied, 'No, thank you; I don't like people who kill spiders. I like them, and I have a pet tarantula at home. He tickles when I let him crawl over my head.'

'But you killed that spider at the theatre.'

'I didn't, Armand; I stamped my foot and told you I did. He's probably happy back in the chair by now.'

Armand didn't invite her again. *I won't enquire if he hasn't asked again because I said no, or a tarantula on my head is too horrible to contemplate. I lived with creepy crawlies as a child; the people in Belgium kill them to live sterile lives in a terrifying world. As Ashina said, they aren't our kind of people.*

To Lisa, Brandon seemed more mature, an engineer studying management, handsome, and well-built. *However, he's a bit flabby and needs sunshine.*

They talked in the canteen, and she learnt he had travelled; he had worked in Africa during his engineering degree, gaining the required industrial experience with French construction companies.

She accepted when he asked her for an evening meal at a nearby restaurant where she knew many students went in the evenings. It started well, but after the main course, Brandon took a little box from his pocket and extracted six pills that he laid in a row on the table.

'What are those for, Brandon?'

'Vitamins and mineral supplements, Lisa. I take them every day.'

'Exercise and ten minutes of sunshine a day are enough, Brandon, as long as you eat correctly.'

'I don't have enough time for exercise, Lisa. I go for my flu jabs, and my vaccinations are all current. I've taken these for years. I'm never sick.'

Lisa couldn't imagine life with a hypochondriac pill popper, so she refused his invitations after that. *Europeans in Belgium prefer to live indoors. Spain and Italy might be different. I like the wide-open sunny places. None of the men I've met is my kind.*

Although Lisa once said she would not discuss her boyfriends with her parents and would not bring one home until she was sure he was permanent, that didn't apply to past ones. Lisa told her mother about Armand and Brandon when her mother, sensitive to her moods, asked what was bothering her. Rosemary agreed when Lisa said the men were not her kind, but that night, when she told Gaston, she added, 'When Lisa qualifies, we must encourage her to take a job outside Europe where she will have a wider choice of the kind of man she wants. Otherwise, hormones might push her to marry the wrong man.'

Leo didn't waste time after settling in for the third term. He called Lisa.

'Hello, man, what is it this time?'

'Hello, darling, I have a report to make. I spoke to the History Professor about Butterfly Bill. He told me about a naturalist, James Petiver, who collected specimens from many countries. He received them from amateurs in the field. The Professor suggested I read Petiver's papers to see if he mentions Butterfly Bill. I'm sure I've collected everything in university libraries; I scrapped those published before 1700 and after 1725. There's not a mention in the thirty that remained.'

'So Petiver is a dead loss?'

'I thought so, but he had a correspondent and collector in Africa called Edward Bartar, and as the prof suggested reading anything by people Petiver mentioned, I did. Bartar was a slave trader who collected insects and plants and sent collections to Petiver. However, he didn't mention Butterfly Bill. The Professor also said that the owner of the Petiver collection donated it to the Natural History Museum, so my next step is to visit the Museum and ask if they have any unpublished papers.'

He's going to invite me.

'Would you like to join me?'

'Can I come and return in a day?'

'The fastest way to London is two hours by Eurostar. The Museum is open at ten, with an hour's time difference; if you leave by eight-thirty, we'll visit, have lunch, and you can return to Brussels by six. You can study for four hours on the train.'

He does want me to come; he checked all that before calling. I do miss him.

'When Leo?'

'Choose a weekday date so the curators will be there.'

'I'll check my schedule, Leo, and SMS a date. If you insist on an endearment, try *my love*.'

'Thanks, my love, I'm looking forward to it. Bye.'

'Me too, Leo. Bye.'

14

Leo read the SMS four days later.

> May 1 – Holiday here, not in the UK; check if the Museum
> is open.

He sent an email.

> Hi Lisa,
> I enclose the link to your return ticket. I'll meet you at
> the Lovers statue.
> Love, Leo.

Leo strode forward, smiling as Lisa walked towards him. She had to push her shoulder bag to one side when he took her in his arms. 'Hello, my love. Can I kiss you?'

'The statue's not kissing.'

'The Lovers can't tell us not to.'

'Then you can.'

'Leo, in the station rules, it says extended embraces by the statue are *not approved*.'

'Us pirates never obey the rules unless it suits us.'

'Oh...

'We must go, Leo.'

'Okay, I have a car waiting. Taxis are impossible at this hour.'

A uniformed security agent guarded the door. 'Good morning, Sir,

Ma'am. Can I have your names, please?'

'Poussin and Calmette.'

After checking his register, the uniformed security man waved at a person in a museum uniform and said, 'Doctor Dankworth is waiting for you. The usher will show you the way.'

Lisa's assessment was medical when the usher showed them into a book-lined room with a desk, an office chair, and two leather armchairs. She did it without thought. *Overweight sixty, paunch, sees little sun, almost bald, ruddy face, so above normal blood pressure, watery eyes behind those spectacles.*

Leo was kinder. As Doctor Dankworth stood, he thought, *about a metre seventy-five and moved like the squash player he once was forty years ago, he would have played in the same squash courts as me.*

'Mr Poussin and Miss Calmette, it's a pleasure to welcome students from Cambridge and Brussels. I rang Professor Restolomew. He's an old friend, and he requested my full cooperation. Can you tell me what you want to learn about James Petiver?'

Leo answered, 'I've listed every publication by Petiver I could find, sorted them by date, and read the remaining ones published between 1700 and 1725 that refer to Africa, seeking a reference to a man buried in 1721 as Butterfly Bill. I found nothing and wondered if the Museum might have unpublished papers or diaries.'

'I wish I could help, but we don't have any of his writings; if they exist, they will be in a private collection. What we have is a collection of insects and plants. They're of historical interest, not scientific, because the conservation was poor in 1700, and Petiver made no effort to improve it. He sold most of the specimens he received. We have what he kept. We keep his collection in the basement. Can I take you to see what we have?'

Lisa replied, 'I would like to see it; I came from Brussels this morning, and learning nothing would be a terrible disappointment.'

'Then come with me.'

The basement lighting glowed a dark red, making the place look spooky to Lisa; as they walked in single file behind Doctor Dankworth along several corridors between collections of weird items and the occasional statue, lights sensed their passage and lit up, dying behind them. Lisa shied twice when the lights revealed a statue leaning over her.

'Here we are. This cupboard contains boxes of corals, shells, and skulls, most of them still unclassified, although every item carries an ID number with an entry in the catalogue. Perhaps only the word *skull*.

'The following two drawer chests have insect specimens, and the third has small birds and bats. That tall box contains card plates with leaves and plants. One on top of the other, and the cast iron mass on top keeps them pressed tight.'

Leo remarked, 'The cabinets are massive.'

'Each drawer contains specimens from a particular area. Considering the number of insect species worldwide, this is only a tiny fraction.'

'Is that a label on each drawer?'

'It is. Alfred said you were interested in East Africa or Madagascar; there is a drawer for East Africa; let me look for it.'

Leo momentarily wondered how Dankworth could read the labels in the dim light, but when he took a small torch from his pocket, Leo realised he must carry one when in the basement. After peering at one label after another, Dankworth announced, 'Here it is.'

When he pulled it open, Leo saw scores of small walls creating tiny boxes of varying sizes, and in each, an insect lay. The boxes carried an ID number. On one side, the insects were butterflies. Lisa stepped forward to look at them. 'Doctor, how many items are in the trays?'

'Twenty trays each with one to two hundred insects, so two to four thousand per cabinet. Say, six thousand in total. Then, a thousand birds and bats, eight thousand leaves, two thousand bones and coral. You could work through the catalogue for the name you want. The order is ID number, so that's not helpful.'

Dankworth was puzzled when Lisa asked, 'Is there WiFi here?'

'Yes, it's necessary for safety and specimen identification.'

'Can you connect my phone?'

'Of course.'

'Then please do so; I must make a call.'

Leo asked, 'Who will you call?'

'Princess Bora.'

A confused Doctor Dankworth asked, 'Who is she?'

Leo explained while hearing Lisa say, 'Andry, it's Lisa Calmette here; I occupied bungalow three when I was there, and on the wall was a glass-covered frame with a butterfly inside it. Can you or someone else photograph it and send me the photograph? I need it urgently. I'm in the basement of a museum in London, and I'll use WhatsApp to send my email address.'

....

'Thanks, Andry. I hope to see you all before long.'

'Doctor,' Lisa pointed. 'That butterfly looks remarkably like one I saw mounted in a bungalow on St. Marie Island off Madagascar. It was new, with glorious iridescent colours, but if you can compare the photo the hotel will send me with that one in the drawer and declare a match, that's the ID number we should look for in the catalogue.'

Her phone pinged. Dankworth fetched a magnifying glass, compared and declared the two matched, and they returned to his office, where he removed a thick, leather-bound book from a shelf and paged through it. Leo approved of his search method. Try halfway, then back or forth halfway repeatedly until he turned a page and said, 'Here it is. The ID number is 23678-445-659-44, as on the basement sample, and a comment: Butterfly. Unclassified. Petiver collection. – Collector William Gastrell.'

Leo cheered, 'Whatta girl, Lisa, you're marvellous. That's fantastic.'

'Thanks, Leo, we now have Butterfly Bill's name.'

Dankworth added, 'I'm staggered, Miss Calmette, you're brilliant. Do you realise what else you've achieved? I have the assurance that an unclassified butterfly exists in Madagascar, and I have a photo and example of it. I must apply for a classification and a name.'

'Please remember, Doctor. William Gastrell discovered it circa 1715. We must now find his family.'

Doctor Dankworth accompanied them to the door from the Museum; when he shook hands with them, he said, 'I shall call Alfred Restolomew and tell him how brilliant you are. Thank you again.'

Leo answered, 'Doctor, if you want a live specimen, call Professor Restolomew. I can arrange it.'

'Lunch, Leo, and then I must catch the train.'

'We have two hours. We'll have lunch at the Savoy; I booked a table. It's quiet and we can talk.'

Leo didn't give his name when they entered the Savoy restaurant, yet the maître d' greeted him with 'Good afternoon, Mister Poussin, your table is ready.'

Lisa sensed a pervasive feeling of luxury and discretion and wondered. As they sat, she asked.

'Leo, how can a hiker who stayed at a backpacker's lodge when

we met afford the Savoy and a chauffeured car? And the maître d'
knew your name.'

'That's not unusual; I've been here several times with my dad.
You know I live in Oman. I have a cave there like Ali Baba. It's full of
sparkling jewels and rare objects. I raid it if I need to.'

He won't tell me.

'Does it have a lamp with a genie?'

'Of course. All caves should have one.'

'Did your genie give you three wishes?'

'No, that's Disney. Only one, and I haven't wished yet.'

'Why not?'

'With only one, it must be for something that will last forever.
I'm being careful. Now, let's order, and then we'll discuss what we
will do next.'

'Leo, a Tournedos Rossini, medium rare. It says on the menu that
Chef Escoffier created the Tournedos Rossini, and he worked here
from 1890 to 98.'

'He did work here, but he might have brought the dish with him.
I'll have one, but rare. The waiter will bring a selection of vegeta-
bles.'

'Leo, how will we find Butterfly Bill's family?'

'I'll try the genealogical sites, but since I tried to find the other
two, I've learnt they only have the people who've submitted DNA; if
there are a thousand Gastrells, they may list twenty, I shall try to
establish a list of living Gastrells from telephone data.

'What are you doing this summer, Lisa?'

'Studying, trying to learn ahead for the third year. I need a scholarship to continue, so I must do well in the finals. How about you,
Leo?'

'I must ride a camel in a twelve-hour desert race. It's staged
every four years in one of the Emirates. It's also a social occasion,

like Ascot, but only for one day. The prestige of winning is significant to the winning country. And this year, Oman is the host.'

'Well, I hope you win.'

The food was as delicious as Lisa expected; she ate more than usual. After another visit to the Lovers statue, Lisa dozed on the train while returning to Brussels.

Before the term ended, Leo knew the best time achieved in earlier races was fractionally under eleven hours, and his camel trainer had sent other data.

The report gave the camel's body temperature at different speeds, using a GPS to measure its speed over five kilometres. Another table showed the water quantity his camel drank after a forty-kilometre run at different speeds; one, only ten kilometres, was at maximum speed.

Leo worked out a plan. He knew a camel stored its water in the bloodstream.

It will drink before the start but slow down if its blood becomes too thick. It will need water to finish that distance in time; the trick is not to run out of water before the race ends.

On the appointed day in the summer break, Leo and his camel were ready at the start on the edge of the Wahiba Sands. A festival atmosphere reigned amongst the colourful tents surrounding the start-finish line, although it was only an hour after dawn. Thick carpets with intricate designs covered the sand in the tents, and some tents had carpets outside where mothers sat with young children. The men wore traditional Omani clothes, but others from the Emirates wore *thobes* of assorted colours. They all had headcloths, some with *agals*. Women sauntered in groups, dressed in intricately embroidered robes, some with gold or silver threads; necklaces and jewellery were abundant. Between the tents, braziers heated and perfumed the dry morning air with fragrances of sandalwood or frankincense when someone threw some onto glowing coals. To one side, gathered around firepits tended by young boys, the cooks tipped fat over sheep rotating on spits turned by other boys.

Leo was well behind the start line, leaning casually against his kneeling camel, with his mother, father, and grandfather, who, as the Sultan's son, had dressed to suit the public occasion in desert garb, a blinding white ankle-length outer *thobe*, headscarf and golden *agal*. His parents had dressed carefully to be less noticeable. Louis remembered his father-in-law dressed similarly the first time he met Soraya.

When Leo's mother asked, 'Asad, shouldn't you mount and be at the start line? They'll leave you behind.' He replied.

'No, Mother, that's part of my plan. I shall cross the start line at a canter, a second after the gun, to be ahead of the others. I'll let them pass.' *And exhaust themselves.*

His grandfather looked pleased.

He mounted, rode away from the line, circled and returned, gaining speed. He crossed the line a second after the gun and was fifty metres ahead before the others managed to control their camels that had bolted after Leo.

His camel ran comfortably, steady at twenty-two kilometres an hour; he checked it on his handheld GPS but already felt the gait and temperature of the beast were correct.

Eight hours later, after taking several measured sips of water, each time resisting the urge to drink more than his calculated amount and the increasing desire to accelerate, he had passed all but two competitors. He came steadily to a halt and gave his beast all the water, which it drank rapidly.

Remounting, he urged his camel up to speed, and thirty minutes later, a fraction faster. After thirty more minutes, he passed one of the two remaining competitors. When the array of tents and flags at the start line came in sight, he could see the remaining camel in the race ahead of him. He thought he was catching it, but instead of accelerating, he waited.

Between Louis and her father at the finish line, Soraya asked, 'Why is he not going faster?'

Her father replied, 'It is the moment of judgement; his camel will try its hardest to reach the other, so he must hold back until it can do so just before the line. – *Look, there he goes!*'

Leo released the restraint on his camel, his voice an encouraging caress as he yelled, '*Yalla! Yalla!* Go, my girl.'

His mount, finally freed from restraint, fixed its eyes on the camel ahead and, within a few strides, reached the sixty-five kilometres per hour peak speed of a camel. The other rider, hearing the muffled hoofbeats, looked back and began whipping his exhausted mount furiously, to no avail. A hundred metres before the line, Leo swept past him and then over the line to resounding cheers.

'You see, Soraya, my grandson has learnt restraint is a valuable tool, and he calculated it perfectly.'

Soraya could hear the pride in his voice.

Leo dismounted, thanked his camel with a stroke of affection and a few words, and called for water. Only after his mount drank did he join his parents. A hawk-eyed man had watched him with interest.

An hour later, Asad bin Rachid Al Said met Sheikh Abdullah Al Nahyan at the prizegiving. Leo's grandfather presented him, 'Asad, please meet Sheikh Abdullah Al Nahyan, the race sponsor.' Leo bowed. 'It is an honour, Eminence, to meet someone of great renown. May Allah pour blessings upon you.'

Leo was surprised when Sheikh Abdullah called him Sheikh Asad.

'Sheikh Asad, you won that race with skill, and your camel seems as fresh as when you left. I noticed you didn't use your whip.'

'I never do, Eminence. I love her; she loves me and does what I ask.'

'Allah rains his blessings on a man who loves his camels. May I present you with your prize?' He gestured to an assistant who presented a black velvet cushion with a little gold bar in the centre.

Leo knew the bar was worth a little more than three camels. 'Eminence, your stables are famous for producing fast camels. I'm a mathematics student and don't need a gold bar, but sometime in the future, I shall need three camels. Please keep the gold to pay for improvements in your breeding programme, and whenever I'm ready and need one, I shall ask for a camel.'

'I'm surprised you don't ask for a profit.'

'I will, Eminence; I ask for a handshake. Then the camels will be the best you have.'

Sheikh Abdullah roared with laughter and put out his hand. 'I must watch you, or I'll lose the shirt off my back!

'Sheikh Rachid, you have a bold grandson. I like him.'

15

The day after the race, Soraya reminded him of his duties as an Omani Prince. 'Asad, a Prince of Oman, must undertake the pilgrimage to Mecca. Hajj is in ten days, and you're now old enough. Take some of the guards with you.'

Leo left with a group of young guards ten days later and returned with the right to the title Hajji. An aide informed Sheikh Abdullah, who said, 'I'm not surprised; Sheikh Asad has earned the respect of men.'

'Shuchang, can you find out how many people in the UK have the surname Gastrell?'

'What sources, boss?'

'Try the UK electoral rolls. There may be some who've died and are still registered and others who haven't. Those electoral rolls are notoriously inaccurate.'

'I can compare them with the births and deaths register, although that may be misleading as any addresses will be outdated.'

'And Shuchang, UK residents born in foreign countries might not be in the register.'

'How about telephone directories?'

'Those might be more current, although fixed lines at rented accommodation are usually in the owner's name. Cellular phone data may be the best of all. Cross-reference everything you can find.

'We must phone them because there are so many messages, emails, and SMSs from only God knows who these days; it's normal to delete an email or SMS when it's from an unknown sender.'

'Okay, boss, I'll see what I can do.'

Shuchang found thirty-four fixed line numbers. As the directory is online, it was easy for a computer to access the service in each county. Then, he used another tactic to find cellular numbers from all the cellular providers.

Removing the duplicates where a Gastrell had both was the last step. The cellular providers had a fixed-line number or address in their FICA data.

The Births and Deaths and the electoral rolls gave no more.

In total, he had forty-two numbers.

Leo phoned Lisa.

'Hello, man. Did you win the race?'

'Of course, Lisa, by a hundred metres.'

'How long was it?'

'Two hundred and forty kilometres.'

'Then that was close. I'll bet you were tired. Why did you call?'

'To tell you I have forty-two telephone numbers for a Gastrell.'

'That's *lucky*! There would be thousands of Smiths.'

'There would. We can phone the forty-two several times if they're out and ask if they have an ancestor called William Gastrell about 1700.'

'Why not the date on his tomb?'

'They may not know when he died, so it forces a negative response.'

'I can't do the calling, Leo. I must concentrate on studying.'

'That's okay, Lisa. I'll let you know what I learn. I'll call them once I've returned to Cambridge.'

A telephone advertising service phoned them all.

'Mr/Ms Gastrell, I'm calling from Cambridge University…'

Leo received the column of telephone numbers with the gender of the callee and their name, and then the response in a third column. The list was overwhelmingly negative.

Gender	Name	Response
F	Gertrude	Negative.
M	Edward	Rude Negative.
M	Peter	Fixed phone disconnected; cellphone number not attributed
F	Evelyn	She has her family history and could look, but she was busy.
M		I called multiple times on the fixed line, but there was no answer.

Etc…

Shuchang found the address of the woman who had a family history.

I must call Lisa.

'Hello, man.'

'Hello, my love. Of the forty-two numbers, only one didn't reply negatively. A woman who said she has her family history and can look. I feel it would be best to visit her. Evelyn Gastrell lives in a manor house near Chalfont St. Peter outside London, about an hour's drive. Would you like to come with me?'

'I'd love to, but I can't, Leo, finals are looming.'

'Then I'll report back. Bye, my love.'

I can't argue that when he's doing my work for me.

'Bye, Leo.' *I hope PegLeg will forgive me.*

Although Leo had told Lisa that Chalfont St Peter was an hour's drive from London, he also had to travel from Cambridge. With no Lisa to collect en route, he looked at a chart, found a direct route at a low altitude, and decided that a thirty-minute helicopter ride was a far better solution.

Leo phoned Evelyn Gastrell, told her why and agreed on a date and time to meet her. Then, he asked if he could land a helicopter on the field behind her house.

'Have you been here before, Mister Poussin?'

'No, ma'am, I looked on Google Earth.'

'The grass in the centre of the driveway is better. We have had a helicopter visit.'

Surprised, Leo could only agree.

Evelyn Gastrell's manor was impressive from the air: three stories, a dozen chimney pots, and a carefully laid out garden. The sweeping U-shaped driveway around a smooth lawn was a perfect helipad; when he stepped from his helicopter, he saw two things. A signboard that announced the building housed '*E D Interior Architects*' and a woman standing beside it. He noticed her elegant dress, necklaces, and bangles as he approached her. Closer, he realised she looked younger than the sixty-two years her FICA data revealed.

'Good morning, are you Evelyn Gastrell?'

'I am, young man, you must be Mister Poussin. I'm surprised

you're so young, but on second thought, I should have expected it. University researchers are rarely old. Please follow me. The front of the manor is now the showroom and offices for my son's business. He has shunted me into the rear.'

Leo remarked as they walked through the showroom, 'Ma'am, the *décor* is outstanding. Is this your son's work?'

'He creates the volume and the mood, and his wife creates the details. Now come through to my rooms. They're also responsible for the decoration, although I specified how I wanted to feel.'

They entered a lounge where a table with a silver tray and teapot, porcelain cups and saucers and a plate of cakes lay ready. 'Ma'am, comfort is the theme, and the style is a mixture of items that broadcast that feeling. I recognise items from several countries.'

'Well done, Mr Poussin; few people relate the items to the theme. How do you like your tea?'

'A little milk and no sugar, Ma'am, please call me Leo. It's far easier.'

....

'Now, Leo, take a cake or two and tell me about your research.'

'It started with a tomb in Madagascar, inscribed Butterfly Bill; he died in 1721. It's a pirates' cemetery. Because he might have known some of the pirates buried there and written about them, I asked the History Professor, who suggested reading everything a Naturalist named James Petiver had written, as he collected specimens of plants and insects sent from other countries by amateur naturalists. I found nothing in published documents, but Petiver's collection is in the Natural History Museum. I went there to find further documents and saw his insect collection from East Africa. My girlfriend was with me and recognised a Madagascan butterfly. The Museum Catalogue notes William Gastrell collected it.'

'From there, how did you find me?'

'There are forty-two Gastrells in the telephone directories, including you. Of them all, when we telephoned them, only you said you knew about your family tree. Here's a copy of the list we have. There may be Gastrells that you don't have in your tree.' Leo handed it over.

'Leo, I have my file here; I've built the tree over many years and visited many graveyards. After the phone call, I looked. I have everyone in the early 1700s unless there was an illegitimate child. If you read that list slowly, I'll check if I have all the current Gastrells.'

....

'Gertrude.'

'I have her.'

'Edward.'

....

'Ma'am, the last is a second Edward.'

'I have him, too. So I have all of yours, but you're missing one.'

'I wonder how that's possible?'

'John may not have a phone. I'll tell you about him.'

'Please do, ma'am.'

'There was a cousin named William Gastrell who died in 1682. In my ancestor's memoirs, he's mentioned as being a *bad lot* and, without any details, an implication that he participated in the slave trade. The words my ancestor wrote were:

> The Lord will never forgive one who builds a fortune on
> the misery and death of other races.

'As a result, the Gastrells decided to forget him, and no mention of him or his descendants has existed in any family document since then.'

'So, how do you know about John Gastrell?'

'He has a son, Christopher, who has a rare eye deformity. The family is poor as they have spent every penny to improve his eyesight before he goes blind; he must be sixteen now and will be blind by twenty. When I met them, the boy had glasses like the bottom of a bottle. Their doctor obtained a DNA analysis and sent it to every eye specialist he could find, with no success. That was three years ago. In desperation, John sent the analysis to one of the heritage websites and saw me. Suspecting a scam, I checked the DNA match. The study says we descend from a Gastrell in the mid to late 1600s, and as John has no DNA link to anyone in my tree, I have assumed he's a descendant of the *bad lot.*

'I have done what I can for the family; they live on the breadline.

'Whether John can tell you about an ancestor called William Gastrell or Butterfly Bill, I don't know. If he had any worthwhile documents, he would have sold them if he could.'

'Ma'am, you've at least provided another lead. As he has no phone, can you give me his address? Forenames often repeat from generation to generation, so there's an encouraging sign.'

Evelyn used a slip from a pad and wrote the address after looking at her file. 'Leo, will you tell me if you find anything?'

'Of course, Ma'am, but it might take a long time. Research often does.'

'I'll show you to your flying machine. It's been an interesting morning. I wish there were more.'

Leo told Lisa about his visit and asked again.

'Darling, a boy named Christopher with badly deformed eyes is involved. I would feel happier if you came with me to see them.'

'I'm not studying ophthalmology, Leo. That would happen during specialisation. Can you find Christopher's Doctor?'

'I won't hack the National Health records, Lisa. Tell me what else I could try?'

'The boy must have some prescribed medicines, and they will use a nearby pharmacy. The prescription will have the Doctor's details. Then, ask the Doctor about his problem. I'm sure you can cook up a story. There's a riskier method. Commission a survey about people's satisfaction with their medical services, door-to-door kind. Ask them to name their doctors.'

'I can try, Lisa, if I can find out, will you come?'

He needs encouragement. I'll excuse the darling.

'Yes, Leo.'

With only the Lent term and half the Easter term to the end of his Bachelor's tripos, Leo couldn't afford any diversions except exercise.

Leo took the first step –

'Shuchang, I'll send you a physical address. Identify pharmacies, starting with the closest, and find me a prescription in their records for Christopher Gastrell; I want the Doctor's details. He will be an Ophthalmologist. Be invisible.'

A week later, Shuchang sent a name, address, and comment.

No security.

And the second step –

'Can you copy the medical file for Christopher from the Doctor's records?'

After another week, it arrived with a comment.

No encryption.

Leo sent it to Lisa as an attachment to a short email.

Darling, is this what you want?

Lisa read the medical file and understood nothing except the first line.

> Christopher has *Oval Eyes*.

I'll discover what Oval Eyes means.
    She found a reference in the Lancet.

> Oval Eyes: a singularly rare condition caused by bone growth in the upper orbital region during the first months after birth. Only five known cases and all were premature births. The ensuing protective tissue layer applies pressure to the eyeball and continues to grow, restricting eyeball movement and eventually leading to blindness. Visible as Oval Pupils, which are a more frequent symptom of brain trauma.

Then, she read the summary of the following article.

> **On the Forefront of Eye Surgery.**
> Like the past revolutionary advances in organ replacement and dental surgery due to advanced electronic imaging, microsurgery of the brain has made enormous strides with remotely operated robotic arms while viewing a camera image of the operational area. The focus now falls on eye and ear microsurgery, promising a revolution from the marriage of micro-miniature electronics and a surgeon's skill. Unfortunately, it will be many years before the enormous cost of the necessary machines will make such procedures available at a price below the astronomical cost of research procedures. However, without such research, medical practices will stagnate.

Leo read her SMS and phoned.
    'Hello, man.'

'Hello, my love, that was quick. What have you learnt?'

'I don't understand much, but I have read an article in the Lancet about Oval Eyes.'

She told him about both articles. Silence followed.

'Leo, do you think John Gastrell will know anything about Butterfly Bill?'

'I don't know, Lisa, I can't even guess. Why do you ask?'

'Because if he has anything, he will ask for treatment for his son, and that will cost a fortune. Must we cross John Gastrell off the list and look for another route, or delete Butterfly Bill from our research?'

'Let me think about it, Lisa. We have nothing unless the Professor pulls a rabbit from a hat or we spot another of my medallions in a shop window. Never knowing if John Gastrell could have given us data will leave us wondering what might have been – forever.'

He said that when we made our promises to PegLeg.

'Okay, Leo, call me when you have an answer. Bye.'

'Bye, my love, you're marvellous.'

That night, Lisa dreamed the pirate dream again. She was in a rowing boat, praying for rescue and waving her skirt at an oncoming ship. Lisa recognised it at the last minute and saw the Pirate glaring at her from the rail moments before the bow wave swamped her frail craft. She woke, panting, with a racing heart.

After her breathing and heart slowed, she thought. *PegLeg wants Leo and me to see John Gastrell. He must have known Butterfly Bill.*

She SMSed Leo at daybreak.

Leo, we must see John Gastrell, PegLeg insists.

Leo dialled her number.

'Hello, man.'

'Hello girl, why the change of heart?'

Lisa explained.

Lisa feels stressed due to the finals. 'Then I'll arrange it for the first days of the summer break; we must pass our exams with high marks. PegLeg will understand.'

With no telephone to call, Leo sent a man to investigate, and a week later, the report said.

> They are always at home after five-thirty pm except Wednesdays, the discount day at the supermarket. The weather was fine on Saturday, and they took a bus to Hyde Park with a picnic bag. The neighbours say they are penniless. Mrs Gastrell works when she can as a cleaner, and Mr Gastrell takes his son to a school to learn Braille twice a week. Two neighbours admitted to taking them food parcels.

Now, to wait until the break.

16

Leo at Cambridge and Lisa in Brussels studied long hours as the June final exams approached.

In Brussels, Ashina told Lisa, 'I think we should take a break; we're saturated, and you can't learn when you're already full. I need to see your father as well.'

Lisa phoned, and they went on Saturday. She told her father that Ashina wanted to talk, so after dinner, Gaston said, 'Ashina, do you want advice?'

'Yes, Doctor, I've considered all my options and what I want to do. I want to return to Katanga, but not immediately, so I need a scholarship. I would love to be a medical teacher in Africa, firsthand training at small country clinics, but I have no idea how to become one.'

'Ashina, that's an incredibly worthwhile ambition. Hold that in your mind until after the exams are over. I'll investigate and ask a few people. Maybe I can propose a scholarship and a course of study. The most difficult problem will be field experience, which comes later. We'll take it a step at a time.'

'Thank you, Doctor, that's marvellous.'

Leo passed and was accepted automatically into Part III of the tripos for a Master of Mathematics degree. Lisa's term ended after Leo's, so he waited and, on the day after, phoned Lisa.

'Hello, man, are we going to see the Gastrells?'

'Hello, darling. That's why I called.'

'Could you try using *My Love?*'

'Delete or Replace?'

'I think Replace will be more successful.'

Lisa grinned when he replied, 'I pressed "[*Replace All*]", my love, do you prefer to visit London on a weekday or Saturday?'

'Saturday.'

'Then, any Saturday when the forecast is rain. The Gastrells picnic in a park if the weather permits. This Saturday, it's forecast to rain.'

'Call me on Friday evening to confirm. I'll plan nothing for Saturdays except study. Bye.'

Lisa smiled when he said, 'Bye, my love.' *Maybe I prefer darling.*

Sheltered by the umbrella Leo held over their heads in the light rain, they reached the front door of a house in Newnham, London's East End. Visibly without maintenance for several years, the sound and kaleidoscope of light they saw on the drawn curtains confirmed someone was home. A dishevelled, damp cat they hadn't noticed, sheltering on the doorstep, yowled and leapt away as Lisa reached forward to press the doorbell.

Ding-dong-ding-donggggg....

The man who opened the door, wearing slippers and baggy trousers that might have fit him years ago, held up by suspenders surmounted by a stained orange wool vest over a collarless green shirt, looked at them in surprise.

Leo asked, 'Mr John Gastrell?'

'Yes, what do you want? If it's a donation, we can't afford anything.'

'I'm a history researcher, Mr Gastrell, from Cambridge University. We're *not* canvassing for any charity. I'm Leo Poussin, and my girlfriend is Lisa Calmette; she's studying to be a doctor.'

'So, what do you want?'

'To ask about Butterfly Bill or William Gastrell, who died in 1721.'

'I don't know when he was born or died; how do you know about him, and how did you find us?'

Lisa asked, 'Can we come in from the rain, sir? It's a long story that might take half an hour.'

Leo thought Gastrell was about to turn them away, so he said, 'We have seen his grave, and Evelyn gave us your address.'

After a pause, Gastrell said, 'Then come in. My wife and son are in the parlour.'

Gastrell led them into the room. Lisa saw the boy from behind, his head turning from side to side as he watched the TV; then Gastrell said, 'Christopher, sit on the floor; Maud, switch off the Telly; we have visitors.' He pointed to two visibly ancient, stained orange armchairs and said, 'You sit there; I'll sit with Maud on the couch.'

The suite must be thirty years old, and the couch has the same horrible colour and stains. As the boy stood and turned to look at them, she thought, *Bottle glasses, and they magnify his oval pupils.*

Gastrell introduced his wife and son and asked, 'Give me your names again.'

Leo did, and then Gastrell asked, 'Did Evelyn tell you about Christopher? She helped us a lot.'

'She did, so you needn't explain. Lisa will tell you our research story.'

Twenty minutes later, with amazement and wonder, Gastrell said, 'So the legend is true. I've always thought so, but I had doubts.'

'What legend, Mr Gastrell?'

'Call me John; you're family if you've been to Bill's grave. I'll tell you.

'I have an ancestor, William Gastrell, who married and had two children, both boys; I descend from one of them; that's in the family Bible. The other boy left England to make his fortune. He became wealthy, and the legend says he did so by trading human beings. He returned to England with another son, whom he named William Gastrell. The family in those days were regular churchgoers, so they and the church shunned our branch of the family, so the Bible has nothing more to tell us. The legend says that William Gastrell the Younger left England, and we never saw or heard anything until his father died and left all his effects to his brother, my ancestor. In his effects was a wooden box. His brother sealed it, for it supposedly contained blasphemous writings. Passed on from generation to generation, it remains unopened. The only thing I can tell you is that on the outside, burned into the wood, are the words – "*The perambulations of Butterfly Bill*". Today is the first time I've heard he survived and died overseas.

'When we learnt of Christopher's affliction ten years ago, I took the box to Christie's. They said it was worth only a few pounds as it contained unknown content from an unknown person. I wish I'd known then that he found an unknown butterfly and it's in the Museum. It might have helped.

'They offered to have the box opened and the contents preserved and would then consider if they could place it at an auction. The price they quoted was twice my annual income from social assistance.

'Two years ago, Evelyn hoped to collect enough money to send Christopher to a doctor in Germany. She said the doctor offered to examine Christopher for free. She even got us passports. It was a waste of her money because she couldn't collect enough.'

Leo replied, 'Maybe not, John. Lisa, you're the doctor; what's John's problem, and who could do something?'

'He has *Oval Eyes*, Leo. It's super-rare. I can ask my father, or perhaps Evelyn remembers the name of the German doctor.'

'John, if we can arrange an examination, who will accompany him, you or Maud?'

'Maud, she's much better at caring for him.'

'Then let Lisa try. At least you will learn if Christopher is treatable.'

John and Maud had tears glistening in their eyes when he said, 'Let me fetch two things.' He returned with a deep box and an ancient leather-bound Bible that closed with a brass clasp.

'I won't turn the pages, but the family tree is inside the cover and on the first page.'

....

'At a guess, William Gastrell left England at twenty in 1680, so he died at sixty-one, which explains why the box is so deep; it must have forty years of writing inside.

'Leo, after Christopher returns from the examination and if the operation is possible, will you take this box and try to raise enough money to cover the operation?'

'That's a promise, John.

'Lisa must catch a train back to Brussels, so we must leave. Do you know how to use a mobile?'

'Yes, but I don't have one.'

Lisa took a phone from her bag. 'You do now; one of us will call you when we have arranged the visit. My number is on the contacts list, and the phone's number is on the label on the back. The code is 123456. We keep one in case one of the people we talk to about our research is like you. Here's the charger.'

'Nice people, Lisa, sacrificing their lives for their son.'

'They are. I'll speak to my father tonight.'

'Then we've one last thing to do before you take the train.'

Lisa smiled, then licked her lips. 'Visit the Lovers statue?'

'Right, first time, my love.'

'Dad, I need some help.'

'What's the problem, Lisa?'

'Leo wants to help a boy with an eye deformity called *Oval Eyes*; his name is Christopher Gastrell. Leo sent me his medical file because I'm studying to be a doctor and asked who might do an examination. I can't understand it. Can you help?'

'I'm not an eye specialist, Lisa. I know one at the WHO who's an expert on river blindness and one from Germany; we met at a conference in Abidjan.'

'That's a parasite, not an epidemic.'

'True, but it behaves like one; it flares up and then dies away. The WHO asked if I could model the dynamics.'

'What was the German doctor doing?'

'Researching operative action to correct the parasite-induced damage.'

'That sounds like someone who might be able to help. Can you call the German doctor to ask for advice?'

'I must look up his name, Lisa, so I'll call him tomorrow. Why is Leo doing this?'

'He's like that, Dad. He likes helping people who deserve help.'

That night, Gaston told Rosemary, adding, 'What amazes me the most is what she said about Leo. Do you think it might be true that he likes helping people?'

'I do, Gaston. Lisa is astute, and she's growing up. She's known him too long to be fooled. But there may be something else in what he's doing, and she may be involved. I have an odd feeling that PegLeg is in the background.'

Gaston phoned Doctor Meyerling's number, and his secretary told him that Herr Doctor was operating. She took his name and number and asked him to call back after five pm.

Doctor Meyerling called Gaston at five precisely.

'Doctor Calmette, your call was a complete surprise. I'm delighted to talk to you again.'

'Likewise, Doctor Meyerling, since this morning, I have read several articles about your successes. Congratulations on your research.'

'And I have read about you and your successful fights against terrible disease outbreaks. Your courage in the face of Ebola is admirable. Have you called for professional reasons?'

'A mixture, Doctor. My daughter is studying medicine, and she and her boyfriend would like to help a London teenager with an eye deformity called *Oval Eyes*. She has received his medical file but must study for years before knowing what is possible. She asked me who to ask, and as I know you, I phoned for a recommendation.'

'Doctor, what's the boy's name?'

'Christopher Gastrell.'

'I've seen his file. His specialist in London sent it to me two years ago. I replied that I had operated on two such cases; today, I can say three, all successful. However, it requires two operations per eye at fifteen to twenty-day intervals, with a minimum of two months in hospital. I have research staff and must have an assistant surgeon and a whole team for each operation. It takes a month to plan. The cost is beyond the British National Health allowance, and Christopher's parents cannot afford it. I offered to do an examination free of charge for research reasons, but they would have to pay for travel and accommodation here for two nights. I have heard nothing further.'

'Doctor Meyerling, thank you. I shall tell my daughter. Between doctors, what would be the total cost of such treatment?'

'A budget of half a million Euros for the boy, not including any costs for persons accompanying him.'

'Thank you again, Doctor; I'm not surprised. My budget for a vaccination campaign can be far more, but the number of lives saved justifies it.'

'And thank you for calling. I hope we will meet again at another conference. Could you give my regards to your lovely wife? Goodbye.'

'Goodbye, Doctor.'

'Hi, Dad, did you call the German Doctor?'

'Yes, he saw Christopher's file two years ago.'

'What did he say?'

Gaston told her.

'Is that expensive, Dad?'

'Not if you consider the cost of the equipment and staff he and the hospital would use.'

'Then I'll tell Leo.'

When she told him, he replied, 'You're marvellous, Lisa, I'll talk to John. I imagine any date will suit them, but I'd better confirm.'

'Hello, John, Leo here.'

'Hello Leo, that was quick.'

'Lisa's dad knows your German doctor, who will examine Christopher for free. Her dad can make an appointment. It's a day's travel, a day to do the examination and tests, and a day to return. My research budget will pay for the trains, and Lisa's will pay for the hotel. When can Maud and Christopher travel?'

'Leo, I don't know what to say. Any day is fine. Just tell me when. We can take the bus to St Pancras.'

'Ok, John, I'll call you.'

'Hello, my love. Any day for the appointment. Ask your dad to make one.'

'Will they travel alone?'

'No, I'll employ a German-speaking nurse and a bodyguard to help the boy; he's too old for the ladies' toilet and young enough to be prey.'

'John, it's all arranged for Monday the twenty-third. A car with a woman and a man who can speak German will fetch Maud and Christopher at seven am. They return late evening on the twenty-fifth.'

'Thanks, Leo, they'll be ready.'

John phoned Lisa on the twenty-sixth. 'Lisa, I promised, and I don't need to wait for the report. You want to know what's inside the box, so can you arrange for Christie's to collect it?'

'It won't be Christie's, John; they add a commission. Leo will send a courier from the conservator-restorer Christie's employs. It will take months and will need a modern English adaptation.'

The examination report was positive, and Leo phoned John.

'Have you received Christopher's examination report, John?'

'I have Leo, what do we do now?'

'If you sign a document that says Doctor Meyerling can use anything he learns or does for research or publication, the operation can happen in a month. It takes two months. You will receive train tickets by courier, and you have a full-board hotel booked for you and Maud for the whole period. All you need is pocket money. Tell Evelyn. She might help; her number is in your phone contacts. You must use a bus to St Pancras.'

'Leo, how's your box?'

'Not mine, John, yours. Conservation and language adaptation may be complete when you return.'

'I promised, Leo. It's yours.'

Leo returned to Oman. His private project was beginning to show promise, but he had more development work.

Lisa and Ashina passed with distinction. They returned to visit Lisa's parents when the university published the results.

Rosemary produced a festive dinner that, being a fine evening, they ate in the garden.

Gaston raised his glass. 'Lisa, your mother and I will always think of you as our girl, and I'll include Ashina when I say, Girls, now Bachelors, our congratulations. We're proud of you, and I'm sure Ashina's parents must be too.'

'Thanks, Dad. Do you have any scholarship information for the next stage of our careers?'

'Lisa, you have a WHO scholarship for a two-year medical management master's degree. When you pass, the scholarship requires you to join the WHO to improve hospital management wherever the WHO sends you. However, once you have the masters, you must take a job in a hospital for practical experience before they send you into the field.'

'And Ashina?'

'She has one as well, a one-year management diploma to learn the basics of organising a small clinic and staff. Then, she has a year at a teacher training college to learn the dos and don'ts of teaching adults; it's mostly psychology. The WHO will then give Ashina a position to train staff at small, remote clinics.

'Lisa, the practical hospital management you can learn here won't be relevant in developing countries. I'll persuade Gary Somers that experience overseas will be worth double what you learn here.'

'I thought he was a by-the-book civil servant?'

'He is, but a good one. Given a valid argument, he will decide because he dislikes passing the buck up the tree.'

Ashina stood, turned to Rosemary, and said, 'With your permission, I want to kiss your husband.'

'Go ahead, my dear; I think he deserves it.'

Ashina did, saying, 'Thank you, Doctor, thank you, I'll not disappoint you.'

'Thanks, Dad,' said Lisa, 'I'll kiss you too.'

A well-kissed Gaston then said, 'Now, I have another announcement. Rose and I have decided that you deserve more than a certificate, so we'll offer you a holiday in Africa to visit Ashina's family.'

Ashina had tears in her eyes as she said, 'That's the most wonderful present I've ever had; thank you, thank you, thank you.'

17

When Ashina explained the alternative flights, Lisa asked, 'Ashina, we've never seen Victoria Falls. Can we route that way and see the Falls?'

'I'll search for flights. It might be expensive.'

Ashina told Lisa the next day, 'We can fly to Johannesburg and then the Falls, but my dad says he'll drive us to Chililabombwe, twenty kilometres into Zambia. He said we'll have no problems at the border because he's well-known there. Then he'll find us a taxi or a bus to Ndola; it's about four hours. Then, we fly to Livingstone, take a taxi to the Falls, and walk across the bridge into Zimbabwe. We'll fly back from there.'

'Then let's make the bookings. It should be interesting. What clothes should I take?'

When she showed Ashina her necklaces, Ashina picked several, including one Lisa hadn't considered; it was too glittery, a long loop of rhinestones, but Ashina said, 'That's just the kind of thing to wear on an evening in Lubum.'

Leo didn't forget to ride his camel and took a week off to make a five-hundred-kilometre round trip around the oases. And each time he had an internet link, he read about Lisa's exploits in Katanga.

Ashina's father met them at the Lubumbashi airport, dressed in his chief inspector uniform, so the formalities were minimal. Lisa thought his body language said. *Behave yourself; I'm the Chief Police Inspector.*

Ashina's parents lived in an old house on a wide street lined with magnificent old trees. Ashina explained that the Belgian government built it for civil servants in the colonial era. All on the road were the same design, but extensive modifications made them look different. The gardens were significant, but owners had built supplementary buildings and workshops in some cases. To Lisa, it was familiar.

She and Ashina shared a room. A quasi-continuous stream of relatives visited for five days, always in the garden or on the wide colonial veranda, with copious amounts of food and drink. Ashina said, 'Don't try to remember all their names; I'll give them to you when you need to speak to one.'

To Lisa, the pride Ashina's family showed in her qualification as a doctor was overwhelming.

On the first Friday night, Ashina asked, 'Lisa, I'm sure you've had enough of my relatives, I have too. Would you like to visit a nightclub tonight?'

'That sounds great; where?'

'I'll ask Dad; maybe the places I visited three years ago aren't open.'

Her father took them personally and early to a nightclub. He took them in, introduced them to the bartender, and said, 'Ashina, if you have any trouble, ask Keita to help. Call me when you want to come home, and I'll fetch you.'

'We'll be no later than ten, Dad; I know it's sometimes rough later.'

Lisa wore her rhinestone necklace; she had to double it, for it fell to her waist, but Ashina made her wear it as a single strand. 'Let it swing free, Lisa.'

Lisa enjoyed the evening. The music, typically African, had a strong beat, and while she and Ashina danced several times, the dance floor area slowly filled. When they missed a dance, Lisa noticed an unusual arrival, a giant man – Lisa thought *over two metres and one-fifty kilos*. He had several long necklaces and rings on his fingers, twinkling under the bar lighting and entered with a woman almost as big. Three other men accompanied them. He went to a corner where a couch, designed, Lisa thought, especially for him, allowed him to relax with the woman beside him. Ashina said, 'We must leave soon; that's Tiny Toomah, the most notorious gangster in town.'

'What's he do?'

'The illegal trade in cobalt and copper.'

When she and Ashina returned to their table after the next dance, they received unwelcome attention from two young men who had watched them. Lisa had been looking at the giant when she spotted something seconds before one of the annoying pair called, 'Hey, white girl, you lookin' for some black meat?'

Lisa hardly heard it; she stood, said to Ashina, 'Come,' and walked straight towards the giant.

Ashina had no choice but to follow. The annoying pair, seeing where they were going, fell back.

'Excuse me, sir, can I ask you a question?'

'Who are you?'

'I'm Lisa Calmette, a doctor.'

'And your friend?'

Ashina answered, 'I'm also a doctor and the Chief Inspector's daughter.'

Tiny grinned. 'Then I shall be polite. Your father and I have had several meetings.'

He waved an arm, and two chairs appeared magically. 'Sit and ask your question.'

They sat, and Lisa asked, 'That chain you have wrapped around your hand and the medallion, where did you buy it?'

Tiny unwrapped it from his hand; the polished bronze medallion, with a skull and crossed bones, hung from the chain and glinted in the lights.

'Interesting that you should ask. Four or five years ago, I was on my way home from Dar es Salaam, and on the road from Mwenda, I gave a ride to a young backpacker. Halfway here, in the middle of nowhere, the car stopped. The guy looked under the bonnet, found a burned wire, took a piece from somewhere else, reconnected it, and the car ran fine. When we arrived, I offered him one of my necklaces. He refused and said, "I can't accept a reward for what I did; if I do, I must give you something in exchange."

'He took this medallion from around his neck and gave it to me; it made us equals, although I'm twice his size.' Tiny laughed, his laughter as big as he was.

'We became friends, if only for a few hours. He stayed to eat with me and told me he had bought it in a Djibouti market, although it's ancient. The date on it is 1710.'

'Do you remember his name?'

'No. Something short, I think. Hey Freddie, do you remember the hiker we took on board from Mwenda – way back? What was his name?'

'Leo, I remember thinking his father must have liked Simba beer.'

Tiny laughed again. 'That was it – Leo. Do you know him?'

'Very well, Tiny, we're co-researchers trying to discover the real name of a pirate called PegLeg Jon.'

'Hey, that's cool. Did this medallion once belong to the pirate?'

'It might have done; Leo has two others: one in copper and another in silver that he wears.'

'So you're his girl?'

'Yes, I am.' *At least, I hope I still am.*

'Then, take the medallion; it should be with the others. The chain's too short to fit around my neck, so I keep it around my hand if I take it. When you see Leo, give it to him, and tell him that Tiny remembers him well.'

'I can't take it without giving you something in exchange.'

'You and Leo must be from the same tribe.'

Lisa lifted the rhinestone necklace over her head. 'Same something, maybe not tribe. Here, please accept this in exchange.'

Tiny extended a giant paw, dropped the medallion in her hand, then took the necklace, hung it around his neck, and turned to his companion.

'Hey, Lucia, how does it look?'

'Like it was made for you, Tiny.'

Lisa put the medallion's chain around her neck and tucked the medallion out of sight as Tiny turned to her. 'You girls stay for a drink, and my guys will take you home; those two excuses for manhood won't bother you again.'

Lisa almost missed the slight gesture but did see the rapid departure of the two annoying men.

Tiny's girlfriend said her name was Lucia Ilunga, and over the following hour, they became friends; they learnt how difficult life had been for an oversized girl and how gentle Tiny was with her. It confirmed Lisa's feeling that he might be ruthless with enemies, but he was a good friend to have, and the women agreed to meet at a café the next day for coffee. When they left, Tiny told Ashina, 'Tell your father you met me, and I hope to have a long chat with him soon.'

When Ashina told him, her father chuckled, 'I'll see him soon. He may be a rogue, but I like the guy too.'

Lisa looked curiously at the medallion the next day; she turned it over in the sunlight, tilting it back and forth. Sometimes, it gleamed like gold. *I think it's happy around my neck. I must tell Leo.*

The following day, Ashina said, 'Dad's given us a car and a driver. I want to visit my teacher at my primary school, and you should see the kind of problems we have with medication in Katanga.'

Ashina's old teacher greeted her like a grandmother would when, after visiting her house, they found her in what Ashina called her treatment room. Lisa didn't want to interrupt the pleasure of the meeting between Ashina and the herbalist, who wanted to know everything. As she couldn't follow the conversation, she looked around the small room with its many bottles, jars, pots and calabashes, with herbs strung from strings below the roof. At first sight, it looked terrible, but then she realised it was neat, orderly, and spotlessly clean.

They had been there half an hour when the door opened, and a young man looked in, visibly a recent arrival as his pale face and forearms were lightly sunburned.

He asked, 'Hello, who are you?'

Lisa seized the opportunity, stood, and instructed, 'Come outside, there's not enough room for four, and I'll tell you.'

They exchanged information; Francis Poulain was a recently qualified doctor. Although he had registered in Belgium, he had signed a contract with *Médecins Sans Frontières*, the charity known elsewhere as *Doctors Without Borders*, and they had sent him to Katanga. He was on a year's contract, saving money, and would return to set up his practice and buy a house in a country town that needed a doctor. He even knew which town.

So, some men plan where to live and work for the rest of their lives. Like a spider, he'll sit in his hole and trap a passing woman. Ugh.

Lisa asked, 'Why are you here in this village?'

'I'm not attached to any village in Katanga; I'm still trying to decide where to base myself. I received a message saying an extremely sick man was here, so I came to see if I could help. Unfortunately, I can't speak his language, and he can't speak French, so I can't ask about his symptoms.'

'Where is he?'

'Two shacks down towards the river.'

'We don't say *shacks*, Francis; we say houses; the people are proud of the little they have.' *Now, why did I say that to a stranger?* 'We'll ask Ashina.'

Ashina spoke to her old teacher, who told her about the man she had been treating for years. Ashina understood the problem at once.

'He has bilharzia; he's had it for years and has been treated with herbal concoctions because there's nothing else.'

Lisa objected, 'But Bilharzia has a prescribed treatment, *Praziquantel*. Why is it not available?'

Francis told them, 'It is available, in limited quantities, and it's costly, about a thousand dollars for a course that brings recovery. At least, that's what MSF told me.'

'It doesn't sound right to me,' said Lisa, 'why isn't the WHO doing something?'

'It's endemic, which means the same number of people catch it as die of it; it's not an epidemic. Also, it's a liver fluke; *Praziquantel* can cure a person one day, and the person can contract it again the next day. Unlike a virus, there is no antibody buildup, so there's no end to a treatment programme without other physical measures like sanitation improvement or snail elimination.'

'Then I'm going to find out why it's so expensive. Ashina, what can we do for the sick man?'

'Nothing much; the herbal treatment is decades old; it slows the development of the parasites and the consequences, but little else.'

'Francis, there's your answer. Ashina and I are returning to school in less than three weeks. I'll study this when we're back in Belgium. If I learn anything, I'll let you know.'

'Where are you going from here, Lisa?'

'Ashina can answer that.'

'To visit three more villages where I have childhood friends, then we'll be back in Lubum for our last six days. We're leaving on the nineteenth.'

'Then I'll try to meet you in Lubum.'

18

After discovering that the three villages had the same problems and inadequate medical care, Lisa and Ashina returned to Lubum. Connected again to the internet, she phoned her father. 'Hello, Dad, we're fine, but I've found that medicines cost a fortune. Especially the rarer drugs. Can you tell me why?'

'No, Lisa, I can't, but I can ask. I'll call you back when I know something. Your mother wants to talk to you.'

'Hello, Lisa; I just want reassurance that you're taking your anti-malarial drug.'

'Mama, you've said the same thing to me for years whenever we travelled; I don't think I could break the habit that easily. We have much to tell you when we return.'

That evening, her father returned her call.

'Lisa, the drugs are expensive for many reasons, primarily because of crime. There's a massive worldwide market for illegal drugs, and stealing them is lucrative, some from hospitals, much during shipment, often at the airport of arrival. The price for a single purchase is exorbitant, sometimes multiples of the base price, because the supplier must reship without payment if the first shipment vanishes. Insurers know this, so their premiums are sky-high. That makes it worse.'

'Thanks, Dad; I must think about this. But can you confirm why the WHO doesn't treat Bilharzia like an epidemic? There are millions of people with the disease. Francis gave me two reasons; I want to be sure they're right.'

'Who's Francis?'

'He's an MSF recruit, a newly qualified doctor looking for experience. Not a bad guy, but I think he's discouraged by the size of the problem here.'

'I'm not surprised. Bilharzia is endemic; treating people who have it would be a massive task, and they would catch it repeatedly if, as in some parts of Africa, there are no adequate sanitary facilities. The WHO considers that there are other more important tasks until countries improve their sanitation.'

'I'll study it when I'm back, Dad. When you see it in the field, it's horrible, especially in women.'

Lisa met Francis the next day for a coffee. Lisa felt he wasn't thinking about medical things when she told him what her father had said.

Francis phoned again two days later; he had something to tell her.

'I checked with the health ministry and the hospital; all the government-imported drugs are solely for hospital use, and all the doctors complain of shortages. The pharmacies say they have the same problems. They can't afford to stock expensive drugs that no one will buy.'

Then Francis invited her for dinner. Lisa felt pity for him; she thought of him as a young Belgian man out of his depth outside Belgium, so she accepted on condition that they go early. *He may be a doctor in Africa, but he's not part of my world.*

As they left the restaurant, the neon lighting opposite was flashing, and Lisa recognised the nightclub she and Ashina had visited. They hadn't walked twenty metres when a large black SUV drew up outside the neon-lit door, and she saw Tiny, Lucia and their entourage leaving the vehicle.

'Lisa, it's high time I took you home unless you come to mine. That giant is Tiny Toomah. My boss told me to avoid him; he's a gangster.'

Lisa had an idea. 'Well, I want to talk to him.'

'You'll go in there alone?'

'Yes, why not?'

'This is Africa, Lisa; anything can happen. Especially if a white woman goes into a place like that.'

'Francis, return to Belgium. You don't belong here while I do. I've been to countries like this with kids of every colour. I speak twenty or more dialects and don't notice skin colour. I feel safer here than in Belgium. I'm going in there. I'll ask Tiny a question or two and for an escort home. Good night.'

There were piercing looks when she entered the nightclub, but the interest died when she went to Tiny's corner.

'Hello, Lisa, I'm surprised to see you again. Sit, where's Ashina?'

'Trying to convince an aunt that the food in Europe doesn't cause sterility in women.'

Tiny laughed his huge laugh again. 'What have you been up to?'

'Ashina and I went into the country to visit several villages where she has friends. You know we're doctors, and we learnt the people out there are dying because there are no medicines. I phoned my dad, who says the theft of drugs is the problem.

'I saw you come in and thought I might ask if you can tell me anything.'

'Not much, Lisa; I don't touch that business.'

'Why not?'

Tiny frowned. 'I don't mind screwing big corporations out of their profits, but screwing sick people is not my idea of fun.'

'You know, I thought you would say something like that. If you feel that way, why don't you do something to stop the others?'

'I could do that, but why? There would be repercussions. I leave them to their business; they leave me to mine.'

'So, set up your business, import medicines without allowing theft, and sell at a low-profit margin.'

'I could, but who will supply me with the goods?'

Lisa smiled at him. 'Tiny, that's all the encouragement I need, knowing you'll be here to help. I'll find someone.'

'Lisa, are you trying to make me an honest businessman?'

'No, Tiny, give you a chance to be the nice guy you are. Lucia, you must know of the thousands of women who have painful genital infections that need treating.'

'I do, Lisa; I'll tell Tiny.'

Tiny asked, 'Lisa, you said you were researching with Leo; why not ask him to find out?'

'I don't know if he can; he's studying maths and economics.'

'Then he should be able to discover the size of medicine theft; maybe it's in many countries. I don't know if they steal in Dar or Zanzibar, but my guys there have told me illegal drugs come through those ports.'

'Then I'll ask him, thanks, Tiny.

'Now I'll leave you for the evening; I'm leaving in two days to return to university. If I can find a solution, I'll let you know or come and tell you.'

'Goodbye, Lisa. You're a hell of a woman, and Leo's a lucky man.'

Will I be a lucky woman?

The following day was busy. Fortunately, Ashina had spare baggage space for the trinkets and souvenirs Lisa had bought, but before breakfast, she sent an SMS to Leo.

Call me.

Then, the wait for his call seemed interminable, and the day passed slowly for her as she said goodbye to all of Ashina's family members who came to wish her success in her studies.

Leo phoned at six pm.

'Hello, man.'

'Hello, girl. Have you met PegLeg's wife in Lubumbashi?'

'Leo, I'm breaking my rule unless you accept that meeting Tiny Toomah and trading for PegLeg's bronze medallion is a legitimate reason for calling.'

....

How will he answer that?

'Darling, any call from you is legitimate, any time. I thought that rule applied only to me. How's Tiny?'

Lisa smiled. 'Leo, *darling*, is still forbidden. Tiny asked me to give you his regards, and he hopes to meet you soon.'

Her voice is smiling.

'I'd like to meet him again. Is that why you called?'

'No, although Tiny suggested I call you and ask. The price of medicines here is sky-high; my dad says it's because of theft. I asked Tiny, and he said it might not be local and might happen in many countries. You know I'll study hospital management for two years; I don't want to fail in my first job due to theft of my medical supplies.'

'Then I'll investigate. Is that worth a darling or two?'

Lisa grinned, 'Maybe, but you've used up two.'

That's a happy voice.

'Only one, *darling*. I counted. I'll tell you if I discover anything. Bye, Lisa.'

'Bye, darling. Now we're equal.'

The drive to the Zambian border was uneventful; the two girls dozed, and the bus to Ndola was a journey into Lisa's past, although slightly different. In the past, as a little girl, she had often sat or slept on the lap of a dark-skinned woman passenger; this time, she had a little boy on her lap, and Ashina cradled babies while their mothers ate.

At nine am the following day, the girls arrived in Livingstone, and after a taxi left them at the border, they crossed the Victoria Falls bridge on foot into Zimbabwe. The activity in the middle interested them; they learnt they could do a bungee jump for a hundred and fifty dollars.

'Ashina, I've never done a bungee jump. Would you like to do one? I'll pay for us both.'

'Let's watch one first.'

Ten minutes later, a young woman jumped.

The jumpmaster heard Ashina say, 'Lisa, I won't do that; I'd freeze from terror and not jump.'

The jumpmaster asked Lisa, 'How about you, miss?'

When Lisa didn't reply, he added, 'It's an experience of a lifetime. After a jump, one of the girls told me it's better than sex.'

Lisa laughed. 'And the guys?' *Is it an orgasm that's cheaper than paying for dinner?*

'They say that free-fall parachuting is better. Have you done a parachute jump?'

'No.' *I can understand that – it lasts longer.*

'Then do the bungee and a parachute jump another day; then you can judge.'

Sensing he had a customer, he produced an indemnity form. 'Here, sign this. Please provide your email address; we take photos and record videos. If you want them, we send them to your email; that's an extra fifty bucks.'

'Lisa, you're nuts.'

'I'll jump, Ashina.' Lisa signed, and when the jumpmaster moved away, she whispered, '*I haven't had an orgasm for three years.*'

Ten minutes later, she stood on the platform looking down, took the medallion from her bra, kissed it, tucked it safely away, and then jumped.

Ashina heard her yell, '*Madagascar!*'

With her arms spread, head back, and adrenaline pumping, she thought *life should always be like this: a leap into the unknown.*

Half an hour later, with a fancy certificate in her bag, she and Ashina walked into Zimbabwe. 'Lisa, was it better than sex?'

'No, not for me, but it might be for others. It's an incredible thrill.'

'Why did you yell "Madagascar"?'

'That's where I last had an orgasm.'

Ashina put two and two together. 'So, where's Leo?'

'I don't know, Ashina, he moves around a lot. I've met him twice on day trips to London. We're waiting for the preservation of some documents to finish, and then I'll meet him again as we have something to do together. I can now help as the worst part of the workload is over.'

She posted the bungee experience on Facebook, with photos and a video.

They boarded the Kenyan Airways flight three days after touring the falls, David Livingstone's monument, and other attractions. The stopover in Nairobi was long, and Lisa looked at her Facebook page and posted something different. She wrote about the Bilharzia case, how frustrating it was to find no medicine because of the cost and to learn the cause was drug theft, shipped to other countries where people could pay for the drugs. *I must be growing up,* she thought.

They arrived in Brussels with over three hundred photographs; she had posted selected ones on Facebook when she or Ashina took them. She had included a post about meeting Tiny Toomah but didn't mention the medallion. That was private, but her mother noticed the chain around her neck. Some weeks later, her mother saw the medallion. *Lisa seems to wear that permanently.* 'Lisa, where did you find that St Christopher you're wearing?'

'It's not a St Christoper Mama, it's a pirate medallion, once it was Leo's.'

'Then why haven't I seen it before?'

'Leo traded it in Katanga for a necklace when he fixed a man's car. When Ashina and I met the man and his wife, I saw it, and he tried to give it to me, so I traded it for a necklace.'

'Will you give it to Leo?'

'No, he has a silver one. Mine is dated 1710. I like wearing it.'

I'm sure it brings Leo closer to me.

Leo read all her posts, including the Bilharzia story, and talked about it with his mother because she was the Minister of Health.

By the end of the summer break, he had received reams of information; the production figures and the market sales were available. The program he ran gave a rough estimate of profits. However, the profits didn't end up in the producers' accounts. The leakage, in billions, was worth investigating.

It's not the money; the human hardship it causes is disgusting. If I can help Lisa, it might bring forward the day we revisit PegLeg, and if medicine prices drop, it will help my mother.

Leo wrote a specification of what data he needed and handed it to the company doing his other factor research. It might take some time, but he would have convincing numbers if required.

Meanwhile, he had something else to do. He registered a company in Muscat that, moments later, owned the internet domain *Generics.com*. His mother owned half the shares, worth one cent each, and a motley connection of companies worldwide owned the other half.

That's a start; next is how to eliminate theft.

19

Leo phoned Lisa a few days before their fourth year began. When he heard the call connect, he spoke first.

'Hello, my darling.'

'Hello, man, you're mixing up darling and my love. Are you ill?'

'Not at all. *My darling* expresses my feelings with greater depth. I'm hoping it will bring a response like *my dearest heart*.'

'Have you been reading chick-lit romances again?'

'No, do they use that?'

'And a lot of other soppy ones.'

'Then I'll think of something less soppy. Have you read Butterfly Bill's story?'

'Not yet, there's so much it'll take me a week, but what I've read is superb.'

'The bit we're interested in is in the middle; it's a letdown because he doesn't say who PegLeg is, but he met him multiple times.'

'Then read it to me.'

1709.

Dear Father,

After my last report to you, despatched on a Dutch ship from Sumatra, I boarded a dhow to voyage to Zanzibar in Africa. For the first six weeks, calm interspersed with terrifying storms that appeared seemingly from nowhere without warning diverted us to the south until, eventually, expecting the final hour, the captain followed sea birds to find the most northern of the Mascarene Islands. After a month of repairs and victualling, we set sail again and, pushed by steady winds, reached the coast of Madagascar, where we landed in a bay named Toamasina. Having endured great hardships, I decided to terminate my voyage for two reasons: the countryside is lush and has unique plant and animal species, a naturalist's dream, and the people accept me as one of them due to the characteristics I inherited from my mother.

I learnt that to despatch this report, I should travel north to St. Marie Island or south to Fort Dauphin. I chose north, collecting specimens as I travelled. I wish I had the means to preserve examples of the abundant and exotic fauna in this tropical paradise with endless coral sand beaches. After five months, I reached a fishing village with my destination in sight across a wide bay.

The crossing, in three canoes, each hewn from a whole tree with outriggers in the Pacific style, although a fatiguing paddle, passed without distress, and the canoes with my collection of specimens crossed safely.

We arrived at a small inlet with a guardian island before it, and after unloading, a French citizen informed me I should see PegLeg Jon, the settlement administrator; I did so immediately, as rudeness has consequences.

A man of imposing stature, with black hair dressed in the sailor fashion with a tail at the back and deep blue eyes, although one he keeps covered with an eyepatch. His left leg includes a wooden appendage, as he lost his leg during a sea battle. Surprisingly kindly, he is admired by all, for he was a ship's captain and lost his vessel recently in a storm such as I experienced.

I found lodging and storage for my collection. I must tell you that PegLeg Jon did more than most to assist me in my research, allocating a woman to keep my lodging in suitable condition, as the tiny houses are of palm leaf construction. She also makes me papyrus sheets from a reed, which I believe is at least a cousin of those that proliferate in Egypt. I pin my insect specimens on them with thorns or sharpened slivers. After a week, I learnt one reason for the respect shown to PegLeg Jon: he has some knowledge of medicine. He does not consider it below him to intervene with minor surgery when a man has a wound that, in this climate, becomes the seat of offensive odours. I find his treatment interesting, for after removing the infected flesh with a knife and dousing the cleaned wound with the potent rum distilled here, he insists a pad of boiled cloth be applied hot and bandaged hot with another boiled cloth.

He is a supporter of the small church with a unique Madonna carved from a palm tree, although the churchgoers told me that in the church at Fort Dauphin, which is now under the control of a Mahomedan, there was a Madonna that will soon arrive here.

It may be many months or years before a suitable ship passes on a voyage to Europe. Still, I shall remain here, collect specimens, and continue this report until I can despatch it to you with the specimens for Doctor Petiver.

'Thanks, Leo, at least we know what kind of man we're looking for. Butterfly Bill's mother must have been African; we should copy this to Father Benjamin. It proves what he said.'

'I agree, and I feel sympathy for Bill; in 1700, the English would have called him a Moor, and more than Evelyn's description of his father as a bad lot, that would have been why they shunned him.'

'What will you do with the box?'

'I don't know.'

'Then I suggest you give it to Doctor Dankworth. Raid your Cave again, pay for binding with a leather cover and gold lettering, and ask Dankworth to set up a display in the Museum with the box, book, and butterflies, with a prominent label saying *Donated by John Gastrell and family*. You could also give John money to buy a new lounge suite.'

Leo laughed. 'How about my amazing, beautiful, genius darling?'

'You'll give me a fat head.'

'Geniuses have fat heads.'

Lisa laughed. 'You're incorrigible. Bye, *dearest!*'

....

That silenced him.

Leo met Lisa at the station again; they met at the Lovers statue but didn't notice it.

'Leo, we'll be late for the Museum.'

'They'll wait for us.'

'They can wait for you; where's the car?'

'Same as before.'

....

'How much did you give John?'

'Enough for a lounge suite, I had a better idea.'

'Tell me.'

'I registered the modern English adaptation we received of Butterfly Bill's book, *The Perambulations of Butterfly Bill – forty years of collecting specimens,* with an ISBN. I named John as the copyright owner of the adapted edition. There'll be a photographer and someone from a publisher there this morning. John will receive an income from royalties for life.'

'There are times when I can't help but like you.'

'Not always?'

'Almost, but.'

'I'll keep trying.'

John, Maud, Christopher, who wore regular spectacles, Leo, Lisa and Evelyn met Doctor Dankworth at the Natural History Museum to unveil the Butterfly Bill exhibit designed by Evelyn's son. Doctor

Dankworth told Lisa he had sent a copy of the adapted book to Professor Restolomew. Choosing who was the happiest person there would be difficult, Evelyn said in an aside to Lisa, 'When Leo came to see me, he came in a helicopter.'

'He does that often. I should call him *Butterfly*.'

'I can't think of a name that fits him. You have the most marvellous man I've ever met.'

John overheard her and said, 'Maud and I will second that.'

Lisa thought, *I think so too, but is he too marvellous for me?*

Lisa began the first year of her management degree in high spirits. She felt she was progressing along her planned career path and now had the time to learn another language. Once again, Lisa decided to study Arabic and signed up for an online course. Finding her progress slow, she went to see the secretary of the language faculty.

'Yes, miss, how can I help you?'

'I'm Lisa Calmette, doing the management masters. I'm trying to learn Arabic through an online course, but I want to meet an Arab-speaking student doing French or English for practice.'

'Why don't you register for an Arabic course?'

'I already have classes during the day, so I can't.'

'Let me have a look at something.'

After a minute of tapping keys on her computer, she said, 'I have an Arab speaker who might suit you, but we have evening classes for an hour three times a week, Mondays, Wednesdays and Fridays. The teacher is from Tunisia. The courses are at an intermediate level in the first term. Why don't you try one? I can give you a note for a week's free attendance.'

Lisa had a printed slip with the classroom and the schedule in less than a minute.

She enjoyed the first lecture, found it matched her ability, and a week later, she signed up.

Lisa thought the class teacher was handsome, but he paid no more attention to her than the other students, and when she saw him with a stunning woman wearing a headscarf, Lisa learnt he had a girlfriend or wife. Of course, she posted her language-learning activities on Facebook.

Leo flew to Oman and divided his time between hiking the mountains and analysing numbers before returning to Cambridge after Easter.

Lisa studied. However, many groups that completed the first three years were still at the same University, starting the second three years. Lisa found she was still part of a tightly knit group she met in the canteen, although she was on a different career path. At lunch one day, Marlene told them about a DNA lecture and said, 'I've sent a DNA sample of my saliva to a genealogical group for analysis.'

Olivia replied, 'I could never do that; imagine the horrible things you might learn – like the alcoholic neighbour is your father. Lisa, would you send a DNA sample for analysis?'

'I will do. It will be interesting to know where in the world my ancestors lived.'

We promised to find out about PegLeg. I won't open his tomb for DNA, but I don't know where to start without knowing his real name. I hope he's not upset with the delay.

Louis phoned Leo.

'Leo, I'm close to finishing in Rwanda, and I must refuse to back the project, but the people are keen to develop the country. I don't know if you can help. They have applied for a loan extension from the World Bank. If I can persuade the Bank to sanction you coming as a student to study the country's budget, you'll at least record much more data for analysis, and you might aid my decision.'

'Dad, helping you will be a pleasure. I've never been to Rwanda; they have gorillas there.'

'I'll see what I can do, Leo.'

Leo arrived in Rwanda at Kigali airport on a Wednesday. Although the plane's tail carried the UN logo, the UN didn't pay for the flight.

Louis met Leo and his two assistants and, after checking into the hotel, took them to the finance minister, who had agreed to supply the information Leo wanted. They began loading and transmitting the data directly to Leo's computer centre in Oman using a private satellite link.

That night, Leo had dinner with his parents and said goodbye, for they were flying home after telling the finance minister that a report would take two to three weeks to complete.

Lisa was studying at home during the holiday when, at dinner, her mother said, 'Lisa, your father and I are going to Rwanda to do a vaccination readiness assessment. Will you be alright alone, or would you like to invite a friend to stay while we're away?'

It surprised Lisa, so she asked, 'Mama, why now and why so suddenly?'

Gaston replied, 'Rwanda is only two degrees south of the equator, so it has an equatorial climate with a rainy season after the sun crosses the equator twice a year, March-April and September-October.

'That's when the insect density soars, so checking the vaccination readiness in March makes sense. – Why us? Because the couple scheduled have cried off. He's ill, and she's staying to nurse him. We happen to be here and available.'

'How long for?'

'Less than a week, the WHO is not worried about the sparsely inhabited areas; an epidemic is only likely in one or two cities, principally Kigali.'

'Then, if the visit is that short, can I come too? I can learn what the vaccination facilities are like. It will be relevant to my studies.'

'I'll confirm the day, Lisa, once Gary Somers does. It will be next week.'

Saturday was Umuganda, a Rwandan tradition of mandatory nationwide community service on the last Saturday of every month, when everyone, including Ministers, participated in a countrywide clean-up. Leo and his colleagues joined in and then continued with their budget analysis.

Leo read Lisa's Saturday post that night. Her announcement that she was flying to Rwanda on Monday with her parents surprised him, and in the morning, he asked reception if they had a reservation for the Calmette family; they didn't. *If Lisa introduced me to her parents, that would be okay. I don't want to barge in and introduce myself. She might have a boyfriend with her.*

Leo's analyses improved as the following week progressed, and wherever he found data missing, he requested it, surprised at how quickly the data arrived.

The Calmette family arrived on Monday and checked into their hotel, unaware that Leo and his team were at a hotel only ten minutes away. After a light lunch, they met the Minister of Health, mapped and agreed on a programme, and visited Kigali's main hospital.

Lisa's task was to inventory the vaccines in stock at the hospital and the expiration dates and types. Her parents were to assess the personnel and skills available to combat an epidemic.

Lisa felt the overworked matron saw the imposition of a young doctor with questions to answer as too time-consuming, and minutes later, Lisa found herself with a young nurse with an instruction to 'Show the visitor whatever she wants to see.'

20

On Friday morning, Leo asked for a meeting with the Minister of Finance, and he met him an hour later.

The minister was visibly unhappy at what Leo said.

'Minister, your government didn't spend the earlier loan as per the budget and specifications used to obtain the loan. I know it was not you, but I can only justify numbers to the World Bank; I'm not a judge. The bank should agree to a reduced loan, as the budget numbers I have analysed show nothing new except a continuation of current and past activity.

'I'll also add that in many cases, the different government departments spent on projects other than those budgeted. Your budget and the use of the funds, a part of which is the current World Bank loan, are subject to intense scrutiny by the Bank's officials, who will remark on this.'

'Mr Poussin, what you have said is disappointing. I must tell the President, and I don't particularly look forward to doing so. I hope that you're wrong.'

'Minister, I'm only a mathematician; my job is to analyse the situation, not suggest what to do. However, I'll add that some avenues might lead to the loan renewal or an increase; I suggest you consider discussing possibilities with the Bank.'

'Thank you, Mr Poussin; I shall consider your words.'

Lisa, who now had a good friend at the hospital, had learnt that there was no control; the stock was distributed amongst a dozen refrigerators in various places, although the total matched the hospital stock list. However, the quantities in each fridge and the number of expired units were unknown. Lisa had also carefully noted that medicines, even simple ones like aspirin, were in short supply. It reminded her of Lubumbashi.

She spent Friday writing a report.

The Minister of Finance relayed a message that the President had asked to meet Leo at 8 pm that evening.

Leo was impressed. Very tall and slim, with an ascetic face, from a minority ethnic group, his position as President didn't follow the usual African pattern where presidents come from majority population groups.

Projecting an air of calm and politeness, he said, 'Mr Poussin, my minister reports you doubt the World Bank will renew our loan in total, but you may have suggestions. Can you remove your World Bank hat and tell me what you have in mind?'

'Mr President, I'm not a politician, but I know how things work. The UN has several agencies that support each other. I can offer an example. Your citizens need better health care. Suppose you request expert advice and help from the WHO to improve your health care. Let me emphasise not money but physical help, staff, and advice, and try to make it their project. They will jump at the chance. Then, follow what the WHO recommends by requesting the IFC to finance it. The WHO will pressure the IFC to support *their* project. If, in addition, your budget showed an increase in annual budgeted expenditure to cover ongoing health costs, I feel sure you would receive cooperation from all three agencies. Health improvement also has a secondary benefit, for it improves a country's rating for IFC loans.'

'What is that, Mr Poussin?'

'Each project assessment has a success rating; the IFC won't finance a project that will fail. One item in such a rating is the probability of an uncontrollable epidemic, and IFC funds are limited.'

The President thought about Leo's description, then asked, 'Another example?'

'Mr President, I'm not a health expert or an agriculture expert, nor am I qualified to run a country; I'm a mathematician. But if you have a project to propose to the Food and Agriculture Organisation on the same basis I have suggested for health, I believe the result would be similar.'

'And the new road project for which we requested IFC finance?'

'Sir, please confirm that the road, if I understand the reason, is to access an area of your country for tin mining. I know Rwanda was a tin producer three millennia ago.'

'That is the intention.'

'Your budget for road maintenance is insufficient. The IFC will not support it.'

'Mr Poussin, you may be a mathematician, but you seem to have, let me say, more political understanding than most. When are you scheduled to leave?'

'Next Friday, sir.'

'Then I'll arrange for a meeting on Thursday.'

Gaston and Rosemary finished their data collection and were surprised by an invitation to see the Health Minister on Saturday.

With nothing to do, Lisa asked reception about the gorillas and left Friday afternoon with other tourists to find the gorillas.

Gaston's Saturday meeting expanded into three meetings with different members of the Ministry, so on return to the hotel, they decided to draft their report over the weekend and present it to the Health Minister on Monday or Tuesday.

Leo had missed the tourist's departure to visit the gorillas, so he booked a private tour on Saturday.

Picked up at his modest hotel at one pm, he and the guide, with a driver, travelled to a lodge close to the volcano national park, to the south of the volcano Sabyinyo. During the drive, he received a carefully prepared and much-repeated lesson on gorillas and, most importantly, how to behave when close to them. The guide assured Leo several times that the gorillas tolerated the presence of people but, if disturbed, were dangerous.

Lisa was at a different hotel. After spending Saturday on a fruitless climb and descent to spot gorillas, she retired to bed early after telling reception that she wanted to try the other side of the volcano on Sunday. *I don't know why I'm so keen to see gorillas.*

Leo spent a relaxing evening in the lodge, reading a book about gorilla experiences by a renowned researcher.

As the tourists and Leo gathered for dawn coffee and pastries, Lisa arrived, saw Leo and almost ran into his arms but stopped suddenly a metre from him and struggled to stay upright.

She's afraid.

'Hello, man. Are you alone?'

Leo smiled. 'Hello, girl, I am, and I'll ask the same question.'

Lisa grinned. 'I was, but now I'm with my boyfriend.'

'Then we'll climb together.'

'I'll tell PegLeg to find the gorillas. He must have brought us together again.'

They left in a group of seven tourists with four guides, Leo and Lisa, together after the first guide in a single-file column. By midday, Leo felt that the gorillas had gone to another volcano.

Then, the guide raised his arm in a stop signal.

After a pause that built tension, Leo's guide moved slowly forward. The guide behind Lisa motioned her to step back several paces. Leo's guide signalled, using the signs that he had taught Leo to crouch and walk slowly and quietly. Leo drifted to the right, or the guide drifted left, without noticing the gap increasing between the two men. Leo could see nothing in the thick jungle; when he saw the guide stop and crouch, he assumed the guide had seen something, so he looked in the same direction and, with his view blocked by vegetation, unwarily raised himself slightly from the crouch.

The colossal silverback gorilla came from under a thick clump of bamboo-like plants; Leo had looked at them and seen nothing. It charged forward with a series of bellowing grunts. The urge to run was overwhelming, but Leo had listened to the instructions, so he sat, then lay on his back in submission.

The gorilla stopped, and seconds later, Leo looked up at a face that showed curiosity. Told repeatedly not to talk or make sounds that a gorilla would not understand, he remained silent. A tendril of fear vanished after the thought. *His expression is almost human. What will he do now?*

Lisa, ten metres away, terrified, her heart beating furiously and her breathing hard to control, almost moved forward to help, but the guide behind her reached out and seized her leg, then gestured urgently. *Down, down.* She could only kneel, watch and pray.

The gorilla turned its back and sat, almost touching Leo.

The book Leo had read recounted a similar incident. The researcher had simulated gorilla behaviour by grooming the beast, so Leo began to do the same, parting the hair on its back and looking for insects. He came to a matted patch and, after carefully spreading the hair, bit by bit, found what looked like a small twig almost protruding from the skin, surrounded by infection and leaking pus. Leo continued to separate the matted hairs while thinking of what to do, feeling that the gorilla was no danger. He was sure another gorilla had tried to remove the twig, as the end at skin level looked like a chewed stick.

Leo used his left hand to draw a multitool from a leather pouch on his belt and eased open the pliers. Carefully using the pointed ends to grip the piece of wood tightly, and as the gorilla hadn't moved except to grab more foliage to eat, Leo took a deep breath and yanked the stick out in one movement. The gorilla bellowed, then turned, and Leo lay back, looked down and offered the twig, still in the pliers, for inspection.

Lisa gasped and then rammed the palm of her hand against her mouth to avoid a scream.

After a tense few moments, Leo sensed the beast turn back again. He sat slowly up, shrugged off his backpack, and extracted his emergency pack, removing a small bottle of antiseptic. He poured it into and around the wound, now bleeding pus and blood, wiped it clean with a cotton wipe, and sat back with an involuntary sigh.

The gorilla moved slowly away without a glance at Leo, then disappeared into the bush twenty-five metres away. Leo thought it was a bit ungrateful and, forgetting the injunction not to say anything, gave a Tarzan yell. '*GreeeGah*.' He thought the gorilla's double grunt was *Goodbye* or *Thank you*.

With his pistol still in his hand, the guard rose. 'Boss, what did you remove from his back?'

Leo looked. 'I think it's an arrowhead,' and gave it to the guide. 'I'm glad these gorillas are used to people; I would hate to meet a wild one.'

'It is an arrowhead, poachers hunting bushmeat. They only try for the juveniles, so your gorilla attacked a poacher and was shot by another. I've never seen him before; he must be a wild gorilla from somewhere. I must tell the office.'

'He's not a habituated one?'

'No, unless he's from another habituated group, and that's unlikely; you did everything right, boss. I didn't need to fire into the air or at him; no one knows if that works. Can we descend now?'

'Yes, I've had more gorilla than I expected.'

As her adrenaline level dropped and her heart slowed, Lisa felt faint, then felt enormous relief. Finally, she stood unsteadily and joined him. 'Leo, that was amazing; how did you know what to do?'

'I read it in a book at the lodge last night. They're different from us, but I'm sure that one is not aggressive. He was hurting, and I had to do something.'

Leo became an instant celebrity at the lodge; the manager refused payment, and he learnt he was now the *Gorilla Doctor.*

Lisa returned to Kigali with Leo and his guide. She left him at her hotel, promised to call him the next day, and told her parents what had happened.

Rosemary said later to Gaston, 'Lisa decided at the last minute to come with us and to see the gorillas. What chance is there that Leo, the wounded gorilla, and Lisa could be at the same place and time on the side of a volcano?'

'I don't know; it's infinitely small. I'm only glad Leo was there.'

'So am I, but I believe it's more than that, and so does Lisa.'

That night, Lisa had trouble sleeping; she tossed and turned until she fell asleep in the small hours. She woke with a start when, in her dream, the charging gorilla gained a pirate's hat and an eye patch a moment before turning away.

Leo took Lisa to dinner the following night; their conversation covered what they had done in Rwanda. Lisa understood that Leo's actions would improve the lives of the Rwandan people. Leo learnt that Rwanda experienced the same medicine availability problems as Katanga. When he asked detailed questions about the vaccine controls she had checked, it reminded her that she had asked about medicine theft.

'Leo, did you learn anything about medicine theft?'

'I did, Lisa, it's worldwide and well organised. I've been collecting figures. Many countries are paying more than twice what they should for medicines.'

'That's not the worst. Pharmacies don't order because the costs are too high to stock, and hospitals run short when an order is lost and must be re-ordered. The patients suffer. Do you have any ideas on how to stop it?'

'Yes, it seemed easy at first, but trying to find a way the criminals can't circumvent security is not. There's no point in doing something that you know will fail. Three IT guys who run my financial analyses are brainstorming the problems. The only idea so far is to make the medicine worthless. I don't know how to do that.'

'What do you mean worthless?'

'Worthless to the thief. It would be worthless if he couldn't sell what he stole.'

'Leo, the worth of a pill is less than zero if no one knows what medicine it is because it could be poisonous. Half the problem in hospitals and pharmacies is how to dispose of expired medications. If I ever have the chance, I'll ensure the incineration of expired packaging after discarding the contents in a bucket of water.

'But the doctors and nurses must know, so that's impossible.'

'I know, but expired stuff could be nearly eliminated with accurate control and statistical consumption analysis.'

'I'll leave you to think about it, Leo.'

As their evening ended, and before she entered her hotel, she said, 'Leo, I think PegLeg may be trying to tell us that we aren't keeping our promise to learn about him. He can't know what our world is like, and if he's the cause of our meeting on a volcano, it may be dangerous if he tries again. Is there anything you can do to learn something about him? I would, but I don't have the time. I'll be in a lecture after we return tomorrow.'

'I'll try, Lisa; I *have* asked the history professor.'

'Thanks, Leo, bye.'

If she believes that, I must do something while waiting for the professor.

'Bye, Lisa.'

Wherever Lisa goes, she will need a better medicine supply; I'll start up Generics.com. I'll also try to discover the makers of my medallions.

21

Leo and his team were complete by Friday, and the President said little on Thursday.

'Mr Poussin, thank you for coming. Can you delay your report by saying you're waiting for information on a pending health project?'

'I can, sir; how long do you need?'

'Will three months be possible? Our loan expires then.'

'I'm sure that will be possible; if you can provide me with some information on what you propose before then, a short-term rollover on the same terms should be acceptable to the World Bank.'

'Excellent. I have spoken to Doctor Calmette, who is reviewing our vaccination readiness in the country and has promised full co-operation.

'Thank you again, Mr Poussin,' then he smiled broadly. 'And you're welcome in Rwanda whenever you wish; I have informed the minister in charge of immigration that you have citizen status. Our gorillas often need medical treatment.'

Leo left the palace wondering how the President had learnt about his gorilla encounter. On returning to the hotel, he phoned Private Wings. They promised a departure the next day.

A man handed him a Rwandan diplomatic passport as he passed through the pilot's channel dressed again as a pilot and said, 'With the President's compliments, Doctor.'

Leo flew to Oman, wondering about something probability theory couldn't explain.

His father naturally asked how the budget research had progressed, and he explained what he had done. 'So, Dad, hold off on your report; I think there will be a different project to improve the country's health, and Rwanda will ask me to review a new budget.

'You might hear about an incident, so I'll tell you. I doctored a gorilla with an arrow in its back, so the President made me a citizen of the country.'

Louis was speechless but later dialled the finance minister and heard the whole story, including who Leo was with. When he told Soraya, she replied, '*Mashallah*. Elisabeth Calmette, the girl in Madagascar.'

With only the final dissertation to present for his MMath degree, Leo applied to the London School of Economics for a doctorate by research on a subject titled:

> The use of advanced statistical methods in state budgeting

An SMS from Professor Restolomew's secretary said Leo should make an appointment.

I told Lisa the professor was searching. I'll call her.

'Hello, man, this is unexpected.'

'Hello girl, the history professor has asked me to see him about PegLeg. If you can take the day off to accompany me, I can collect you in Brussels with my magic carpet.'

'What day?'

'You choose, and I'll try to make the appointment for that day.'

'Then let me look at my calendar.'

....

'Try for November, the eleventh or twentieth; they're holidays here.'

Leo made the appointment and SMSed Lisa, thinking she might be in a lecture.

The following evening, the doorbell rang before Lisa's parents returned home. She answered the door and was surprised to see an attractive young woman with a suitcase who said, 'Good evening, I'm Clo; I've come to see Doctor Calmette.'

'There are two, me and my mother.'

'Then it's you. I've come for the fitting.'

Puzzled, Lisa asked, 'Have you come to the right house? I'm not expecting a fitting.'

'Then the agency hasn't told you, so I will. I'm from an airline tailor; I have an order to fit you with a cabin attendant's uniform for a private charter company.'

Leo – I'll kill him!

'Please, come in. What do you need?'

The visitor lifted the case. 'I have uniforms here. One should fit but might need adjustment. Can you try it on?'

Twenty minutes later, Lisa stood in front of a mirror wearing a navy skirt, cream blouse with single bar epaulettes, a gold wing badge, and a pillbox hat with a simulated veil. Her visitor said, 'That looks lovely; I'll take the skirt in by a centimetre. Any black low-heeled shoes will do. I'll bring you two uniforms tomorrow.'

'Can I have a photo, please, for visas, both with and without the hat?'

The camera clicked, and Lisa showed the young woman out.

Lisa would have used the tallest font available if satphones allowed different fonts.

CALL ME IF YOU CAN.

His call came three hours later. Lisa had cooled.

'Leo, why did you send a woman to dress me as aircrew?'

'I was going to tell you today, Lisa, was it Clothilde?'

The temperature dropped sharply.

'She said Clo, so maybe. Is she your girlfriend?'

'Married with two kids, Lisa,' the temperature rose, 'you know I'm a pilot. Aircrews pass through a separate channel at airports, with no queues – and no questions.'

'Leo, I'll forgive you, but tell me first next time.'

'Did Clothilde take photos?'

'Yes, she said they were for visas.'

'That's true, but the driver who collects you will give you an aircrew card and a Muscat airport pass. It makes travelling far easier. A car will collect you at nine-thirty.'

Lisa chuckled. 'I'll be ready.'

When the chauffeur opened the car door, Lisa stepped out, and she turned to enter the Execujet Terminal at Brussels International. Leo came out of the door and took two paces forward. The door sighed as it closed behind him. They stood silently looking at each other, and then Lisa smiled.

'You look just like an airline captain.'

Leo seemed to hurry as he came down three steps to her. 'And you're the most beautiful cabin attendant I've ever seen.' She dropped her sports bag as he took her in his arms, their eyes locked together and murmured, 'Captains aren't supposed to kiss female crew members in public, but LPAir has special rules; it's mandatory.'

Lisa grinned. 'Then must I obey those rules?'

'Absolutely.'

....

As their lips separated, Lisa gasped, 'Leo, the uniform hasn't changed you.'

'Nor you, Lisa. All we need is PegLeg's tomb. Now let's fly.'

He picked up her bag with one hand, and they held hands as they walked through the terminal to the apron and the waiting jet.

It's like walking the beach in St. Marie once again.

'Where?' Lisa asked, 'Did you find a magic carpet, and where will you take me?'

'In my cave, like my buddy Ali Baba. It's one of the smaller carpets. We'll land at Cambridge Airport.'

'Good morning, Professor. May I present Doctor Elisabeth Calmette, my brilliant assistant.'

'Doctor Calmette, it's a pleasure to meet you; he should have said beautiful and brilliant.'

'Thank you, Professor, but please call me Elisabeth. Although it's been months, I don't feel like a doctor yet and don't intend to practice as one. I'm studying hospital management for my masters.'

'Then I'll give you some advice. Titles are honorifics unrelated to employment. They are recognition for learning or competence gained over the years. An HR manager may carry the title of "Captain", which he earned during military service.

'Worldwide, the title "Doctor" is recognised similarly. I was a "Doctor" before becoming a professor. You would have the title the day you begin working as a junior doctor at a hospital. Most countries have government departments that require a masters degree for doctors who charge for their services. Fewer countries, as in Europe, have organisations that have grown from guilds to restrict competition in the field, and countries with National Health Systems collaborate and profit from this because they can employ overworked junior doctors at low rates.

'You worked hard to earn the right to that title, be proud, and allow others to show their respect for your achievement. You have a Caduceus pin on your blouse. If you work in a medical field, honour it and insist on the title. Sometimes, it brings unexpected assistance.'

'I will, Professor. Thank you.'

'And I will thank you for Butterfly Bill's book, an outstanding addition to historical knowledge. Historians will pore through it and the original to update our history books. Dankworth told me how you found his name. Please write about how you found the documents for my research file. I would recommend writing a thesis if you had registered as a history researcher.

'Mr Poussin. I heard you had deserted us for the London School of Economics. I have a reply from a colleague regarding PegLeg Jon; it's a starting point, not more. If you continue this research, will you do so with me or someone in London?'

'With you, sir. I have registered with the LSE for a doctorate as an external statistics researcher. Cambridge is my alma mater, and I hope you will assist if required.'

'I will, but first, I want to know something. You said you had read treatises by Arab mathematicians; I have checked, and there are few translations. Have you read only those?'

'No, Professor, Arabic is my mother tongue; I was born in Oman.'

'That explains it; I'm afraid there's little in historical records about PegLeg Jon; historians surmise he was a lieutenant to Captain Kidd, who sailed to Madagascar in 1698, and there are fragments from around the early 1700s. Still, we don't know anything about him before the fragments from Madagascar; we don't know if or when he joined Kidd.

'There is only a suggestion, call it a deduction, by Yves LaSalle, a French researcher who wrote a paper about French warships that sailed to the Caribbean in the late 1600s.

'A French medical officer, Lieutenant Raymond Jean Calmel, on board the *Vengeance,* lost a leg in a sea battle and consequently became a patient in Tortola, an English haven, which is likely because the French and English were cooperating to eliminate pirates from the Caribbean. La Salle studied the Tortola hospital admissions list that covers the pirate period, expecting to find that Calmel died, but he recovered. After the hospital discharged him, LaSalle could find no further trace of Raymond.

'Captain Kidd's ship, the *Adventure Galley*, was in Tortola for repairs. The hospital discharged Calmel before Kidd left for Madagascar.

'There are a few fragments about PegLeg Jon and an attempt to found an independent republic in Madagascar. A researcher said that from the number and context of the mentions, PegLeg Jon appears to be an eminent figure in the pirate haven, and the size of his tomb proves it. Butterfly Bill has provided proof that he was the administrator of the colony.

'I'm sorry to disappoint you, but history often hangs on unproven suspicion, and linking Calmel with PegLeg Jon based on the date of his disappearance, the sailing of Kidd's ship, and the first mention of PegLeg Jon in Madagascar is risky, but it's all we have.'

'Sir, I can clarify what you have said. In the St. Marie cemetery is a small tomb engraved with *William Kidd, 1701*. As the English court hanged Kidd in England in 1701, that tomb must date from 1705 or later, after the news reached St. Marie; Mr Farquhar suggested it's a memorial. I believe PegLeg Jon built it, for I found the crew list of the *Adventure Galley* in the legal archives of his trial, now in the British Museum, and the Quartermaster on the list is Lieutenant Jon. His mark or signature is Jon prefixed by a Y drawn as a U with a central leg like the prostheses worn in that period by amputees.'

'Good heavens, Mr Poussin, congratulations. Please send me copies of those lists and tell me how you found them. That information alone is worth a degree in history.'

'I will do, sir, though I'm not a history student.'

'You will be if you continue. How on earth did you find that information? The legal archives are all microfilm.'

'The index is digitised, sir, with comments from the technician about what he was photographing. A keyword search highlighted forty items, including two crew lists for the *Adventure Galley*, so I ordered microfiche copies and read them.'

'Mr Poussin, you and Doctor Calmette are already historians; your research has a touch of genius. As you're fluent in Arabic, I suggest you approach Arab historians. They will, I'm sure, have preserved accounts of voyages southwards along the African coast around 1700, and you might find a mention of PegLeg Jon.

'Do you have any key dates that may be important?'

About to reply no, something made Leo pause, and a thought came from nowhere.

My medallion, initials, skull and crossed bones. PegLeg's tomb, skull and crossed bones. Medallion date 1710. – 'Only one, 1710.'

'Then search the archives of the Dutch VOC, the British Admiralty archives, and the National Museum of the Royal Navy for ships that sailed the Indian Ocean before, during, and after that year. The French have similar records kept in Brest. Remember that a report or a ship's voyage log, despatched by sea, might not arrive for two or three years.'

'Professor, thank you for those suggestions. It might take us ages, but at least we have something positive to do.'

'Mr Poussin, please keep me in the picture with what you learn. We might turn you into a history graduate in addition to maths!'

About to leave, Leo remembered Lieke and then asked, 'Professor, I learnt that only accredited researchers have full access to the VOC records; the other archives may also have restrictions. Can you help?'

'I can. Ask my secretary for a Cambridge application form to register as a History Research Fellow. Fill it in and come this afternoon to collect the accreditation. Submit copies to all libraries that require it, and let me know if one of them refuses.

'Doctor Calmette, it's been a pleasure to meet you. If you intend to research history with Mr Poussin, please register as a history research fellow.'

'Thank you, Professor. I intend to research and accept your offer with pleasure.'

'Lisa, you didn't say much.'

'What the professor said shocked me. When he said PegLeg was Raymond Calmel, I knew it was true, and he might have been a distant cousin. It took me back to the day we met by his tomb, and I remembered what I did.'

'Do you mean lying beside me?'

'Yes, I should have run, like most young girls would have. But I didn't, and I finally know why.'

'Please explain.'

'I had my hand on his tomb, and he told me I was safe.'

'That's certainly one explanation.'

And I thought it was my animal magnetism.

'Why do you feel you might be related?'

'Calmette could mean little Calmel.'

'That's possible. I was shocked, too. My medallion has the same initials as Raymond Jean Calmel. I wonder if there is a connection. Let's have lunch, collect our accreditations, then fly to Brussels, where my super magic carpet should be waiting to take me to Oman.'

Leo landed in Oman the following day, went directly to his cave, and registered with four libraries an hour later. 'Shuchang, which of the new programmers is a hotshot search programmer?'

'Kabir has a knack for finding an answer faster than the others. He found the crew lists.'

'Then I have a job for him.'

'He's finishing a faster search routine in the medicine sales program. I'll tell you when he has finished.'

Lisa's Lent term soon changed from interesting lectures to hours when concentrating became something physically demanding. After hours of reading text that she had already read, trying to identify those details she had forgotten, her mind repeatedly wandered; being alone in her tiny apartment made it worse. She reverted to the method she had used before. Instead of making tea every ninety minutes, she left her apartment for a walk, bought tea and a biscuit in the canteen, and then returned.

Sometimes, she met one of the other women she knew, but often, she sat alone, sipping her tea and watching the students. Several times, one of them approached her.

She sensed the younger men were only interested in sex, but some were much older, and some were married. They had worked for some years and wanted to improve their qualifications and open the route to new careers. Half a dozen proved interesting, and she would have stayed to talk, but after glancing at her watch, she had to break away with the statement, 'I must return to the grindstone. Nice talking to you.'

Philippe Daurain was a student who introduced himself in the canteen. His ploy was simple: ask for advice on a first-year subject and then ask about her.

She found him attractive, a surprisingly gentle character with a fund of knowledge about the entertainment industry, an industry she knew little about. He was studying management because his ambition was to manage a theatre, not the building or the accounts, but the stage crews and performers. He must have noted when she came; he often joined her. After a dozen discussions in the canteen, where he described the avant-garde theatres of Brussels, he invited her one evening to see a stage production.

22

The theatre was small; the set decoration was minimal, with the actors dressed in garish colours. Lisa had begun to grasp the overall theme by the show's end. After the show, Philippe asked in the theatre bar, 'How did you like the show, Lisa?'

'I didn't understand it at first, and then I thought the cast should be in ancient Greek togas, like Greek tragedies. Then it made sense; the show's theme is the Greek story of Oedipus, who married his mother.'

'I knew you'd understand. Avant-garde is often telling an ancient story from a different viewpoint.'

'But why the garish-coloured clothes?'

'The director wanted to tell the ancient story in a modern or futuristic setting.'

Two weeks later, Philippe took her to another show; the theatre was more spacious, and she thought the set decoration was excellent, but she couldn't grasp the theme. She was careful not to say so.

When Philippe asked her to a third show, he added, 'There's a little restaurant next door where everyone goes after the show. The show is at 7:15. Can you come for dinner?'

She agreed but didn't like the show; something upset her; it was just a feeling. She understood it was a spoof of the movie *Pirates of the Caribbean*. Still, the pirate, a caricature of Captain Jack Sparrow, was far more effeminate than the sexual ambiguity of the film character, and the entire crew of his ship were, too.

During the interval after the first act, Lisa said, 'Philippe, I'm going to the ladies.'

In the ladies' room, Lisa filled a basin with cool water, took a bunch of paper towels, dipped them, and began to wipe her face; then, she splashed water on her eyes and patted them dry. A woman moved to the spare basin between Lisa and the wall and spoke quietly, 'I'm Leonie. I saw you with Philippe Daurain, and I don't think you belong in this crowd.'

Lisa glanced at a sympathetic face in the mirror. 'I'm wondering that myself.'

'I'll warn you. I went out with Philippe a dozen times and then slept with him twice. The third time he wanted anal sex; I'm not into that, so I refused, and he tried to force me. I managed to kick him in the balls and left. I found out afterwards he's bisexual, half gay, and sex with a gay person is against my religion; I'm warning you because I'm not sure a kick in the balls will work again.'

Lisa felt nauseous. 'Thank you.'

She didn't return to Philippe after she thought, *I don't like the show; I don't want to be here, so why stay?*

She walked out of the theatre and took a taxi home. When she arrived early, Rosemary asked, 'Are you feeling alright, Lisa? You don't look well.'

Lisa burst into tears. Between sobs, she told the story.

'Lisa, stop crying; you're unhurt; you never had sex with him, and thank God you found out in time. I want to thank that woman.

'You're walking in a minefield, Lisa; go out with your women friends and keep the men at a distance until you find the one you want.'

'But if I never accept an invitation, how will I meet such a man?'

'He'll appear when you're ready. You can try my method. Whenever a man invited me to join him for something, I asked myself a question. "Do I want to accept?" If the answer was yes, I asked myself why. Only if there was no reason would I accept.'

'That's crazy, Mama.'

'That's the first sign of love, Lisa. I still can't tell you why I love your dad. There's no reason, but I do. That first invitation may not grow into the love of a lifetime, but if there's no beginning, it's a waste of time and may be dangerous. You can also try another method. Ask yourself if a man you respect and like would have taken you to that theatre. If you know he wouldn't, don't go.'

Lisa thought, *Leo wouldn't; that's a valid test.*

That night, Rosemary told Gaston, then said, 'No harm done, Gaston. And Lisa has learnt another lesson.'

'What was the name of the woman who warned her?'

'Leonie.'

'I don't know how or why he's doing it, but I'm glad he does.'

'Who?'

'Leo...nie.'

'My god ... do you think he's watching over Lisa because he loves her?'

'No. Leo might have had strong feelings when they met, but today, five years later, he may be doing the same thing for a dozen girls. He won't be actively watching, but if he hears what they're doing and spots anything endangering them, he does what he can to help.'

But Rosemary had doubts. Lisa said she felt sick before Leonie spoke to her. *Was she reacting to the spoof of the pirate Jack Sparrow?*

Gaston, too, was close to the truth. When Lisa posted that she had met someone called Philippe Daurain, a student in the management school, Leo had sent a copy of the post to an email address. A week later, he received a reply and did nothing; that Lisa should meet a bi-sexual acquaintance was her business.

When Lisa said, in a Facebook post, that she was going to dinner with him, he sent a two-word message.

Tell her.

Lisa didn't accept another invitation, but as the summer break approached, she discussed with Jennifer what she might do during the summer break. Jennifer proposed visiting London to see her grandmother.

'I've always wanted to attend Cowes Week, the first week in August. Although it's for yacht racing, it's an enormous party. So, after a week of visiting the crown jewels, changing the guard at the Palace, and Windsor Castle, we could drive to Cowes. We could return with the ferry to Le Havre from Portsmouth and then drive back via Normandy.'

'That would be great. Could we do that in reverse? Then it would be the first two weeks in August instead of one in July and one in August.'

'Yes, why not ask those coming which way they prefer?'

Lisa posted their planned trip on Facebook.

Jennifer made the bookings, including an Airbnb apartment for four in Cowes. Marlene's parents lived in Dieppe, where they spent the night, and Marlene joined them for the ferry ride to Newhaven from Dieppe.

After unloading the car into the apartment on the outskirts of Cowes, Jennifer and Lisa drove away to find a parking space and walk back. They crept along narrow streets for ten minutes, looking for a place to park without success. Annoyed, Jennifer grumbled, 'We must try farther out; we might be luckier in East Cowes.'

'That means a drive to Newport to cross the river or the ferry called the Floating Bridge. Try farther out first.'

Jennifer looked for a place she could turn around, and fifty metres ahead, she saw a side entry and a sign '[*No Thru Traffic*]'. As they approached, Lisa said urgently, 'Turn in here.'

Jennifer read the '[*Private Road*]' sign as she turned. 'Why?'

'It's a close. Look, a circle's ahead, with cars parked around it.'

Two-thirds of the way around, one parking space between two driveways stood empty. Jennifer claimed it. As her car was left-hand drive, she stepped onto the pavement to see a gentleman holding secateurs, watching them from the nearest garden.

'Good morning. Can we park here?'

'Usually not. A notice by the turn says this is private, but the owner is away on holiday, so I'll say you can.'

'For three nights?'

'Five if you wish.'

'Thanks, parking is impossible during Cowes Week.'

He was reproachful. 'The brochures suggest parking on the mainland and taking the ferry.'

As the two girls walked out to the passing road, Jennifer asked, 'Lisa, what made you decide to turn in if you saw the private sign?'

'I didn't see it; I only saw the street sign, "[*Calmel Close*]".'

'Oh, is that a relative?'

'I don't know, he or she might be.' *I'll tell Leo.*

'Unless we can find a bus, we must walk into Cowes,' Jennifer told the others when she and Lisa returned, 'it's too crowded.'

As the day trippers poured in the next morning, they discovered how crowded it would become. 'We must eat lunch early,' suggested Olivia, 'we'll never find a table near the waterfront if we wait.'

They found a table with five chairs and ordered drinks while waiting for a menu.

'Excuse me, if I can find an extra chair, could we join you? There are no free tables.'

The speaker, a girl Lisa thought was only a year or two older than her, and another girl the same age, dressed in tight T-shirts and short pants, looked at Olivia hopefully.

'If you can find a chair, you're welcome.'

The two girls introduced themselves as Greta and Susan, and the conversation continued with introductions and details about where they were from. Greta was the most forthright; after saying that London, where they worked in a supermarket, was empty except for tourists, she added, 'Everyone is down here, and I fancy the tanned sailors; maybe one will invite us for a cruise, or at least, a cruise on board a boat,' she grinned, 'if you know what I mean.'

Olivia remarked after lunch when the two girls left, 'I know what she means; they don't have a place to stay in Cowes and must take a ferry back unless they can find a couple of sailors who invite them on board for the night.'

Jennifer said, 'Let's watch the next race start; that's the most exciting few minutes of a race.'

Later, they strolled along the Cowes parade; it seemed the entire world was there, and they found the Regatta village and the Clubhouse crew bar. Jennifer found a table with benches under an umbrella, and they ordered drinks.

Lisa thought the two suntanned young men who came to their table improved on Greta and Susan. Greg and Theo sat down after asking, and Greg said, 'You don't look like English girls; where are you from?'

After they explained, Lisa asked, 'And where are you from?'

Theo, whom Lisa thought was the more handsome of the two, sitting opposite her, replied, 'All over, we're professional crew, so we go where the work is.'

'Please explain what professional crew do.'

'Mostly, we do boat maintenance. It's been the same for centuries: sailors scrub decks. We have skipper tickets, so sometimes we sign up to do a delivery job, sailing a yacht from one port to another, even across the Atlantic, usually to the Caribbean.

'Then there are jobs crewing for a rich guy on a big yacht who wants to sail somewhere, and we look for jobs crewing on boats in yacht races.'

'So, are you racing here?'

'No, we've just returned from Grenada and haven't had the time to look for a berth.'

'So, where do you stay?'

'There are many boats we've sailed in the harbours we visit, and there's always one where we can sleep. We're on a luxury cruiser we skippered last year; the owner left us the key and the bar.'

Greg drew a bottle of wine and small plastic cups from his satchel as if on cue. 'I have a bottle of his exclusive wine here. Would you like to try it?'

Lisa refused. *That's asking for trouble, although we're four. They must have practised this ploy.* But the others agreed, and Greg poured large samples to taste; then Theo asked Lisa, 'If you'd like to board our boat, I can take you past security to visit.'

'I'm not sure I want to break the access rules. Have you won many races?'

'Yes, quite a few, once we won all three trophies in a regatta.'

'Where was that?'

'In the bay of Cannes.'

'That sounds like a tall story.'

'No, I promise you it's not.' Theo swung a small bag from his shoulder, unzipped it and dug inside. 'I keep my licences and stuff with me; I never know when I'll need to prove my competence to an employer.' He paged through a photo wallet. 'Here, this photo proves it; it was four years ago.'

All twelve men in the photo had blue striped tee shirts with *Jolly Roger* embroidered on the chest; in front of them, three gold cups stood in a row on a wooden chest, but Lisa didn't look at them; one of the men had a three-cornered hat. Lisa couldn't make out his face, but it looked familiar.

Theo pointed. 'See, that's me, and that,' his finger moved to another, 'is Greg.'

'Who's the man with the hat?'

'A young guy that the owner brought on board. He was once the Cannes junior sailing champion. He said he had sailed the Solent, so I watch for him when I'm here.'

'Was the boat the *Jolly Roger*?'

'The *Anemone* with the company's name plastered all over it, but the company had a tourist boat called the *Jolly Roger* that we slept on during the regatta, and on the last day, the *Jolly Roger's* captain gave us those teeshirts, he sold them to the tourists. He put his pirate hat on the owner's head for the photo. The owner took it off and put it on the young guy's head, saying, "You won us these trophies; you wear it."'

Lisa finally posed the question she was dying to ask, 'What was his name?'

'I can't remember.'

Lisa felt disappointed until Theo asked, 'Greg, you remember the young guy who won us three trophies in Cannes?'

'The one we called *The Navigator*?'

'Yeah, him; what's his name?'

'Leo.'

That was after we met; PegLeg must think Leo is a pirate.

Lisa spotted Greta and Susan, who had just taken a table vacated by a couple.

They don't seem to have any success.

Then Theo asked, 'So, Lisa, will you come with me to see the boat?'

With Leo watching? Never.

'No, Theo, if you're looking for company, you have the wrong person, but those two girls over there are Greta and Susan; they told us they wanted to look at the inside of a boat.'

After saying, 'Nice meeting you, ladies,' the two men left quickly. As he stood, Greg reached out, lifted the wine bottle, and held it up to check the contents. As he did so, the label faced Lisa for a few seconds.

Olivia remarked, 'I guess when you have no plans for the future, finding a guy to provide for you is your only fun.' The others murmured in agreement.

Lisa was speechless. She had read the wine producer's name on the label. *Calmel and Joseph.*

That night, Lisa had a pirate dream; she was on a yacht, and the pirate ship was overtaking her. The pirate was wearing a three-cornered hat with a parrot on his shoulder. He seemed angry as he passed. The pirate ship had a name, the *Jolly Roger.*

In the morning, she didn't post about what she had learnt; that was private, and so was the thought: *PegLeg is watching me. He's angry again.* That led to another. She grabbed her phone and checked the moon's state. The full moon would rise that night. *I'll ask him to call tonight when the moon rises in Oman, and he can describe it; it's too cloudy here to see the moon.*

Puzzled by the odd instruction, Leo waited until the moonrise began.

'Hello, man, thanks for calling.'

'Hello, girl. I didn't expect a message.'

'There's no moon here to remind me, so you can tell me what it's like, and I'll tell you something about PegLeg.'

'It's huge, halfway above the desert horizon, and a deep red colour that's changing as it rises. It's not yet bright enough to block the stars close by, so twinkling lights that fade as it brightens surround it … it's now silver with a pink tinge, and the moon is shrinking; the bottom is rising faster than the top … there, it's now silver and beginning to light up the land with moonlight, there's a path across the desert from me to the moon that's shimmering with star reflections inviting me to walk there.'

'Don't you dare leave me; I'll imagine we're watching together, and I have my head on your arm.'

....

'Will you take me into the desert for a moonrise one day?'

'Say when, and I'll bring you here on my magic carpet.'

'Thanks, Leo, I won't forget. I'm in Cowes with the girls. I should have asked you to bring us here on your carpet because we couldn't find a parking place until I spotted a road named Calmel Close. It's private, but we found a place there. Could the Calmels have come from England?'

'As Normandy and England were once a single kingdom, and Calais was part of England for two centuries, the same names must occur on both sides of the channel in a band close to the coasts.'

'When I can study genealogy, I'll find out.

'We met two of your old sailing buddies, Greg and Theo, and they had a bottle of wine with the label *Calmel and Joseph*.'

'Now that's improbable.'

'I know; I think PegLeg is pushing again; maybe he tried to bring you here.'

'Greg and Theo were deckhands when I met them; where did they find the wine?'

'From the boat they're staying on.'

'That fits with what I remember of them. I've registered on four maritime databases, so I hope PegLeg knows we're trying. I have a search specialist to help. If there's anything to find, we'll find it.'

'Thanks. Good night, Leo, I'll dream of the moon.'

'Good night, Lisa.'

I must start the search.

23

Leo asked the next day. 'Shuchang, is Kabir free yet?'

'Yes, boss, Kabir has finished. The guys are running performance trials.'

'Thanks, Shuchang; I'm sorry I haven't asked sooner. How far is the medicine sales program from completion?'

'Ready for a core demo, but we still have work on the ancillaries. Help and a learning simulation, logging in using face recognition, a menu item so users can ask for missing products, allowing discounts to charities, and controlling transport costs by switching to CIF with a fee for import agents who deliver to the end user.'

'How will you manage sales where the end user has no internet?'

'I've spoken to a manufacturer of satellite systems for boats; for limited compressed data, they can make a tiny system for us. They're waiting for confirmation before making a prototype.'

'Then order a thousand, subject to prototype approval. Encode and lock message routing to the logged-in route.

'Please bring Kabir to me.'

'Kabir, it's simple but laborious. There are four marine databases to search. I don't know what we're looking for. It might be a ship's log, a report on a sea battle, a burial at sea, or a passing boat. You'll need to translate the docs between 1700 and 1720 and list those vessels that never arrived. Then, expand the search by including references to those ships and their crews or passengers. Any mention of pirates or the skull and crossed bones, Madagascar or St.

Marie is a red flag. So are the names PegLeg Jon, a one-legged man, Raymond, Jean, and Calmel. The date range is between 1695 and 1715, but the database entry may be years later than the sailing. Send any red flag item to Shuchang.'

'I'll do my best, sir. Can I ask for a local server near each database to run the search programs I write? I might overload the Oman to Europe cables.'

'Thanks, Kabir, I should have considered that. Shuchang, rent a server in a local server farm near each database.'

I don't have much time to solve Lisa's medicine supply problem, but I promised to help.

Leo arranged a meeting with his father, grandfather, and the health minister, whom he knew well – he was a grand-uncle. *I must start now to be ready when Lisa needs it.*

His grandfather asked, 'Asad, what do you want to discuss?'

'Sir, do you know anything about the worldwide black market in stolen medicines?'

Rachid turned to his brother. 'I don't. Do you, Ahmed?'

'I know it's enormous, in the tens of millions of dollars. Much of it is stolen medicines; some are counterfeit.'

Leo replied, 'Quite right, but not tens of millions, *billions*.'

The following silence lasted until Rachid asked, 'So please explain how you will avoid the problem and what you want of us.'

'I'll supply in sealed plastic bags or liquid containers with only a random code number on the bag or container. All orders, transactions and payments are via a secure website. After delivery, the person receiving the goods must pay before learning what medicine the bag's code number refers to. If possible, all the products will look the same. With no identifying packaging, the product is unusable. The medical specifications will not be in a box but will be available online to authorised persons. I could tell you about the security my programmers are discussing, let me say that it will be outstanding.

'Initially, I want a large warehouse near the airport; it will import medicines in bulk and then supply them in smaller bulk parcels. Sales will be via the web.'

'Initially means what, Asad?'

'Once sales are high enough, I want to add chemical processing to manufacture the generics.'

His uncle asked, 'So you'll only sell generics?'

'No, sir, only manufacturing the generics, but I'll continue bulk importation of others subject to patents if there's no generic.'

His uncle replied, 'Then there's only one site – opposite the proposed police hospital.'

'I consider that site excellent, sir. As this will be an import/export business, I need the factory classified as a free zone with no import or export documents or clearance procedures. Nothing will show the packages' contents; we will label everything as water treatment chemicals. When the company manufactures generics, Oman will receive them free of charge, and before then, the price of all medicines to Oman will be at cost. In return, I'm hoping for military-quality security at the factory, from aeroplanes or cargo ships to the factory and vice versa.

'And the company?'

'Generics.com. An address, a bank account in Muscat, and a bank account in various countries where clients and suppliers live. Members of the royal family and approved investors will hold the shares. Our family will not buy the shares.'

'Where will you find the staff?'

'A few selected managers will train Omanis. Until manufacturing begins, the skills are no more than running a warehouse. I shall recruit an expert from Amazon's warehousing.'

Ahmed added weight to Asad's argument, 'Rachid, I support this; I'm sure our father will approve it.'

'If I can't persuade him, I'm in trouble. My daughter will hear that Asad wants to give free medicine to Omani citizens, and I'll never hear the end of it. Asad, go ahead; let us know whenever you need something. When will you begin operations?'

'About a year to build and put the equipment in place, but once we have the software bug-free, I'll roll out a small operation to check everything in a few months.'

Louis asked, 'Ten years from now, how big will this factory be, and how many people will work there?'

'I can only guess. Several square kilometres and twenty thousand people.'

'Then I suggest we include other ministers and form a planning committee with roads, housing, water, and electricity in its portfolio. Perhaps a port expansion, even a separate freight airport. We must manage a major project of this nature correctly. Asad, can you supply an estimate of the size and personnel numbers in five, ten, and twenty years?'

'I can try. Thanks, Dad. I'm all for it, but wait until I have a trial business operating with just the import/export operation. That's the unknown; the manufacturing is not.'

Leo miscalculated. When Soraya learnt of his plans, she decided to become involved. Every Oman hospital, clinic and pharmacy had to send a list of the medicines they used or sold. Within two weeks, Leo's team had a database of the drugs and the amounts. Work began on an automated warehouse, and an office with a dozen employees began working on suppliers and bulk orders to stock the warehouse. Six months later, Oman hospitals obtained all their medication from Generics.com.

Leo thought. *One thing about being the Sultan's granddaughter is that what she wants happens. At least the system has had a thorough trial. Making the generics will keep Mother busy, and I can return to PegLeg's research.*

Leo phoned Professor Demirci's secretary, told her he was a Cambridge research fellow working with Professor Restolomew and asked for an appointment, 'Ma'am, I can meet Professor Demirci anywhere in Türkiye, and I'll adjust my schedule for any date he accepts. I'm sure the meeting will be less than an hour. However, if he's too busy, can you give me an email address? I'll send the question I want to ask, and you can forward it to the professor.'

He received the email address and sent the message.

> Dear Professor,
> I have attached four photos of the front and back of a copper and a bronze coin, and I have also attached the spectroscopic analysis of the metals. My question is, where were they made? Professor A G Restolomew suggested I ask you.
> Leo Poussin.

Leo was unsure if it was Restolomew's name or something about the medallions, but the secretary returned his call and offered a meeting in Sanliurfa a week later.

He made a day trip, leaving at five thirty from Muscat. An hour after touchdown, he stepped from a car at a temporary building near the *Göbeklitepe* archaeology site.

Suspecting a cold and formal meeting, Leo was pleasantly surprised at the warm welcome tone as the professor, who appeared younger than LinkedIn reported, said, 'Welcome, Mr Poussin. I spoke to Restolomew, and he referred to you in flattering terms. So much so I couldn't resist a meeting.'

'Thank you, Professor. I hope that means a positive answer to my question.'

'Archaeologists are rarely positive, although they behave as if they are. The analyses of your medallions are intriguing. The copper could be from anywhere, but the tin in the bronze is the key, as it matches the output of ancient artisanal mines in Rwanda. Although not mined today, their cassiterite ore had low impurities, so it was easy to produce ninety-nine per cent pure tin; some of the best bronzes in antiquity used Rwandan tin.

'Given that, and assuming the same copper in both medallions, the impurities are in the copper, which suggests a mine in eastern Oman. The Al Hajar mountains were a major source of copper in the Bronze Age. Copper corrodes slowly and is highly recycled; little goes to waste.'

Leo raised his hands to his neck and pulled the silver medallion from inside his shirt. 'Professor, this is an identical design and size but in silver.' He took a folded piece of paper from a pocket and handed it to the professor. 'Here is the metal analysis. I have taken photographs of all three coins and overlaid them. The skull and crossed bones match perfectly.'

'You've answered a question, Mr Poussin. The photographs you sent showed two small holes near the side. Did they have chains?'

'They did, Sir, heavy ones that corroded. I replaced them later.'

'Mr Poussin, you're complicating the problem. Let me look up historical silver analyses in a reference book.'

Professor Demirci rose and pulled one volume titled *Historical Analyses-Silver* from a row of similar reference books.

After turning a dozen pages, he said, 'This is a match: a silver deposit called the Kapagula Intrusion. South of Kigoma near Lake Tanganyika.'

'That's marvellous, Professor, but where were they made?'

'The first question to answer is, *how* were they made? And how many of each?'

'The silver one is unique, Professor, as it has initials engraved on the reverse side instead of the debossed date. I would expect three thousand copper and two thousand bronze.'

'Then I'll tell you how, in 1710, a foundry might have minted them. They would start with a metal die, possibly gold or silver, made by a jeweller. After preparing boxes of foundry sand with flat tops, they press the die, debossed date down into the sand, then cut a channel for the molten copper or bronze to flow and fill it. They would have an iron scraper that they would use to wipe any excess molten metal away and leave the coin with a flat surface and even thickness. They might have advanced to using a flat sand upper mould with a feed funnel. They would make a baked clay master of the opposite side of the metal die, press it into a sandbox, and cast a single Wootz steel punch that, using a hand-operated press, could impress the skull and crossbones into heated but not molten copper and bronze coins.

'I'll suggest that your silver medallion was the original, and later, after a jeweller filed off the debossed date and polished it, he engraved the initials and added the chain.

'I can't tell you where to find the foundry that made the coins, but I can suggest. A foundry melts copper at about a thousand degrees and tin bronze at about nine hundred degrees. Both require coal. Such foundries were close to a port and coal imports. Rwandan tin came in ingots to Mombasa or Lamu and then to Djibouti, where traders bought it and shipped it north up the Red Sea or to the Gulf. Metalworking was and still is a traditional craft at the ports along the southern coast of Arabia from Aden to Sur; I feel confident,' he smiled, 'although not positive, that if you check for foundries along the coast, you will find one, and that one will tell you of others.

'The silver medallion is different. Like gold, silver finds new uses. Zanzibar, Lamu, and Djibouti are the sites most likely to have had a silversmith using that silver. However, it might be anywhere on the Arabian coast or on either side of the Red Sea. Britain made silver teapots that they exported worldwide. Never discarded, they became a myriad of items.

'So, you have a major task to uncover the information you seek, but Restolomew does say you have an uncanny search ability.'

'Only logic, sir; as a mathematician, I can't reach an answer if I ignore a step in the calculation.'

'An admirable attitude. I shall leave you to look. If you find some coins, please send me some copper and bronze ones in the exact state you discover them.'

'I will, Professor, thank you.'

Leo's analyses of Rwanda's data were now in the sixth refinement loop, and he spent more time working on his doctoral thesis, interspersed with camel rides.

Leo was fifty kilometres from home in the desert when his satphone beeped SAT+0. He phoned his father on schedule.

'Hello, Leo. Are you interested in another but different problem?'

'Where are you, Dad?'

'Dakar. Senegal has applied for IFC support to replace the Dakar to Tambacounda road.'

'I know why: a colonial road built when trucks were few and never more than three tons.'

'Yes, and I must refuse. There's something wrong with the figures; the income is far lower than in a comparable country. If you're interested, I might swing a World Bank investigation. They're impressed with what you did in Rwanda.'

'I'm interested, Dad; see what you can do, but can we do something to avoid a future bottleneck?'

'What?'

'I'll need a dedicated Oman satellite to manage the data downloads. Rwanda will be an annual contract.'

'Now, that's a great idea, maybe not entirely for us; it could also serve other users in Oman.'

'Why? What's wrong with one for us?'

'I could use a commercial satellite company and guarantee sufficient usage from Oman to have them launch a satellite for us. You can't do it in your name. I could persuade the Oman Ports Authority to make a request, including a camera to provide images of the ships in the ports and the approaches, and as the project consultant, I could promote it for port usage, and other Omani companies could chip in with usage guarantees. They need not meet their guarantees because we will use the available data capacity.'

'Dad, please investigate it. I also need to expand the cave; I'll deepen it where it's cooler for some new hardware, but I must visit a professor at the LSE to discuss my thesis. I'll stay in Wight for a week or two.'

24

Two weeks after returning to Oman, Leo and his local team, now seven people, ran analysis programs on the Rwanda data multiple times, with improvements each time. Fully alert to the possibility of medicine theft, Leo asked for an in-depth analysis of the health budget.

Then Shuchang came to see him with pages of information.

'Boss, I have data from the VOC. One of the documents stands out. It may not be what you want, but it fits your requirements.'

'Shuchang, please. Summarise.'

'The first reports are standard documents and logs regarding the departure of a Dutch vessel, the *Eenhoorn*, from Amsterdam to Jakarta. Nothing unusual, except the process trace shows the system selected them after another.'

'So, what triggered the backwards search?'

'The *Eenhoorn* left Jakarta on November 2, 1710, and vanished. There are reports before it left, including the cargo lists. The reports show delayed cargo deliveries to the ship.

'I asked for a list of all the ships that left Jakarta for the Netherlands shortly before the *Eenhoorn*'s departure. The list is conclusive; a fleet of cargo-carrying boats with armed escorts sailed three weeks before the *Eenhoorn*, which departed late due to the delayed cargo.'

'Was it armed?'

'I checked on its design. It was a Dutch Fluyt design, built for cargo and with only six light cannons on each side. It might have frightened a dhow, but nothing bigger, they sailed with escorts.'

'That's no help – you haven't said what triggered that search.'

Shuchang smiled. 'But another document refers to the *Eenhoorn*, the *Eenhoorn* captain's report, written and filed in Amsterdam two years later.'

'How can that be?'

'You must read it. A storm drove the *Eenhoorn* onto an island reef, and a year later, another ship rescued what remained of the crew.'

'Shuchang, send me the link and stop being mysterious. Is that what I'm looking for?'

'I don't know, but I've added keywords from the report to the search criteria. It may be a year or two before we find something else.'

Leo downloaded the document.

A report by Captain Maarten J Hulft. Master of the Merchantman *Eenhoorn* dated January 16, 1713.

Interpreted from handwritten Dutch text and then translated into English.

After shipwreck and rescue, I submit this report to the *Heeren Seventien* board of directors and beg their indulgence.

I am confident that the examination of documents completed at the port of Jakarta, including the bills of lading signed by me, will prove that the *Eenhoorn* sailed late due to cargo delivery and loading delays. The fleet had left three weeks before with armed escorts, leaving the *Eenhoorn* at the mercy of rogue raiders.

The Indian Ocean from November to April spawns mighty rotating storms, and the northeast coast of Madagascar is a known pirate haven. My decision, agreed by my officers, was to sail directly towards Africa without descending southwards where storms might occur and, once within sight of Africa, to sail southwards along the coast, assisted by the current that flows near the shore.

All went well for the first two months; the easterly trade winds carried our vessel north of the Mascarenes and south of the Seychelles. Despite several calm spells, our heavily loaded steed (sic) made satisfactory progress. As Christmas approached, I agreed with my officers that a giant tortoise Christmas dinner to celebrate the birth of our Lord Jesus would break the voyage's boredom.

As longitude is an estimate, the navigator did not know when we might see the island, but he confirmed we were at the correct latitude for the atoll with the tortoises that the Arab seafarers named Al Khadra. I ordered extra lookouts who searched the horizon for land.

The masthead lookout, staring westwards, with the rising sun in the east, almost missed a sail three leagues to the northeast.

As the other craft grew closer, I recognised a heavily armed English brigantine design. I ordered the preparation of our cannons and readied for a course change to bring my guns to bear. When the raider flew his black flag with a white skull and cross, I considered surrender, for we had little hope against such a foe, but he luffed at the last minute and fired from our starboard quarter as I ordered the helm over to starboard.

I was sure he intended to capture the *Eenhoorn*, for he fired but one cannon loaded with chain shot that caused significant entanglement and damage to our sails and rigging. Without the ability to manoeuvre, I had no choice but to order the lowering of our flag and to await a boarding party.

To my surprise, the raider came close to our starboard side but did not attempt to grapple. I read the French name, *La Fleche*, on the bow and saw the captain on the poop deck, a handsome (impressive) man with hair blowing in the breeze. Puzzled, I could only watch until he raised an arm and swung to gesture to the east. I looked where he pointed and saw a dark band of cloud on the horizon, and I understood he would allow us to brave the coming storm without further damage.

He saluted, and as custom demands in such circumstances, I raised my hat and bowed to thank the rascal.

He sailed northwest, and I ordered the crew to prepare as best we could for the storm that carried us helpless in its furious grip until we foundered on the reefs of an island.

When the company vessel *Jonge Thomas* visited Al Khadra for water and tortoise meat, they rescued us, and we learnt the name of our island.

Of *La Fleche* or her crew, I know no more.

Attached is a list of the crew members who survived the island landing and the five whose bodies we found on the shore; the names of those who later died on the island I have marked with the letter D, and those who drowned with a V. The remaining crew members are missing.

Signed by the Captain.

'Shuchang, there may be other interesting items, but it's a start and encouraging; I'll report this to the history professor in Cambridge *and Lisa* and ask for ideas. I must explore two other avenues; I'll let you know if I need help. I must talk to my dad; we need a significant expansion of our facilities. I'll consult with you if he approves. This time, we'll add enough power to last many years.'

The information may be the key we need. I'll tell Lisa.

'Hello, man. Are you sending another girlfriend to see me?'

'Hello, girl. No, I'll come myself. If you can give me a date when you can visit Cambridge, I'll make an appointment with the professor and fetch you. I have some documents from the Dutch archives.'

'I'm in my last year. My last term and finals are looming; I can only manage time off during the easter break.'

'Beginning or end?'

'Beginning, please.'

'Mr Poussin, Doctor Calmette, you continue to surprise me. What do you need now?'

'First, professor, I have some documents for you filtered from the VOC archives. They provide information on a Dutch merchant ship that vanished on a voyage from Jakarta to Amsterdam in 1710, and the crew was rescued a year later from Aldabra, though it then had the Arab name Al Khadra.'

'With a link to PegLeg Jon?'

'The captain reports encountering a pirate ship called *La Fleche* shortly before a cyclone.'

'Fantastic, incredibly well done. I shall enjoy reading the reports. Historical research is changing; instead of years of reading in a dark library, digital records allow far faster searches, with, I must warn, an increased likelihood of error.'

'Why, sir?'

'The transcription to digital text and the translation to modern languages are open to error. Fortunately, *La Fleche* is likely correct. Pirates rarely sailed ships built to the captain's measure; they captured ships and traded them with each other. I remember something about a British vessel called the *Arrow* that fell into pirate hands. Find it if you can. There may be many *Arrows* in the naval archives.'

'Thank you. I will do, sir. Lisa has another question.'

'Go ahead, Doctor.'

Lisa spoke, 'Professor, you told us PegLeg Jon might be Raymond Jean Calmel. I have looked at genealogical websites, but how do I find someone who is an expert in searching family name data and might provide a clue as to his origins?'

'If he were French, you need a French researcher. I'll ask a historian I know well at the Sorbonne in Paris to recommend someone; I'll SMS the contact details. Several researchers are tracing the movements of the French who moved from France to their colonies. Unfortunately, they may not be in Paris but in a French-speaking territory anywhere.'

'Video conferencing solves that problem, Professor.'

'True, I tend to forget. The best of luck in your search; I live in anticipation of your discoveries.'

'Goodbye, and thank you again, Professor.'

'Thank you, Doctor Calmette, Mr Poussin, what you're doing is fascinating and impressive. Goodbye.'

Louis obtained authority from the IFC for Leo to conduct a study. After he told the Senegal finance minister that Leo had done a survey for Rwanda, and the minister had checked and learnt Leo was a Rwandan citizen called the *Gorilla Doctor*, Leo had a job.

At the end of June, Leo flew to Dakar with two other pilots, three men and two women from his growing data collection team, and a technician with a box of satellite communication equipment.

The finance minister gave them a large office with internet. They didn't use the internet; instead, a technician installed a direct satellite link to Oman, and then they began collecting data, a more significant task than in Rwanda. Leo had set a collection period of three months. The same problems in obtaining data cropped up, but Leo only had to visit the finance minister twice before total cooperation reigned. He left for Oman and, a month later, sat scrolling through figures from Senegal. He could see a leak in receipts and could not match numbers to physical events, but data was still arriving.

Lisa and Ashina finished their formal education when the University published the results. She and Ashina passed with honours; they had dinner with Lisa's parents that night.

'Dad, we have a problem.'

'Explain, Lisa.'

'Our scholarships now end, as I'm supposed to find a paying job for experience, and Ashina has no income until she starts to work for the WHO. Can you tell us whom to see?'

'I'll see Gary Somers tomorrow. If you ask, you'll have an appointment after the summer break; I can barge in. I'll call you once I know. Stay here tomorrow morning.'

Gaston remembered his conversation with Rosemary when she had said, 'When Lisa qualifies, we must encourage her to take a job outside Europe. Otherwise, hormones might push her to marry the wrong kind of man.'

'Hello, Lisa. I have the information you need.'

'Hold on, Dad, I'll put you on speaker, and Ashina can listen and take notes.'

....

'We're ready, Dad.'

'Ashina must see Mrs Anneke de Bakker in the WHO office this afternoon at four. She must bring her passport, degree, and references for the last two courses, including bank account details for her salary. Mrs de Bakker will help her complete the WHO employment forms.

'She should receive the contract next Friday and then fly to Lubumbashi to see the Katanga Health Minister for an appointment.

'Lisa, you must see Gary Somers tomorrow at eleven. He has a job for you out of the country if you are interested. If not, you must find a hospital in Belgium for experience.'

'You're a star, Dad.'

Gary Somers welcomed Lisa enthusiastically. 'Doctor Calmette, congratulations on your medical and management degrees. I know the terms of your scholarship specify that you should now find a post in a medical institution for practical experience; however, I have a problem you may solve. I'm sure you know what your parents have done in Rwanda. Their project to build multiple small clinics is accelerating. The designs and sites are approved, and the first clinic is complete. The IFC backed the project, and now Rwanda is impatient to see the clinics operating and has received a World Bank loan to fund materials, medicines, and staff. Your father told me you have visited Rwanda, and he has confidence in your ability to take on such a job. So, if you take it on, you'll have a contract.'

'Starting when, sir?'

'There's paperwork to do here, a UN passport to issue, and I must obtain Rwandan approval once you have a contract. A work visa may take another month. Say in about two months? If you accept, your contract will begin today.'

I won't tell him I have a friend in the hospital.

'Sir, can you ask Rwanda to allow me two months to study what and how they do things? I'll meet resistance if I try to implement our country's practices. I prefer to learn theirs and modify them.'

'I will, and I'm encouraged. So, you will accept?'

'Will I be employed by Rwanda or the WHO?'

'The WHO will appoint and pay you. We will recover the costs from the World Bank loan. I understand your concern. I'll ensure the appointment letter mentions your authority to specify how to spend the loan money.'

'Then I accept.'

'Then please see Mrs de Bakker for the paperwork.'

On the way home, Lisa reviewed her meeting and thought. *Rwanda has a World Bank loan, and Leo was doing their budget; he's somehow involved. I have some spare time; I can ask Leo what I can investigate about PegLeg.*

Ten days later, after tearful farewells, Ashina landed in Lubumbashi to a rapturous welcome and presented the WHO letter of appointment to the Provincial Health Minister the following morning.

The letter said:

> The WHO has appointed Dr Ashina Kisula as its medical training representative for Katanga.

As the Minister of Health in Kinshasa hadn't bothered to tell him, the Minister had no idea she was coming and had no training department. However, achieving a ministerial position in government requires quick thinking. He solved the problem diplomatically.

'Carry on.'

Ashina found nothing had changed since her visit with Lisa, but this time, she knew all about Bilharzia; she had researched it with Lisa and knew the Bilharzia in her area was *Schistosoma haematobium*. The sample Lisa had taken to her father proved it. One way of breaking the bilharzia cycle of the strain was to stop people from urinating in streams and rivers. She decided to tour the area around Lubumbashi to count the villages and cases. Her primary school teacher helped.

25

Leo received Lisa's SMS and dialled.

She answered, 'Hello, man, how and where are you?'

'Hello, girl. I'm in Oman, and I checked on your results. Congratulations. What do you do next?'

'I have a job in Rwanda.'

'That's unexpected.'

'Totally. I must equip, start, and manage the newly built clinics.'

'That will be fun. If you need help, ask.'

'That's why I'm calling; I promised to help with our PegLeg investigation. I have two or three weeks before I leave for Rwanda; what can I do?'

'Are you ready to travel, Lisa? Around France, the Caribbean, and India?'

'Why, Leo?'

'Professor Restolomew gave me four names. Two are in France, Brest and Cannes, one in St Barth, and another in India, Puducherry. They're genealogy experts – the two experts in Puducherry and St Barth specialise in French families that emigrated to the Indian Ocean and the Caribbean, respectively.'

'Can't I consult with them by video?'

'You can, but you only see a face; if you visit, you may see things that give you ideas.'

'Send them to me; Raymond Jean Calmel sailed from Brest. Should I visit there first?'

'He might not be PegLeg. I would try St. Barth; proving that

Raymond is the PegLeg who sailed with Kidd is the first step. Let me know where and what day. I can't come because I'm due to leave for Senegal, but I'll send my magic carpet for you. Where are you now?'

'At my parents' home, but I can make bookings, Leo.'

'Magic carpets are far better; they can take you wherever you want without a booking.'

Why am I not surprised?

Lisa grinned to herself. 'I'll check the contacts, make an appointment and call you. How much notice do you need to fetch a carpet from your cave?'

'Two days is fine. The car driver who comes to fetch you will give you two diplomatic passports, one from Rwanda and the other from Oman. They make international travel easier.'

'I know you're Omani, why Rwanda?'

'I'm a citizen since a minor incident with a gorilla, so I asked.'

Lisa laughed. 'What did you tell them?'

'That as we were going to marry, I want you to come with me through the diplomatic channel.'

'Shouldn't you have asked me first?'

'No, I worked out that PegLeg is backing me, and I only need to wait.'

I'm sure her laughter is happy.

Five days later, Lisa departed for St Barth. She appreciated the chauffeur-driven limo from her house to the Execujet terminal.

She had often travelled with her parents on private jets, but boarding as crew with no formalities was still new, and the G650 with a small bedroom and a bathroom with a shower was a step up in comfort.

After a night's sleep, they landed in Guadeloupe. Lisa transferred to a smaller aircraft for the two-hundred and thirty-kilometre flight to St Barth and another limo ride to the Eden Roc Hotel in St Barth, feeling cosseted.

That afternoon, a taxi took her to the house of Darius du Chantauvent.

When she rang, the woman in a light floral dress who opened the door said, 'You must be Doctor Calmette. I'm Genevieve; I'll take you to my husband; he's in his study.'

The study was as Lisa had imagined it: a long room with glass windows overlooking a lush garden. Lisa wondered if it wasn't once an orchid house. The opposite wall had sheets of many sizes, stuck or pinned in place, many overlapping others, each clearly a family tree.

Darius rose from his chair behind a massive office desk as they entered. He was tall, spare, bald with frameless spectacles, and his ears appeared to stick out. Lisa liked his soft eyes.

'Doctor Calmette, welcome. Please call me Darius.'

'Thank you. I'm pleased to meet you.'

'Doctor, since your enquiry, I've done some research. Are you interested in what I've done or only the results?'

He wants to describe how difficult it is. 'Please give me the full story.'

'Over many years, I've collected the telephone directories of Caribbean countries, not only the French territories. They were in printed form, but I managed to purchase the punched cards and tapes used by the printers; others I have only recently converted through scans.

'When you contacted me, I programmed an extraction of every Calmel entry in the database with the date of the directory. I'll put the map of the Caribbean on the big screen behind you and add all the plot points.'

'There are only two clusters, Darius, St Martin and Guadeloupe.'

'Yes, it makes things easier, for after finding the earliest entry in each cluster, I used voting registers to find the date those two arrived. I'm sorry to say both came from France after the revolution. From the Calais region, where the Calmel name has a cluster.'

'Were there no Calmels in the Caribbean before 1800?'

'There were, but another way we can search is hospital registers. Recent entries are easy, but old ones require a human to sit and search. I have a researcher in Tortola who is collecting historical records, and he found the record you referred to in your mail; Raymond Jean Calmel was there, recovering from a shipboard amputation.'

'That's a relief.'

'I'll disappoint you again: John Richardson, a British sailor, another amputee, was discharged from the hospital only days before Raymond, so your PegLeg Jon may be either.'

Lisa was ready to deny the suggestion. 'Our evidence suggests our PegLeg had at least some minimal medical instruction, might have known how to navigate, captained a ship, and had respect in his community. He's also titled Quartermaster in Kidd's crew list. Those characteristics are compatible with Raymond, an officer in the French Navy. What about Richardson?'

'That I must research. There are church records of deaths and baptisms. Many are digitised, but some are not. Fortunately, we have digitised records of all cemetery occupants. I'll ask for assistance, and the records are only accessible for a fee, but I may find the grave of Raymond Calmel or John Richardson.'

'Please do; my office will pay the costs and your fee if you send an invoice as specified in my email.'

'Thank you, and I have a snippet of free information for you. Your name and Calmel are related. I did a rough check. The Calmels came originally from the north of England; DNA evidence of current Calmels indicates Scottish genes. I found your DNA unless there's another E Calmette; the origins are similar. The Calmels in the Calais-Dunkirk region lived through the border changes when the Spanish Netherlands became the rulers of part of the region. I can only guess why they would one day be Calmel in France and the next be Calmette in the Spanish Netherlands without changing their address. I found a baptism certificate for Gustave Calmette, whose father is Philippe Calmel.'

'What is your guess?'

'The English Calmels were not Catholics, and the Spanish Inquisition was relentless. Changing religion and name was a frequent practice to escape persecution.'

'Thank you, Darius; perhaps that's why I sense Raymond is our man. If you find anything further, please email me.'

Lisa couldn't resist the beach, changed, and minutes later, after a cooling dip, stretched out on a lounger five metres from the calm sea.

'Good afternoon, Doctor; I have a drink and beachside lunch menu for you.'

The young waiter placed both on the small table beside her.

'How do you know I'm a doctor?'

'It's our job to know, ma'am.'

'Do you have a lime drink that includes lemongrass and mint? No alcohol.'

'I'm sure the bar will have what you want. Can I fetch one?'

'Bring me a little to taste; I might want less sugar.'

....

'Thank you, that's perfect. I'll order lunch in an hour.'

Thanks, Leo. I'm behaving like a spoiled brat, but I love it! What will I do next?

She hadn't finished the first glass when the waiter arrived with another. 'Your drink must be warm, Doctor; I've brought another.'

'Thank you. How far is Tortola?'

'Closer than Guadeloupe, but there are fewer flights.'

'Thank you.'

I'll see where Cousin Raymond landed.

She called the agent and explained.

'Certainly, Doctor. What time tomorrow?'

'As early as possible, I'm living with jet lag.'

'Seven from the hotel, seven thirty for takeoff, you will have breakfast in Road Town.'

She was ready in the lobby. Once in Road Town, Lisa had eaten breakfast by nine-thirty at the Village Cay restaurant with a view over the inner harbour: her destination, the hospitals and the museum were less than a kilometre away. She left her overnight cabin case with the restaurant owner and walked.

'Good morning, I'm Doctor Elisabeth Calmette. I'm visiting Tortola and want to know where to find the first hospital on the island.'

Flustered by the unusual request, the receptionist said, 'Please, Doctor, at the end of the corridor behind you is the main office; ask there.'

After a receptionist, a matron, and two doctors, she received a sensible answer. 'That hospital might still exist as a building, but even the outside will have changed. Everything inside would have gone on auction, except items earmarked by the Museum authorities. If those are anywhere, they will be in the Old Government Museum or its warehouse.'

The Museum was close by, and the only person in the building was, Lisa thought, a museum piece himself. 'Good morning, I'm Doctor Elisabeth Calmette.'

'Good morning to you, Doctor. How can I help?'

'Do you have any relics from the hospital that existed in 1695?'

'I might; I've never sorted through the stuff from that hospital. There's a doctor who does that in his spare time, Doctor Kerring; he likes the old knives.'

'Where can I find him?'

'At the Eureka clinic, beside the old harbour.'

Lisa sighed, 'That's where I've come from. Can I call a taxi?'

'I'll call for one.'

'Good morning. I'm Doctor Calmette; where can I find Doctor Kerring?'

'The young one or the old one?'

'The one who collects old medical instruments.'

'That's the old one; he's on the second floor. Room 232.'

'Good morning. I'm Doctor Calmette; I'd like to see Doctor Kerring, not for medical reasons but to ask about his collection of hospital relics.'

'He's doing his hospital rounds; if you wait for half an hour, he should be back.'

'I'll do that.'

'Would you like some tea?'

'No thanks, I had breakfast less than an hour ago. I'll take a glass of water from the machine here.'

Professor Restolomew was right; the title Doctor *helps.*

Lisa read a magazine that extolled the virtues of the hospital until a measured tread followed by the door opening signalled the doctor's arrival. She stood when he turned to look at her, and the secretary said, 'Doctor Calmette to speak to you, Doctor.'

'Then come in, Doctor.' He entered his surgery, hung his lab coat on a hook and said, 'Please, sit. How can I help?'

Lisa had decided to stretch the truth. 'I'm related to a man who sailed in 1696 aboard a French Navy ship to the Caribbean. On the crew list, he's the doctor. The log says Raymond lost a leg in a battle, and the captain unloaded him in Tortola. The hospital, wherever that was, treated him and, after recovery, discharged him, and he disappeared. I'm trying to find out more about him.'

'Well, as the last rites were a more usual result than a cure, he might have been a priest; most ship doctors were priests in the seventeenth century. He might have gone to a church. Also, you're standing in the hospital, although the owners bulldozed the old building and the new one expanded while I did my clinical studies.'

'And the contents of the old hospital?'

'They sold or scrapped most of it. They donated the surgical equipment to the Museum. It lay in a shed for fifty years. I'm working my way through it when I have time to create a display room in this hospital for visitors, like a museum. When they see some of that equipment, they'll realise how lucky they are today.'

'Please, this ancestor, what were his initials?'

'Raymond Jean Calmel.'

'Then either God or his ghost guided you to me unless I'm the luckiest man alive.'

Doctor Kerring stood. 'Please, Doctor, come with me, we'll visit the Museum; my car is in front.'

26

At the museum, Kerring drove around the back to a massive shed. 'It's not all medical relics. They occupy a small section.' He had a key, and minutes later, Lisa looked in amazement at a collection of lethal-looking instruments.

'There's a wooden box back here with those initials carved on it...

'Here it is.'

An artisan had burnt the initials R J C on the top of a box about sixty centimetres long, with thirty-by-thirty sides and top. 'I'll pull it out, then we'll carry it to a table and open it.'

'Is it locked?'

'Yes, but the locks rust inside. A screwdriver will open it. A marine surgeon's instruments were bronze.'

When the lid creaked open, Lisa stopped breathing until Doctor Kerring said, 'A bronze bone saw, in excellent condition, engraved with the initials RJC. Do you inherit?'

'I don't think so, but if you put it in your display, I won't claim it.'

He carefully lifted out three similarly engraved scalpels, then said, 'We have a problem. There's a Bible here. It has a leather cover and gold lettering, but it will collapse if I touch it. I must fetch the museum curator; he'll call a preservation expert to remove and vacuum pack it, then tomorrow you can take it to Europe, where laboratories know how to preserve it.'

'I'll call my travel agent to delay my departure. Where should I stay?'

'I'll leave you at Maria's by the Sea; they will have a room, and I'll ask the museum to deliver the packet early tomorrow. I must return to the hospital. I have patient appointments this afternoon.'

'Thank you, Doctor. I'll tell you what I learn.'

After returning to the Village Cay Restaurant, she had lunch on the terrace, looking over the inner harbour at the Marina on the far side. *I'll register at Maria's, leave my case, and look around.*

The following day, the room phone rang at eight am. 'Doctor Calmette, this is the Museum. I have a package to deliver. It's in a sealed cardboard box. If you take it as cabin baggage, can I put it in a cloth carry bag for you?'

'That would be perfect, thank you.'

'Then the courier will be at Maria's at nine.'

'I'll meet him in the lobby.'

Lisa phoned her travel agent, who said the car and the plane would be on time. Then she went for breakfast, paid her bill, and went to the front door at nine to await the delivery. She was on one side of the lobby with a view out the door.

Moments before the courier arrived in a small car, a noisy motorcycle stopped on the far side of the road, and a man dismounted and then leaned against a wall. Lisa thought it odd.

Perhaps he's waiting for someone.

The courier arrived in a little van, stepped out and came to the hotel with a brown cloth carry bag in one hand and a clip pad in the other. Lisa went out to meet him.

'Good morning, I'm Doctor Calmette.'

'Good morning, doctor. Can you sign the receipt, please?'

Lisa did, took the bag, looked inside, and then said, 'Thank you. That's fine,' and turned to enter the hotel. *That man is still watching.*

She dressed in her attendant uniform in her room, packed her trolley cabin suitcase, brushed her hair and attached the pillbox hat, and then looked out the window to see if the car had arrived.

That man has disappeared, but his motorcycle is still there. He must be on this side of the road.

Lisa looked at the Bible in its carry bag, and the thought came from somewhere: *I won't lose Raymond's Bible now, especially as he's family.*

She opened her cabin case, removed some dirty underwear, took the box containing the Bible from the brown carry bag and packed it carefully in the trolley case. Then she looked around for a replacement. *That Gideon Bible on the bedside table is perfect. Raymond would approve.* Wrapped in the underwear, she placed it in the carry bag and thought, *It looks right.*

She rechecked the window. *The motorbike is still there, the man isn't, but my car is arriving.*

Pulling the trolley case with one hand and carrying the bag with the other, she took the lift, crossed the lobby floor and walked out the door. The driver took her trolley case. The man must have hidden behind a pillar, for Lisa heard six or seven footsteps and began to turn when he ripped the carry bag from her hand and ran around the front of the car and across the road to the motorcycle. Her driver yelled and tried to run after him, but the motorbike roared to life and disappeared down the road.

Her driver returned. 'Doctor, I'm sorry, we'll call the police.'

'No, it's only dirty washing. Drive me quickly to the airport before the thief finds out. He might return.'

Determined to regain self-respect, the limo driver drove well, but two wheels were faster than four in traffic. As Lisa entered the airport building, she heard the motorcycle roaring up the road and then recognised the man. She went directly to the crew passage to immigration and the apron. A large security officer stood there, and on seeing the airline uniform, he stepped to one side. Lisa stopped and saw the man run into the building and look wildly around. 'Officer, if the man over there with a brown bag comes here to say I left the bag behind, tell him I don't want it, and he should read the book and give the clothes to his wife.'

'I will, Ma'am. Have a good flight.'

The immigration officer recognised her from the day before, remembered she had a diplomatic passport, and waved her past him to the waiting pilot, who took her trolley case. And Lisa said, 'Let's fly. A madman is trying to steal my suitcase.'

Five minutes later, the Twin Otter began to taxi.

In Guadeloupe, she switched planes without entering the airport terminal. The G650 crew took her trolley case, and she asked the pilots of the smaller plane to watch them take off before entering the terminal.

An hour after Lisa arrived home, Leo phoned. Surprised, Lisa answered.

'Hello, man, does the travel agent report on where I am?'

'Hello, girl, no, but Private Wings sends me an invoice when the flight ends. Why did you visit Tortola?'

'To fetch Raymond's Bible.'

That shocked him! The silence dragged on until Leo asked, 'Does it require preservation?'

'Yes, it's vacuum-packed by an antiquities expert but needs treatment before opening.'

'You're fantastic, Lisa, what a find! Can you visit Cambridge? I'll see if the Professor is there and can see you.'

'Can't you come, Leo?'

'I'm in Senegal. I should finish in a week.'

'The Bible has waited over three hundred years. It can wait another week, but I must put it in a safe place.'

'Why?'

'A man in Tortola tried to steal it, but I fooled him. He must have believed it was valuable, as it came from the museum. I don't know if he has accomplices here.'

'Are you alright?'

'Yes, Leo, don't worry.'

'You'll have two security men there in an hour, twenty-four seven. Tell your parents.'

'Thanks, Leo. I could have taken the Bible to a bank.'

'It's not for the Bible. I'll tell you when I fly.'

He's worried about me! That's nice.

Leo called Cambridge; his secretary said the professor was on a fly-fishing holiday in Scotland, but she gave him the professor's mobile phone number. Leo waited until he reckoned the Professor would be having lunch in a pub, then phoned.

'Good afternoon, Professor. Leo Poussin here.'

'Mr Poussin, what a surprise. I cannot imagine what you will tell me, so please do.'

'My colleague, who may be a distant cousin of Raymond Calmel, has returned from an expedition to Tortola with Raymond's Bible. An antiquities expert has temporarily preserved it, but further treatment is necessary before examination. I'm calling to ask what to do with it.'

'Mr Poussin, your colleague has surpassed you. What a team you make! I return to Cambridge in another week and will have a lab expert available for a meeting. Can you meet me in my offices on the eighteenth?'

'I can, sir, and I agree, she has outclassed me.'

'I can hardly wait to hear her story.'

'Hello, girl.'

Leo sounds happy. 'Hello, man.'

'I've organised everything. A car will collect you at eight am on the eighteenth, wear a uniform and bring the Bible. I'll meet you at the Execujet terminal, and we'll fly to Cambridge to meet the professor and the lab guy.'

'Wilco.'

'Is the uniform changing you?'

'Something is. I'm having more fun than I could have imagined.'

'Then hold on to your hat; it's just beginning.'

When her parents arrived home, Rosemary exclaimed, 'Lisa, you look radiant. Where have you been, and what's happened?'

'I've been to St Barth via Guadeloupe, then Tortola, and home via Guadeloupe.'

'But you've only been away four nights!'

'That's right. I phoned Leo and asked what I could do to learn more about PegLeg. He said I should meet a man in St Barth.

'I've not had as much fun since my eighteenth birthday.

'Leo is Omani and has a magic carpet that took me there. I discovered PegLeg is a distant cousin and found a box with his medical gear and a Bible in the museum warehouse on Tortola. Next week, Leo will take me and the Bible to Cambridge to meet the history professor.'

Gaston grinned. 'On his magic carpet, I suppose.'

'Of course, Dad. He magicked up two diplomatic passports for me and a cabin attendant's uniform so I could pass through the crew channel at the airport.'

'What nationalities?'

'Oman and Rwanda.'

'I'm glad you're so happy, Lisa.'

'Rose, does Lisa know Leo is the Sultan's great-grandson?'

'I don't think so. We must let Leo decide when and how to tell her. Lisa has much to learn to become a princess. I'm glad he gave her those passports; it will encourage her to work outside Europe, whether or not they marry.'

Leo opened the car door for Lisa when she arrived at the airport, took her in his arms, and kissed her. 'Leo, should a Muslim man be kissing a woman in public? Especially one wearing a headscarf.'

'Absolutely not, but I had to check if kissing you is still the same.'

'Is it?'

'No, far better. Now let's fly.'

'Good morning, Professor.'

'Good morning, Mr Poussin. Doctor Calmette, you brighten my day. Beside me is Giles Smale, who studies the details of Mr Poussin's and your discoveries, and Martin Glover from Antiquaries, whose company restores anything.'

'Now, please tell us how you discovered the Bible.'

Lisa did and put the box with the Bible on the desk. 'The box is only protection; the Bible is in a vacuum pack with a chemical liquid, and that's packed in foam in the box.'

Martin Glover remarked, 'Excellent, that's our usual procedure with fragile artefacts. I know what the liquid is. It will take at least three months before we can hope to read anything. The soaking periods in three different solutions are long.'

The professor replied, 'Whatever it takes. Martin, please call

Giles when that day comes. Doctor, what happened to the instruments in the box?'

'I have photos, but Doctor Darius Kerring, at the Tortola hospital, is trying to create a museum in the hospital lobby. He'll clean and polish the instruments and send the latest photos with any manufacturer's markings. I've said he can use them in his museum.'

'Admirable, I couldn't think of a better solution. What will you do next?'

'Visit Puducherry.'

'Ah, yes, my other contact. What do you hope to find?'

'I'm convinced we have the right man, professor, but we have nothing to prove Raymond is PegLeg. Puducherry was a French enclave captured by the Dutch, and in 1699, after Raymond reached Madagascar, it became French again. I wonder if pirates visited and left traces of a one-legged captain.'

The professor replied, 'I'm impressed again, Doctor. It is possible, even likely. Pirates had booty to sell and couldn't take it to Europe. They sold to a passing ship at a discount or found buyers in ports like Djibouti or the Gulf states. Puducherry would have been attractive. I wish you luck.'

27

'Lisa, how much time do you have before you must leave for Rwanda?'

'Eight days, but I need three to pack and organise everything.'

'Then I'll offer you a three-day cruise on the Norfolk Broads starting now. I rent a cabin cruiser and potter along the waterways, watching the birdlife and eating at various waterside pubs.'

'I would love to, Leo, but I might be miserable company; my period is starting.'

'Lisa, with or without sex, having you with me will be fantastic.'

Lisa smiled, then replied, '*Inshallah.*'

Leo grinned, hesitated, *I'm not supposed to know*, and replied in Arabic, 'Have you been learning Arabic.'

'Yes, Leo, how's my accent?'

'Superb, though Tunisian.'

'Then please speak Arabic for the three days.'

'Then Leo translates as Asad; my mother calls me that.'

Once Leo pushed away from the quayside, they returned, figuratively, to Madagascar. The cockpit was long enough to lie in, and once the sun rose high enough to feel warm, Leo and Lisa lay naked, warmed by the sun, her head on his arm, with the boat in a hidden inlet. They tied up beside a pub at night for dinner and breakfast and ate a salad lunch purchased from stalls beside the pub.

They slept in each other's arms in the forward cabin, unaware that Ashina in Katanga was about to trigger a train of events that would change their lives.

After inspecting the area surrounding Lubumbashi, Ashina devised a plan. First, she needed enough *Praziquantel* to treat a dozen people. There was none available in Lubumbashi, so that evening, she phoned Lisa.

Lisa and Leo had just finished dressing after the second afternoon of sunbathing on the boat, and when her phone rang, it was a WhatsApp call.

'Hi, Ashina, are you calling from Lubum?'

'Yes, I need help. Where are you?'

Lisa pressed the speaker icon. *She might mention orgasms when I say Leo is here, and he can hear without the speaker.*

'I've switched on the speaker, Ashina. I'm on a boat with Leo on the Norfolk Broads in England. We've been to Cambridge to see the history professor about PegLeg. I went to Tortola and found a Bible that might have been his.'

'Wow, that's fantastic, but I thought you were going to Rwanda?'

'In a few days, Ashina. What's your problem.'

'I can't buy *Praziquantel* here. I need, say, twenty tablets for an experiment. I'll pay for them. Where can I buy them? It hasn't changed in Katanga; medicines are extremely expensive or non-existent. I called, hoping you might find some in Brussels.'

'I can try when I return, Ashina, but I think it will be a special order because there's no Bilharzia in Belgium. I'll try the tropical diseases hospital.'

Leo interrupted, 'Ashina, can you WhatsApp your home address to Lisa? I can buy them for you and have them delivered.'

'Thanks, Leo. I've never met you, but I know all about you. You're a star.'

I'll bet she does.

'I'll send it now. Thanks, Lisa, thanks, Leo. Have fun. Bye.'

'Bye, Ashina,' they chorused.

Leo grinned and switched to Arabic, 'Darling, does "have fun" mean she knows?'

'Yes, we're close friends. But where will you buy the pills?'

'From a Muscat medical wholesaler. One of my guys will arrange to send some.'

'Why?'

'Because I like to help and want a happy sailor on board.'

'I suppose you want a kiss in payment?'

'Of course. I shall send a thousand pills, and I want a kiss for each one.'

'How will you arrange transport into Katanga?'

'A courier can hand carry them; he shouldn't have much trouble; a small bribe will work.'

Lisa remembered Tiny. 'Call Tiny Toomah. He'll have someone at the airport to meet him.'

'That's a great idea. I have Tiny's number unless it's changed.'

'I have his girlfriend Lucia's number if it has.'

Lisa's phone pinged. 'I have Ashina's home address.'

'Then SMS Lucia's number and the address to my SMS number while I fetch my Satphone.'

Leo dialled Tiny. The number worked, and Tiny answered, 'Toomah here, who's calling with a Satphone?'

'Hi, Tiny, it's Leo, and I'm with Lisa; she said I must call.'

'*Leo*, what a pleasure. Lisa's a fantastic woman. When will we see you both?'

Leo smiled. 'Probably sooner than you imagine, Tiny. Is Lucia with you?'

'She is. She's dying to speak to Lisa, but why did you call?'

Leo answered, 'I must send a parcel of medicines to Ashina. I was going to send it via courier, but Lisa said I should ask you to send someone to meet him at the airport.'

'Which airport will it leave from?'

'Muscat.'

'Then address the parcel to Lucia Ilunga with her phone number on it and send it by air freight on a direct flight to an address in Dar. My agent there will collect it and send it here, where my guy will collect it. That's a guaranteed delivery. Lucia can send the Dar address to Lisa. Ashina's doing great here, and Lucia can tell Lisa about it. We'll help all we can.'

Leo remembered what Demirci had said about Tanzanian silver and Dar.

'Tiny, thanks. Before I hand the phone to Lisa, do you have any contacts in Dar or Zanzibar who can tell me if a jeweller or silversmith has been in the same place since before 1700?'

'Lisa said you have a silver pirate medallion. Do you want to find who made it?'

'Yes, the silver was mined near Kigoma.'

'Then I'll ask around.'

'Thanks, Tiny, here's Lisa.'

'Hello, Tiny, I'll add my thanks as well.'

'It's a pleasure, Lisa. Here's Lucia.'

Lisa closed the call after a rambling discussion about what had happened since she and Lucia last met, and then a WhatsApp message arrived with an address in Dar.

'Lisa, you surprise me every time.'

'Well, you do, too. Do you think Tiny can find your silversmith?'

'If anyone can, I imagine he will.'

'Then motor to the pub before it's dark.'

Lisa's Arabic improved steadily as her vocabulary expanded. Leo knew the names of the birds in Arabic and gave them to her. Watching the bird's behaviour was an unexpected delight, as Leo lyrically described the activity in classic Arabic.

It pleased Leo when she began using the Omani and Emirati expressions, but her accent remained Tunisian.

On the last day of their short idyll, Leo returned the boat and drove to Cambridge airport, where a chartered aircraft took them to Brussels. He said goodbye to Lisa at the airport as the G650 was waiting.

Rosemary welcomed Lisa home. 'It took four nights to visit islands in the Caribbean; where have you been for the last four?'

'We had a meeting in Cambridge as planned, and then Leo invited me to spend three days on the Norfolk Broads. It was fabulous; it was like being in St. Marie again, and we spoke Arabic the entire time.

'I must now pack; I'll call Mrs de Bakker to confirm the flight to Rwanda.'

When Rosemary told her husband, she added, 'Leo is teaching her to speak Arabic properly. He wants to eliminate any excuses to say no. I hope he succeeds.'

Five days later, Lucia carried a package to Ashina with a content declaration stuck on the outside that read water testing pills. They opened it together and found two plastic bags with hundreds of pills in each. The bags had a skull and crossbones stamp in black, the word POISON in red, and numbers in black marker.

The skull and crossed bones on the packets brought a strange thought. *The pirate medallion that Lisa recovered from Tiny was Leo's. I suppose the skull and crossbones warns others, but is Leo the wholesaler?*

A sheet of paper in the box had a one-sentence instruction, the web address Generics.com, and a password. The instruction was: -

Choose a username, enter the password, follow the instructions, and run the demo.

For two days, Ashina and Lucia ran demos and read menu items.

That evening, Ashina read Lisa's Facebook post, which said she had arrived in Kigali. So she sent an email telling Lisa about her pills and Generics.com.

Lucia returned home late. 'Tiny, I want to start a business.'

'That's a new idea. What business?'

'Ashina needs an agent to import her medicines, and I want to help; I can be the agent; all I need is a thousand dollars and some protection. I won't earn much, but it will do good where needed.'

'Only for Ashina?'

'If you can send a salesperson to pharmacies and the hospitals, I can supply them too. The commission is higher on supplies to pharmacies.'

'I will, Lucia, and then I'll expand your sales all over Katanga and the DRC.'

Lisa read Ashina's email. *Leo wasn't joking. He sent a thousand pills, so I owe him a thousand kisses.*

Then Lucia brought Tiny to visit her medicine store. Afterwards, he told Lucia, 'You'll need a bigger store with bank-type security. I'll see to it.'

That night, Tiny said, 'Look up Generics in the Oman company register.'

'Do you think it's an Oman company?'

'I'm sure it must be.'

'Yes, it's here, the majority shareholder is Soraya bint Rachid Al Said.'

'Look up her name.'

'The Minister of Health for Oman and the Sultan's granddaughter.'

'Leo will need help; he's a pirate. Only a pirate would take on the odds he's up against.'

'Why do you say that, Tiny?'

'The moment I saw the skull and crossed bones on those bags, I thought of Leo, and Leo is Omani. I guess Leo's not only helping Oman to prevent medicine theft but must fight it anywhere. When we have control of the medical supply in the DRC, we'll look at Tanzania and Zambia.'

'Okay, Tiny, but you've promised to ask about silversmiths. Do that first.'

'I'll call Akida tomorrow. I'll tell him it's important.'

Leo had dinner with his crew at the airport, and the wheels left the tarmac on the way to Oman at midnight. He touched down just after midday in Muscat.

After spending the afternoon and evening with his computer team, checking on the progress of his analysis programs, Leo joined his parents for dinner.

He had to listen to his mother recount all the local news before his father could speak.

'Leo, I think your net worth is now greater than mine; how do you manage it with all your other activities?'

'I don't, Dad. My AI programs are smarter than I; I only need to feed them new opportunities, and they take care of it.'

'Could they manage my investments as well?'

'If you duplicate my facilities – yes.'

'What part?'

'All of it, Dad; you'll need another solar panel farm with the power control room, a new underground cave with aircon, and the same computers. Plus, extra aerials in the mountain crater. It should take about two years using only Omani labour.'

'And what about staff?'

'You won't need any; I now have over three hundred employees, although only the nine you know work here. The others are spread worldwide and have never met me or each other except at web conferences. We manage their work from here. The research teams are independent contractors.'

'I suppose they work for different companies as well?'

'Yes, several are Gulf registered, but none in Oman.'

Soraya asked, 'Asad, have you met any girls that interest you?'

'No, Mother, you must wait a few more years to become a grand-mother.'

28

Christmas loomed; Lisa SMSed, and Leo responded.

'Hello, man.'

'Hello, girl, are you visiting your parents for Christmas?'

'I have Christmas and then two weeks off starting on Saturday. I'll be free. How do I uncover the secrets of PegLeg Jon? Do I try Puducherry?'

'Lisa, start by studying some history. I remembered my school history: Zanzibar became an Omani sultanate at about the same time that PegLeg reached Madagascar. Puducherry is three times farther from St. Marie than Zanzibar and even more in the days of sail. There are several ports in Zanzibar; it has been a major trading centre, including the slave trade before 1815, for two millennia. If the pirates had something to sell, they would have tried there, and ports keep records.'

'Right, let me read about it. How do I find an expert?'

'The university is like all the recent ones in Africa; they're either religious or offer programmes that lead to employment in business or industry. There are very few history departments. Find museums and libraries with stores of old documents. There will be several in Stone Town.'

'Will you come?'

'I'm tied up in Oman right now; I'll try to join you in Zanzibar as soon as possible.'

'Will you send your magic carpet?'

'Of course, and a bodyguard named Moustapha, you must speak

Arabic. Call me with the day you want to leave.'

Moustapha impressed Lisa when she met him in the Execujet terminal at nine-thirty on Sunday evening, four days after Christmas. She guessed his age at forty-five, thought his expression severe, and his eyes friendly. He looked like a bodyguard. About a metre ninety, he smoothly glided forward to greet her.

'*As-salaam alykum, Tabiibu.*'

She replied in Arabic. She didn't know Moustapha had specific skills as a bodyguard; he understood and could speak English but had trained to hear the accents of Arab speakers from many countries. Surrounded by a crowd, he could pick out someone who said something with an identifying accent. Forewarned is forearmed. When Lisa replied, he noted her accent was Tunisian.

Eight hours later, Lisa, Moustapha and the crew deplaned in Zanzibar. The pilots went to the airport hotel as they would fly to Oman after a break, and Lisa found the promised greeter with the placard saying:

Serena Hotels, Doctor Calmette.

Lisa's first surprise was when the driver greeted her in Arabic, 'Welcome to Zanzibar, *Tabiibu*. I'm Faraji Suleiman, your driver during your stay.'

His Arabic is like Leo's.

Forty minutes later, Lisa was at the Zanzibar Serena Hotel in a luxurious corner suite with an expansive balcony and a view over the sea. *I should be here on holiday! Why must I work?*

She had insisted Moustapha join her for breakfast, so after washing and changing from her crew uniform, she met him at the restaurant.

'Moustapha, I've listed the museums and libraries I found online. If we visit four to six a day, we should cover them all in the time I have.'

'*Tabiibu*, we must ask at each place for a recommendation of which one on your list might be best. Only a few will have a history dating from the Omani occupation. We should ask for the oldest ones.'

'That's excellent advice. If we have no success in the region of Stone Town, and we have the time, we can try nearer to another port.'

Lisa thought from that conversation onwards that her Arabic was still far from perfect because, at intervals, Moustapha would ask what she meant, giving her an Omani expression or an Omani-accented word. She made rapid progress.

Five days later, a dispirited Lisa, despite lengthy discussions with Moustapha, who she had learnt knew something about everything and much about people, said, 'Moustapha, it's hopeless. The earliest records we have found are 1760.'

'We should not surrender, *Tabiibu*; you suggested other ports. If we ask at the docks or the Malindi fish market, someone will tell us which port the sailing ships visited.'

'That's a great idea. We'll have lunch first; ask Faraji for healthy food.'

Faraji dropped them off and told them to walk up the narrow Stone Town street to find a Lukmaan restaurant. Halfway there, Lisa stopped in front of a small shop. 'Moustapha, the sign says Maritime Museum, but it's not on our list.'

'I see that.'

The open carved wooden door seemed to invite them into a cool interior with a dozen tiny lights illuminating Perspex cases covering model ships. The venerable gentleman who shuffled forward to meet them bowed and asked, 'How can I assist a beautiful woman?'

'Please, tell me what is in these cases?'

As she had spoken in Arabic, he replied, 'Examples of an ancient art, *Sayidati.* Carving or building model replicas of ships began before Muhammad. Mauritius is today's modelling centre, although we have a small workshop and workers from three countries here.'

'Are they all sailing ships?'

'That is the tradition, for they're the most difficult and artistic.'

I'll chance a wild question. 'Do you have an English brigantine called the *Sahm?*'

'I don't; I've never seen that name.' Lisa's hopes plummeted. Then he continued, 'An English ship would have the name *Arrow.* There was once a French ship with the name *Fleche.*'

Lisa's adrenaline soared, and for a moment, she felt dizzy. 'Please tell me where you saw it.'

'I sold a model some years ago. Let me see,' he counted on his fingers, 'about forty years ago.' The adrenaline dropped.

'Was it made here or in Mauritius?'

'Here, at our workshop near Fumba. It was a port for many sailing ships when the monsoon winds blew. If you want a model of that ship, go there and order it. I'll ship it to you in three months.'

'Please give Moustapha the address.'

'Moustapha, if the factory can make a model of *La Fleche,* surely they must have some records of the first one?'

'*Tabiibu,* one can hope.'

'Then we'll have lunch, and Faraji can take us there.'

Despite several bags of sawdust and wood shavings outside, the workshop floor had a thick cushioning layer. The building accommodated an office, a store, and six workspaces. In each, a man sat working at a low table with a growing model in front of him and an array of tools spread around it. The man who came to the door to meet them spoke Arabic, but Lisa was sure he was from further east.

'*Sayidati*, I'm Ahmed Budi. I received a warning about your coming; please enter. Can I offer you coffee or tea?'

'I'll try your coffee.'

'And you, sir?'

'The same.'

After instructing a young boy, he led them to a collection of overstuffed cushions in a corner. 'Please relax while my nephew brings the coffee. The shop said you were interested in a ship called *Fleche*.'

'I am. Do you know if it was of English brigantine design?'

'I'm sorry, I never saw it. It was before my time. We have the record box with the engravings, dies, patterns and jigs so that we can make another. If you order one, I can photograph everything in the box.'

'I'll order one. Moustapha will tell you where to send it. Now, can we see the box and its contents?'

As Ahmed laid down the box, Lisa exclaimed. 'Is that label silver?'

'Yes, these boxes can be hundreds of years old. Tradition is that the modelmaker carves his name with the date on the box top and the model's keel when he uses a box's contents. When the box deteriorates, we replace the wood and add a silver plate for the old names. The last man to make a model from these contents is on the plate with the date; it is 1979.'

Lisa remembered Leo asking Tiny to search for silversmiths. 'Who makes the silver plates?'

'Once, it was a silversmith at the port, but his business closed two hundred years ago. A smith in Stone Town supplied this one. They have modern rolling machines.'

I'll tell Leo.

As Ahmed lifted the items from the box, Lisa realised there were no paper drawings; thin sheets of resin-soaked wood with burn marks, not ink, replaced the drawings. She photographed everything and asked, 'How does a model maker work with these?'

'I can ask one to tell you, but I cannot understand; it is because they know how the pieces they make will fit together.'

'I must photograph the plate; what is the date by the first name?'

'1709. He was Malagasy because his name is Rakotoarimanana.'

'Didn't they keep patterns for the sails?'

'They do now, but in those days, they were meticulous. Look at these waxed blocks. The modelmaker stretched cotton cloth across them and waxed them to hold the shape before cutting them.'

Lisa picked up the largest, turned it over and almost dropped it. 'There's a skull and crossed bones burnt into the wood.'

'We have several pirate ships in the archives. The modelmaker fills that design with paint before stretching the sailcloth over it.'

'Mr Budi, thank you very much; you have provided some valuable information, and I look forward to receiving the model. Will you paint it?'

'The modelmaker decides. Without a photograph or an artist's painting, his idea is all we have.'

'Can I email you if I can identify any extra details?'

'Of course, *Sayidati*. Thank you for your order.'

'Moustapha, at least we haven't failed; that was a piece of luck. We'll return to the hotel; I must send a message.'

Lisa sent the SMS and answered in Arabic when he phoned, 'Hello, man, I've bought you a present.'

She smiled at the silence.

'Hello, girl, I can't guess what it could be.'

'I ordered it today. You'll receive it in three months, a handmade model of *La Fleche* with the pirate flag on the mainsail.'

Lisa thought his voice was hopeful. 'Lisa, I can say nothing except, shall I come and fetch you? Then you can tell me all about it.'

'That depends. Can you propose something better than the Norfolk Broads this time?'

'Are you still at the Serena? And when must you return?'

'Yes, it's convenient for museums, and I should be back in five days; I have a report to submit to the WHO before returning to Rwanda.'

'On the other side of the island, north of Pongwe Beach, there's the Tulia; I'll book a beachside bungalow there for four nights.'

'Leo, are you trying to seduce me again?'

'What do you mean again? You asked, Lisa.'

'That was PegLeg.'

'Then I'll bring him with me. Hold on a second...

'Lisa, can you pack and move to the Tulia? The bungalow will be ready. I'll arrive early tomorrow morning.'

Lisa checked out, and Faraji drove her to the Tulia. After dinner, she sat on the beach watching the stars and the rising moon until she finally went to bed.

Leo arrived before daylight and waved at the receptionist, who recognised him as a bungalow owner. When he reached the bungalow, he undressed on the beach and eased open the door. The smell of ylang-ylang filled his nostrils, and he stopped to savour it.

Lisa's voice was a shock.

With hormone levels climbing as she anticipated Leo's arrival, Lisa had woken an hour earlier, her senses tuned to detect his arrival; she had heard his footsteps, the strash of a heel falling to the sand, the rustle of his shirt, the slither-schlock as his trousers fell, and when he slid open the door, the change of airflow that carried a whiff of his cologne confirmed it was him. After two weeks of speaking Arabic, she continued.

'If you don't climb into bed instead of creeping around like a thief, I'll call security.'

'Won't.'

After a short silence, piqued, Lisa asked, 'Why not?'

'Because I want to sit on the beach and watch the sunrise.'

'Is it better than me?'

'No, but if you watch it with me, it'll signify a new beginning.'

....

Leo backed off the veranda to the sand, then Lisa came out carrying two towels and stepped forward to him. He couldn't see her expression but heard her plead, 'If you kiss me, you can sit on one.'

The clinch and kiss lasted over a minute. Leo heard happiness when Lisa said, 'You've earned a towel; where do we sit?'

'A bit closer to the water where there's more sand and less coral.'

'Take my hand. I've seen the sunrise here once before. I was alone, but it will be our special memory with you beside me.'

....

The moon had set, and the horizon was a faint line between the pitch-black sea and the star-filled sky. With only light zephyrs riffling the sea, the stars reflected like a million tiny twinkles. Reluctantly, the horizon became sharper as the black star-filled curtain began to rise, leaving a yellow-tinged grey that lifted as the line between sea and sky passed from the grey through yellow, rose, and red and then raced towards them across the ocean like a bedspread ripped from the horizon and as the first red tinge reached them, turning the tops of curving wavelets every colour of the rainbow, the first narrow arc of the flaming sun like an inverted saucer announced daylight with a sudden blinding flare. Minutes later, the last of the blood-red orb dragged the sea above the horizon before releasing it to drop back, and the orb began to lose its glorious crimson to orange, then yellows and finally a blinding white.

'Come, Lisa.'

They entered the bungalow, walked through a cool shower, and after a quick rub with towels, Leo pulled the sheet off the bed and lay down with an arm stretched out for Lisa to lie on. She lay on it, and Leo said, 'Come.'

Lisa rolled into his arms....

29

'Leo, must we leave this bed?'

'No, I'll call and ask for breakfast in bed.'

'That will be a waste. The beach pictures are beautiful. It was dark when I reached here.'

'Then breakfast on the beach.'

'In an hour, Leo, you have something to do first.'

'Can I call you my darling yet?'

'No, but we could try – *My love.*'

'Then kiss me, my love...'

When they walked onto the beach, wearing swimming costumes, they found a table, two chairs, an umbrella and a smartly uniformed waiter ready to serve them breakfast.

Lisa told Leo about her investigations, the model, and her conclusion that the first modelmaker, in 1709, had copied the ship in the port. Then she said, 'A Silversmith near the port once made the labels on the boxes. But he stopped ages ago. Has Tiny uncovered anything?'

'He called me two days ago; I think he might have identified the same guy. He said the only information he had to pass on was that the silversmith closed and went to Lamu Island after Mokotini, near Stone Town, replaced the Fumba port. There's a museum there that might be worth a visit.'

'We have four days, can we visit?'

'Let me check the nearest usable runway.'

....

'The runway is good. I'll book a hotel.'

'The Red Pepper House has rooms. The airport is Manda, and the flight time is fifty minutes. We must take a ferry to Lamu Island. The guys must clear our visit and check fuel supplies. Do you have your uniform?'

'Yes.'

'Then, if we leave at four, we can spend a night in the Red Pepper, visit the Museum and fly out that night. Shall we go?'

'Yes, it should be fun, and we still have two days here.'

'I'll call, and then we'll swim.'

'What do I tell Moustapha?'

'Tell him to meet us at the airport.'

She phoned Moustapha, and Leo admired how well she spoke his mother tongue.

They visited the tourist highlights for two days, swam, sunbathed, and made love. Then, they flew to Lamu and took the ferry to the Red Pepper House.

A taxi took them to the Lamu Museum after breakfast. They arrived at nine and had eight hours to search for something that might remind them of Leo's Medallion. Four hours later, Lisa grumbled, 'Leo, I'm hungry; my water bottle is empty, and I don't think we'll find anything. There are hundreds of fascinating items; we should return for three or four days to see everything.'

'Okay, there's a seafood café close by. We'll go there.'

Lisa felt better after large mango fruit juices, a plate of lobster and rice, and a cooling ice cream. When Leo suggested a final two-hour visit, she agreed.

It seemed that Lamu slept the first part of the afternoon, for there were no visitors in front of the entrance, and the doorkeeper was seated beside a cannon under the shade of a tree with a guide they had seen earlier with a school group.

The doorkeeper greeted them in Arabic; Lisa thought he must have heard Leo talking to her. 'Sir, returning so soon is unusual. Do you seek something specific?'

'I do.' Leo took his medallion from under his shirt and explained, 'This medallion was made somewhere on this coast. We tried Zanzibar, and they suggested Lamu. It is ancient, so we look in museums for anything that might give us a clue.'

The guide asked, 'May I look at it?'

'Of course.'

....

'There is a small display in one corner on the upper floor. It has a collection of silver items, including a circular picture frame. There is no picture, but the writing inside the frame resembles this engraving. If you come with me, I'll show you. I'm Ahmed.'

'I'm Leo, and my partner is Lisa; we will be forever grateful if you can show us something.'

Once up the stairs, he led them to a corner where a section of the wall, with a simple table between two tall cabinets, displayed the silver items. Leo saw the frame immediately, about twice the size of his medal, and the carefully painted letters RJC in a black script. He held his medal up and compared the two.

'The script appears the same. This drawing would be the design given to the jeweller who engraved the medal. Thank you very much.'

Lisa was standing to one side. In a breathless, tight voice, she said, 'Leo, that's not all. Step back towards me and look at the side of the cabinet.'

'*Alhamdulillah.* Thank God, that's a drawing of PegLeg Jon!

'Ahmed, can you say where he was when the artist drew it?'

'I don't recognise the quayside. Other paintings in the Museum show the old quay.'

'Can we take a photograph of it and the silver frame?'

'Photographs are not allowed,' Ahmed glanced around. 'But if I turn my back, no one will see you take the photographs.'

He did; both Leo and Lisa took photos, and then they left. Before joining the doorkeeper, Leo took a wad of notes from his pocket and gave four hundred dollars to Ahmed. 'Your help is appreciated.'

'Thank you, Bwana. My wives will be delighted.'

Leo gave the doorkeeper fifty dollars as they left.

I hope he has only one wife.

'Lisa, let's return to the café and summarise what we have learnt.'

'I'll have a pineapple juice. After that excitement, I must visit the ladies.'

Leo had a lime and Lisa's pineapple juice ready when she returned.

'Lisa, look at the picture of PegLeg. I can't tell if the artist exaggerated anything, but he was handsome. The image matches Butterfly Bill's description, with his hair tied back in the seaman style. He lost his lower left leg and knee.'

'It's marvellous, Leo. The background is a quay, and I'll suggest that *La Fleche* visited Fumba in Zanzibar, where the Malagasy artisan made a model of the ship. While PegLeg waited for the silver medallion, an artist drew the picture. What we saw today must have come with the silversmith when he left Zanzibar for Lamu and ended up in the Museum years later.'

'We have another link tying PegLeg to *La Fleche* and my medals. We're also confident he used the silver medal to have bronze and copper coins minted. We must find out where. We must also discover the wreck of *La Fleche*. Although we know PegLeg left Tortola with Kidd, and Raymond was out of the hospital before Kidd left, we still don't have proof that PegLeg and Raymond are the same person. Although we know Raymond and PegLeg were in the Indian Ocean, we know each lost a leg.

'We'll return to the Red Pepper, have dinner, then fly. I'll call the guys for takeoff at eleven. That will mean landing at six in the morning.'

'Will you tell Restolomew?'

'Of course, as soon as I reach home.'

They flew to Brussels; Lisa left the airport in a waiting car, and Leo and Moustapha returned to Oman.

When Lisa reached her parents' house, she made coffee. Her mother rapidly descended the stairs in her dressing gown to the kitchen.

'Hello, Mama.'

'Lisa. What a relief! We haven't heard from you for days, and when I dialled your phone last night, it didn't ring. How are you?'

'I'm fine, Mama; I was flying from Lamu with Leo. He dropped me off an hour ago and left for Oman.'

'What have you been doing? I thought you had gone to Zanzibar for five days.'

'I did, Mama. I must tell you about it later, but we decided to visit Lamu before the return flight. I'll pass out from hunger if I don't have a good breakfast. The flight was seven and a half hours.'

'Then have a shower, and I'll make breakfast.'

'I had a shower on the plane, Mama; I'll take my bag to my room and unpack. After breakfast, I must work on my report.'

Rosemary made Lisa's breakfast and then returned to bed. 'How is Lisa, Rose?'

'Having fun, Gaston, she was with Leo, and she's changed; she doesn't dither anymore, she's brimming with confidence and thinks flying in a private jet with a shower is normal. I'm not sure if that's good or bad.'

'I've sensed it coming, Rose, she's grown up. Mothers must accept that it happens. You should talk to Soraya; from what I've heard at the offices, Leo is considered a rising star in the World Bank. I'm glad they were together; this is the age when they grow apart. We can only hope they don't.'

Leo arrived in Oman that evening and called The Professor's secretary. 'Good morning, Ma'am, Leo Poussin here. When can I have a few words with the professor?'

'He's away for two days, Mr Poussin, at a conference in Cairo. If you can call on Friday at nine-thirty, I'll add it to his appointment list, and he should see it. He'll tell me to alter the time if he can't make it.'

'I can, Ma'am. You can add that it's for a status report.'

I must call Tiny and thank him.

'Hello, Leo. My phone recognises your satellite phone number now.'

'Hi, Tiny, I'm calling to thank you for the silversmith info. Lisa and I went to Lamu, and although there was no silversmith, we went to the museum and found more than we expected. After the business closed, the owner gave the relics to the museum.'

'That's great, Leo, a pleasure. Lucia's doing well, and the Dar transfer hasn't lost a shipment yet. I'm considering whether I should start another business there. Can you suggest how to do it without the agents ripping me off?'

'Tell me when, Tiny, I'll add you as the sponsor for Tanzania, and any order originating in the country will appear on a list you can view.'

'That should do it, Leo.'

'Tiny, if there are changes Lucia or others would like to the website, tell them to use the support menu item, even if it's only asking for a better description of an item under help. The guys who wrote the software are beginning to think they've done a perfect job, and you know that nothing stays the same.'

'You're dead right, Leo. I'll tell Ashina and Lucia. I hope to visit Oman one day and say *Asante Sana* to your mother.'

'I'll tell her, Tiny. Bye.'

'Bye, Leo.'

Two days later, Leo phoned the professor.

'Mr Poussin, I'll put you through.'

'Good morning, Mr Poussin. What startling announcement do you have today.'

'Good morning, Professor. There are only two items. Lisa and I visited Zanzibar and Lamu for several days. She unearthed a company that makes hand-carved replicas of sailing ships; I expect you've seen the kind of model they make.'

'I have one I bought in Mauritius that stands on my mantlepiece. Wonderful work.'

'The Zanzibar artisans copied *La Fleche* in 1709, with the pirate flag on the foresail. So it was in the Fumba port then. She ordered a model.'

'That's marvellous; I hope you will send photos when you receive it.'

'I will, sir. Professor Demirci said my silver medal was likely the die for the foundry that made the other medals and many coins. He said the silver came from Tanzania, and the information I received confirmed there was a silversmith at Fumba, but he closed and went to Lamu when Fumba lost its shipping to the Stone Town port. So we went to see the Lamu Museum. I'll send you photos of a drawing of PegLeg Jon and the proof sketch of the initials on my medal.'

'Mr Poussin, you and Doctor Calmette should be historians; I'm in awe. What will you do now?'

'It will depend on what we can find in the archives, sir. We still need a link between PegLeg and Raymond. Then, to learn Raymond's story and discover what happened to *La Fleche*.'

'Then I shall live in anticipation of your discoveries. Thank you.'

'My pleasure, sir.'

Ten days later, Shuchang came to see Leo. 'Boss, when searching the British Admiralty archives, the AI found a reference to three ships named the *Arrow*. It seems like a chance in a million.'

'Why, Shuchang?'

'The AI's process trace shows three ships were active simultaneously from 1650 to 1750. The AI built crew lists and searched for references to the crew names.

'The bosun on one of the *Arrows*, Thomas Chenoweth, has a reference tag on his name. The AI read the referenced item and red-flagged it. I downloaded the docs and think it's what you want.'

'Shuchang, you do it every time, don't keep me in suspense, what is it?'

'Letters to a girlfriend in Plymouth, England; Thomas was Cornish, I would guess under twenty-five. He wrote the last when in St. Marie in 1711. He mentions the *Arrow*; he might have signed as crew when it had that name, but it had changed to *La Fleche* by 1711, like the model you received.'

'Send me the link.'

30

Item 1847-692. One of twelve letters written by Thomas Chenoweth, bosun of His Majesty's brigantine, The Arrow.

Donated in 1847 to the Admiralty archives by his family – adapted from handwritten English period text.

My Dearest Morwen,

I missed sending last year's letter, for fate struck a heavy blow. We sailed north in June; the winds carried us rapidly to the coast of Arabia, and we anchored in Aden, for the Captain had business there. We stayed for seventy-nine days and sailed in November after we installed two massive cannons amidship with chain shot and loaded a cargo of eleven iron-bound chests; ten were excessively heavy and went in the bilges, but two *eabd* [slaves] carried the larger eleventh to the captain's cabin.

We sailed with a warm wind until the captain ordered a course due south after passing Kilmia with Socotra on the bow.

With the current and the wind favouring our route, I believed we would arrive in St. Marie before Christmas. But fate stepped in.

Our lookouts sighted a Dutch merchantman at dawn on December 19. At first, our captain said we would leave the Dutchman, but when the Dutch ship maintained the same course, although we were rapidly overhauling him from his starboard quarter, our captain, desiring to observe the result from a discharge of chain shot, ordered the preparation of the port cannon. We broke out our flag and observed the consternation of the Dutchman who opened the ports of his six cannons.

The helmsman luffed on command, our cannon fired, and the wildly swinging chain shot, aimed high, brought down the Dutchman's aft sails and cut the mainsail free. Bereft of control, the Dutchman lowered his colours in surrender.

To my great surprise, the captain ordered a change of course instead of engaging with our prize and saluted the Dutch captain as we passed. It was then that I noticed the clouds on the eastern horizon.

Sailing with audacity, using the changing winds of the terrifying storm, I prayed and believed we would prevail, but we knew not where we were, and the blinding rain and screaming wind hid the reef on which our ship foundered. The crew were all on deck as massive waves swept the ship landwards, and all but the ship's cat reached the beach after gripping a spar or broken beam.

After the terrible anger of the great storm abated, we found the carpenter's chest of tools washed ashore as the carpenter said it should if unbreached, for he had sealed it with pitch, and the first thing we did after thanking the Lord was to carve a new leg for the captain.

We cut a road through palm trees to a lagoon in the island's centre, carried all the ship's timber to safety, built a boat, fitted a palm tree as a mast and cut the mainsail to a lateen. We set sail through a southern passage with a boat full of palm nuts and, five days later, sighted land that proved to be Madagascar. We arrived in St. Marie too late for Christmas.

As our captain has no ship, he will command the garrison here, and I shall sign on to the first vessel that can carry me to England. My heart tells me I must be the postman for this letter and your love.

Your loving Thomas.

'Shuchang, I wonder if he married his Morwen?'

'I doubt it; like all ship's boys, he would have left home at twelve or thirteen, and Morwen would be married with three kids by the time he returned – if he reached home. Love dies when people are separated. But exceptions abound.'

Will that be Lisa and me?

Leo rang Lisa. It took half a minute for her to answer.

'Hello, man. Where are you taking me this time?'

'Hello, girl, I wish I were. I'm still planning the tropical island, coconut cocktails and music to suit. My search specialist has discovered letters from the bosun of the *Arrow* to his girlfriend. It's the last of them that tells the story that's important to us. I'll send it to you. Then I'll call the professor and tell him.'

'That's marvellous. Tell me what the professor has to say. I must attend a meeting. Bye.'

'Bye, my love.'

'Good morning, Ma'am, Leo Poussin here. When can I have a few words with the professor? I must tell him what I'm sending.'

'He's presiding at a supervision but should finish in thirty-five minutes. Can you call then?'

'I will do, Ma'am.'

'Good morning, Professor.'

'Good morning, Mr Poussin. Do you need more help, or will you shock me again?'

'The latter, sir, although I never refuse help. I have twelve letters for you; I think you will enjoy reading them. They were written in the early 1700s by the bosun of the *Arrow* to his girlfriend. The one that interests me recounts that after leaving Aden in 1710, the *Arrow* attacked a Dutch merchantman, which I believe was the *Eenhoorn*, as the descriptions match.'

'And the link to PegLeg Jon?'

'Not conclusive, sir, but two things indicate the link.

'The *Eenhoorn* captain described *La Fleche* as a pirate ship, and the Bosun writes that the *Arrow* ran aground in the storm and states the first thing the crew did after thanking the Lord for their lives was to carve a new leg for the captain.'

'Mr Poussin, for a historian, that's more than enough to support a doctoral thesis. Congratulations. What do you expect me to do with the documents you're supplying? Will you author a book or sign up for a doctorate?'

'Neither, sir. If there is sufficient fresh information in the documents for a thesis, please encourage a student to write one. My interest is the truth, nothing more.'

'That's generous in the extreme. What is your next step?'

'I shall attempt to find the foundry that made the medallions I have. Professor Demirci suggested where I could search, and the letter from the bosun mentions heavy cargo and Aden. I shall try there first.'

'Good luck, Mr Poussin.'

Leo didn't consider looking for a foundry; he took photos of the copper medallion and employed an investigator. Mahmoud Al Zaheri, an Emirati from Abu Dhabi, would visit every foundry from Aden to Abu Dhabi and ask one question.

'Did you make this?'

The answer arrived after two weeks. – Shaykh Uthman is a semi-industrial area of Aden; the foundry's name was the Arabic equivalent of *The Melting Pot*.

He asked Mahmoud what the foundry made and learnt they made forged bronze screens with traditional Islamic motifs.

Leo rang Lisa again.

'Hello, man.'

'Hello, girl, I shall arrange a visit to a foundry outside Aden, where they make ornate bronze screens, but the owner says they made my medallions.'

'You must go alone, Leo; I'm bang in the middle of a switch to a new medicine control system.'

I should ask. 'What system is that?'

'It's called Generics. It's marvellous but quite different to what they've done here before. Ashina says you know all about it.'

'I'll tell you if I learn something new, my love. Bye.'

He didn't deny his connection to Generics.

'Bye, Leo.'

Dressed as businesspeople carrying briefcases, Leo, alias Karim Khawar, and Mahmoud Al Zaheri flew to Aden, where Leo had to brush off the approach of a man who asked, 'Taxi, *sayidi*? Where can I take you?'

The arranged driver took them to the foundry, where they examined ornamental screens displayed in a small garden after a ceremonial coffee with the young manager and his aged owner-father. Leo regretted Lisa's absence; the screens were beautiful. For nearly an hour, the young manager described the different methods used to make them, and they watched an employee grinding and polishing a screen with various tools. Then they visited a strongroom to see a screen in silver, a delicate filigree web.

Leo asked, 'The quality is superb, but no more than the designs deserve; who is the artist? He's a genius.'

'My second son, he's young but gifted.'

'Then I shall ask my architect to specify the screens needed and to ask you for designs and manufacture. I have another question: can we retire to your office?'

'We can, sir. I remember the first question asked by Mr Al Zahari; I have further information.'

'Sir, this foundry has kept its records since it began melting metals, and after Mr Al Zahari's visit, I searched for the records about the medallion. The records are in this wooden box. In our dry climate, Ebony wood lasts for centuries. Please examine the contents, but use the silk gloves on the box because the documents are on parchment. I can tell you there is an order, signed by the captain who sailed here, and a delivery note, also signed, that includes two items not on the order: one is a gift, and the other is a chest without mention of the contents. However, a letter from my ancestor, the foundry owner, states he gave it to the captain for delivery to any French ship.'

The order made Leo's heart turn somersaults; the signature in a flowing French ecclesiastical script was:

Raymond Jean Calmel

The delivery note, signed similarly, listed four cases of bronze and six cases of copper coins, each weighing twelve hundred *Ūqiyah*. Leo knew his Arabic measure and read it as a hundred and fifty kilograms.

Then, a gift box with three medallions.

And one captain's chest for onward delivery to any French ship.

The letter was intriguing.

> My father, Moustapha el Haddad, may Allah guard his spirit, received a chest in 1699 for sale as payment for the rudder pintles and chains supplied to repair the boat *Alyaesub*. I, Suleiman el Moustapha, a *mu'min* fearing the contents of such a chest from a ship of *kefirs*, give this chest to the captain of the *Sahm* and ask him to give it to any *Fransiun* vessel. I leave this account as proof that I have passed on the chest and its contents, as my father promised to any suitable person who passed.

Leo noted the ships *Alyaesub* and *Sahm* were literal Arabic. *Sahm* could mean *Arrow* or *Fleche*, and *Alyaesub* mean *Dragonfly* or *Libellule*.

'Thank you. The signature is the proof of something I needed. May I photograph the order, delivery note and letter?'

'Of course.'

After taking the photographs, Leo asked, 'Sir, can you show me where you store your archives?'

'The rooms are dusty, as most records have remained untouched for centuries.'

'I don't mind some dust.'

'I'm amazed; historians will adore your archives. Would you agree to an offer by a university to examine every item, record and classify them? After they finish, they will place them in a museum here in Aden for others to visit.'

'I feel sure that will please my ancestors.'

'Then I'll suggest it at a university. Can I take a photograph here?'

'Please do.'

On returning to Oman, Leo emailed Professor Restolomew and included the photos.

> Dear Professor,
> I appreciate your support in obtaining help from Professor Demirci; he provided critical information and narrowed down the area where I could find the foundry that made my coins. It is in Aden, and they have a treasure trove of archives that would bring a historian to tears. The photos are attached. The owner supplied the other items photographed and has advanced my search for the story of PegLeg Jon.
> The foundry owner will accept a university research programme to digitise and classify his archives and store them in a museum in Aden. Universities in the Gulf do not have history programmes, although Muscat University could be encouraged to begin one. The Minister of Culture and Tourism is a keen supporter. Witness an archaeological expedition last year to uncover vestiges along the Frankincense trail. However, before discussing the idea with others, I felt I should tell you.
>
> Regards,
> Leo Poussin.

Then, he sent copies to Lisa.

Lisa sent an SMS, and her phone rang minutes later.

'Hello, man, that's marvellous news about Raymond, but I have a problem and need help.'

'Hello, my love. Tell me about it.'

'I thought it would be marvellous, but this new medicine control system will likely fail. I called Ashina, and she has Tiny Toomah protecting her imports. I have no one; the thieves may throw away what they steal but will continue until I surrender.'

'Then I'll come and help.'

'What can you do?'

'They'll listen to the World Bank, Lisa; I'll don that hat and talk to the Minister of Finance. I'll take you with me so you will have met him if you need to ask for anything else.'

'You've made me feel confident again. I'll send you the address of my apartment.'

'Send it now, Lisa; I'll ask for an appointment and tell you my arrival time. Bye, my love.'

'Bye, Leo.'

Leo stepped out of a taxi two days later with an overnight bag. Lisa opened the door when he rang, and moments later, he pushed the door closed with a foot when he took her in his arms, and a minute later, she said, 'Leo, we can't stand here all night.'

'I don't intend to. Are we going out for dinner?'

'Maybe we should; I'm still learning to cook something other than student meals. I bought steaks, oven fries, and peas. Will that do? The steaks are Halal.'

'That's a lot better than my student efforts. I can heat a Pizza.'

'Then put your bag in the bedroom, and I'll switch on the oven for the fries.'

Leo removed a bottle from his bag. 'Here's a bottle of your favourite wine.'

'I don't have a favourite,' then she looked at the bottle he handed her. '*Calmel and Joseph!* Where did you find this?'

'I bought a stock from their winery. When I told them you were a relative, they gave me two cases for free. Bring two wine glasses while I open the bottle. We'll taste it.'

'Lisa, my love, we have a meeting tomorrow at ten. You must tell me the details.'

'I will, but when I saw the order, delivery note and letter, I wished I had been there. How did you feel when you read those documents?'

'Enormous relief and excitement. And you?'

'Amazement, I've been wearing PegLeg's medallion for years and feel closer to him now. It might explain my pirate dreams. But what was in the chest?'

'I don't know. PegLeg must have thought it valuable to have it placed in his cabin. We know that Thomas Chenoweth wrote that two men carried it, so I would guess the weight was under one hundred and twenty kilograms. If we knew its size, I could guess the weight of the contents after allowing for the chest and iron straps. As the foundry owner specified a French ship, I suggest stolen church symbols like chalices or candlesticks, but not gold, perhaps gold plated, for gold would be heavy. Guessing is a waste of time when you have a more pressing problem.

'Tell me about it, Lisa.'

'I lost a shipment. It was only a shoebox-size, but I must order it again, and the clearing agent won't pay. He says it is the courier. The thief will have thrown it away, but once they realise that those shipments cause their income loss, they'll steal all of them until I stop.'

'I'll consider what I say to the Minister tomorrow, but don't worry; we'll find a solution.'

'I hope so. The oven is hot. I'll do the fries; I know you like rare steak, then we'll eat.'

After the meal, Lisa insisted, 'You use the bathroom first while I wash up.'

....

31

'Good morning, Mr Poussin. It's a pleasure to meet you again.'

'Good morning, Minister, this is Doctor Calmette; a gorilla introduced us to each other.'

The Minister laughed. 'I know, a unique introduction. Doctor, we haven't met, but I know what you're doing in Rwanda, and successfully, I hear.'

'Thank you, Minister, I'm doing my best.'

'Mr Poussin, what is the problem you wish to discuss?'

'The clinic project is progressing well; it's within the budget so far, and I hope that continues. If not, the road project may not receive the hoped-for funding. Doctor Calmette told me she fears that medicine costs may exceed the budget due to theft.'

'Doctor Calmette, what makes you believe that?'

'Minister, the customs officer, the clearing agent, or the courier from the airport to the hospital stole a small medical shipment last week. The shipper sent me a copy of the signed receipt as it left the aircraft. I must now order again, doubling the cost of those medicines.'

'Was it expensive?'

'Fortunately, no.'

Leo intervened. 'Minister, the project budget for medicines is six million dollars annually, and the re-order may also disappear, so the possible overrun is significant.'

'Then it's serious. Do you have a suggestion?'

'I do, sir. The shipper will send all packages addressed to a police or army office at the airport, and they will deliver them to the main hospital. If the police or army loses a shipment between an aircraft and the hospital, the police or the military will pay the loss from their budget; the respective Ministers must take that responsibility. Leaving the integrity of the clinic project unaffected.'

'I like that solution, but I must discuss it with the President. Doctor Calmette, is changing the delivery address a problem?'

'No, sir, a five-minute task.'

'Then don't order again until I give you an address.'

'Thank you, sir.'

'I have heard you have a Rwandan passport because our Gorilla Doctor requested one for his fiancée. Have you fixed a wedding date?'

'Not yet, sir. I need to concentrate on the clinic startup. Once it's running, I'll have the time to choose a date.'

'Then I shall make sure you have the support you need. Thank you both for coming. Mr Poussin, I shall try to see the president tomorrow; he may wish to meet you again.'

'Then I shall wait for two days, sir.'

'Thank you.' He smiled broadly. 'Goodbye, Doctors.'

The president didn't request a meeting, but Lisa received an army address at the airport.

Leo left for London and the LSE.

'[*Shuchang requests a conference call. Click here to begin*]' popped up on Leo's screen.

'Hello, boss, I have a new lead. One of our team members found something in the French Naval data. She deserves a bonus.

'The crew list for the *Vengeance* shows Raymond as the doctor, but it wasn't his first ship. The *Glorieuse*, a vessel under repair, had a staff list including Raymond as Chaplain. He served in this post for several months, and another search of the paymaster's records shows the navy paid his salary, at his request, to his mother, Madame Sylvie Calmel; her address was a farm in Normandy, in the St Malo area, and the farm still exists.'

'How would Raymond live with no income?'

'As a priest and a doctor, while his ship remained in the docks, he could easily earn enough from the occasional confession or minor treatment.'

'Who owns the farm now?'

'We're four years too late to talk to the remaining Calmel. He had no descendants, so the executors sold the farm, and the proceeds went to the local church.'

'I wonder if he had a guilty conscience?'

'We'll never know.'

'Give the lady a bonus, Shuchang; I might visit the farm to ask if they know anything or if there are any relics.'

Leo rang Lisa.

'Hello, man. Will you whisk me away on your magic carpet to romantic places again?'

'Hello, my love. I'll whisk you away whenever and wherever you wish, but it's not romantic this time. A woman working for me has found data in the French Naval archives. Raymond's mother lived on a farm not far from St Malo.

'I'm about to call Restolomew to tell him because he called to tell me the Bible preservation is complete and invited us to visit.

'They will open the Bible shortly. He sent me a surprising cover photo. The text says in gold:'

> For my dearest friend and everlasting love, Raymond Calmel, with all my heart, Florimond.

'That's a male name, Leo. Do you think they were gay?'

'We must accept it's possible. We know the church, with its ban on sex and marriage, was no stranger to gay activity. And then sailors, with no female contact for months, were known to indulge. The high ranks had young cabin boys aboard, whom the sailors called bum boys.

'Can you come to Cambridge?'

'I can take a Friday off, but I'm in Rwanda.'

'I'll tell the captain to slow down so you have a good night's sleep. You can fly on Thursday evening. I'll meet you in Cambridge.'

'Tell me which Thursday.'

Leo was waiting on the parking bay apron as the G650 carrying Lisa stopped.

'*Marhaba, habib albi.*'

'Leo, that feels more than *my love* that we agreed on.'

'It's the usual translation, but since the days of Scheherazade, Arabs have perfected the caress in those words.'

'I'll accept that; it sounds more poetic than *my love.*'

'How was the flight?'

'Super smooth, we were high, and I slept well. Joe will bring my bag to the terminal. Where are we having breakfast?'

'Fitzbillies. For those who overeat, reaching Queens College is a short stagger.'

'Good morning, Professor.'

'Good morning, Doctor Calmette. Mr Poussin, are you now a doctor?'

'I am, sir. We have discussed the possibility that Raymond was gay, with mixed opinions. What further information have you uncovered from the Bible?'

'First, my congratulations on your doctorate.'

'Thank you, Professor.'

Restolomew continued, 'As expected; it is French, the Port Royal version, so Raymond receiving one as a gift corresponds to the period. The Port Royal translation was published in instalments and finally finished in 1696. They were, however, expensive, and only the aristocracy could afford to buy gold leaf hand-printed covers. That suggests Florimond was an aristocrat. The information from Brest you sent me says Raymond's farm was in a county called *La Vicomte sur Rance*, at the inland end of the St Malo estuary. The name *La Ferme des Ronces Rouges* suggests it was close to the estuary and once supplied red reeds, commonly used for roofing.

'The *Chateau de la Bellière* is nearby. It has a chapel and several graves, and the French digital grave records mention one at the *Chateau*, Florimond Etienne, 1680-1722.

'There is a handwritten note on the Bible's first blank page; it was hard to decipher, but this is what the expert has sent.'

> Florimond will never be mine; I leave my mother with a heavy heart, though with pride that I exacted the ownership of our farm as payment for my departure to foreign lands. I go with nought, but I shall care for Florimond's gift as I would have cared for him.

'That's conclusive, Professor. Lisa or I will visit the farm to be sure we haven't missed something.'

'Lisa, will you come with me to the farm? You're a far better detective than I am.'

'I will, Leo, if we fix a date. I'm due for a break at Easter.'

'Then we'll make it Easter. I'll make the arrangements.'

Leo parked their rental car at the gate with the *La Ferme des Ronces Rouges* sign. Their feet stayed dry as they walked thirty metres to the farmhouse door, stepping from flagstone to flagstone. Lisa remarked, 'This is a picture postcard farmhouse.'

'It is; I hope there's someone in. We should have brought boots to walk around to the barn.' Leo knocked, and after a short pause, they heard footsteps.

When the door opened, a plump, rosy-faced woman smiled at them. '*Bonjour*, can I help you?'

Lisa replied, '*Madame*, I'm Elisabeth Calmette. The previous owner of this farm was a relative. As we were in the area, I came to ask if there was anything that Jean Calmel left behind when he died.'

'I must disappoint you; there was nothing. When we received the keys, the house and barn were empty.'

'So, who removed the furniture?'

'I don't know. The *Notaire* who sold the farm to my husband must have ordered it.'

'Then we shall see him; what is his name?'

'Damien de Vedrine, his *etude* is in the town.'

'Thank you, Madame. Your farm is so beautiful, many must stop to photograph it.'

'Thank you, many do.'

'There, Lisa, across the road, that office building has a brass plate beside the door.'

The receptionist in a tiny room with three chairs and her desk looked up as they entered. '*Bonjour, Monsieur-Dame*. Can I help?'

Leo smiled and replied, 'I hope so. We're passing through and would like to ask *Maître* de Vedrine a question about the passing of Jean Calmel four years ago.'

'I'm sorry, but you must make an appointment.'

Lisa added a plea, 'I'm a relative of *Monsieur* Calmel, and we're travelling to Nantes. Is it possible to have a few minutes sometime today?'

'I don't believe so, but I shall ask *Maître*.'

She stood and walked down a corridor.

A minute later, she returned. 'If you come before closing at four, you may wait for *Maître* to finish with his last client, and then he'll grant you a few minutes.'

'Thank you very much. We shall be here.'

Once outside, Lisa declared, 'That's the Town Hall opposite; let's ask for the best restaurant in town for lunch. The seafood here must be super.'

The wait after the secretary left at four was only fifteen minutes, and then *Maître* de Vedrine showed a client out and invited them into his office. Lisa thought that if the *maître* wore a beret and carried a long loaf of French bread, he would be an archetypical Breton.

Leo introduced himself and Lisa, and then she asked, '*Maître*, Jean Calmel was a relative of mine, a distant cousin. As we were passing, I decided to look at his farm and found it exceptionally beautiful. The current owner says that when they bought it, there was nothing there. I assume your *etude* sold everything.'

'I did; he required the sale under the terms of his will, and the money was bequeathed to the Sisters of Charity, so nothing remains. Except, of course, his will and the associated documents we must store for ten years.'

'Can I see his will?'

'*Bien sur*, it is now in the public records, but I'll fetch it for you.'

....

'*Maître*, what is this item in his will?'

'Which one?'

Lisa read it. 'I order my executors to keep the casket of my ancestor for twenty-five years at the charge of my estate, then hand it to the Sisters of Charity unless claimed by a family member.'

'I'd forgotten about that. We must have the casket somewhere, but unless you can prove you're a family member, I cannot give it to you. I'll fetch it for you to see.'

....

The ornately carved casket with an oversized lock had a small envelope taped to the top that partially covered some letters. Excited to see the first letter, Lisa asked, '*Maître*, can you remove the envelope? There are initials carved into the top.'

'There are two lines of initials and a heart between them. I suppose they're from a family member and his wife or girlfriend.'

Lisa answered, 'The first is F E B for Florimond Etienne Bellière; his tombstone is in the Chateau de la Bellière cemetery. The second is R J C for Raymond Jean Calmel. They were lovers, and Florimond's family drove Raymond out of France but paid for him to leave by giving the farm to his parents. The casket's contents may be letters from Raymond to Florimond, and if he sent any after he left, they may reveal what happened to him.'

Surprised by what she said, the notary asked, 'Doctor Calmette, tell me of your relationship to the Calmel family.'

'*Maître*, the first Calmels were two brothers from England in the 1100s, after Normandy conquered England; our DNA is Scottish Gaelic. One came to Calais; the other continued to Languedoc, where the name is common. The Calais branch split over the years, with one man moving to the farm here and others moving to Dunkirk, where they eventually found themselves in the Spanish

Netherlands, which became Belgium. They changed their name to Calmette to avoid persecution by the Spanish Inquisition, as the Calmels were not Catholics. Raymond Calmel had no children, but his brothers did, and they descended from the same English Calmel immigrant as I did.'

'Doctor Calmette, that history is too complex to be a fabrication. I believe you; I'll ask you to sign a receipt.'

Lisa signed, and the lawyer said, 'I hope you find some useful information; I'll add something. To sell the farm, I had to prove ownership. Searching the records back to 1695 was a complex process, but I found the record in the Bellière county register signed by the *Vicomte*, ceding ownership of the farm to Pierre Calmel. The register is now in the publicly available records of land transfers. Your statement on why he did it proved your association with the family.'

After thanking the *Maître*, Leo and Lisa left carrying the casket carefully. 'Lisa, what do we do now?'

'I can't wait to read what's in the casket, find us a hotel in St Malo.'

'Dinard is better; I'll try the Castelbrac.'

The Castelbrac had a room, and an hour later, they had a room key.

'Leo, I can feel the casket key in the envelope; open the casket.'

....

'I can't. It's glued closed with sealing wax.'

'Can't you break it?'

'No, I'll ask the hotel for a gas lighter and a knife; if I warm the wax, I can scrape it off.'

....

'Hold the box, Lisa; I need two hands to warm and scrape.'

....

'That's one side done ...

'Hold tight, I'll see if I can break the remaining seal; it's thin.

'It's coming ... there.'

Leo lifted the lid. 'There are letters tied in bundles with ribbons. Please don't touch them, Lisa; they may fall apart. There's a loose one on top.'

'Can you photograph that one?'

'Yes ... I've sent it to your phone.'

'Leo, can you read it?'

'Sort of, it's in Norman French, so I'll have to guess some words.'

'Then read it to me.'

> Knowing that my brother Raymond must have died, I
> will place this notice and Raymond's letters in his

casket according to his instructions before sealing the box.

Driven by bigotry to leave our Patrie, Raymond could but write to our mother to tell of his travels. Some, intended for Florimond, remain undelivered due to the danger of doing so, and then Florimond died. My Mother, consumed by her love for Raymond, has read Raymond's letters to Florimond at Florimond's grave; in so doing, she has received consolation. This casket will remain here at our farm until no Calmel lives here.

Signed.
Jean Louis Calmel 1736.

The enormity of the find brought a deafening silence until Leo said, 'Lisa, we must take this to Professor Restolomew.'

'I agree. It needs preservation. Can you call the professor?'

'It's too late to call today. I'll reseal it with tape and put it in the hotel safe during dinner.'

'Leo, I've figured out why the Normans aren't fat. They would be enormous from the butter and cream, but they counter that by stuffing themselves with enormous basins of mussels or oysters.'

'True, and they speed up the digestion with glasses of the apple brandy they call calvados.'

'But the seafood is superb.'

'It comes straight off boats a hundred metres away.'

'Talking of boats, Leo, can't we find the island where the *Arrow* sank?'

'There are thousands of reefs. If Raymond wrote a letter to his family, it might mention something that would give us a clue. That's worth trying first.

'The alternative is to ask the Cambridge Digital Technology Group for help.'

'What can they do?'

'Model a cyclone in the Indian Ocean based on our few facts, and suggest an island. The problem is a complex variation of a simple navigation technique. Draw three straight lines that cross each other. The answer is the centre of the formed triangle. But our lines aren't straight. Also, they're moving, so the answer is lines of equal probability.'

'I'm glad I learnt some math; that's like epidemics, chasing a moving target. I hope the professor can see us tomorrow.'

Leo phoned after breakfast. 'Good morning, Ma'am, Leo Poussin here. Can you tell Professor Restolomew that Doctor Calmette has found another casket requiring preservation, and we want an appointment to deliver it?'

'Hold on, Dr Poussin...'

'The Professor says any time after three-thirty this afternoon. What time will suit you?'

'We'll be there at three-thirty, Ma'am. Goodbye.'

'Goodbye, Dr Poussin.'

'Leo, if we're going to Cambridge, can you make an appointment with your Cambridge Digital Technology Group? Maybe we won't need to wait for Raymond's letters.'

'Okay, I'll try. I'll tell them we are visiting Restolomew.'

'I'll call Salim, takeoff at ten for Cambridge.'

'How long is the flight?'

'Forty-five minutes.'

'There's an hour time difference. If takeoff is at two-thirty, we have enough time for a walk around historic St Malo and a plate of mixed seafood for lunch. Salim can collect our bags and take them to the plane.'

Leo grinned. 'You're enjoying this, aren't you?'

'I am. I never realised how much fun you can have with a magic carpet.'

And I'm learning how much fun it is to be with Lisa.

'Good afternoon, Professor.'

'Dr Poussin, Dr Calmette, you have me on tenterhooks. I couldn't concentrate this morning. Giles is hopping from one foot to another, and Martin is praying you haven't damaged anything. What have you discovered?'

'It's Lisa's discovery. We went to Calmel's farm inland from St Malo.'

Lisa told the story to an audience sitting on the edge of their seats...

'So, Leo removed the wax sealing and opened the box at our hotel.'

Martin Glover looked anguished. 'How did you do that?' Then he sighed with relief as Leo replied, 'I heated the sealant with a small gas flame and scraped away the softened wax. When the wax was thin enough, the join failed easily.'

Lisa continued, 'When Leo opened it, we saw packets of letters tied with ribbons and a single sheet of paper with writing. We photographed that without a flash, then closed and sealed the box with tape.'

Leo took three copies of the photograph and handed them to the three men. 'This may be difficult to read, but it explains everything.'

Silence followed as the three read. The professor was the first to finish. 'Stupendous, utterly amazing. I don't know what the letters will say, but a first-hand account of events in the late seventeenth and early eighteenth centuries is an incredible find. Where's the casket?'

Leo lifted the cardboard foam-filled box with the casket inside and gave it to Martin. 'Here, I'm glad you now have the responsibility.'

'Three or four months of it until I have recorded all the letters for posterity. What will I do with the casket afterwards?'

Lisa answered, 'Legally, as I signed the receipt for the box, they're mine. I want them back, intact, in the casket; I'll decide then. The casket and some letters I might hand over to the Museum in Tortola, the love letters, I'm not sure.'

'Doctor,' said the Professor, 'I suggest Martin preserves everything, but you leave that decision to later. Once Giles has all the information, I'll authorise a historical paper that covers your discoveries; you will both be co-signatories. I suspect the letters, and even one or two love letters, will feature boldly in such a treatise; that will be your decision.'

Lisa agreed, and the professor said, 'I'll ask that question again: what will you do next?'

'Find the wreck of the *Arrow*, professor, and recover its cargo.'

'An impossible task, except for you two.'

'We have an appointment with Professor Johanneson at the Cambridge Digital Technology Group this afternoon. It's a long shot, but with computer modelling of the weather and the few facts we know, I hope he can indicate the reefs that might have sunk the *Arrow*.'

'Johanneson's team are excellent. I'm sure he'll have an answer for you. I wish you luck. Thank you.'

Lisa thought Professor Johanneson looked like his accent. His accent was Swedish, although he had been born in Iceland. Years at Stockholm University had taken the harshness from his speech and added words from other European languages. Love of the sea, unavoidable for those born in Iceland, had guided his career. Taller than average, with long, red-tinted blonde hair almost to his shoulders, his pale skin and blue eyes completed Lisa's image of a Viking.

Leo introduced Lisa. 'Good afternoon, Professor Johanneson; it's good of you to see me. With me is Doctor Calmette, who is partnering with me in my investigation.'

'Good afternoon, Doctor Poussin, Doctor Calmette. I could hardly refuse your call this morning; after I mentioned at a staff meeting that a mathematics graduate had asked for a meeting, Professor Restolomew said I would regret refusing and wished you had studied history.'

'That's kind of him, sir. We're still researching and want to know if anyone in your group can propose the probable track of an Indian Ocean Cyclone experienced by two ships in mid-December 1710.'

'My God, Restolomew was right; what a question! What do you know about it?'

'Several things, sir.'

'Let me call Tim Barker; he's a cyclone expert.'

'Tim, this is Dr Poussin and his colleague, Doctor Calmette. They have a fascinating question to solve. Go ahead, Dr Poussin, let's have your data.'

'There was a ship in the Indian Ocean a few days before Christmas in 1710. The captain's report stated their position was on the same latitude as Aldabra, longitude unknown, but he expected to reach Aldabra for Christmas. The ship spotted a cyclone cloud bank to the east, and without sails, the vessel foundered on Aldabra before the cyclone passed. Where on Aldabra, I don't know.'

'What kind of ship?'

'A Dutch Fluyt design, heavily loaded.'

'We can calculate a speed and drift. Those cyclones are clockwise and track plus or minus southwest at ten to twenty knots; we can program that, but assuming a range of central pressures and speeds, we'll have a large area where the cyclone centre could be. But why do you want to know this?'

'I don't, but I can also say that an English brigantine, the *Arrow*, was at the same spot as the Dutchman when they saw the cyclone. It tried to outrun the hurricane, beginning with a northwest heading. It ended on the reefs of an unknown island. I want to know what island.

'Have you looked at possibilities?'

'Yes, ruling out Aldabra, there's Assomption to the south, Cosmoledo directly east of Assomption, and Astove south-southeast of Cosmoledo.'

'No others?'

'The Seychelles outer islands are too far east, the Comoros population was significant, and the survivors reached Madagascar after sailing south for five days in an open boat with a lateen rig. They would have known little about currents. It must be one of those three islands, but which is the most likely? Searching for underwater remains, even with a magnetometer, can take years.'

'Are you treasure hunting?'

'No, sir, unless you consider copper coins of historical value to be treasure. We promised them to Professor Restolomew and Professor Demirci in Türkiye. Our interest is personal and historical; the captain of the *Arrow* was Lisa's distant cousin.'

'I'm amazed! However, Tim can program everything you've given us and try to find the answer. The cyclone would first carry the Dutch ship south-west, then, once in the main flux, north-west, even north. I would guess the south coast of Aldabra. The other, sailing northwest, might have maintained the latitude until forced to alter course to follow a circle, continuously altering course to starboard; a northwest coast is the most likely. The survivors' voyage is vague because we have no idea where they might have landed in Madagascar. Still, after considering currents and possible winds, data on a lateen-rigged boat might eliminate one of those islands. It'll take a few days to obtain the performance data on the vessels, and Tim can call you.'

'Thanks, sir, thanks, Tim.'

'Leo, I must return to Rwanda.'

'Me too, Lisa, I must see the finance minister about some budget items.'

'I'll be working, Leo.'

Leo grinned. 'Me too, but not at night, my darling, and only for two days. Do you want to visit your parents first?'

'I should, if your carpet can take me to Brussels, I can stay two days with them.'

'That works well. I'll then fly to Rostock in Germany. They have the sonar, and I must buy it now that we might be hunting for underwater treasure.'

After the plane levelled off en route to Kigali, Leo came to sit with Lisa. 'How are your folks?'

'I think they're missing me. I told them to come to Rwanda and visit whenever they wish.'

'That's good. You can explain what you're doing. I'm sure your parents will be interested.'

'Leo, what will we do if Cyclone Tim gives us a place to search?'

'I looked up the activity in the area. It's a top fishing spot for Giant Trevally. The season is November to April, which restricts us to the off-season. We must make two trips. The first will be reconnaissance to identify the exact spot and learn what equipment we need. If possible, I'd like to do that before November.'

'Will you update me on what you will arrange? You can call any evening after seven.'

That's a radical change from 'Don't call me unless you have something to report about PegLeg.'

'Of course, my love.' Leo grinned. 'Will the cabin attendant make coffee for the pilots?'

Tim sent an SMS the evening before Leo left Kigali.

> There's only one place that fits both ships and the sur-vivors – the northwest corner of Cosmoledo.

'That gives us all we need, Lisa. I need an ultralight seaplane, a magnetometer, and the means to reach the island. I'll work on it when I land in Oman. Now, how about wishing your diving buddy a warm goodnight?'

'I can't.'

'Why?'

'For lunar reasons.'

'Oh... then a warm cuddle.'

Leo bought the slowest seaplane he could find, a two-seater ultralight on inflatable floats with a hook to hang it from a crane. He purchased a magnetometer, ordered brackets to attach it to the floatplane, then dismantled, boxed and shipped everything to Durban, South Africa.

Lisa SMSed.

> Watch Al Jazeera News.

He did, then dialled her number.

'Hello, man. Have you watched the news?'

'Hello, girl. Yes, but why are you watching Al Jazeera, and what should I look for?'

'The local TV speaks *Kinyarwanda,* and I'm practising Arabic. There was an announcement about pirates. It'll come again, then you can call me.'

> Al Jazeera news.
> Yesterday at 06:15 Oman time, pirates captured a cargo ship passing three hundred kilometres off the coast of Oman en route from the Red Sea to Bombay. The boat has changed course, and authorities suspect its destination is a Somali Port. Details on the ship and its cargo will follow.

'Hello, man. Did you hear it?'

'Yes, it's a problem. I won't take you where there's a risk of capture by pirates.'

'I can't stop you, but I'll say we would be stupid to go without a naval escort.'

'That would require political approval and clearances and create other problems.'

'With thousands of satellites in the sky, why don't the navies know about every pirate ship?'

'I don't know, Lisa. I'll ask the experts and call you back in a day or two.'

Shuchang had the information three days later.

'Boss, the satellites have two methods for identifying ships –from the AIS signals they transmit, position, ID, heading and speed, and the other is a photo, and that's all there is when the pirates switch off their AIS.'

'Why isn't the photo enough?'

'I checked Landsat 9. It's seven hundred kilometres up in a ninety-nine-minute polar orbit, and the size of the photo it takes covers a patch of the earth one hundred by one hundred nautical miles. That calculates to sixteen days before a second pass at the same spot. A ship seen on a pass will have disappeared.'

'That makes it useless for identification, but if it sees a ship and there is no AIS signal, then it should be investigated.'

'That's another problem. It doesn't see a ship; it takes a photo and transmits a bundle of data that someone on the ground must look at and match with an AIS map. By the time that happened, the pirate ship would be miles away.'

'Well, that explains why satellites are no good. Let me think about it.'

I told Lisa I would tell her.

She answered his call, 'Hello, man, what have you learnt?'

'Hello, girl. No satellites can see ships that don't transmit an identity, and the pirates switch off their transmitter.'

'Why?'

'The low-level satellites can take sixteen days to cover the Earth's surface, and the geosynchronous ones are so far away that the photos aren't much good, and they don't receive the ship's ID transmissions.'

'Is there nothing you can do?'

'I'm thinking about it, Lisa; I'll tell you if I find a solution.'

'If you can't, Leo, buy a battleship.'

'That would solve the problem but bring on many more.'

'Leo, you don't have to find all the pirate ships in the world, only those within range of us.'

'Lisa, you're a genius. I'll approach the problem from that view. Bye.'

'Bye, Leo.'

He immediately asked Shuchang, 'What's a ship's radar range?'

'About fifty miles. A ship could identify another following it using radar. Without AIS on the other ship, with the right software, radar could tell you if the other ship was on a collision course.'

'So I wouldn't know a pirate was on my tail until he was less than fifty miles away. What speed would they likely do?'

'There are reports that their high-speed skiffs can do forty-five knots. They could catch a twenty-knot ship in two hours if they launched from a mother ship at the radar limit, but they would launch at twenty-five miles, which takes an hour.'

'Shit.'

'Shuchang, the low orbit satellites all have specific tasks, but our Oman satellite is geostationary and over the equator. It has a camera that photographs Oman with zoom and GPS positioning; I've seen the photographs. Can you experiment and see what quality picture is possible at full zoom?'

'If you can obtain permission and access codes, I will. How small a picture do you imagine?'

'A two-hundred-mile circle. Double the radar range. Those skiffs can't have four hours of fuel at top speed.'

'Boss, a two-hundred-mile diameter image is possible.'

'Great, Shuchang, what's the resolution?'

'About sixty metres.'

'That's no good. Can multiple overlaid images give better resolution?'

'I can try.'

'The resolution is about four metres with overlays, but transmission is slow. I can upload an AI that identifies anomalies and only sends them.'

'That's brilliant, Shuchang.'

'If you can authorise some experiments, boss, maybe we can do something worthwhile to avoid the pirates, but they're wily bastards and can hide behind islands. I recommend some firepower in reserve.'

I'll tell Lisa we can go.

'Hello, man, what can you tell me?'

'I have a solution, Lisa, thanks to you. It will take my IT guys about a month to complete the software and update the Oman satellite. We might manage the first inspection after all.'

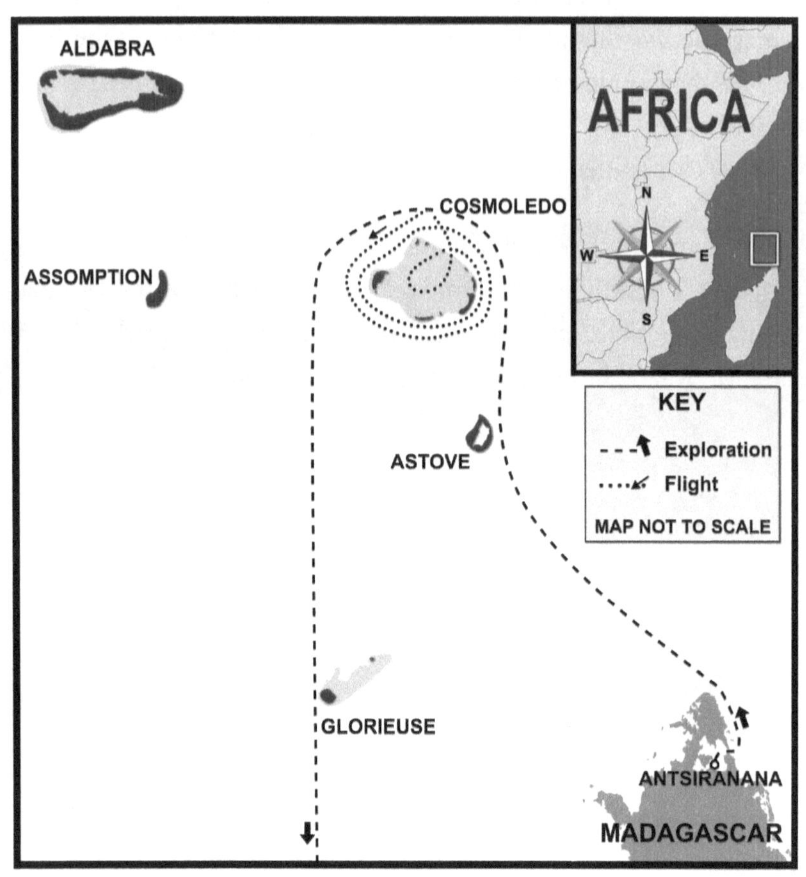

Leo and Lisa's voyage in the Indian Ocean searching for
the early 1700s shipwreck of the *Arrow*

33

It took Shuchang and two assistants a month.

'Boss, can you look at what we've done?'

'What am I looking at? A radar screen?'

'No, what we discussed. The camera focuses on a two-hundred-mile circle around the base GPS point I've set at a hundred miles off the Oman coast. It transmits twenty images with a tiny incrementing jitter. Each image is blank except for identified anomalies, so the data is minimal. The receiver calculates the GPS coordinates from the base point to each anomaly. The total picture includes the wake. With a four-minute update, a ten-knot ship moves six-tenths of a mile, then we can calculate direction and speed.'

'Can you realign the camera so the base point is the centre of Cosmoledo island? I'll find the coordinates ... 9.7088 S, 47.5153 E.'

'It'll take six minutes; the camera moves five degrees a minute.'

The picture on the screen froze, and six minutes later, the first wedge appeared; after four more minutes, Cosmoledo appeared as a tiny island in the screen's centre, surrounded by a light blue sea.

'That's superb, Shuchang, though I doubt it has a high enough resolution to spot a fishing boat.'

'Wait for several repeats; the AI will flag a pixel if it reappears in the same spot in four minutes or as an adjoining pixel.'

'Thanks, Shuchang; see what improvements you can make, and then we'll sell a service to the Navy or Coast Guard to protect Oman's waters. Now I can plan my trip.'

I'll warn Lisa.

'Hello, man.'

'Hello, my love, we're on our way. I must charter a yacht and have it pick up my ultralight in Durban, then sail to Antsiranana, where we will meet it. I've been there and know it's ideal.

'My satellite view will warn us enough to avoid trouble as we will stop at Cosmoledo for only two hours.'

'Okay, Leo. Let me know when I must be ready.'

Leo chartered a motor yacht with a rear deck that carried a motor-boat launched using a crane, then arranged for the eight crew to sail it to Durban, leave the motorboat, and load his seaplane before sailing to Madagascar.

Leo flew to Kigali a month later, collected Lisa, and continued to Antsiranana. During the flight, Leo told Lisa what they would do. He added, 'As we won't be landing, we don't need to enter the Seychelles territory, although if they learn what we're doing, they would claim we need flight permission, which would take ages, and when other government departments become involved, we will have to take an observer and hand over any data we collect. Then, if we recovered items from a wreck, we'd have to hand them over. It's far better to behave as tourists looking at the island, but we'll first check that no one's looking. I have a satellite terminal to install so we can watch for intruders.'

A crew member collected them with an inflatable after a taxi ride to the Antsiranana port. Lisa climbed the ladder while Leo and the seaman motored around to the crane on the other side to lift the satellite receiver box.

As she stepped onto the deck, Lisa recognised the epaulettes of a captain and then his face…

Captain Jacob de Vries stepped forward to greet her, but she spoke first.

'Captain Jacob, you're a surprise. Leo said nothing about you being here.'

'Then I must assume you're Lisa. Welcome aboard. Leo doesn't know; I was offered this job at the last minute.'

'Then we must surprise him; how do you know my name?'

'When we were on Kili, he said your name in his sleep the night before he phoned you, and I asked when Leo said he would call.'

He never told me that.

'I'll tell my crew I'll be in the lounge with you.'

When the crate with the satellite receiver swung over the deck, the inflatable returned to the ladder, and Leo boarded. As he stepped onto the deck, a seaman pointed at the glass doors and said, 'The Captain and the lady are in the lounge, sir.'

Leo's eyes hadn't adjusted from the bright sunshine to the cool shade of the lounge where, on seeing two figures, he said, 'Good morning, Captain. Thank you for being here on schedule.'

Leo recognised the voice instantly when Jacob replied, 'I wouldn't be late for a meeting with you, Leo.'

'*Jacob de Vries!* What a fabulous surprise. I thought you would be in Tariq's security.'

'I'll tell you, but would you like a THB or a Simba? I remember you drank that on Kilimanjaro. Lisa has an Iced tea.'

'Simba. Let's sit, and you can tell us your story, then we must install the satellite receiver.'

'I did join Tariq's security, and thank you for that introduction. I stayed with him for four years, first in Iraq and Syria, guarding commercial interests, and then he sent me to Bahrain. With a lot of free time and the sea available, I studied for a skipper's ticket. Then, I spent a year ferrying rich Emirati yachts to various ports before finally returning to South Africa after I qualified for a Captain's licence.'

'So, have you found a *Meisie*?'

'Not yet, Leo. Oddly, I don't feel as happy in South Africa as I imagined. I might return to the Emirates.'

'We'll talk about that later, Jacob. Show us our cabin; then, we'll look at the satellite receiver and decide where to put it. Tomorrow, we must take the plane from its crate and assemble it. Can we move to a remote part of this inland bay and anchor while we do that?'

'Now I know it's you. Why the secrecy?'

'I'll tell you later. The satellite connection first.'

...

'Wow, this cabin is as big as the lounge!'

Jacob answered her, 'These luxury yachts always have an over-sized owner's cabin. If they pay millions for a yacht, it's a social necessity.

'Leo, the schedule says we'll be here tomorrow, motor about two hundred nautical miles the day after, arriving at dawn, then less than a day later we'll return to Mayotte, then Durban. Is that right?'

'If all goes well, yes. I can only confirm once the satellite connection is working.'

'Then we must do that – today.'

It took longer than planned as the yacht's engineer had to make extra brackets that night before Leo was satisfied with the aerial component installation on the flying bridge roof, with a connection to a computer on the bridge. Early the following morning, Leo switched on the PC. After logging in to the satellite, a circular picture of the area around the yacht appeared on the screen.

'Jacob, think of this as a two-hundred-mile circular radar picture around our position. At sea, it will show ships and boats. Click on one, and it will pop up speed and heading.'

'Why do you need it?'

'We haven't applied to Seychelles for permission to fly around Cosmoledo, which is what we want to do, and we don't want anyone other than ourselves to know. We must do it before the fishing season starts in November, but there might be illegal fishers, and they switch off their AIS.'

'I've never seen or heard of anything like this. Where does it come from?'

'Lisa gave me the idea. I'll tell you later. Where will we park while I assemble the plane?'

'There's a spot in the north of the *Baie du Tonnerre*. There's a beach, we can swim.'

'Then let's move.'

Once the anchor dropped, the entire crew, except the cook, assisted with the assembly process. After inflating the floats, two crewmen held the frame and seats in place while others bolted them to the floats and then the tailplane and fin followed. Finally, Leo inserted the pins to connect the wings to the frame and added two struts. The most time-consuming item was locking all the nuts with wire, including the control cable connections. Two men lifted an engine and propeller assembly into place on one wing and then repeated it on the other while Leo made the fuel and control connections.

Lisa, who had helped the cook prepare the table on the deck for lunch, thought it was a carnival atmosphere.

Jacob asked, 'Leo, what's next?'

'Lisa and I will strap in, and then you lower us to a metre above the water. I'll start the engines and signal; you'll lower us into the water and drop the hook until I can unhook the sling. Lisa will stow the sling, and I'll taxi away and then take off to fly around.

'Lisa will lower the magnetometer four metres below us; we'll check that the magnetometer is operating, then return. Lower the hook with the buoy, and I'll catch it between the floats and switch off the engines.'

'That might work here, but if there are waves, it would be safer for the rubber duck and two crew to grab you. They could have the hook in the inflatable before you land. Once you cut the engines, you will be at the mercy of the waves. You can stop several metres away, and they can come to you.'

'Okay, Jacob, you're the captain, we'll do it your way.'

'Put on your goggles, Lisa, there's no windscreen.'

'I will, but first, tell me how you will judge our height over the water. If I lower the magnetometer and you're too low, it'll hit the surface.'

'That altitude indicator on the panel between us is a radio altimeter. I asked the supplier to calibrate it to metres between zero and fifteen below the floats. We'll fly at five. A red line on the yacht's transom is five metres above the water. We'll fly past and check the calibration before you use the magnetometer winch control.'

The trial was faultless. After taxiing around in circles while checking the controls, Leo headed for the bay's far side and opened the throttle. At maximum power, the aircraft accelerated slowly for the first metres. It increased as the front lifted until, after a hundred metres, only the rear of the floats supported the aircraft. With backwards pressure on the joystick, it lifted from the water, and Leo circled to fly past the yacht's stern. The radar altimeter read 5. Lisa lowered the magnetometer, and pulses showed on the tiny screen beside her. She hauled it up, and then Leo landed.

When the crane lowered the plane to the deck, the crew covered it with a tarpaulin. Jacob remarked, 'I could see the top of the wings when you were on the water. The grey-blue camouflage is perfect. I'll give you a portable ELT. Then, we can find you with the drone if something goes wrong. When do we leave?'

'Tomorrow morning, we need daylight for the satellite view, so as soon as it's safe to pass through the channel.'

'I'll check the tides, and we'll discuss it over dinner.'

'Leo, I'd rather leave at four am. The tide is slack then, so the channel has no current. Our radar will guide us. Also, no one will see us leave. Once out, I can idle beside the Emerald Sea until your satellite picture is clear. Then what course and speed do you want?'

'Course to Cosmoledo, speed ten knots. Above that, the Satellite picture has difficulty keeping up. It gives us about two hundred nautical miles of range. If a boat shows up, we'll decide what to do. If the picture is clear at sunset, it's back to a few knots until morning with a radar watch. I don't want to take risks, so we run away if anything appears on the radar. If the satellite view is clear in the morning, a quick run to a spot close to the Cosmoledo coast, launch the plane, and we will fly three forty-minute circuits before we return and leave.'

'The swell is running southeast to northwest. The northwest corner will be the calmest. Will that do?'

'Perfect, Jacob. Lisa, if I must wake up at three thirty, I'll crash now.'

'I'll come too.'

'You shower first, Lisa.'

'Okay, you can shower while I brush my teeth.'

Leo slid into bed, and Lisa rolled on top of him, so he wrapped her in his arms as she said, 'Darling, I have an idea that needs your approval.'

'That depends.'

'On what the idea is?'

'No, on what you do next.'

She kissed him.

'That's a good start.'

'Only a start?'

'Yes, you have a long way to go before I can approve anything.'

....

'My love, I approve.'

'You haven't heard what it is.'

'Then tell me what I've approved.'

'Must we end this trip in Mayotte? It will take only three more days to reach Durban.'

'Approved, even if Jacob needs to call at Mayotte for fuel. Now I need convincing before I can agree and certify the change.'

....

As the yacht ghosted slowly through the channel to the open sea, Leo said, 'Lisa, once we turn north and the sun rises, look at the sea on the port side. Between the reef and the land, it's called the Emerald Sea because of the colour.'

While they stood silently in the wheelhouse, the cook brought mugs of coffee or cocoa to them and the crew on watch. As the first rays of sunlight skittered across the sea, Lisa looked.

'It's beautiful.'

'Wait until the sun is high enough to reflect off the bottom, then the sea will light up and glow as if floodlights are below.'

An hour later, Leo said, 'Jacob, we have a clear run on the sat pic.

No fishing boats are out this early, so go to ten knots. Set a course fifty miles east of Astove and curl around the north of Cosmoledo to the northwest. North of the island is a good place to spend the night.'

'You're right, Leo, this *is* a good place to spend the night.'

'You mean north of Cosmoledo?'

'No, I mean in this bed.'

...

With a clear satellite view, Jacob brought the yacht to a halt off the northwest corner of Cosmoledo by applying a touch of astern thrust. When stationary, the crane lowered the plane over the water. Leo started the engines, and two minutes later, he taxied towards Cosmoledo and took off to make three forty-minute circuits of the island, the first halfway between coast and reef, the others over the reef and lagoon.

Lisa kept an eye on the magnetometer needle as Leo flew as slowly and steadily as he could, only five metres above the water. The magnetometer recorded continuously, but she wanted to know when it sensed metal. There was one place on the northwest coast where, on both circuits, the magnetometer buzzed, and the needle oscillated for a few seconds. Lisa looked down; the sea surface was an opaque blur, even at their slow speed. After the second circuit, Leo flew around the lagoon inside the island to the place where the magnetometer signal had blipped. As he left the lagoon, the needle wavered wildly and buzzed loudly for a few seconds. Ten minutes later, Leo landed beside the yacht and cut the engines. The inflatable and its crew hooked up the plane and towed it to the yacht, and minutes later, they were on the deck.

Leo grinned after he looked at Lisa and remarked, 'You look like a female Bleriot.'

'Why?'

'Go and look in a mirror.'

Then he went to the wheelhouse.

'Are we still clear, Jacob?'

'No, there are three small boats about forty-five miles to the east. I've watched them. I think they're fishers from the small village on Assomption Island. If we turn south and do twenty knots for an hour, they won't see us, and I'm sure they're too small to have radar.'

'Then let's go. If you don't need fuel, you can bypass Mayotte and sail directly to Durban. I'll join Lisa for breakfast after she's removed the two-stroke oil from her hair and face.'

In the saloon, the computer screen showed a map of Cosmoledo; then, a line began to extend from the starting point of their survey, showing the track they had followed. The line remained thin, with now and then a tiny sideways blip as the magnetometer registered a magnetic object.

'How can it sense copper and bronze?'

'It can't, Lisa; I'm hoping for the iron on the boxes, the rudder, and the anchor. The cannons must show.'

They did. As the track passed the hot spot, the track widened and then shrank, leaving a triangle with a base on the beach and a point in the sea before the reef. The second pass extended the triangle from the coast to the reef. 'That's it, Lisa, at least that's an iron-containing wreck and the only one on Cosmoledo. It shows the impact site and a spreading debris field from there to the beach. Watch the track as we fly back across the lagoon.'

As the trace approached the inner lagoon beach, the trace wavered significantly to one side. 'What's the cause of that?'

'I'll guess they built their felucca there, and there are iron tools and nails in the sand and iron pots between the trees.'

'So what comes next?'

'We're lucky the wreck is on or over the reef; we don't need to dive in deep water, so no scuba. We return to work while I figure out how to dive into this area without interference. We don't want what we find confiscated or stolen.' Leo grinned and licked his lips. 'So we have a three-day luxury cruise next.'

Lisa smiled. 'I'll tell Jacob to slow down a bit.'

The jet awaited when they arrived in Durban, where Leo told Jacob, 'I've extended the charter. Please arrange to ship the plane to Oman. I'll mail you the address in two days and then shore leave for the crew and yourself. I'll call with the next step.'

Leo left Lisa in Kigali and then flew to Oman.

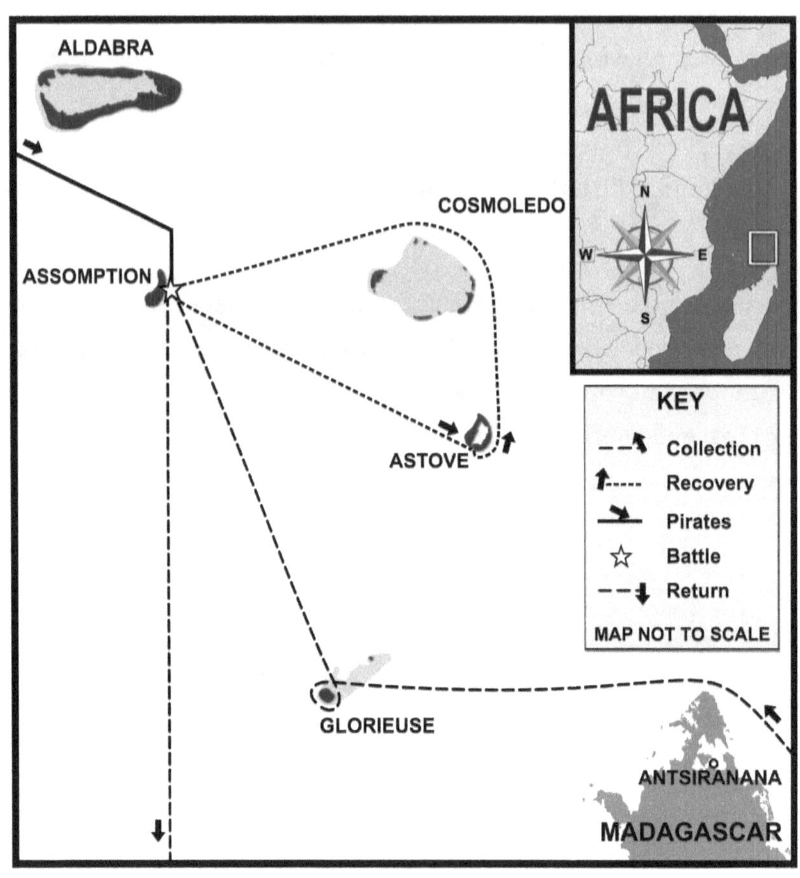

Leo and Lisa's voyages in the Indian Ocean recovering items from the shipwreck of the *Arrow*

34

Leo remembered Shuchang's words. 'I recommend some firepower in reserve.'

He phoned Jacob. Then Tariq. Jacob arranged for unique mounting points on the yacht to drawings supplied by Tariq, then sailed to Toamasina on the east coast of Madagascar, where the port had cranes for three containers that arrived on a small cargo ship to transfer to the yacht with no customs formalities.

'Hello, my love, I've worked it out.'

'What?'

'How to dive for the *Arrow*. Astove Island is a top fishing area fifty kilometres from our dive site. People live on Cosmoledo during the fishing season, so we'll visit when they leave the island at the end of the fishing season. I'll apply for fishing licences and send three flybridge sport fishers with Omani crews and camping gear to Astove. We'll fly via Mahe for the formalities, board the boats and motor to Cosmoledo. We can disembark, camp, and dive while the crews fish and watch for intruders. They will carry recovery gear as well.'

'When?'

'I must organise it. Because the sport fishers will need refuelling multiple times, I'll send them two months earlier to fish around the *Iles Glorieuses*; it's French territory and only four hours motoring from Astove. I'll tell them when to meet us in Astove. Be ready by the last week of April.'

Before the end of the Trevally fishing season on the first of May, Jacob, with a crew including three past colleagues from Iraq, sailed from Toamasina to the *Iles Glorieuses*, a hundred and twenty-five miles south of Cosmoledo, and the same from Assomption.

An hour and a half after leaving Astove, the three sport fisher boats slowed as they approached the position Leo had set on the GPS and unrolled thin tarpaulin covers over the sport fishers from bow to stern.

'What's that for, Leo?'

'It's Kevlar with a radar reflecting paint coloured to look like the sea. We know there are no boats near us, but satellites pass above, and we don't want someone warning the government of activity, although, because we're close to the deserted fishing camp, the satellites must pick up boats and people here. When they begin trolling, the crews will remove the covers to look like legitimate anglers.'

The crews retrieved three inflatables from inside lockers, loaded them with camping and diving gear, and then left to navigate two hundred and forty metres to the narrow channel between the *Ilot Lacroix* and the main island. Leo and Lisa set up camp in a secluded lagoon bay, a short walk from the sea, and the three inflatables departed.

Lisa asked, 'What will they do?'

'Fishing at the three corners of a triangle with Cosmoledo in the middle. They will keep a twenty-four-seven radar watch with military strength radars and warn us if a fishing boat approaches.'

'They'll be far away, and we may be swimming; how do they warn us?'

'I have a Satphone beeper that vibrates. They won't use the radio as others can hear. Jacob is also on watch with the satellite view; he's near the *Iles Glorieuses*.'

'Leo, you're full of surprises.'

'It's far safer not to talk about something if you don't need to. You never know who's listening.'

Lisa made the first discovery. She removed a portable magnetometer from a bag, switched it on, and said, 'Leo, I'm going for a pee. I'll see if this thing beeps.'

'It should do; this is where PegLeg built their felucca.'

Lisa was back in minutes. 'It doesn't just beep, Leo; it warbles continuously.'

'Show me where.'

Followed by Leo, Lisa walked along what might once have been a path to the sea or, during a cyclone, a river between the lagoon and the ocean. As the beach came into sight, she turned right into a sandy patch, and the magnetometer in her hand began to chirp. Three steps farther, and it became a continuous warble.

'Lisa, move around the patch, find where it's loudest.'

'Here, on this side.'

Leo fell to his knees and began to scrape the sand away with his hands. After a few centimetres, he stopped. 'I'll fetch a trowel; the top was loose but hard with sharp coral below. You look around for other spots while I fetch it.'

....

'There aren't any other places, Leo. I must have chosen the right place for a pee.'

Leo dug and soon hit something solid. 'Lisa, this may be one of the money chests. PegLeg must have recovered one or two and buried them here. We must at least clear off the top.'

Leo continued while Lisa walked back and forth with the magnetometer, then said, 'Unless there's space between chests, it's more than one or two. I think five. Shall we dig them out?'

'No. This one is too small to be anything except a money case. We'll cover this one and disguise this area as our toilet. We'll recover the cases at the last minute. Tomorrow, we begin swimming.'

'What do we do?'

'Wear full protective gear; coral is dangerous, and cuts don't heal well. The magnetometer is waterproof; you take that. I have a Sonar that will see what's under the coral. It records, and we can look at the recording after the day's swimming. You put the beeper in an ear and then flipper along the search area, holding a short rope between us. If you hear a beep, tug the rope, and we'll investigate. My wrist GPS will display the programmed track.

'We'll take it slowly and rest every thirty minutes, else we'll exhaust ourselves.'

'I'm hungry, Leo; what do you want for dinner?'

'There's an hour before dark; I can catch a fish.'

'Not too big, please.'

On his third cast, a fish struck Leo's spinner. 'It's a Trevally, Lisa, a small one.'

The fish jumped, flashing gold as the setting sun reflected on its scales.

'Big enough for two, Leo, don't lose it.'

'Lisa, we'll start close to the beach, and after each pass, we'll move seawards. We'll soon learn what sound level indicates something worth investigating; a mild chirp might be a lead, but we should continue without a significant signal. We can't investigate every nail.'

'What about sharks?'

'We'll be inside the reef; we might see a small one. Ignore it.'

'And if it's a big one?'

'There are so many fish that sharks aren't hungry but swim to the beach if one seems curious. You're a tasty nibble.'

Lisa grinned. 'So you're a shark! I wondered.'

'I said *nibble*, not nipple!'

They swam until lunchtime, had a break and ate, then swam until four in the afternoon. Leo fished and returned with two small trevallies. 'I think the lagoon is a nursery; they're easy to catch.'

The following day, they started where they left off. The length of each swim was shorter as their search moved into the deeper water nearer the point of the triangle. The first shriek came only an hour later. On the seaward side, Lisa pulled the rope. Leo joined her, dropped a line with a float and weight, and they dived into three metres of crystalline water. Leo probed into the coral with his knife; Lisa swam around hunting for the loudest signal, then waved at Leo, pointed and rose for air, so he joined her. After two minutes of deep breathing, he said, 'I'll take a look.' He was back a minute later. 'It's the rudder. We must keep swimming.'

Then the signals came every few metres as coral-covered cannons lying in odd positions caused the magnetometers to whoop. Leo dived to examine a cannon that screamed, then surfaced. 'This is the *Arrow*, that cannon is a giant, bigger than the others.'

Lisa was ready to stop at four pm. 'One last pass, Leo.'

Fifty metres later, about to reverse her course as she passed beyond the GPS-marked triangle, she heard another signal. Below her, about four metres below in the growing gloom as the sun dropped to the horizon, she saw a sizeable coral outcrop.

There must be something lying beside it. After one last dive to check the signal, I'll swim to the beach.

She dived and skimmed over the top of the outcrop at minus four metres to look on the other side. As she did so, she received four distinct whoop-whoops as she crossed it. Nothing was on the other side, so she rose to the surface where Leo waited.

'Leo, a massive coral lump below me, gives four separate whoops.

Mark this spot, and let's return to the camp. I'm exhausted. Tomorrow you can look.'

'Okay, Lisa, I'll make a pass with the sonar while you swim to the beach.'

That evening, they looked at the sonar trace. The canons showed clearly, and the last images showed the coral outcrop. 'Lisa, it looks like a hollow outcrop. Either there's something there, or there was something that has rotted away. We'll look in the morning.'

They returned to the marked position the following day, and Leo dived. 'Lisa, it may be a coral-covered chest two metres long with four iron straps; I'll fetch a bar and a float from the camp.'

Forty minutes later, with a small air bottle and extra weights on his belt to allow him to stay down, Leo dug under the rock with a metre-long iron bar until he could pass a rope through and tie it on top; he then hooked a deflated ball onto the rope and triggered its gas charge, so the rock had a one-metre diameter ball tugging it upwards.

Leo continued to break coral away from the rock, where it joined the floor. Lisa fetched another air bottle, and when Leo was tired and ran out of air, she attacked the remaining coral. Leo rested on the surface while breathing through a tuba, watching her and a curious three-metre shark. He saw the block tremble, dived, and pulled Lisa away from the rock as the float pulled the coral from the floor, tearing at the seaweed that held it until suddenly it accelerated.

They surfaced; Leo noticed the shark had gone, *scared by the float.*

'Lisa, it's not a solid rock; for that ball to lift it, it must be hollow and weigh less than a ton.'

An hour later, they had towed it to a shallow pool near the beach.

'What now, Leo?'

'I'm inclined to call in the heavies, collect this and the buried stuff, and leave. The longer we stay, the more likely we'll encounter some trouble. Illegal fishers come here in the off-season, and I don't want a war. You found it, you decide. Leave it like this, or break it open?'

'Let's do it properly, X-rays first.'

'Right, I'll deflate the float to hide it.'

Once back in their camp, Leo used his satphone to tell the lead captain, 'Early tomorrow, do a drone scan; if you're clear, come and fetch us. We have several one-fifty kilo loads, so prepare the long ropes, the carbon fibre skids and the hundred-litre floats.'

'What's a drone scan for?'

'The island blocks the radar from southeast to northeast when the boats come here. The drone flies up and can see over it.

'We put the coral rock and whatever we find buried under the sand onto skids attached to a float and then winch it down the beach into the sea and the boat. Then it's like pulling a marlin from the sea.'

'Do you do this often?'

'No, but we practised.'

'Are we returning to Astove?'

'We must, but by then, we'll have caught and released some giant Trevally to prove we've been fishing, and the booty will be on board Jacob's yacht on its way to Oman.'

'Where's Jacob now?'

'Idling along near the *Isles Glorieuses*. About five hours from rendezvous. We'll meet up with it in Muscat.'

The extraction operation began after dawn, but Leo's plan changed when Jacob buzzed on their secure radio link.

'Leo, I have an unidentified threat. We're leaving the *Glorieuses* for Assomption. The intruder is on a line from Dar to Cosmoledo, about one-seventy-five miles from you. I estimate he will be in radar range in about eight hours.'

'Okay, Jacob, keep me updated.'

The extraction operation ran smoothly, and six hours later, the three boats began the run to Assomption to meet Jacob.

'Leo, I can see you. We'll be fine if you meet me before the target passes Aldabra; if not, he will see you on his radar. If he turns towards us, I'll assume he's not a fishing boat, and we may have to fight.'

'We can't increase speed; the wave height is excessive, and we'd break something.'

'Then we'll prepare.'

Lisa had listened. 'Prepare for what, Leo?'

'Jacob is military, Lisa; he has prepared for terrorists and pirates.'

Leo could see the yacht at three miles when Jacob buzzed again.

'The target has spotted you and is turning. Run between me and the shore; I've left enough deep water for you. When he's within drone range, I'll launch the spy.'

'Copied.'

The sport fishers fell into line astern behind Leo and slowed as they passed between the island and Jacob. Leo saw the drone lift and head north as they stopped, wallowing in the waves two hundred metres from the reef.

A tense ten minutes ended when Jacob phoned to say, 'The drone photos are clear; it's a fishing boat with no fishing gear, and the aft platform has three high-speed skiffs. I'll wait until he stops to launch his skiffs. He probably thinks you're fishing.'

The yacht began to move, rapidly accelerating as Jacob applied full power.

'Leo, he's slowing; I'll decide as soon as I can turn to face him. If the skiffs come for us, I'll sink the target and hope they'll head for the island.'

Lisa disagreed, 'Tell Jacob that leaving armed pirates on the island will bring the death of the fishermen and families living there.' Leo did.

Jacob had to admire the speed at which the ship launched the three skiffs, and they headed straight for the yacht as it turned to face them.

'I have a confirmed lock at ten miles, Captain.'

'Fire one.'

The Exocet missile reached nine hundred kph in seconds, and a minute later, the target ship vanished in a cloud of smoke. A roll of thunder reached them a minute later as the smoke cleared to reveal an empty sea.

The three skiffs slowed; they didn't notice the drone five hundred metres above them that showed them abreast, almost touching, with ten gesticulating men in each, all carrying automatic weapons or RPGs, arguing violently.

When the skiffs accelerated and headed for the yacht, Jacob leaned forward and ordered, 'Guns, wait until you're sure, but take them out before they launch their RPGs.'

At a thousand metres, the skiffs split to pass on both sides of the yacht. One launched an RPG that fell way short. The starboard 20mm cannon fired a dozen rounds, and the outboard of a skiff exploded and took the stern with it, followed seconds later by the port cannon and another skiff. The third turned to run towards Assomption.

Jacob ordered, 'Guns, take him out.'

The helmsman asked, 'Why, sir?'

'Those guys would slaughter the twenty or so fishers and families on the island. If they can swim, they'll have to ditch their weapons.'

After the yacht had loaded their booty and left for Oman, the sport fishers, including Leo and Lisa, fished for four days within close range of Astove. Lisa caught a giant Trevally, and then Leo caught another. They took photos to show their families and the Astove Island staff, then released the fish. The boats departed for South Africa, where Jacob would sell them, and then Leo and Lisa took the local flight to Victoria on Mahe Island, where the G650 awaited.

Once the G650 levelled off, Leo left the cockpit and sat beside Lisa.

'Leo, will we meet your parents? I know of your father, though we've never met; I know nothing about your mother.'

'Lisa, does any of that matter?'

'If it were just us, Leo, it would not, but if, one day, there will be little Leos, as a mother, I must know they will be fine.'

'You know me as Leo Poussin, and that's true; we don't use de la Vallee Poussin, but I have two other names.'

'What are they?'

'The first is Karim Khawar, an ordinary Omani. That's the alias I use to avoid any suspicion that I'm Sheikh Asad bin Rachid Al Said, the great-grandson of the Sultan and a Prince of Oman.'

'Are you pulling my leg, Leo?'

'No, Lisa, that's the truth, and tomorrow you'll meet my mother, Soraya; she's a princess and the Minister of Health responsible for Oman Hospitals.'

After a long silence, Lisa inhaled deeply and said, 'You could have told me sooner. What do I call your mother?'

'She'll tell you, Lisa; I expect she'll say, "Call me Soraya."'

'Must I wear a headscarf?'

'Not with my parents, and Oman is not fanatical. Headscarves are considered a polite acceptance of other people's beliefs.'

35

Lisa looked out the window as the aircraft slowed to a stop and saw the couple waiting for them. Heart beating rapidly, she stepped down the G650 stairs after Leo, who took her hand, pulled her forward, and said in Arabic, 'Mother, this is Elisabeth.'

Soraya stepped forward and, without asking, took Lisa in her arms and, speaking in Arabic, said, 'I have waited years to meet you. I know your parents well, but I don't know why we've never met. Call me Soraya. Don't be surprised when Louis kisses your cheeks; he can't escape his French upbringing.' She stepped to one side as Louis came closer.

'Lisa, I imagine you've dreaded this moment; welcome to Oman and our family. Call me Louis.' He kissed her on both cheeks.

She replied in Arabic, 'Thank you both for making me feel at home; I'm sure you're waiting to hug Asad.'

They did, and then Soraya said, 'If I didn't know better, I would think you're Omani from your speech. How did you learn Omani Arabic?'

'I find languages easy; I learnt Arabic and adapted to the Omani accent.'

Leo added, 'Lisa's multilingual and has spoken Arabic with Moustapha and me for weeks.'

Once driving to the palace, Leo asked, 'Dad, where's our booty, and when will we have X-Rays?'

'The cases are at the X-ray lab. Shuchang will receive the scans this morning, and the cases will arrive at the palace tomorrow.'

As the limo drew up in front of the porticoed palace entrance with four smartly dressed Omani guards, Soraya asked, 'Lisa, I must visit the hospital; if you want to come, I can wait half an hour for you to freshen up.'

'I would like to come, and I had a shower before landing. I can come now.'

'Then we'll stay in the car.'

Louis turned to his son as the car drove away with Soraya and Lisa. 'She's a beautiful and talented young woman, Leo. Have you proposed?'

'Not yet, Dad, I want to fetch a camel for her and finish what we're doing first.' *A camel will know what I hope is true.*

In the car to the hospital, Soraya asked, 'Has he proposed?'

'Not yet; I'm sure he will, but not until we have finished our research.'

Soraya smiled as she remembered. 'Louis never proposed to me. The second time we met, he told my father it was Allah's will. – I didn't say yes; I knew it was true. I had rejected a dozen proposals before then.'

Lisa thought. *The first time I met Leo, I lay on his arm half-naked and knew I could stay there forever. Is that still true?*

'The hospital we're visiting is the main Muscat hospital. There are others and many smaller clinics. My responsibilities are the buildings, maintenance, medical stocks, and nursing staff. The medical treatment, surgery and any speciality requiring a medical degree fall under a different Minister of Health.'

'That's unusual.'

'It is, but it works well once the men accept that a woman can play a role in government and do her job instead of them trying to take over. I have succeeded with the added protection of being the Sultan's granddaughter.'

'Where do you buy your medicines?'

'We don't buy. Asad's company delivers free of charge.'

'That's generous, what company?'

'Generics.com. Ask Asad, and he'll take you to visit. It's massive.'

After a pause, Lisa struggled to say, 'They supply Katanga, Rwanda, and Senegal.'

'I know, and many more countries.'

I'll kill him again.

Lisa had imagined a grand affair with a flunkey behind each person; it was a relief to find lunch was held in a small palace dining room.

Leo passed around photos of the coin boxes and coins and remarked, 'We have three boxes of copper coins and two of bronze. The other five must be near the reef and buried in coral. I don't think recovering them is worthwhile. I'll give some of these coins to Professor Demirci and Professor Restolomew, and we'll donate the rest to Tortola and the Foundry Museum. Now look at the X-rays and ultrasound scans.'

Lisa looked at the first image and passed it to Soraya. 'It looks like a statue; do the others show it as a mother and child?'

'I'm not one hundred per cent sure, but that's my conclusion. Look at these. The report says the ultrasound scan corresponds to the density of wood. There is lead content in a thin layer; I guess that's paint, then a natural wax covering that varies in thickness. The lab suggests it's beeswax. Then there's wax-impregnated multiple-layer linen wrapping as a cushioning layer and an outer carapace in a tree pitch and natural fibre composite.'

Louis remarked, 'Someone went to extreme lengths to preserve it. Do you have any idea where it comes from?'

Lisa answered, 'The only carving we know of was lost from Fort Dauphin in the late 1600s. Leo, I'm a metre eighty, and I just fitted in the alcove of the St. Marie church; how big is this statue?'

Leo looked at the report. 'It gives the chest's internal dimensions; the length is a metre seventy-seven. That's conclusive; I'll contact the Lazarists and ask someone to come here when we unwrap it.'

Soraya asked, 'What will you do with it?'

'If it's the lost Madonna, we'll take her to the church in St. Marie.'

'Don't they have one?'

'They do; it's carved from a palm tree trunk and is three hundred years old. I shall buy it. I think it might make a suitable exhibit in a museum.'

Louis asked, 'Where?'

'Lisa can talk to Doctor Kerring in Tortola. That's where this story started, and he's interested in museums.'

That afternoon, Leo showed an amazed Lisa around his cave, introduced his staff, showed her his workspace surrounded by computer screens, and then showed her the lower level, filled with humming servers and three supercomputers in separate alcoves with flashing LEDs. *He didn't lie; if the lights were dim, it would look like a cave of sparkling jewels.* Lisa came away with one thought. *There's more money in that cave than I imagined existed.*

'Lisa, the Lazarist will arrive in two days, and tomorrow, I want to collect two camels.'

'I thought you had one.'

'I do, but she's old, and I don't like to ride her long distances. The Emir of Abu Dhabi owes me three, and I asked him to have two ready tomorrow; he said about eleven o'clock.'

'How far is it?'

'An hour by car.'

'What's he like?'

'He's one of the richest men in the Emirates, a faithful follower of Islam, and a powerful ruler.'

'Must I hide my face?'

'No, he's progressive, a supporter of women's rights, and an admirer of beautiful women. I'm sure he likes women who don't hide their faces, only their hair. I've never asked. Have you ridden a camel?'

Lisa smiled. 'I wondered if you would ask. I spent two months in Niger when I was seventeen; I rode with my parents to remote camps when they took blood samples.'

'Then follow instructions, and everything will be fine. The Sheikh has a superb camel trainer. He'll make sure you don't fall off. The stable hands all say he talks to the camels.'

'They do that in Niger.' *It's my turn to surprise him!*

When the white Rolls stopped beside the stables, Sheikh Abdullah Al Nahyan came from a side door to meet them.

'Sheikh Asad, welcome. You look well, and with such a beautiful woman to accompany you, I'm not surprised.'

'Sheikh Abdullah. May I present my companion, *Tabiibu* Elisabeth Calmette? Lisa, Sheikh Abdullah Al Nahyan.'

As Soraya had advised, Lisa kept her eyes averted until he spoke, then looked up at him.

'*Tabiibu* Elisabeth, welcome to my stables. I doubt I have a camel to suit such a beautiful woman.'

She looked beyond the signs of age and saw the rugged hawk-eyed face of his youth. *Women must have adored him when he was thirty.* 'Thank you for your welcome and kind words.' Lisa noticed a sign of his surprise at her accent.

Two almost white camels came from the stables, led by a man wearing a blue robe and black headcloth. One was female. Lisa asked, 'Which one is for me?'

'It is for you to choose.'

'Then I'll take the male.' Lisa smiled at Sheikh Abdullah. 'Men do what I tell them. Women argue and disobey.'

The sheikh laughed as Leo replied, 'It depends on the handler. In my hands, females are obedient.'

Lisa stepped forward and took the lead of her camel from the trainer as he walked past her to Leo. Sheikh Abdullah tensed, expecting the camel to react to the stranger by turning to spit or bite. It swung its head towards Lisa but did neither as before it had turned sufficiently; Lisa hit its upper lip with the palm of her hand under the nose, driving it painfully upwards while speaking in a language the Sheikh felt was familiar. 'We will be friends if you behave yourself, my handsome beast. Now *Kneel*', then slapped and thumped the camel on its neck. The shocked camel knelt, and a surprised Sheikh relaxed and looked at the trainer, who was looking with approval at Lisa as two more men appeared carrying saddles and reins.

Leo had missed the brief interaction and wondered who had told her camel to kneel, but seeing the saddles, he ordered his camel to kneel, which she did with a loud groan. Once the saddles were tightly attached, the trainer watched with appreciation as Lisa climbed into the saddle with an effortless fluid movement sequence he recognised, foreleg, thigh, chest, then neck, and arranged her skirt over crossed legs that locked her to the saddle, before thumping the camel again with a sharp word. The camel obediently rose, back first, then front.

'*Walk.*'

As her camel carried Lisa away, and Leo mounted and followed her, Sheikh Abdullah stepped forward to the trainer. 'The *Tabiibu* is a remarkable woman. Does she speak your language?'

'I do not know, Eminence, but she has lived in the Great Sahara with my people, mounts as do our women, and speaks camel language. Your beast is safe, Eminence.'

'Both camels. I have wondered if Sheikh Asad would find a woman who loves camels as he does. I should not have doubted. Allah will bless their union, and I or my son will present each child with a camel once they're old enough.'

'When they return, deliver the camels.'

'I can see a dust cloud, Eminence; they return and are racing.'

'The male may be stronger with greater endurance, but the female is still young and faster in a short race.'

'He'll slow it, Eminence. He loves his woman as he does his camel.'

On the drive back to the palace, Leo said, 'Lisa, this was the most surprising morning I've had in years.'

'You mean seeing how well I can ride a camel?'

'Yes. The Sheikh was impressed, and the camel trainer adores you. How did you learn to talk to camels?'

'I had to; how else could I persuade a camel to do what I wanted? I'm sure it's the remains of an ancient language; there are few words, but everyone across the Sahara uses those words. Luckily, the trainer is a Tuareg; otherwise, my camel would not have understood. Each girl I rode with in the desert had her camel. The girls must have thought me gawky, but they told me a girl with a camel could marry a better class of man, so they taught me, and I enjoy riding a camel; they're as intelligent and as friendly as a dog.'

'I've heard that bit about girls with camels, Lisa, although I thought it was ancient.'

'The Sahara and the people there haven't changed much in five thousand years.'

'Leo, your mother said you would show me Generics if I asked you. When she did, I decided to kill you for not telling me about it. Why did you start it?'

'You asked me to.'

'I didn't.'

'You did. You asked your dad about the cost of medicines, he asked mine, and Dad asked me. I investigated and decided that effectively managed generics would be profitable, good for people, and would help you. Then you told me, "I don't want to fail in my first job due to theft of my medical supplies." The next minute, my mother took over here, and you and Ashina were doing my marketing. She asked Tiny because you told her he would help.'

'How do you know that?'

'Tiny told me. Lucia runs the business, and he's expanding the sales there.'

'So killing you alone is pointless. I'll say thanks. Now let's have lunch, then visit the factory.'

36

Three hours later, a subdued Lisa returned to the palace with Leo.

'Lisa, there's a rooftop lounge; come with me and watch the sunset; drinks are in the fridge.'

Relaxed, side by side on a comfy mattress with their drinks on low tables, Leo asked, 'Do you still want to kill me?'

After a long pause and an exaggerated sip of her drink to allow time for thought, Lisa asked, 'Leo, that visit was beyond my comprehension. Did you build that yourself?'

'No. I had to find the right people, find the correct solution, and oversee the startup, including the first two packets of pills sent to Ashina. But once that worked, hundreds of others worked to build the business. Oman may receive free medicines, but it allows import and export without duties or paperwork, doesn't charge rents on the desert we use or ask for tax money, and the police provide rock-solid security.'

'Who knows about Generics.com, Leo?'

'All the people who use it, and the WHO, but no one except you and my family know of my involvement. I prefer it that way. Now, watch the sunset; it's only minutes away.'

As the sun vanished beyond the desert horizon, Leo said, 'That's it. The night falls quickly in the tropics and the temperature drops. Let's descend. Dinner will be early, and we have the unveiling tomorrow.'

He said that the first night we met in St. Marie.

Two separate conversations developed at dinner; Soraya engaged Lisa in a discussion about Generics.com and how she hoped it might evolve. When Lisa heard about extensions to the University, degrees in chemistry and biochemistry, and Soraya's ambition to open a branch of the Pasteur Institute, she felt she was in another world where things would happen if you wanted them to. And then Soraya, who had spoken to Rosemary, adroitly steered the conversation into hospital management and let Lisa talk about her ideas, finally asking, 'Did Leo take you to see his cave?'

'Yes, I'm unsure if his cave or Generics.com is the most incredible.'

'I'm counting on that computer power to run the hospitals and clinics Oman needs.'

Louis and Leo discussed something else. 'Leo, are you ready to settle down yet, at least enough to listen to a proposition?'

'It will depend on Lisa, Dad, but I'll listen.'

'I've been thinking about your mother and me travelling as tourists. Amina will be leaving home soon, so we'll have more liberty. The project evaluations are now so tightly integrated with your budget analyses that we could take them on jointly. You do the math, and I'll do the presentations.'

'That would be great, Dad, if not tomorrow, in a year or so.'

Father Matthias was a few grams more than skeletal, with the pale skin of a librarian, white hair cut short around an otherwise bald head, and a gaunt face with vague brown eyes.

He seemed relieved to meet Leo and Lisa, a French-speaking couple. When Leo asked if he had slept on the flight, he replied, 'I don't often fly, and it was the longest flight I've ever made.'

'We'll visit the lab; it's quite close. The coral growth on the box is ready for removal; the contents will be visible shortly. Once it's unwrapped, do you have a way to identify it?'

'I'll give you photocopies of the documents I found in our library. They're fascinating to read, but the proof is on the back of the Blessed Mary. We should find the code "*MC170-EG-1645*". The "*EG*" is the sculptor Eugene Gaviscon.'

In the lab, they met an engineer, who introduced himself as Samir Hassan and saw the massive coral block crisscrossed with cut lines. Samir said, 'The cuts may look random, but we carefully planned them to avoid the internal package. We have photographed the block from all sides, and we can lift off the coral pieces with the iron bands and wood.'

'Then take off the coral and take photos at each step; we'll move out of your way.'

....

'How will you unwrap it?'

'The first step is to remove the protective carapace; we have plaster saws from the hospital. They vibrate, so if they touch the cloth below, they will do no damage.'

'Then continue...and the last stage?'

'We must turn the statue many times as we unwrap the bandage, so we'll first place it on an inflatable mattress.'

....

The tension and amazement grew as a delicate foot, a hand, or a section of her headdress peeped from the wrappings. Lisa whispered, 'She's beautiful and perfectly preserved.'

As the wrapping fell from the Madonna's face, Father Matthias placed his palms together and prayed silently, tears falling from his eyes.

Leo waited until he finished, then asked, 'Please, can we turn her over?'

Her back had no markings, only flesh-coloured paint. Lisa could not believe it and stood silently staring. Leo reacted first. 'Please, give me a sheet of paper. I'll place it on her back, and I want an X-ray and ultrasound scan of that area. Also, I want a high magnification image of a paint patch on her back and another on her hand.'

'Certainly, sir.'

'Why, Leo?'

'I don't know who did it or why, but I'm sure that's not the original paint.'

Father Matthias was shuffling papers in his file. While Samir and his assistants wheeled the Madonna out, he said, 'There is a report here dated after the Madonna reached Fort Dauphin; it says she was damaged, and they made a small repair to her back. I hope the code remains. There should be a report by the repairer in this file.'

Samir returned with two images and the Madonna. 'There was writing, and bits remain where it was deepest. The repairer removed a damaged surface piece and fitted a replacement.'

'So what is left?'

'The enlargement shows "M 2 E - 46" under the repair. The "2" could be a "7", the "E" could be an "8", and the "6" could be a "5".'

'That proves nothing either way. Father Matthias, is there nothing else?'

'Give me a minute; four-hundred-year-old French handwriting is difficult to decipher.'

....

'I'm sorry, I can't understand the writing; I need reference books.'

Lisa asked, 'Please, can I see it, Father?'

'Of course.'

The despairing silence grew as Lisa looked at the incomprehensible paper, but she recognised some words. 'Father, I'm a doctor, and medical terms are Latin. There seem to be several Latin medical words here.'

'Please, Doctor, show me.'

'This one, for example, *Pedem*, the Latin for foot, and *Spina* is the Latin for spine, where the repair is.'

'Then a priest, not an uneducated artisan, must have written this. Let me look.'

....

'Doctor, would you know what *Pittacium* means?'

'That could be a medicine bottle's label or a signature.'

'Then look at one of the Madonna's feet.'

All eyes moved to look at the feet. Samir said, 'There's still wax there. I'll clean it off.'

....

'There's nothing there.'

As the despair deepened again, Father Matthias said, 'Doctor, it's not *pedem* alone; it has *parvum* in front – is that *small foot*?'

Lisa didn't answer as Leo was the first to look at the only visible foot of the baby Jesus. 'There's something there. Samir, a magnifying glass, please.'

'Father, can you look for us?'

....

'It is the code, followed by the letters P-F-S-S. The repairer was a priest; he begged forgiveness for his work; the letters stand for *Pater et Filius Spiritus Sanctus.* I declare this to be the lost Madonna. You should return her to the Lazarists in Paris.'

Leo replied, 'Father. You don't know her story. She left Fort Dauphin for St. Marie in Madagascar on board a ship we know was the *Libellule.* After a storm damaged the ship, she spent eleven years in an Aden foundry storeroom. A pirate ship, *La Fleche*, loaded the Madonna with a promise to hand it to a Catholic church or ship. A cyclone wrecked the ship on an island, and we found where the Madonna lay in her sea chest for three hundred years. We shall take her to the Catholic Church on St. Marie, where an alcove has waited since 1857 for the Madonna.'

'Then it is better to say nothing in Paris until the Madonna is in St. Marie. I recommend you act quickly.'

'Thank you, Father. Samir, can you finish cleaning the Madonna and then pack her with foam in a ply box for airfreight? I'll tell you where and when to deliver it.'

'Of course, sir. I'll have it ready tomorrow morning.'

Lisa said that night on the rooftop lounge, 'Leo, do you remember asking me, "Would you know how to help this church and ensure the people think they saved it?"'

'I do, and I remember you replied, "Then it needs a miracle."'

'I have a better answer now.'

'Then tell me.'

'Mount the Madonna on a platform supported by four poles so four men on each side can carry her. Place the platform on a table at the right height, in one of those planes where the back lowers.

'We'll arrive two hours before and call Father Benjamin to ask him to bring eight young men to carry a present for his church. I'm sure they'll carry her, and thousands will join the procession.'

'That's spectacular, but why the secrecy, and why will the people believe they're responsible?'

'If the bishops don't know, they can't come and claim responsibility. And we have only to say to Father Benjamin that God listened to the prayers of his flock and showed us where she lay. We should ask him to avoid saying we searched and found her.

'You can tell him if he asks, or later if he doesn't, that any who doubts the Madonna is the original should speak to Father Matthias.'

'Lisa, that's brilliant. Thanks for reminding me. We'll do as you say. I'll add that Moustapha can visit St. Marie and check that Father Benjamin is there. I'm sure Sunday will be the best.'

'Father Benjamin, good morning.'

'Father, it's Leo, and I have Lisa with me.'

'Good heavens, it's been years since you came to the church. Are you coming to the service today?'

'Yes, Father, but can you first come to the airport with eight strong young men and carry something to the church?'

'Can't you put it on a truck?'

'It's not here yet, Father. The plane should arrive at nine, and it's too fragile to risk a bumpy truck ride.'

'What is it, Leo?'

'You will see, Father, I don't have words worthy of a description.'

As Leo had instructed, the C-130 landed on time and stopped after swinging around until the gate into the parking area was directly behind. Leo, Lisa, Father Benjamin and the eight young men walked toward it. The rear platform descended, revealing the dark, cavernous hold with something in the shadows.

Lisa said, 'Father, please remember this is a gift from God, who Leo and I believe has listened to the collective prayers of your flock. We're no more than couriers.'

Father Benjamin's eyes widened. 'Is this…'

He didn't finish his sentence; the floodlights switched on in the hold. Father Benjamin stared for thirty seconds, then fell to his knees and began to pray, 'Almighty God….'

The eight men with him knelt and bowed their heads as well.

37

Knowing what might happen, Leo and Lisa negotiated a *tuc-tuc* ride to the church, where they waited. The parade occurred, as Lisa had forecast. The Madonna, borne on the shoulders of the eight men, followed the road to Ambodifototra. It seemed the entire island's population joined in. Before the halfway mark, the singing began, and then the parade became a dance that would shame the Rio Carnaval. From the platform on which the church stood, Leo and Lisa watched the parade as it wound across the bridge to Madame Island and the causeway to the town and the church. 'Did you expect this, Lisa?'

'No, but I'm sure the people believe God has answered their prayers. What will Father Benjamin do when they arrive?'

'We must wait and see.'

....

'He's sent other men forward; he'll say a prayer outside, welcoming the Madonna and set up a single-line queue to view the Madonna as soon as she's in her alcove. It will take all day.'

'Then we'll wait until the prayer ends and slide out of here to our bungalow at the Princess Bora.'

The following morning, many more visitors were queueing to see the Madonna and Father Benjamin, but when he saw Leo and Lisa arrive, he excused himself and joined them. 'I didn't have a moment to thank you, and my thanks will never be enough. I also know you weren't alone, so please thank all those who must have helped. Can you come back in a week or two when things are calmer and tell me about it?'

Leo answered, 'We can't promise, Father, but I'm sure we'll meet again. There's something we must tell you and something we must ask. If anyone questions the authenticity of the Madonna, refer them to Father Matthias of the Lazarists in Paris.'

'I had no doubts when I saw her, but I suspect others will refuse to believe the truth. Father Matthias has seen her?'

Lisa answered, 'Yes, and he has the proof. The other item is the sale of the Palm Madonna. We have a bank draft for you from a company that will place her in a Caribbean Museum dedicated to the history of pirates.' Lisa handed him the draft; he looked at it and turned back with tears in his eyes. 'This is more than I ever expected. I shall never forget these two days or you. Henceforth, this church will include you in its prayers.'

Leo grinned. 'Not too loudly, please; otherwise, we'll have hundreds knocking on the door for help. You can refuse the draft, but if you accept, please make whatever arrangements you wish to say goodbye to the Palm Madonna and then message me to collect her. To avoid claims from the bishops or other churches, announce the amount and state that it's exclusively for refurbishment, and the bank will pay against invoices.'

'Leo, I understand why. We may not need so much. With the Madonna here, many will volunteer to assist.'

Lisa replied, 'Accept such offers; participation is part of faith. Use what remains for improvements. We must leave, Father. May the Force of God be with you.'

They walked away, and Leo said, 'There's only one thing left to do. Tell PegLeg we've fulfilled the promise to learn about him.'

'I'm sure he knows. He didn't want us to learn his history but to finish his failed task, bringing the Madonna to the Church. We asked him to witness another promise, and that isn't over. It's also a full moon in five days.'

'I know,' Leo replied, 'and I've decided; I'm ready to marry and must tell you I'll visit his tomb as promised. Will you come?'

'I'm not sure, but if you stay at the Princess Bora until after the full moon, I'll stay with you to discuss whether I should come.'

'You have a deal.'

It was like the days after their first meeting but without the evenings in the cemetery. They talked about anything that came to mind. Many things were memories that began with 'Do you remember...' And sometimes those memories were awkward.

'Leo, are you serious about wanting to marry? Is there a woman I don't know about, or do you want to marry me?'

'Lisa, since we met, there has never been another.'

'That's hard to believe; no girls at all?'

'Some I helped when they had problems, but they were all brief encounters.'

I'll bet I know what that means. 'What *help* did you give?'

'When I went skiing the first winter, I was going to bed when I heard a row and a door slam, and when I looked in the freezing corridor, I found a barefoot girl in a bathrobe, crying. After she came to my room to keep warm, she said her boyfriend had tried to force her to accept bondage and kinky sex.'

'So you helped her. I had a man take me to a theatre once, but I felt sick and took a taxi.' *That's true, but Leonie told me he was bi ... I never connected Leonie to Leo; was he behind it?*

'Leo, you saved me from a gorilla. Did you save me from anything or anyone else? Please be honest.'

'A bisexual creep.'

So it was him!

'How did you know?'

'You posted on Facebook; becoming a friend is easy.'

'Which one?'

'I'll let you work that out....'

Then came the day Lisa asked, 'Leo, what will you do if I don't come to the cemetery?'

Leo had his answer, although it wasn't attractive. His reply was expressionless; Lisa thought it hurt. 'I shall ask my mother, and she'll search for a woman who will suit my life. I know I'll never love another as I love you.'

The day of the full moon arrived, and Leo asked at breakfast, 'Lisa, will you come tonight?'

'I still don't know.'

'Then I'll pack my holdall and leave it by the door to collect it to-morrow morning without disturbing you. I'll take my backpack now and leave you to think about it during the day; I'll be in the cemetery before sunset and will sleep there.'

Lisa sat on the beach before the bungalow, remembering her dictum.

> Live the life you want to live, not the life others expect you to live.

She thought, considered every angle, and then phoned her mother.

'Mama, Leo has told me he's going to the pirates' cemetery and has said there is no other woman in his life, so he's asked me to marry him and expects me to join him.'

'What is your decision, darling?'

'I won't go. I won't marry Leo.'

'Lisa, we'll back you if you're sure. Why have you decided to refuse?'

'Because I want to live the life I want, not the life he expects me to fit into.'

'That sounds like a good reason if you believe he won't let you live the life you want. Is that how you feel?'

'Not Leo, Mama, but he's a Prince and has enormous responsibilities, so I must conform to everyone around him.'

'That's not a valid reason; Leo has asked to marry you, not others. I'll agree if you tell me he'll not support you when you fight against restrictions that others try to impose on you.

'But didn't you promise to meet him if he told you he would be there? I seem to remember you told me you did. And, Lisa, irrespective of any promise, any man who dares to propose expects the woman will have the courage to face him if she says no.'

'Thanks, Mama, you're right. I'll go. Bye.'

Lisa closed her eyes and remembered her words to PegLeg Jon on the final night: *'I'll not marry until I have told him and have visited your tomb on the night of the August full moon to meet him.'* Then, the memory completed itself. *'I promise to come if he tells me he's coming.'*

He said he'd be there, and I promised. I must go.

She dressed and left for the cemetery.

She couldn't see his face, but the view matched perfectly with her memory; he was lying naked in the sun on a camp mattress in front of the tomb.

She felt giddy and faint and had to draw a deep breath; he heard and turned. They stared at each other intensely and silently until he moved to one side and patted the groundsheet as he had done when they first met.

I'll tell him why when the sun sets.

Lisa slipped from her dress and underwear and lay beside him; he stretched his arm under her head as a pillow. She didn't notice his silver medallion, its chain around his neck, lying on the grass below his armpit. Her bronze medallion slid sideways as she lay her head on his arm until it fell and rested on the silver one.

They lay together, remembering as the sun set over the mountains. It seemed the same sunset they had watched years ago, and Lisa thought, *I still feel the same; I could lie beside him forever.* And then words bubbled from her memory.

'*They fought against the restrictions placed on women in a male-dominated world.*'

Leo is a pirate, and he admires women who will fight. He'll support me.

As the last tiny arc of the sun disappeared, he turned, and she did, too. For a minute, they studied each other, noses almost touching; she saw the invitation in his eyes, and he saw the same in hers.

He smiled. 'Hello, girl, you're good company.'

'Hello, man, but I haven't said anything.'

'You don't need to.'

'Have you used your wish yet?'

'Yes, as the sun set. And the genie said he would grant it.'

'Then I don't have a choice.' Lisa leaned towards him and whispered before their lips touched, '*It's forever.*'

And then the moon rose and smiled on them as before when they made love.

She was on the pirate ship again, holding on tightly; it was closing on the shore, tossed by waves and breakers; on the beach stood a pirate with azure eyes.

She knew the ship would run aground. Suddenly, an enormous wave lifted the boat and hurled it towards the beach; she screamed as it hit the land, and she felt the shuddering and shaking.

Eyes closed, Lisa whispered, 'Did I faint?'

'Yeah, us both. Lie still.'

'Darling, I want five.'

'Five what?'

'Children.'

'Why five?'

'The five elements, Earth, Air, Fire, Water, and Spirit.'

'Then, my darling, roll onto your back.'

'Why?'

'Because we'd better start now; I'll ask PegLeg to speed things up and make it twins.'

'Is that all?'

'No, I want to check if being on top is still the same.'

As he felt her warmth envelop him, she looked up and fell forward until her breasts rested on his chest, then reached both hands forward to touch the tomb side above his head. 'PegLeg. *Please* give us twins.' Twenty minutes later, she knew – it wasn't the same, but far better.

They married a month later under a full moon. Jacob was the best man, and Ashina was the bridesmaid. Two hands, one covering the other, rested on the silver medallion Leo placed on the tomb of PegLeg Jon when the wedding couple recited their vows.

A Lifetime Later

Holding Leo in her arms, Lisa had an ear close to his mouth. She was the only person to hear his last whisper, 'Hello, PegLeg.'

Flame, Lisa's eldest daughter, was puzzled when she saw her mother smile happily.

Two months later, Flame heard her mother's last whisper, 'Hello, man.' – And marvelled.

Three men and two women began walking to climb a small hill two hours before sunset.

After a two-kilometre walk along the only road from their hotel, they reached a rotten wooden signpost. It looked like it would cease to exist in a year or two, but it still pointed drunkenly at the path to follow; it said, *CIMETIERE.* What seemed like a skull and crossed bones once burned into the wood was almost invisible. The people carried bags; the eldest, twins, had celebrated their sixty-third birthday three months earlier.

In a single file, they followed the path that climbed slowly upwards through the lush tropical growth that had tried for centuries to cover the track. Arriving at a plateau, they continued with a sea view to the left and a lagoon to the right. Then, a narrow grass path between the sea and the lagoon appeared through a gap between the palms. Almost hidden amongst the undergrowth, the cemetery's tombstones thrust upwards, trying to remain in view and impress the memories they encapsulated into the modern world.

Three metres in diameter, the grassy patch at the very peak of the hill had spectacular views. Beside it, a tomb looked clean, for someone had regularly cleaned off the tropical creepers and plants. On one side, a recent stone plaque read:

> In Loving Memory of Lisa and Leo. Blessed by the Lord, they carried our lost Madonna home. – The Catholics of St. Marie.

One of the men removed a brush from his bag and swept the tombstone; another removed a small scrubbing brush and a scraper from his holdall, then carefully cleaned out the weatherworn lettering on the tombstone and a patch below it.

The lettering was only just readable.

> PEGLEG JON
> PYRAT O CARIB
> 1716

They stood beside the tomb, remembering, not speaking, as the sun's orb began its final dive below the horizon of the distant mountains darkening on the other side of the western sea, a vast sheltered bay; the grassy patch before them, lit and warmed by the sun, slowly cooled.

When only a tiny sun arc remained, they moved to circle the tomb; the women each removed a small ornate stone sarcophagus from their bags and removed the lids. The stone urns had names and dates.

Passing the urns from one to the other in silence, they sprinkled the ashes they contained in a circle around the cleaned patch. The sarcophagi emptied; the eldest man took a large pot of glue from his bag and poured it onto the cleaned area in two sticky pools while two others carefully glued the lids onto the mini coffins. Then they gently laid the stone coffins, touching side by side at the centre, the engraved names uppermost, on the glue patch and stood back. The youngest woman took a silver medallion from around her neck and pressed it face down into the remaining glue pool at the foot of the coffins. It didn't stick, so she replaced it around her neck. No one spoke, but lips moved silently, and then they turned and filed down the path. They didn't see the worm of glue that defied gravity, snaking sideways to run under the end of the touching sarcophagus. One would seem to lie on the arm of the other *forever*.

The gentle night breeze stirred the air much later that night. Palm fronds rustled in secret music, and erratic swirls of the air mixed the ashes thoroughly and swept them into small dunes against and between the urns. The skull and crossed bones imprinted below the coffins remained clear of ash.

Then the temperature dropped, and dew condensed, cementing the sarcophagi to the tombstone – and each other – *for eternity*.

www.ingramcontent.com/pod-product-compliance
Lightning Source LLC
Chambersburg PA
CBHW030936120726
47906CB00002B/586